P9-BZB-545

THE LAND OF MY DREAMS

Also by this author
The Morland Dynasty series:

THE FOUNDING
THE DARK ROSE
THE PRINCELING
THE OAK APPLE
THE BLACK PEARL
THE LONG SHADOW
THE CHEVALIER
THE MAIDEN
THE FLOOD-TIDE
THE TANGLED THREAD
THE EMPEROR
THE VICTORY
THE REGENCY
THE CAMPAIGNERS
THE RECKONING
THE DEVIL'S HORSE
THE POISON TREE
THE ABYSS
THE HIDDEN SHORE
THE WINTER JOURNEY
THE OUTCAST
THE MIRAGE
THE CAUSE
THE HOMECOMING
THE QUESTION
THE DREAM KINGDOM
THE RESTLESS SEA
THE WHITE ROAD
THE BURNING ROSES
THE MEASURE OF DAYS
THE FOREIGN FIELD
THE FALLEN KINGS
THE DANCING YEARS
THE WINDING ROAD
THE PHOENIX

GOODBYE PICCADILLY: WAR AT HOME, 1914
KEEP THE HOME FIRES BURNING: WAR AT HOME, 1915

THE LAND OF MY DREAMS

War at Home, 1916

Cynthia Harrod-Eagles

to Mom
from Michael
2016

sphere

SPHERE

First published in Great Britain in 2016 by Sphere

3 5 7 9 10 8 6 4 2

Copyright © Cynthia Harrod-Eagles 2016

The moral right of the author has been asserted.

*All characters and events in this publication, other
than those clearly in the public domain, are fictitious
and any resemblance to real persons,
living or dead, is purely coincidental.*

All rights reserved.
No part of this publication may be reproduced,
stored in a retrieval system, or transmitted, in any
form or by any means, without the prior
permission in writing of the publisher, nor be
otherwise circulated in any form of binding or
cover other than that in which it is published and
without a similar condition including this
condition being imposed on the subsequent purchaser.

A CIP catalogue record for this book
is available from the British Library.

ISBN 978-0-7515-5632-2

Typeset in Plantin by
Palimpsest Book Production Limited, Falkirk, Stirlingshire
Printed and bound in Great Britain by Clays Ltd, St Ives plc

Papers used by Sphere are from well-managed forests
and other responsible sources.

MIX
Paper from
responsible sources
FSC
www.fsc.org FSC® C104740

Sphere
An imprint of
Little, Brown Book Group
Carmelite House
50 Victoria Embankment
London EC4Y 0DZ

An Hachette UK Company
www.hachette.co.uk

www.littlebrown.co.uk

THE HUNTER FAMILY
of The Elms, Northcote

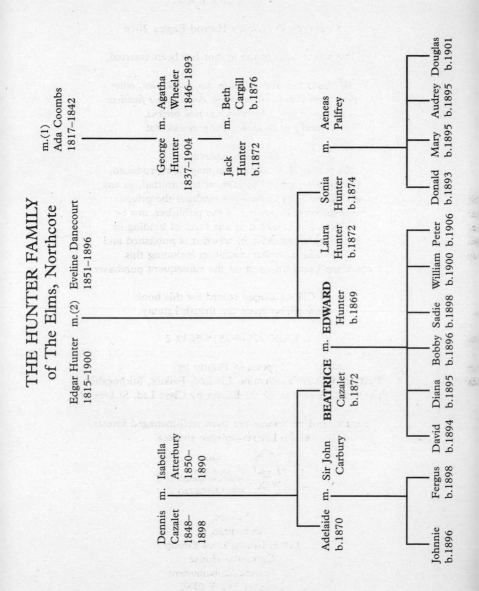

THE LAND OF MY DREAMS

CHAPTER ONE

Sophy Oliphant was nervous. Saying 'yes' to David Hunter had been almost an act of impulse. She hadn't been intending to accept anyone just yet for, at eighteen, she was having too much fun. And she hadn't really expected David to propose. He had seemed too reserved, too diffident.

There was something different about David. All her other admirers liked the same things that she did: tennis, dancing, gramophone records, parties. They spoke the same language. David was almost like a figure from history: a Cavalier, a Crusader. He was so tall, heroic-looking; he read books, he quoted poetry, sometimes in *Latin*; he was serious and thoughtful. And he had volunteered right at the beginning of the war, which was splendid. So when he had begged her, so earnestly, to marry him, she had felt honoured.

She half thought her father would put his foot down – it was no secret he wanted her to marry Humphrey Hobart, the son of a neighbouring landowner. Humphrey was nice, but he wasn't exciting, like David. But Papa had given his blessing, and David had given her a pretty ring of turquoises he had brought back from France, in a box stamped with the name of a Parisian jeweller. Her friends had been very impressed with the box!

And now here she was, walking from the station to his house to meet his family. It had begun to rain, and she was afraid she was getting splashes on her suede boots. She felt he ought to have got them a taxi, but he was holding the umbrella entirely over her, to the detriment of his own uniform. He did look so *fine* in uniform, she thought, with satisfaction.

A girl had only one chance to make a good marriage and secure her future comfort. She knew very little about David's prospects, though she supposed Daddy must have asked about them. She knew his father was 'a banker'. Vaguely she thought about the funny little man behind the counter at the London and Provincial in Melton Mowbray, who wore a wing collar and gold pince-nez, and combed his hair over the top of his bald head. David had said he would go into banking after the war, and that it was a good career. Daddy must think so, or he would never have agreed. The Hunters were well-to-do. It must be a different sort of banking.

They had stopped at last before a house. It was handsome and large, and the door was opened before they reached it by a respectable-looking maid in neat uniform. So that was all right. She drew a sigh of relief.

David said, 'Here we are. Don't look so nervous. I know they'll love you.'

He looked down with infinite tenderness and some awe at the little person over whom he held the umbrella. She was so perfect, so beautiful; innocent and shy, like a delicate woodland creature. Whenever he saw her or thought about her he felt a great surge of love that was almost like sorrow. How could he deserve her? The words of a hymn ran through his mind: she was his pearl of price, his countless treasure. He wanted to do great deeds to prove himself worthy of her. It was lucky in a way that there was a war, because opportunities to conquer mountains and slay dragons were scarce in the ordinary world. But surely in fighting for mankind's freedom, he might achieve something to lay at her feet.

She glanced up at him through her thick dark eyelashes and said, 'I'm all right.' And put her chin up and walked in. She had courage, too, he thought, folding the umbrella and following her.

It was Sadie Hunter's way to stay in the background, to watch and listen before she made up her mind about things. As the middle child, overshadowed by her elders – David's magnificence, Diana's beauty, and Bobby's charm – and with two boys after her, she had always stood rather apart within the family.

She felt she was not pretty enough to make a success of being a girl – especially as everyone must compare her with Diana. She would be eighteen in two weeks' time, and had never had a single beau. She did not particularly want one. She visited wounded officers at Mount Olive convalescent hospital as part of her war work. Some of them died. In wartime, it seemed a perilous thing to become fond of a man.

It was wonderful to see David home on leave. She saw the change in him. He had been in battle, which she thought tremendous, though also sad and rather horrible. He had seen men die – perhaps had killed men himself. Something like that must change a person. Peter clamoured, as a nine-year-old might, to know how many Germans he had killed. David avoided the question lightly, but Sadie would never have asked him that.

It was a shock that he was engaged to be married. Sadie hung back and examined the person he had brought to see them, who would one day be his wife and Sadie's sister-in-law. She was very pretty, that was the first thing one noticed: dark hair, white skin, large eyes; the sort of rosebud mouth men admired, and a very long neck. She had on a pretty dress of dusky-pink wool, the hem a modest two inches above the ankle, showing pink suede buttoned boots

3

– not sensible wear, Sadie thought, for a day of unremitting rain.

So much for how she looked; but what was she *like*? She smiled a great deal, and seemed to say just the right thing to everybody, but that could be just the good manners of a well-brought-up young lady. Probably it was foolish to expect any deeper insight into a person's character on a first meeting. At any rate, David obviously adored her, and that was enough for Sadie. She would do everything she could to get to know and love her. She owed it to David.

Diana was also examining Sophy's appearance. The dress was up to the mark, the colour well chosen, the style not too elaborate. Either Sophy or her mother had good taste. And Diana loved the boots. David ought to have got a taxi from the station.

David, she thought, had grown rather grim – not that he had ever been jolly, the way Bobby was – but there was something about his eyes, and the way he avoided certain questions. He was obviously besotted with Sophy. Diana found herself a little surprised. He had easily resisted the charms of her friends, many of whom had been smitten with him. She saw nothing out of the ordinary about Sophy.

Well, perhaps she grew on one. It had taken Diana a long time to find out the true worth of Charles Wroughton, Lord Dene. Too long. She felt she had only just started to appreciate him properly when he was killed in action at Festubert last May. So she would withhold judgement on Sophy. Not that it mattered anyway. It was hard to take an interest in anyone else's marriage now Charles was dead.

William and Peter, having inspected 'David's crush' and found her as uninteresting as all creatures of her age and sex, sidled out of the room about their own affairs, and the others disposed themselves around the fire to talk politely

4

of war and weddings until Ada should come in and announce luncheon.

'What do you think of her, then?' Cook asked Ada, when she came back to the kitchen.

'Seems a nice young lady. Not as beautiful as Miss Diana, of course, but quite pretty. And Mr David's mad for her, you can see that.'

'So we shall have a wedding,' Cook said. 'Well, not *us*, of course. It'll be *her* family arranges everything. Up in London, I suppose. Two houses, they got,' she added, with a sniff, torn between approval and envy.

'And what then?' Ada said. 'With him away at the war?'

'Probably stay on with her parents,' Cook said. 'Won't seem hardly like a marriage at all, to my mind.'

'Oh, but it's ever so romantic,' said Emily, the kitchen-maid. She clasped her hands in rapture. 'The brave soldier going into battle, wearing the favour of the beautiful maiden he loves.'

Cook sighed. 'I don't know where you get all that nonsense from, I really don't.'

'Everybody loves a wedding!'

'Well, *you* won't be invited, so you needn't get worked up about it,' Cook told her.

'Lucky if there'll *be* a wedding,' Ethel said.

'What d'you mean by that?' Ada said quickly.

Ethel wouldn't elaborate. 'They're sitting down,' she announced instead. 'Are we taking the soup in, or what?'

'Oh, my goodness, go, go!' Cook said. 'Don't keep 'em waiting! What'll Miss Oliphant think?'

Ada and Ethel exited with their trays, and Cook stood a moment, frowning. No wedding? What was Ethel talking about? Was she referring to poor Lord Dene being killed? Or perhaps her own beau that was killed by a wicked Zeppelin bomb. Ethel had been very quiet since it happened, quite a changed character – not that she hadn't needed changing. Too full of what the cat cleaned her paws with, that's what she'd been before, and heading for trouble with her flirty ways and so many soldiers wandering about the place.

Still, Cook would almost have preferred to have the old Ethel back, rather than this stone-faced stranger. You had to forgive her a lot. But she'd no right putting a damper on Mr David's engagement. It was unlucky to talk like that. No wedding . . . ?

'Do you want them taties mashed?' Emily broke into her reverie. 'Will I do it, so?'

Cook snapped back to the present. 'You will not – they'd be all lumps. Fetch me the butter. And stir that gravy, and get the hot plates out of the oven. They won't be long over a drop o' soup.'

Edward was sorry to miss the opportunity of welcoming David's fiancée into the family. He was anxious to do the thing properly, remembering the awkward first meeting with Charles Wroughton's family, how frosty and disapproving Lady Wroughton and some of her relatives had been. But he would have opportunities of seeing her when David had gone back to France. The Oliphants were bound to invite him and Beattie to dinner, and they would have to reciprocate in kind. The wedding itself must be a distant prospect, given that David was in no position to support a wife; so distant, that the nuptials of his eldest son seemed curiously irrelevant to him, compared with the war.

He had a late meeting at the Treasury that evening, so he took supper at his club first. He met Lord Forbesson, from the War Office, bent on the same mission, and they went into the dining-room together, talking about the weather.

'At least we can forget about Zeppelins for a couple of weeks,' Forbesson said, as they studied the menu.

'How so?' Edward asked.

'Next full moon isn't until the twentieth.'

'Oh, of course,' said Edward. Zeppelins needed moonlight to navigate by. 'I should have remembered.'

'One finds oneself aware of the phases of the moon quite subconsciously, these days,' said Forbesson. 'And with any luck, there might be bad weather around the twentieth. A fog in January isn't too much to ask. Or a good rough storm. But the Zeppelins aren't so much of a problem, in any case.'

'The fear they engender is out of all proportion to the damage they do,' Edward agreed, 'but I would have thought—'

'I mean,' said Forbesson, 'not a problem to *us*. The people don't blame the government for the Zeppelins. But there's bound to be a lot of bad feeling when conscription kicks off. It goes against our basic national characteristic: sheer bloody-mindedness.'

'How far along are you?'

'Asquith introduces the Bill this evening,' said Forbesson. 'There'll be no opposition. We should get Royal Assent by the end of the month.'

'It only covers unmarried men, doesn't it?' said Edward.

'Yes, but I doubt that will last more than a few weeks. We're forty thousand men short in France *now*, and we mean to mount a big push this year. The married men will have to turn out as well if we're to get the manpower we need. We have to leave out Ireland – things are too volatile there. And there'll be thousands looking for exemption: widowers with children, starred occupations, ministers of religion . . .'

'You anticipate a rush of young men to be ordained?' Edward said, amused.

'It wouldn't surprise me,' said Forbesson. 'When it comes to finding new methods of shirking, the man in the street has wiles approaching genius.'

'So when does it happen?' Edward asked.

'Assuming the Bill goes through to our timetable, we'll call the first classes at the end of the month, and they'll have to report on the second of March.'

'That's quick work.'

'We've been planning this for months, ever since it became obvious the Derby Scheme wasn't going to cut the mustard. But it won't affect you, will it? Your two eldest have volunteered already, and your younger boys are below age, I think?'

'Yes,' said Edward. 'But my secretary's twenty-eight.'

'Ah,' said Forbesson. He knew how much Edward thought of Warren. 'Bad luck.'

It was very late when Edward got home – something that had become more frequent since the war had picked up pace. The servants had gone to bed but the hall light had been left on for him and he let himself in with his latch-key. He looked in at the drawing-room, where the fire had been banked. A decanter had been left out with some sandwiches wrapped in a napkin, but he wasn't hungry, and trod his way wearily up the stairs. It had been a long day. The Treasury meeting had been hard work. War was an expensive business, and acceptable ways of raising money required a lot of thought and planning.

The lamp on his side of the bed was alight, but Beattie seemed to be asleep, so he went into the dressing-room to undress so as not to disturb her. But when he returned to slip into bed, he saw she was awake, staring at the ceiling; and he remembered what he had forgotten since the morning, that it was the day of David's visit with his fiancée.

Beattie had been upset that he was spending his leave with the Oliphants, and only granting his family one day of it. David was very special to her, and Edward always had to step carefully around anything concerning him.

8

'I'm sorry I missed it,' he said. 'Did it go all right? What's Miss Oliphant like?'

There was a long pause before she answered, in a dead voice, 'She's a pretty girl.' It sounded like a condemnation.

He studied her blank face, trying to deduce the problem. 'Was she well-behaved? Did you like her?'

'Of course she was well-behaved,' Beattie said, avoiding the other question. She had learned the hard way to school her countenance and give nothing away, and it had come in useful over luncheon. She had smiled and talked graciously to Sophy Oliphant, while inside she seethed. Why was David entranced by this commonplace girl? It was true that other men, lesser men, wanted nothing more than a decorative cypher to keep house for them. The girl had a pretty face, youth, and well-brought-up manners – but that was all. How could her darling, her most precious son, throw himself away on such a mannequin? He was so young, not yet twenty-two, and he was tying himself for life to a girl who would never understand what she had caught.

Sophy had smiled, and looked modest and shy. Beattie had sensed the shadowy presence of an expensive governess behind that polished façade. Sophy would always say the right thing. No doubt one day she would ask – modestly, shyly – if she could call Beattie 'Mother', and Beattie would long to break that swan-like neck.

She knew she should be grateful. There were two of her acquaintance in Northcote whose sons were dead. David had come back unharmed. But he had not come back to *her*. From now on, Sophy would have the love that previously had been Beattie's. Sophy would be the one he chose to be with. It was hard to bear – and harder still because they were feelings she could not express to anyone, because no-one would understand. Not even Edward.

He saw the compression of her lips, as though she were

holding back words that wanted to burst out. 'What is it, dearest?' he asked her gently.

And despite herself, she answered, 'It feels like the end of everything.'

He didn't understand. 'But you'll have a lovely daughter-in-law. In time, grandchildren.'

No answer.

'It's a beginning, really, not an ending.'

No answer. She closed her eyes so that he shouldn't read them.

Edward put out the light, lay down, turned on his side and tentatively touched her shoulder, hoping he might hold her, comfort her. But at his touch she turned away, hunching her back against him, moving to the furthest edge of the mattress.

The rejection hurt him. His heart ached with loneliness, but also with concern for her. He lay very still, so as not to come in contact with her, since he knew she didn't want to be touched. Despite his tiring day, it was a long time before he fell asleep. He didn't think she was asleep, either, but it seemed there was nothing he could do for her – or for himself.

Bobby eased his way through the crowd in the Lamb and Flag in St Giles', carefully protecting his pint of beer against impulsive elbows. He spotted his friend Horsey – inevitably called Dobbin – already seated in one of the little alcoves that made the pub so cosy. Trust Dobbin to be early, he thought. Very reliable chap, old Dobbin.

'What-ho, Dob! There you are, old thing! Do you realise you're sitting in the very spot where Thomas Hardy wrote *Jude the Obscure*?'

Dobbin looked startled. 'Am I? Did he?'

'No idea,' Bobby admitted. 'You being such a swot, and having a huge brain, I assumed it'd be the seat you'd pick.'

'I don't really know anything about it. I just thought it was quieter in here than the Bird and Baby,' Dobbin admitted.

It was what the undergraduates called the Eagle and Child. 'Bound to be,' said Bobby. 'That's where the hearty St John's roughs do their quaffing.'

'Quaffing?' Dobbin wrinkled his nose at the choice of word.

Bobby sat down opposite him. 'You know what quaffing is, don't you? Much like drinking, except more of it ends up on the floor.' He punched his friend's arm cheerfully. 'It's so good to see you! It's been an age.'

They had been 'best pals' in school, but since coming up to Oxford, their paths had flung apart. Bobby had gone to Balliol and Dobbin to Brasenose; and then Bobby had volunteered. He'd spent three months doing basic training on a very chilly hilltop in Surrey, before transferring to an officer training unit, which, fortuitously, had turned out to be accommodated in his old college, back in Oxford.

'I see you in the distance now and then,' said Dobbin. 'Hurtling by in someone's motor-car. Generally making a lot of row, it has to be said.'

'One has to make a row in a motor-car – it's half the fun.' He was studying Dobbin closely as he spoke, and knew his friend was doing the same to him. He felt a sort of pang – he and Dob had been as close as brothers all through school, and now there seemed a distance between them.

Echoing his thoughts, Dobbin said, 'You've changed, y'know.'

'Have I? I feel pretty much the same.'

Dobbin shook his head. 'You think you do, but you don't. You're much older.'

'It's the beer and cigarettes. Copious consumption thereof. You're older, too. I suppose that's the greasy grind.' He

11

grinned. 'What a surprise it must have been to the Brasenose dons to find they'd got a genuine scholar on their hands instead of another beefy sportsman!'

'You always talk as if I'm a complete rabbit,' Dobbin complained, 'but I'm a pretty fair cricketer. I don't suppose you've *been* on a playing-field in the last eighteen months.'

'I've been too busy,' Bobby said. He extended his arm to show the ring of braid and the single crown on the cuff flap. 'Got my pip! You're looking at Second Lieutenant R. D. Hunter, in all his glory.'

Dobbin peered at it suspiciously. 'Is it pukka?'

'Course it is! Gazetted yesterday. I'm the real thing, old Dob. What d'you think?'

'I never doubted for a moment you'd make officer. You were born for it. Congratters.' He shook Bobby's hand across the table. 'So, what's next in the illustrious career? Back to the Middlesex?'

'Well,' said Bobby, 'you remember we used to talk about what we wanted to *be* when we finished at Oxford?'

'And you said you wanted to be a tight-rope walker.'

Bobby nodded. 'I'm going for the next best thing. I'm seconded to the RFC. I start my training tomorrow.'

'Flying?' Dobbin looked wondering, and then smiled. 'Yes, I can just see it. It's your métier – flying so high with your head in the sky.'

'Looking down on the poor bloody infantry in their trenches.' He lowered the level in his glass, then said, 'I bet you're wishing now you'd volunteered too, when I did.'

'You know my father would never have allowed it.'

'I didn't think mine would either – that's why I didn't tell him until afterwards.'

'I'm not like you. You never seem to care about consequences, but when my pater gets in a bate with me, I shrivel like a salted snail. Can't help it.' He looked down. 'Lacking pluck, I suppose.'

12

'You don't lack pluck.' Bobby jumped to his defence. 'You're just thoughtful, so you see things coming. I'm too thick-witted to think ahead.'

Now Dobbin smiled. 'You know that's not true. Anyway,' he became grave again, 'it's out of my hands now, from what I hear. It's not just a rumour, is it? They're bringing in conscription?'

Bobby nodded, eyeing his friend with sympathy. 'Our CO says they'll be calling up the first classes within weeks. I'm sorry, Dob.'

He thought it must be awful to be coerced, rather than to volunteer; and he wasn't sure Dobbin would have volunteered anyway, even if his father would have let him. He was the bookish type, whatever he claimed about his cricketing prowess. Always thinking. You couldn't imagine him with a rifle, shooting at Huns – he'd be more likely to want to discuss Kant and Nietzsche with them.

'We've all got to do our bit,' Dobbin said sadly. 'I know that. It's just that I think the army'll be getting an awfully poor bargain in me. You know how cack-handed I am. Probably shoot the CO by mistake.'

'Oh, they teach you not to do that sort of thing in basic training,' Bobby said lightly. 'And, look here, Dob, when you're through basic, why not transfer to the RFC, like me? I know you'd be a bit behind me, but we might end up in the same unit, and the flying boys are much more relaxed about seniority and suchlike, so I've heard. You don't want to go into the trenches, anyway. Awful muddy places, trenches. Shocking hard on the trouser turn ups, y'know, your Flanders mud.'

Dobbin shook his head. 'It's no use. I'd never make a pilot,' he said. 'My eyesight's not good enough.' He saw Bobby about to protest, and went on, with forced cheerfulness, 'I'm not glamorous enough for the RFC, anyway. I'd bring down the tone. I suppose I'll end up where I'm sent,

13

and they'll have to put up with me. So what happens now? Are you staying in Oxford?'

Bobby recognised a change of subject when he heard one. He felt obscurely angry on Dobbin's behalf, though he hardly knew why. The war would not be kind to chaps like him. 'No, I'll be off tomorrow – that's why I wanted to see you today. I had to report to the Air Ministry yesterday, and a jolly helpful captain laid it all out for me. I totter up tomorrow to the School of Military Aeronautics in Reading for basic training. That's a ground school, lasts about four weeks. And then, assuming I don't make a complete ass of myself, I'll be transferred to flight school, and actually get off the ground at last.'

'And when will you be a qualified pilot?'

'Flight training's three months, more or less – depending on how you take to it, duck to water, or ostrich on roller-skates.'

'You for the duck, definitely. And then – France?'

'Most likely. I mean, they do have aeroplanes in the eastern theatre, and there's the home-defence johnnies, but the greatest need is obviously on the Western Front. So, come May or June, I shall be doing my quaffing in the *estaminets* and – look out, Mesdemoiselles!'

'Speaking of which . . .' Dobbin said, suppressing an odd twinge of envy – for, really, he had no desire to go to France, not like that. A cultural tour in peacetime, to visit the museums, monuments and art galleries, perhaps, but in khaki and carrying a rifle? *Non, merci!*

'Which which is that?' Bobby queried.

'*Mesdemoiselles.* Have you been breaking any hearts lately?'

'Oh, Lord, no – there hasn't been time. But I believe discipline is much looser in the RFC, and spare time much more generous, so perhaps I shall be putting a toe in the water soon. What about you?'

Dobbin blushed a little. 'Well,' he began cautiously. 'There is someone—'

'You dog!'

'Nothing like that,' Dobbin said hastily. 'She's a very nice young lady who's studying English literature at Somerville. Her name's Mary Talbot. Her brother's at Brasenose, and we met at a tea-party in his rooms. All very respectable.'

'I'm sure it is. Is she nice?'

Dobbin became inarticulate. '*Nice?* She's – she's—'

'Beautiful as an angel?' Bobby suggested.

'Well, she is,' Dobbin said. 'Dark hair and the most wonderful dark eyes, and such a gentle, *spiritual* look to her face.'

'Dob, you've caught it badly,' said Bobby, seriously.

'I can't think what she sees in me,' Dobbin confessed.

'She's lucky to have you. In fact, I'd love to meet her, to make sure she's worthy of you.'

'I did say I might bring you to see her, if you had time. She's waiting at the Botanic Gardens.'

'At this time of year?'

'It's warm in the greenhouses,' Dobbin pointed out.

Bobby caught the train to Reading the next morning in reflective mood. He had been impressed with Miss Talbot. The three of them had walked for an hour or so in the warmth of the greenhouses, while a very January rain coursed down the glass roofs above them. They had talked of Rupert Brooke, and Webster and Elizabethan drama, and the war had not been mentioned. She was, as Dobbin had promised, handsome, with a quiet understated beauty that he found affecting. There was something serene and strong about her, and she carried on the conversation in such a frank, straight-forward manner that he found himself forgetting – almost – that she was a woman. There were no wiles, or guiles, or foolish foibles about her. He found himself envying Dobbin. He had never known a woman like her – a woman, he felt, whom one could really make a *friend*.

They had walked back together, sheltering under Dobbin's enormous umbrella, and left her at the gates of Oriel. (The Somerville buildings, being adjacent to the Radcliffe Infirmary, had been commandeered by the War Office early in 1915 for use as a war hospital, and the undergraduates had been relocated to Oriel.) They had met again in the evening, for dinner at the Florence Restaurant, making a quartet with her brother for respectability's sake. The evening was jolly, and she showed that she could laugh, too, though Bobby had sensed an underlying seriousness to her, which had made him modify his own high spirits. It emerged in conversation that she helped out at the hospital between reading and lectures. With her calm, gentle manner, he had thought she would make an excellent nurse.

As the train crawled with war-time lassitude towards the beginning of his new life, he imagined what it must be like to win the love of such a woman. He wondered what would happen to them all in the next months and years. Dobbin would be called up, he would have to go, and she would be left behind to fret and worry. Would they get engaged before Dob had to leave? A lot of chaps did. Some in the Middlesex had even got married.

He was glad for Dob, but on the other hand, he wouldn't swap places with him for the world, if it meant not learning to fly. He was going to fly! That was excitement enough, he decided, to be going on with. All the other stuff could wait until the war was over.

CHAPTER TWO

A Police Bill was going through Parliament, and there was agitation, from former suffragettes and their sympathisers, to have some provision for women police included. An MP, Frank W. Perkins, was campaigning for women police to be appointed, sworn in, and given power of arrest, just like the men. The Church was broadly behind him, and some senior policemen, even one chief constable, had said that the women police had made a great difference to the streets.

'I hope we have,' Edward's sister Laura said to her friend Louisa one day, as they got ready to go out, 'but it hasn't been easy.'

'I think it's getting *more* difficult,' said Louisa, trying to wrestle her unruly hair into something more suitable for a woman police officer. 'Don't you think the lower orders are less polite and obedient than they were when we started?'

'They're getting used to the sight of us,' said Laura.

'I think they're bolder in every way. Especially the women. Now their men are away, they don't seem to have any restraint.'

'You may be right,' Laura said. 'I think the war *has* eroded a certain natural deference. If it weren't for the badge and the armband, I don't suppose they'd heed us at all. What was it the sergeant said to us the other day? "If you ask a group of bystanders to move on, never look back to see if they've obeyed you."'

'But we *are* useful,' Louisa said, as if reassuring herself. 'Especially with the children. Those poor little mites the other night!' They had come across two brothers, about eight and nine years old, selling newspapers on a corner after eleven at night. Neither had any shoes or stockings, and their clothes were worn thin, pitifully inadequate for the January night.

Laura shrugged. 'I don't know how much good we do taking them off the streets. You saw the sort of home they came from. No fire or food, the mother out working, the father absent. And those two were just the ones we caught. There are dozens – hundreds, even, wandering the streets at night.'

'One of those philanthropic societies ought to tackle the problem,' said Louisa, adjusting her hat over her curls. 'Provide somewhere for the children to go in the evenings when their parents are absent. A community hall, where they can get warm, have something to eat, engage in useful activities. Like a Sunday school, but not restricted to Sunday.'

'That's a good idea,' said Laura.

'I wonder who'd take it on,' Louisa mused. 'Perhaps we—'

'No time. We have other work to do,' Laura said quickly.

'I was only going to say, perhaps we could suggest it to someone. Well, I'm ready.' She made a face at herself in the glass. 'As ready as I'll ever be.'

Laura laid a hand on her arm. 'I know it will be horrible and distasteful, but we have to do our duty. If we shirk it, it will give ammunition to those who say women can't do the things men do.'

Laura and Louisa had been patrolling their usual beat around Charing Cross and, luckily, had fallen in with a male constable of their acquaintance, one of those who approved of them. They had walked on together for a short while, until in an alleyway they had come across a half-naked youth

18

sprawled across a dustbin, while an older man leaned over him committing an act that caused PC Perry instantly to arrest them both.

Laura and Louisa had been dreadfully shocked, never having imagined such a thing could be. The constable told them grimly that it was far from uncommon in London, but that three-quarters of gross-indecency cases taken to court were dismissed by the jury because *they* didn't believe such things could be either.

'But if you two'll stand witness,' he said, 'it'll make a big difference. If you say you've actually seen it with your own eyes, they'll have to believe you.'

Distasteful as it was, they agreed to give evidence. It was their clear duty – and it was a great chance to advance the Cause. They held on to that thought as, with quaking stomachs, they made their way to the magistrate's court.

Perry met them outside, and looked them over keenly. 'Very smart,' he said. 'You'll do. You look nervous, though.'

'It's a new experience for us,' Laura said.

'You've been in a court before,' said Perry.

'To observe, never to give evidence,' said Laura.

'If it's the nature of the case that's bothering you,' said Perry, kindly, 'you've already gone through the worst bit: seeing the blighters in the first place.'

'I know,' said Louisa, 'but it still goes against the grain to speak about it.'

'Doing your duty's not always easy,' said Perry. 'Just think to yourself, These men have broken the law, and justice must be done. Never mind *what* they've done, just remember it's against the law, same as pickpocketing.'

'Picking pockets,' said Laura. 'Yes, that's how I shall think of it. Well, we're ready – and determined. Shall we go in?'

They hadn't realised that they would not be allowed inside the court before they gave evidence. They sat in the corridor on a hard bench with a lot of other witnesses, most of them poorly dressed and rather cowed-looking. They eyed the women in their uniforms, with the Sam Browne and the black felt hat, and the silver chain of the whistle curved across the front, some with suspicion and some with open-mouthed interest.

'What you 'ere for?' one woman asked them at last.

'We're not allowed to discuss it,' Laura said firmly.

'Coo!' the woman said. Laura wasn't sure if she was impressed, or affronted.

They waited – and waited. Louisa whispered, 'I'm getting awfully nervous.'

'I'm getting hungry,' Laura countered. 'Surely they must get to our case soon.'

But instead of the duty constable calling them in, they were eventually roused by PC Perry coming out, his face set grimly.

'No soap,' he said. 'The old boy won't have it.'

'Who won't have what?'

'The magistrate, Mr Parsons. When I told him there were two eye witnesses, he perked up like anything. Then I told him they were women police, and he went so red in the face I thought his head would burst. "Women?" he says. "In a case like this? It is out of the question for women to involve themselves in matters of such a disgusting nature," he says. So I said you were well aware of the seriousness of the matter and were willing and eager to give evidence, but he gets more hot and bothered, and he says, "I would not allow any female in my court when such filthy cases are being dealt with, far less allow them to speak. I'm appalled they should want to. One would have thought their natural delicacy would revolt against it."' Perry shrugged regretfully. 'So there you are. I'm sorry, ladies.'

'What happens now?' Laura asked. One part of her felt relieved, though she was mostly indignant and disappointed.

'Well, the blighters pleaded not guilty, so it'll have to go

20

to the Crown Court,' said Perry. 'I suppose their solicitor told 'em how unlikely they are to be convicted, so they're ready to take the chance.'

'But will we be allowed to give evidence at the Crown Court?' Laura asked.

'That I can't tell you. A judge is all-powerful in his own courtroom. If he says you can't come in, that's it. All I can recommend is that your chief – what's her name? Miss Dawson – makes a fuss about it.'

'I don't suppose that will do much good,' Louisa said glumly.

'Now, now,' said Perry, 'don't give up so easy. There's lots of us on your side, you know.'

'And lots against us. Most of the Law Society, to begin with,' said Laura.

'Maybe so, but if it'll help get convictions – which it will – the chief constables'll be all for it. Anyway, nobody said it'd be easy, did they? It's a whole new world you ladies are fighting for. But now I got to get back – got another case coming on. Will you be all right?'

'Oh, yes, thanks – we'll be fine,' Laura said.

They left him and walked away down the corridor. Outside, it was raining again.

'What a farce!' Laura said. 'Sometimes I wonder if it's worth going on.'

'I'd braced myself to give evidence,' Louisa said. 'Then to get all the way to court and be turned away!' She turned under her umbrella to look at her friend. 'So, what now?'

'This very minute? Something to eat, I think. Look, there's a nice little café over there. Let's go and get a cup of tea and a sandwich.'

'You're always so practical,' said Louisa, with half a smile. She didn't speak again until they had sat down and ordered their food. Then she said, 'Am I imagining things, or are you cooling off the idea of being a lady policeman?'

Laura hesitated, then said, 'You know me too well. I *am* starting to feel restless. Dealing with drunken soldiers, unruly prostitutes and lost children is all very well, but it doesn't seem to have anything directly to do with the war.'

'We may not be helping to win the war, but we *are* advancing the Cause,' said Louisa. 'Even some of the former Militants are impressed. I spoke to one of them the other day – Milly Hattersley. I think you met her once at Lady Frances Webber's house.'

'Plump woman with a surprisingly hatchet nose?'

'Yes, that's her. She's a good sort, really, only terribly fierce for the Cause. She said she hadn't thought I had it in me, but I should be proud of what we'd achieved.'

'The Militants achieved more than we ever shall,' Laura said. 'At least they got to speak in a courtroom.'

Now Louisa smiled. 'On the wrong side of the dock, and only to say "not guilty".'

'Oh, pay no attention to me,' Laura said. 'I'm just peeved about being thwarted. Here comes our tea. I say, those sandwiches look good.'

She brushed the subject aside and they talked of other things as they ate. But Louisa eyed her friend from time to time, not convinced the issue had been laid to rest. Once Laura got restless, there was no knowing what direction she'd take next.

The grey January weather was making everyone feel gloomy. Diana was longing for a change of scene – occupation – anything. Since Charles had fallen, she had lost a sense of purpose in life, and with it her natural gaiety. Before, she had been dedicated to the search for the best possible match, and being surrounded by suitors had seemed her proper life's work. Capturing Viscount Dene had seemed like a crowning triumph. She looked back almost with shame, now, at how shallow she had been – though, in fairness to

22

herself, most girls of her class would have felt the same way.

But having won Charles, she had come to understand and appreciate his qualities, to realise what an honour it was that he loved her. She had fallen in love at first with the glamour of his position in society, but then had fallen in love all over again, with the man himself. Knowing him had made her grow up; losing him so soon seemed such an unfair blow. The life they would have had together had been cut off, untasted.

An odd relationship had grown up between her and his mother, Lady Wroughton: not a friendship, since it was so unequal, but the countess had summoned Diana to tea at Dene Park one day, and it had become a regular meeting. The countess talked about Charles, and Diana was glad to gain an insight into her lover's life before she had known him. She had thought she saw something more human in the countess, under what had always seemed an inhuman mask of haughtiness.

The meetings had ceased at Christmas, when the earl and countess went to Sandringham, but Lady Wroughton had made an engagement with Diana for a date in the new year.

On the appointed day, Diana walked up to Dene Park with the rain blattering against her umbrella, the bare trees dripping dismally. The deer in the park were nowhere to be seen; even the birds were hiding. The weeping skies did nothing to lighten her sadness. The main door to the house was shut fast when she arrived, and it was a long time before it was answered, by a very nervous young footman. He didn't seem to know what to do or say, so she said, 'Miss Hunter to see Lady Wroughton,' and walked across the threshold so that he had to step back and let her in.

The boy turned red and looked more than ever flustered. 'Her ladyship is not at home, miss,' he managed to say.

Such a rejection would have reduced her to a jelly a few months before, but she had more self-confidence now. 'I am expected,' she said firmly.

The boy gulped, his eyes shot left and right, as if seeking escape. His voice came out as a squeak: 'If you would come this way, please, miss.'

To her puzzlement, he showed her up to the picture gallery, said, 'Would you wait here please, miss,' and made a hasty escape.

The gallery was lined both with paintings – mostly family portraits – and bookcases, and served the house as a library. She wondered if the boy had heard somewhere that visitors to a great house were taken to the library. Presumably he had gone to seek advice from a more senior servant. It was annoying, especially as there was no fire, so the room was chilly.

This had been Charles's favourite place to think, read and work, and there had always been a good fire for him. It was too cold to sit, so she walked up and down, looking at the paintings and the titles of the books. She felt close to Charles here, could imagine him sitting at a table working on estate matters, or in the big chesterfield by the fire, reading.

It was here, in this gallery, that he had proposed to her. Here, in this very spot, he had kissed her – her first kiss. Would she ever be kissed again? She was twenty, approaching twenty-one, and felt as if her life was over already. The portraits looked down at her solemnly. They would have become her family if Charles had lived. She would have been mistress of the house one day, the person to whom the servants came for orders. She would have been queen of this kingdom, with Charles at her side, and little princes and princesses in the nursery above. And now she was merely the sort of visitor who could be left to wait in an unheated room.

There was the click of a door opening at the far end. She

turned, and saw with surprise that Charles's brother, Rupert, had come in.

When they had first met, he had been poisonously, horribly rude to her, for no reason she could understand. Later, after Charles had gone to France, he had changed – in fact, he had been quite attentive to her when she was staying in London, but she had never entirely trusted the *volte face*, suspecting he was only luring her into making a fool of herself. She watched him warily as he walked down the long room, waiting to see what his mood would be today, whether he would jeer, or try to charm her.

'Miss Hunter,' he said. 'What are you doing here?'

She examined the question for traps. He was looking at her intently, *examining* her, she might almost have said. Was he searching for some impropriety of dress or appearance? She felt her cheeks grow warm. 'I've come to see Lady Wroughton,' she said.

'There must be some mistake,' he said. 'My mother is not at home.'

She put her head up, offended. 'So the footman said. But she asked me here today. We had an engagement. I'm not mistaken, I assure you.'

'I beg your pardon,' he said. 'I mean, she is *literally* not at home. She has not been here since before Christmas. She and my father went on to Scotland from Sandringham. There's no-one here but me, and I go to London tomorrow.'

Diana was stranded in the moment, feeling a fool. The countess had not given her enough of a thought to cancel the appointment. She couldn't think what to say that would not give Rupert an opening for satire.

Into her silence he said, more kindly, 'I am sorry. She must have forgotten to tell Auden to write it in her diary.'

Diana thought she detected mockery in his tone. 'It's quite all right,' she said. She was pleased that it sounded cool and haughty.

'No, really,' Rupert said. 'She's been rather distracted since – since Charles died. She would not have meant to be so impolite to you, I assure you. She thinks very highly of you.'

Diana looked her disbelief. The countess thought very highly of no-one. Diana had not been under the illusion that she was anything more to Lady Wroughton than a convenience.

Rupert laughed – a short, unhappy bark. 'Well,' he amended, 'I'm sure she didn't mean to be rude, at any rate. Believe me, when she means to, you're not left in any doubt about it.'

She didn't know what he was up to, but she didn't care to be made the butt of his humour. And she was getting cold. She said, 'It's of no consequence, I assure you. I must go, now.'

'No, please don't,' he said. He put out a hand as if to detain her. 'You must at least let me give you some tea, when you've come all this way. And in the rain. You're shivering. Why on earth the fool brought you here . . . ! There's a fire in the Octagon. Come and get warm and have some tea.' Still she hesitated, and he tipped his head a little to one side and gave her a winning smile, and said, 'Please. I really want you to. I'm pining for a cup of tea, and you must be too.'

He was hard to resist. Wondering a little at herself, she nodded assent, and walked with him down the long room, under the blank, incurious eyes of his ancestors, who never would be hers.

The Octagon was an anteroom off the main hall, furnished as a parlour and, with a good fire, unexpectedly cosy. 'This was always our room – Charles and Caro and me,' Rupert told her. 'When the parents had parties, we'd skulk in here and keep out of the way. And later, when we had parties of our own, we'd set up a gramophone in here and dance. On the terrace, in summer.'

The room had French windows onto a terrace walk between the main house and the orangery. The walls were papered in a Chinese pattern and there was a thick blue and green carpet on the floor. The paintings were all of animals, mostly horses, some dogs, and one or two rather horrid ones of dead game. There were three sofas drawn up in a square before the fire, and a table in the corner covered with periodicals.

'Make yourself comfortable,' Rupert said, and rang the bell.

She wasn't ready to sit down yet, feeling nervous and a little trapped, so she walked about and looked at the paintings. The one she liked best was of a dog, a Jack Russell terrier standing with its forepaws up on a footstool, and an eager look on its face. It reminded her a bit of their dog, Nailer. She had no particular love for Nailer, but he was something familiar to think about in a strange and possibly hostile place.

Rupert came over and stood behind her, looking at the painting over her shoulder. She stiffened, half expecting some scathing remark about her taste in art. But he said, 'That was Charles's dog, Rags.'

'I think I remember him talking about it,' Diana said.

'I wouldn't be surprised,' said Rupert. 'He loved the little beast. Cried when it died.'

Diana didn't know what she was supposed to say to that, so she moved on, and stopped, pretty much at random, before a painting of a fat white pony being held by a groom, who seemed rather too grand for it in a green livery coat and top hat. In the background was a romantic stretch of parkland and in the distance, very tiny, the front of a house, which she guessed, from the columns, was supposed to be Dene Park.

'And that,' Rupert said, having followed her, 'is Charles's first pony, Cobweb. You seem to have the knack of picking out his soft spots.'

She suspected a criticism, and turned to him with a cold look. 'He told me a lot of things about himself. We did *talk*, you know.'

Rupert gave her a twisted sort of smile. 'First rule of a successful campaign – gather intelligence.'

'What do you mean by that?' she asked sharply.

The door opened, cutting her off, and a maid and the young footman came in with trays, which they set before the fire. The maid went out, and the footman paused at the door to say to Rupert, 'Will there be anything else, my lord?'

'No,' said Rupert.

Diana stared at him. *My lord.* Of course, as soon as Charles died, he would have come in for the cadet title. Charles had explained it to her one day. So now Rupert was no longer plain Mr Wroughton, but Lord Dene. It made her scalp feel cold to think of it, for the title had been part of what Charles was, and was no more.

Rupert was busy with the tea things. 'Come and sit down,' he said. 'I won't make you pour. I'm quite handy with the strainer and all the gubbins. When I'm at my friend Erskine's—' He had looked up, seen her expression, and stopped. 'Is something wrong?'

'No,' she said. 'Not at all.' She went over and sat down across the tea-table from him. 'I was startled hearing you called "my lord", that's all.'

'Ah, yes,' he said, handing her the cup he had just filled. 'Gives me a start, too, from time to time. It's a title that seems to belong peculiarly to Charles, doesn't it?'

'That's what I was just thinking.'

'Bread and butter, or cake?' He offered her both, and she took bread and butter. 'Yes,' he went on, 'it must strike you that you chose the wrong brother. Not that you could have known, of course. If you had, I'm sure you'd have looked more kindly on me.'

She was angry again. 'Why are you so determined to be rude to me?' she asked. She felt hampered by the teacup, and put it down with a bang. 'Is that why you asked me to tea, so that you could insult me?'

'No, I really wanted you to have some tea. Insulting you is quite tangential.'

'Oh, really!' She began to rise.

He put out a hand. 'Please, don't go. I apologise. I don't know what comes over me. I say things without considering what they'll sound like. Don't you ever do that?'

'No,' she said.

'No, of course not. You're a well-brought-up young lady. You'll always say exactly what's right. But I'm an unregulated male. You'll have to forgive me – I've never been properly house-broken. It wasn't deemed necessary, you see, given that I was only the Spare. Just an insurance policy. Never intended to be used.'

She felt a twinge of sympathy that was most unwelcome. 'You're trying to make me feel sorry for you,' she said.

He smiled, the smile that might be thought charming if you believed in it. 'Am I succeeding? No, don't answer that. Please, just sit down and have your nice tea, and I promise I'll try to be a good boy.'

She sat, but without fully forgiving him. 'You're hardly a boy,' she observed.

'No, I'm twenty-six,' he said, taking a piece of cake. 'Twenty-six years of being regarded as a waste of my parents' effort. It does things to a chap.'

'I'm sorry,' she said.

'Ah, it's working! Good. I expect you're beginning to feel my attractions?'

'No,' she said.

'*That* was rude,' he said. 'Good for you. But you shouldn't dismiss me too lightly, you know. All that Charles was, I am now. You wanted him, so why not me?'

'I think you're insulting me again,' she said, uncertainly.

'Am I? Can you look me in the eye and tell me you weren't attracted to Charles for his title and social position?'

She reddened, and didn't answer, the more angered because there was an element of truth in it. At the beginning, before she really knew Charles . . . at the *very* beginning . . .

'God knows,' Rupert went on, as though he hadn't noticed her blush, 'poor old Charles missed out on the looks. *I* got the lot. *And* the charm. He was a good fellow, but none of the females of our circle had any time for him. And then, suddenly, this *divine* creature –' he made an expressive movement of his hands in her direction '– this veritable goddess, though not, of course, of our station in life, is head over heels in love with plain, stodgy old Charlie, heir to Dene Park. Now what could that be all about?'

The words burst out of her: 'You're hateful to talk about him like that! He wasn't stodgy or – or dull, or what you said. He was worth ten of you!'

'Oh, I know,' Rupert said.

It took some of the wind out of her sails, but she carried on, though with less emphasis. 'He died a hero's death. He—' She was about to say what Charles had told her once, that he wasn't a natural soldier, and that war was against his nature and hard for him to bear. But she stopped herself. They were Charles's private thoughts and not for anyone else to hear; and Rupert might make sport of him for them. She said instead, 'What are *you* doing for the war effort? Why didn't *you* volunteer?'

'The pater wouldn't have worn it,' he said. 'No heir, you see, Charles not having produced one when the war broke out. Couldn't have both of us risking our lives at the same time.'

30

She was silent, looked at him suspiciously. Could that be true?

'Of course, we're in a very delicate position now,' he went on. 'Still no heir, and the government's bringing in conscription, so I shall get called up willy-nilly. Not a good prospect for the title and the estate.' He met her eyes, and gave a self-mocking sort of grin. 'The mater is beside herself. And she'll start badgering me any moment to get married and do my duty.'

'Well, why don't you?' Diana asked, interested, despite herself.

He handed her cake, and she took a piece absently. 'Waiting for the right person,' he said lightly.

'I thought—' she began, and stopped to consider what she was going to say; then said it anyway. 'I thought that didn't matter to people like you.'

He seemed startled. 'What do you mean, people *like me*?'

'I mean, titled people. Aren't you supposed to marry someone from your own circle and not worry about whether you love them or not?' It was what she had heard said about Charles and her.

'Ah!' he said – and, oddly, looked relieved. 'I see what you mean. Well, you're right, in general, but I don't propose to go down that route. I've looked over the girls my mother considers "suitable" – inspected them when they were paraded for Charles, didn't like them then, don't like them now. And since he's set the precedent of marrying for *love*, it'll be easier for me to wriggle out of the trap. Besides,' he added, 'I'm hatching a different plan. One that will satisfy my mother, and get me out of a hole.'

'And what's that?' she asked.

He examined her carefully for a moment. 'No, I don't think I'm quite ready to tell you about it – *yet*.'

'You might as well,' she said, trying to sound indifferent. 'It's not likely there'll be another opportunity.'

'Oh, don't say that,' he protested. 'I thought we were getting on rather well. I was thinking this could be the start of a long and fruitful friendship.'

'Friendship?' she said disbelievingly.

He gave the 'charming' smile again. 'I think we have the basis of understanding each other very well, Miss Hunter. We have so much in common.'

'We have *nothing* in common,' she said firmly. In truth, she was rather enjoying herself. She had never spoken so boldly to a man before. It was exhilarating, in an odd way, not to care what someone thought of you.

'We both loved Charles,' he said softly.

She struggled, feeling obscurely that this was an unfair stroke. She was sure he didn't mean it, anyway. 'I don't think,' she said carefully and haughtily, 'that I like you very much.'

He laughed. 'Bravo! And you may as well know that I don't like myself very much, most of the time, so we've no quarrel there. Let me refill your cup, and we'll talk of something else. There's lots still to eat here, and I don't want to spoil your appetite. Tell me about your war work.'

She felt he was not really interested, and that he was pursuing some devious end in persuading her to talk, but she was hungry and the tea was good and the fire warm, and as long as she kept her wits about her, she thought he could do her no harm. If he started getting insulting again, she could leave.

But he didn't get insulting, and the conversation did not go down any prickly paths. She made a good tea and left half an hour later, wondering what exactly had been going on, and coming to no conclusions – except that Rupert was odd, possibly mad. But she was unlikely ever to see him again, so it hardly mattered.

CHAPTER THREE

Ada had been to the pictures at the Electric Palace in Westleigh with Len Armstrong, who was an instructor corporal at the New Army camp on Paget's Piece. Afterwards, as it wasn't raining, they took the bus home, instead of the train, and went upstairs, where they held hands, and Len pretended he could see the stars, and told her about imaginary constellations, like Rover the Dog, and Gilbert the Fop. Ada didn't always understand his jokes, but she knew he made them for her, and laughed anyway. They made her feel warm. No-one before had ever cared enough for her to try to make her laugh.

They'd been to see *Carmen*, with Geraldine Farrar and Wallace Reid. In the interval after the supporting film and the newsreel, he had produced a paper bag of Milk Tray chocolates from his pocket, which had touched her greatly. In the second half, during *Carmen*, when the exciting bull-fight scene came on, she had instinctively grabbed for his arm, and he had smoothly transferred the grip to his hand, and had somehow forgotten to let go. It was the first time they had held hands, and if it hadn't been such an exciting picture she might not have remembered much about it afterwards.

Coming out into the dark evening, amid the satisfied crowds, he had taken her hand again and slipped it under his arm, and said, 'You know, I always think you look a lot like Geraldine Farrar.'

'Oh, no,' she said deprecatingly. She had no illusions about herself. 'She's really beautiful.'

'No, I mean it,' he said, looking at her seriously. 'There's a sort of something about you reminds me of her. Especially the eyes.'

She would have liked to return the compliment and say he looked like Wallace Reid, but he didn't, and her tongue was not ready enough to shape truthful compliments.

Into her unhandy silence he inserted, 'I reckon you were swooning over that dago chap, the one who played Escamillo.'

'Pedro de Cordoba?'

He smiled. 'Oh, I see you remember his name. He was a good-looking devil.'

'I didn't notice, really,' she said.

'So how come I heard you sigh every time he came on? Made me jealous, that did.'

She blushed with vexation. 'I didn't – I wasn't . . . Honest, Corporal Armstrong, I—'

'Here, here,' he said, squeezing her arm against his khaki-clad ribs, 'I was only teasing you. And don't you think it's time you called me Len? If I can call you Ada, that is.'

'Oh, yes, please,' she said breathlessly.

'Say it then,' he coached her. 'Yes, please – *Len*.'

'Len,' she said shyly.

'That's better,' he said. 'Ada was always my most favourite name. If they'd asked me at school what I wanted to do when I grew up, I'd've said, "Go to the pictures with a girl called Ada."'

And thence to the bus, the top deck, holding hands and looking for stars. One of the many nice things about Len was that he knew she had to get back by a certain time and made sure she wasn't late.

They got off the bus on the Rustington Road, just past the blacksmith's, and he walked her the rest of the way home. 'So, then – Ada,' he said, after a silence, 'are we going steady, d'you think, you and me?'

Her heart jumped. 'I don't know,' she said. 'Are we?'

''S for you to say,' he said. 'Lady's *pre*rogative. But I like you very much, Miss Ada Cole, and I'd like to be able to say you was my steady girl, if you've no objections.'

He had such a funny way of talking, she thought. She could have listened to him for ever. 'I've no objections,' she said shyly.

He stopped and faced her, took her hand in his again. 'I'm glad to hear it,' he said. 'You do like me, then?'

'Yes, I do,' she said.

'How about a kiss, then, to seal the deal?'

'All right,' she said. She'd never been kissed in her life before, and didn't know how to go about it, but she trusted Len – he was the sort of chap who'd always know how to get something done. Handy as anything, his sort – reliable, steady, good for his word. So she stood still and let him show her how. He put his arms round her, drew her towards him – she came stiffly, like a sheaf of corn – and laid his lips against hers. The sensation made her tingle all over. His lips were warm and surprisingly silky, and she smelt cigarettes and hair oil and something else, a warm, bready sort of smell that she guessed was the smell of *him*, his skin, which made her feel giddy.

It was over all too soon, and he set her back on her feet and, when she opened her eyes, smiled at her, as if he had asked a question and she had given the right answer. 'There we are, then,' he said. 'Gentleman's agreement. You can't go back on it now.'

'I don't want to go back on it – Len,' she said.

'Right-oh,' he said, took her hand under his arm again and continued towards the house. She walked at his side feeling happy, proud, a bit dizzy, and very surprised about the way things had changed in the short time since she'd met him. Forty-one years of everything being pretty much the same, and four months of things being different – but it was the different stuff that felt *right*.

He started whistling – a sound she liked, because she guessed he didn't know he was doing it, but it was the sound of a man who felt things were all right with the world. A person might sing for many reasons, including being sad, but you had to be feeling pretty chipper to whistle.

They parted at the gate, with an agreement to meet again on her evening off next week, provided he could get a pass. 'But trust me for that,' he said, with a wink. She thought he might kiss her again, but perhaps he'd decided she'd had enough excitement for one night, for he squeezed her hand, said, 'Nighty-night, then,' and walked away. She watched him go a few paces, stop and bend his head to light a fag, then walk on, with a jaunty step. She felt good to know she was part of the cause of that jauntiness. It was good to know another human creature was happy because of her.

She walked down the path beside the house to the back door, and as she passed the shadow of the big laurel bush she jumped almost out of her skin because there was someone there, a dark shape lurking against the fence. She let out a little, muted shriek, then saw it was Ethel, not lurking, but leaning.

'Oh, you gave me such a fright!' she said, and then, realising that it was not normal behaviour for Ethel to lurk *or* lean against the fence behind the laurel bush, she said, 'What are you doing out here?'

'Leave me alone,' Ethel said, in a low, irritable tone.

Ada saw she was not in uniform. 'Here,' she said, 'it's not your evening off. Where've you been? Have you been seeing someone?'

'None o' your business,' Ethel muttered.

'Does Cook know you're out? I bet she doesn't.'

'You better not tell,' Ethel said, but her voice lacked its usual vigorous menace. She sounded dull, miserable.

'I've a mind to,' Ada said. 'It's not fair. Why should you get extra time off?'

'I do my work,' Ethel said.

'Only just,' said Ada. 'I'm always having to go round after you . . .' She felt suddenly guilty, remembering the awful thing Ethel had gone through, and her voice softened. 'I know you've not been feeling quite the thing, ever since that Zeppelin, but you've got to pull yourself together, Ethel. You can't just go doing whatever you want. It's not fair on other people.'

'Oh, jaw, jaw. Stop making a row,' Ethel said.

She opened the door and went in. Ada followed her. A lamp had been left on in the rear lobby, and in its light she saw that Ethel's clothing looked rumpled, her hair was coming down, and there was a smudge of something on her cheek. She caught her arm to turn her back. 'What's happened? Are you all right? Did you have an accident?'

Ethel looked at her with a sort of cynical distaste. 'It was no accident.'

Ada's indignation faded into concern. 'Did someone do this to you? Who was it? Did you see who it was?' Getting no response, she urged, 'You have to tell me. He's not got to get away with it, whoever he is.'

Ethel removed her arm, not violently but deliberately. She looked more weary than anything. 'Give it a rest, will you? I'm going to bed.'

She walked away, up the back stairs, leaving Ada feeling confused. She was angry about various things – that Ethel had been out, that she'd been mistreated, that her own sympathy had been rudely rejected. She was worried for Ethel, and didn't know whether she ought to tell or not. Telling would make Ethel mad, but would *not* telling allow her to get herself into even more trouble?

Ethel dragged herself upstairs. Knowing Ada would not be long behind her, she grabbed her nightdress and locked herself into the bathroom to get undressed. She saw in the mirror there was mud on her cheek, and washed it away with cold water. The ground had been muddy in the wood, and he had thrown down his greatcoat over the leaves he had piled together. She remembered him grabbing her face and turning it towards him – that must be when he had left the mark. Courting out of doors was always a problem in winter.

Courting. She caught herself up with the word. It wasn't courting, was it? Andy Wood was a bad lot. And he was married. Why had she wasted her time with him? She needed someone who would marry her and take her out of service, provide her with a nice little house and a decent life. She deserved it. She was pretty. All the boys were after her. But somehow it never seemed to work out right. There'd been some fair prospects, but they'd volunteered and gone off to the war. Then Eric Travers had come along: good, steady job in a starred occupation, and he'd really liked her, treated her right. But the Zeppelin had seen to him, the bloody hateful Zeppelin that had dropped a bomb on him, and her, and destroyed her hopes.

And after that, she had lost heart, somehow. There'd seemed no point in trying any more. And then Andy Wood had come back. He was supposed to be in France, but he'd told her they'd needed him more at the training camp: his was a specialised skill. He'd said it with a wink, suggesting it had been a 'wangle': he was the master of wangling. But whatever the truth of it, he was there again, big, strong Sergeant Andy Wood, with his feral grin and his flattering partiality for her.

She looked at her pale face in the mirror. She had always thought of herself as a smart girl, but she had not been smart tonight. There were bruises on her arms, and her lips felt swollen from his rough kisses, and – and other parts of her felt very strange indeed. She had never intended for things to go so far. She was not stupid: she knew you never gave away the game until you'd got the ring on your finger. She'd assumed she could control him, like all the others. She hadn't reckoned on his determination . . . or that *she* would get carried away. Yes, there was a bit of her had wanted it too. She was lonely. She missed Eric. And this – it was a sort of love, wasn't it? Underneath her tough, care-nothing act, her secret longing was to be loved, as she never had been, not from the time she was born. Andy Wood was no good for her, she knew that, but he offered a kind of consolation. He made her feel wanted, even if only for a few moments.

Well, there was no point in crying over spilled milk. What was done was done. She clenched her jaw, switched off the light and felt her way in the darkness to the bedroom. Ada was already in bed – she could see the shape under the bedclothes. *Let her say something – let her just!*

But Ada didn't speak.

She got into bed, turned on her side, felt tears come up from somewhere and sting her eyes. She forced them back down. Crying was for weaklings. She was tough. They wouldn't get *her*, she thought – and 'they' in that context meant everyone else in the whole world, because that was who Ethel had always had against her. There never had been anyone *for* her, never in her whole life. Except Eric. But Eric was dead.

The School for Military Aeronautics was newly built in red brick in the neo-Tudor style, so that it rather resembled a small Hampton Court Palace; and the residential facilities were excellent, including bathrooms and a supply of hot water an Oxford student would give his eye teeth for. It was the curriculum that seemed both difficult and pointless. How an aneroid barometer worked; how engine parts were manufactured; the correct method of stitching linen onto an aircraft frame – Bobby couldn't see how these were going to be useful to him. And the Lewis gun: the cadets had to know every part and what it did, how to take the gun apart and put it back together, how to replace a broken bolt, even though none of these things could be done while flying an aircraft, and spare parts weren't even carried.

One could see the point, Bobby admitted, of learning about wireless telegraphy and the Morse code. He found he had no natural aptitude for Morse, but the instructor warned that they would be examined at the end of their pilot training, and that if they could not read and transmit at an acceptable speed, they would fail to gain their wings, however good they proved in the air. So he purchased a portable buzzer (the instructor corporal kept a few on hand to sell to the young gentlemen) and practised whenever he had a spare moment.

He had done some map-reading in officer training, and as he liked maps and enjoyed poring over them, he was well up in that branch; and aerial observation lessons were rather fun. In a windowless room, with a map painted on the floor, the cadet rode in a mock fuselage hung from the ceiling, which was moved about on pulleys. There were little lights embedded in the map that could be turned on and off by the instructor.

The one thing they didn't learn, despite the name of the school, was aeronautics. Nothing was taught about the theory or mechanics of flight. One of Bobby's class, Cartwright, opined laconically that they didn't want to spoil the untouched bloom of ignorance on the cadets' minds before they were actually sent up in an aeroplane.

Time on the ground course was spent pleasantly enough. Reveille was at six o'clock, followed by breakfast, then parade and inspection on the nearby playing-fields. Then there were two lectures and two periods of practical work, divided between morning and afternoon, ending at four o'clock, after which a cadet was off duty until the following morning – unless the CO had ordered Study Parade, in which case they were supposed to stay in their rooms swotting.

In practice, however, nobody much minded if a chap didn't turn up to parade, and even missing classes hardly raised an eyebrow. The CO only ordered Study Parade as a punishment, if anyone annoyed him, and they soon learned to tiptoe round his foibles. Leave was freely granted at weekends, and given that most of the candidates were around eighteen or nineteen, the long hours of free time in the evenings led to much merry-making and frequent sore heads the next day. There was no pressure on them to learn: it was said that the exams at the end were really easy, and that if a chap washed out they let him resit as often as necessary. Bobby, however, thought spending more time here rather than at flight school was pointless, and intended to pass first time, which meant doing a modicum of work.

He had thought officer school relaxing, compared with basic training, but ground school was even more of a cake-walk. As they were officially only 'attached' to the RFC, pending full acceptance after training, they wore the uniform of the regiment from which they had come, but without rank badges, and with a white band covering the regimental cap band. Officially they were supposed to wear breeches and puttees, but one or two, getting up late, experimented with long stockings, and when no fuss was made, the easier dress was adopted by most of the cadets. Off-duty they could wear slacks.

And with the town of Reading accessible and on-limits, and evenings and weekends to fill, the cadets enjoyed them-selves to the limit of their bent, or the pay of seven and six a day, whichever ran out first. Cartwright told Bobby there was no hurry to finish at ground school because at this time of year the weather would prevent their getting much flying anyway. 'Might as well enjoy oneself here as anywhere,' he said. 'At least the beds are decent, and there are enough bathrooms. The one thing you can be sure of about flying school – the accommodation won't be as good.'

But Bobby wanted to get there as soon as possible, bad weather and bad beds notwithstanding. Now and then an aircraft passed over, and he would crane his neck and watch, longing to be the airman up there, looking down on the poor earthbound creatures who didn't know any better.

But the time passed, the exams came and were, as predicted, easy, and Bobby passed. On the following morning he was called in to see the CO, was told he had 'graduated', and was posted to a training squadron at Shoreham-on-Sea.

The CO gave his rare smile and said, 'Congratulations, Hunter.'

'Thank you, sir.'

'From this moment, your pay goes up to eleven and six, plus four and twopence daily allowance. Considerable riches, my boy – don't let it go to your head.'

Bobby grinned. 'No, sir.'

'Here's your travel warrant. Better get your kit packed. The tender for the station will be here in an hour.' He stood up and offered his hand across the desk. 'I'm sure you'll do well, Hunter. I've seen cadets come and go this past year, and you've got the look of a flyer about you.'

He sounded almost wistful, and Bobby felt a pang. The Old Man had been a flyer before the war. Why he was not now operational was unknown to the cadets, but Bobby thought it must be the worst thing that could happen to a chap, to be trained to fly and then not to do it. No wonder the Old Man could be crabby and difficult, he thought. 'Thank you, sir,' he said, shaking the hand with an earnest look. 'I won't let you down, sir.'

He raced up the stairs two at a time. The door to the room next to his was open, and Cartwright could be seen within, packing. 'Where have you got?' he asked, as Bobby paused to look in.

'Shoreham. What about you?'

'Wyton.'

'Where on earth is that?'

'Somewhere in Cambridgeshire, I believe. I've to take the next tender to the station.'

'Me too. I suppose we'll travel as far as London together.'

They looked at each other in silence a moment, bright-eyed and eager. 'I say,' Cartwright said, 'this is the start, isn't it?'

'I can't wait!' Bobby said. 'Do you suppose they'll let us fly straight away?'

'That's the idea, I believe. Get us airborne as soon as possible. I heard one of the instructors saying they're shoving pilots through in six weeks, if they've any aptitude at all.'

'God, I hope I've got aptitude! What happens if you haven't?'

'Ground work, or back to your battalion.'

It sounded like a sentence of death.

'I've got a brother in France,' Bobby said. 'Light infantry.'

A look of absolute understanding passed between them. To end up a foot soldier . . . It didn't bear thinking about.

'I'd better get packing,' said Bobby, and scooted.

The train from Reading to London was fast, but there followed a tedious journey by tube from Paddington to Victoria (though a very pretty young woman in the under-ground train smiled at Bobby in his khaki, and an older woman gave him a mint humbug from a bag and said her son was out in Mesopotamia). Then there was a wait at Victoria until the train to Brighton was ready.

At the barrier at Brighton, Bobby fell in with two other officers bound for the RFC Training Squadron at Shoreham, who introduced themselves as Farringdon and Porteous. They were both from the ground school in Oxford.

'What did you think of it?' Bobby asked, as they walked down the platform together.

Farringdon rolled his eyes. 'Shocking waste of time,' he said. He was lean and swarthy, with the restless, hungry air of a stray dog. 'We seemed to spend every waking hour dismantling a Lewis gun. Not a word about flight.'

'I learned more from my aunt who breeds canaries,' Porteous affirmed. He had a round, innocent pink face and butter-coloured hair. 'She used to tell me about flight feathers and downdraughts and so on. I wish I'd listened more at the time.'

'Aeroplanes don't flap their wings, Porker, old man,' said Farringdon, kindly. 'Hate to disillusion you.'

'Have you ever actually been in an aeroplane?' Bobby asked.

'Never,' said Farringdon. 'More's the pity.'

'Me neither. I can't wait!'

'Porker here went up once – didn't you, old chap?'

'Five-minute flight at a county show when I was a kid. Just a "sixpenny sick", really,' said Porteous, modestly, 'but I've never forgotten it. Ever since then, I've wanted to fly – and, well, really, the war's come as a bit of a godsend. Can't see how else I'd ever have learned. I was down to take over my father's business.'

'Porker's papa owns a string of drapers' shops,' Farringdon put in. 'Anything you want to know about ladies' underwear, he's your man.'

'I was at university,' Bobby said. 'Balliol.'

'Me too,' said Farringdon. 'Trinity. Glad to be out of it. This is going to be much more fun.'

'That's the whistle,' said Porteous. 'We'd better get in. Here, this'll do, won't it?'

They got into a carriage which was already occupied by

an officer, a little older than themselves, whose luggage labels, visible on his bag in the rack, said he was heading for the same training squadron, and that his name was Braithwaite. He didn't respond to their cheerful greetings, moving further into the corner seat and staring away from them, out of the window. But the train to Shoreham was very slow, seeming to move almost at walking speed, and once it got dark outside he could hardly pretend to be watching the scenery, so he had no choice but to engage with them.

They asked him about the squadron, and he seemed willing to enlighten them, though in a very superior manner, *de haut en bas*, as if he had been there for simply *years*, and found it tedious but necessary to unbend towards the lower life forms.

It was pretty relaxed at Shoreham, he told them. Few parades, drill kept to a minimum. Mess etiquette not too strict – none of that 'don't speak until you're spoken to' nonsense. Church parade on Sunday was optional. Not many chaps bothered. Lots of free time, and you could pretty much do as you pleased – you were trusted not to make an ass of yourself. In fact, you were treated as a grown-up, as long as you didn't abuse the trust.

'I like the sound of that,' Farringdon said, rubbing his hands. 'I suppose it's easy enough to get into Brighton when you're off duty? Any pretty girls in the vicinity?'

'I wouldn't know,' said Braithwaite, loftily.

'Never mind girls,' said Bobby. 'What about flying?'

Braithwaite looked weary. 'Oh, nobody does much flying at Shoreham. Too few machines, too few instructors. Too many pupils. You lot don't stand much of a chance of getting up. And if you do, you've got to be pretty damn good to get a second shot. A lot of officers give up after a week and go back to their regiments. Most of them without ever leaving the ground.'

45

The three newcomers looked at each other, crestfallen and doubtful. Farringdon rallied to ask, 'How long have you been there?'

Braithwaite's eyes shifted. 'Two months,' he said. They were too polite to ridicule. 'It's long enough,' he went on. 'I've about given up hope of becoming an active service pilot. I'm thinking of going in for admin – the squadron's got an opening for a non-flying adjutant. Better than going back into the infantry, anyway. I wouldn't get my hopes up, if I were you,' he went on, recovering his superiority after the bathos. 'Unless you show out pretty damned impressively, you'll never get the chance to make pilot.'

With that he turned his head away and, notwithstanding the darkness outside, determinedly watched the passing scenery, signalling that the audience was over.

The other three were silent for a while, digesting the information, then began to talk again. In politeness they didn't discuss what Braithwaite had said, but Bobby could see in the eyes of each of his companions the conviction that it couldn't be so bad, or why would they keep sending people there? And that if anyone was going to show enough promise to fly, it would be him.

They pulled in at Shoreham at last, and stepped out into a chilly, damp darkness with a thrilling tang of salt to it. A Crossley tender was waiting for them, and took them on a short drive, to deposit them outside a bungalow near the sea – they could just hear, in the darkness, the sound of waves sighing on the shingle. 'Officers' mess, sirs,' the driver informed them. They got out, heaving their kit after them. Braithwaite hurried away from them in the darkness without a word, and the other three exchanged a look, shrugged, and went in.

Inside all was comfort: warmth, a friendly welcome, a pleasant fug of cigarettes, the cheerful voices of young men in the prime of life. Bobby noticed a bar along one side, a good fire on the other, a number of battered armchairs, an upright piano, a dart board, and a card school in the corner engaged in what looked like bridge. A handsome, dark captain with pain-aged eyes came over to them, leaning heavily on a stick, and introduced himself as Cardoon, mess president. Bobby eyed the wings on his jacket, and wondered if the stick meant he had suffered what he now thought of as the fate worse than death – not to be able to fly any more.

'I'll have you shown to your quarters later, but I expect you want to relax a bit first, meet some of the chaps. This is Hastings, by the way, head steward – he looks after us all.'

Hastings, in his white jacket, eyed them professionally, and said, 'Dinner's over, gentlemen, I'm afraid, but I can do you cheese and biscuits.'

'And I'll stand you a round of beer,' Cardoon said, 'seeing as you haven't your mess accounts set up yet. Hastings, three tankards, if you please – and I'll have another.' He drained the contents of the glass he was holding, and passed it to Hastings, who exchanged a brief look with him, the meaning of which Bobby did not fathom.

'Thank you very much, sir,' Bobby said. He thought he'd better seize the chance while they had Cardoon's attention. 'I was wondering how much flying we're likely to get. Will we get a chance to go up soon?'

Cardoon only shook his head slightly. 'No "shop" in the mess, gentlemen. Does any of you play the piano, by the way?'

'I do, sir,' said Porteous.

'Excellent. You'll be a big asset, then. We lost our best piano-player last week. One or two of the others tinkle a bit, but nothing to write home about.'

'Lost, sir?' Farringdon queried. Bobby had been about to ask the same question. He hoped it meant the fellow in question had got his wings and been posted to an active squadron.

'Crashed on landing,' said Cardoon, neutrally. 'Broke his neck, I'm afraid.'

Hastings arrived at that moment with a tray, and gave Cardoon what Bobby thought might be a reproachful look. 'Your drinks, gentlemen,' he said.

Cardoon took his glass, which now contained a measure of amber liquid, raised it to them, said, 'Cheerioh!' and walked off to talk to another officer.

The three exchanged a glance. 'I say,' said Porteous, in a low voice.

But two other young men came over to introduce themselves, and after that the talk was lively and cheerful until Hastings appeared to say that an orderly would show them to their quarters if they were ready.

There was one more surprise for them: they were shown to a line of railway carriages, converted into narrow but adequate billets. The sound of the sea, and the smell of it in the fresh breeze that had got up, suggested to Bobby that when he woke in the morning, there would be rather a fine view from the salt-scratched windows.

It started to rain as they heaved their kit up into the compartments. It slapped against them and the carriages with a sound like small pebbles.

'I wonder if we fly when it rains,' Porteous said doubtfully.

'A bit of rain wouldn't stop me,' Bobby said stoutly.

CHAPTER FOUR

'They're back! Oh, my Lord, there was another Zeppelin raid last night!' Cook cried, planking down the teapot so abruptly it rattled the bread-and-butter plate. She almost snatched up the newspaper, which she'd had no time to glance at since getting up, what with upstairs breakfast, downstairs breakfast, orders from the mistress, tradesmen at the door, and now the servants' 'lunch' – as their elevenses were called.

Munt, who had sat down early for once, growled, 'Never mind about blimmin' Zeppelins. Get the tea poured, woman!'

'Don't you woman *me*!' Cook snapped back. 'I've a right to see what's in the paper. Oh, them blessed Zeppelins! Look at this – hundreds killed and injured, it says! Oh, my good Lord! I hate 'em! Hate 'em!'

'Only a load of old gasbags,' Munt said. 'Same as some others I could mention.'

Ginger, the boot boy, sniggered, and Munt shut him down with a look. Ginger was an improvement on his predecessor, Henry, who'd had the wits of a landed herring and would never have understood Munt's caustic humour, but Munt was all for the repression of youth and speak-when-you're-spoken-to, which included sniggering.

'I been dreading this,' Cook said, trying to read the paper and panic at the same time, which wasn't really possible. 'They said it'd come the end of the month, and here they are. Raining death down on us!'

49

'I think it was quite a long way away,' Ada said cautiously. 'Somewhere up north. The Midlands, I think it said. A long way from here, anyway.'

'All in good time, girl,' Munt said, pretending sympathy. 'They'll get round to you.'

Ginger sniggered again, and Cook woke up to what was being said and cracked the boy round the back of his carrotty head with a work-hardened hand. She couldn't slap Munt, more was the pity . . .

'What's the government doing about it? That's what I want to know,' she complained, taking her seat and beginning to pour tea. 'Seems to me the Germans just do what they like. Why don't they shoot 'em down? There was supposed to be anti-aircraft guns and all sorts. Bombing people in their own homes, while our boys are risking their lives out in France!'

'I heard Alfie Wendell got his call-up,' Ada said. Wendell's was the haberdasher's in the village. 'And Clewlow's boy.'

'Which Clewlow?' Cook asked, distracted from bombing of the Midlands by this more immediate concern. There were two Clewlow families, headed by brothers. Alfred, the elder, was a chimney sweep, having taken over the family firm, and Arnold was the local piano-tuner.

'Jimmy, the sweep's son,' Ada clarified. 'It'll be hard for Mr Clewlow, doing it all alone once he's gone. Takes a lot out of you, sweeping chimneys.'

'They can start putting boys up, same as they used to,' Munt said happily. 'Plenty o' boys around no-one'd miss.'

'I wunt mind goin' up a chimbley,' Ginger said stoutly. 'Reckon it'd be fun, messin' about with all that black stuff.'

'Nobody asked you,' Cook said automatically. 'Drink your tea and sharp about it. You got knives to clean.'

'It seems like everyone'll be going,' Ada said anxiously. 'There's that Horace out of Stein's the butcher's – he's had his papers. And that nice man with the big moustache that delivers the coal for Charrington's, what's his name, and I don't know who else!'

'My Jack's been called,' said Mrs Chaplin, the charwoman, who had been quietly getting outside as much bread and butter as she could. But she couldn't waste a piece of news like this.

She got a gratifying amount of attention. 'Never!' Cook exclaimed.

'Oh, my Lord,' said Ada. 'Not your Jack!'

'Coo!' said Ginger. 'Wish I c'd get called up!'

'He wunt go,' Munt opined tersely. 'Not once they knows he's the blacksmith.'

'He's appealing,' Mrs Chaplin admitted, 'but he's that worried. He says, "What'll happen to you, Auntie, if I go?"'

'I'm sure Mr Munt's right,' Ada chipped in loyally. 'They won't send *him*. Someone's got to shoe the horses, stands to reason.'

'Don't they have 'orses at the Front, then?' Ginger asked innocently.

To distract from this awkward question, Cook looked across at Ethel, who had been sitting staring at nothing, as she so often did, these days. 'Haven't you got an opinion about it?' she asked her sharply. 'Cat got your tongue?'

'Ah, she's thinkin' about *him*, so she is,' Emily said sentimentally. 'I had an auntie buried her heart in the grave with her husband,' she went on. 'He fell off a cart and got trampled by the horses.'

'Nobody wants to know about your auntie,' Cook said. 'You got all too many aunties.' Her sympathy with Ethel, never very great, was being worn out by the length of her mourning for that chap. When all was said and done, they were only walking out, not even engaged. 'You used to be ready enough with your opinions,' she pursued, scowling at her. 'Whether we wanted 'em or not.'

51

Without looking at her, Ethel stood up. 'I got fires to do,' she said, and walked out.

Ada looked at Cook reproachfully. 'You gone and upset her.'

'She wants upsetting. Time she bucked up,' Cook said. 'Don't she realise there's a war on?'

'She didn't eat a thing,' Ada said. 'Didn't even touch her tea.'

'Can I have her bit o' cake?' Emily asked eagerly.

Munt looked at Cook with rare approval. 'They say salt is good for wounds. Gotter rub it well in, though.'

'Oh, what are you talking about, you tiresome old man?' Cook retorted. 'You mind your business. Isn't it time you got back to work?'

'Gotter have me cake first,' Munt said calmly, taking a slice. He fixed Emily with a sardonic eye. 'I'll have Miss Hoity-Toity's as well, seein' she don't want it.' And he took a second. Emily could only watch wistfully.

Edward's secretary came in with a guilty expression. 'You have the look of a dog with feathers round its mouth,' said Edward. 'What have you done?' Warren reluctantly proffered something that had the look of an official letter, a War Office kind of letter. Edward's smile disappeared. 'Oh, no!' he said. 'Not you, Warren.'

'I'm sorry, sir,' Warren said. 'My call-up came this morning. I've been trying to think how to tell you.'

'I shall appeal,' Edward declared.

'No grounds, sir,' Warren said. 'I'm only a clerk. Anyone can do my work.'

'You are my confidential secretary. You know perfectly well that I can't do without you. I'll get you out of it.' Warren only looked at him, seeking for words. Edward understood. 'You don't want to be got out of it,' he said.

Warren bit his lip. 'My family would be awfully put out if I shirked my duty. And – well . . .'

'You want to go.'

At last Warren nodded. 'I love my position here – you've been very good to me – but I *do* want to go.'

'Then there's nothing more to be said.'

'You're angry with me,' Warren said unhappily.

Edward roused himself. 'God! No. Not with *you*. You've . . .' he hesitated, then said it anyway '. . . you've been like a son to me. It's this damnable war.' He stood up and came round his desk to shake Warren's hand. 'My loss is the War Office's gain. You'll make a splendid officer. But I really don't know how I can manage without you.'

'I'll have a couple of weeks, sir. I can train someone in the basic procedures.'

'And I suppose as soon as I get used to the new man, he'll get called up as well,' Edward sighed.

'Well, sir, I did think about that, and it occurred to me that Mr Murchison is – er – too senior for the call-up.'

'Murchison?' He must be fifty at least, Edward thought, one of the clerks who had been at the bank since the earth cooled. 'Do you think he's up to it?' he asked doubtfully.

'He's slow and methodical,' Warren said. 'That's not a bad thing when you're dealing with money. His overall experience, I think, will compensate for his newness to the position. And you couldn't want a more discreet person. In all the time I've been here I've never known him to gossip.'

Edward thought of the relationship he had developed with Warren, and sighed inwardly. It was not to be expected that that could be replicated. Murchison? Well, as Warren said, he did know the bank inside out. 'Have you sounded him out?'

'I wouldn't speak to him without your permission, of course,' Warren said, 'but I believe he would. It would entail a rise in salary, and he's the sole support of elderly parents. I do think it would be the best solution to the problem – at least in the short term.'

'Very well. You may ask him, and if he agrees, I'll see

him. But you'll be on your mettle to get him set up before you leave me.'

'I'll do my very best, sir,' said Warren. 'And now I'll fetch your coffee.'

'Better make it strong,' said Edward. 'I'll need it after this shock.'

There had been one or two meetings on neutral ground, and Beattie, Edward and Diana had dined with the Oliphants; now it was time to return the compliment. Beattie had secured the presence of the Olivers, who by a lucky chance had their nephew Henry 'Hank' Bowers staying with them on that date, on embarkation leave.

'It'll be nice for Diana to see him again,' Beattie said, as they dressed.

'Will she care?' Edward asked, tilting his head skyward to fasten his collar-button.

'He always was a lively young man. I've never heard her laugh so much as when they were helping with the fête together.'

The boys had been excused dinner. Peter was too young to eat so late, and though William had just had his sixteenth birthday, he pleaded off on the grounds of homework and school the next day. But they were both excited that the Oliphants were coming by motor-car, which they hoped to examine extensively while the owners were indoors.

'They have a chauffeur, too,' Peter informed Cook, leaning beguilingly on the end of the table where she was making pastry. She sometimes gave him the scraps, and he liked raw pastry even more than cooked. 'If I had a motor-car, I'd want to drive it myself.'

'Then you'd get to where you were going all messy. Grand gentlemen don't drive themselves.'

'Lord Dene did,' Peter pointed out. 'He was grand, wasn't he?'

Cook didn't want to remember the disappointment of

losing Lord Dene. 'You'll have to move,' she said tautly. 'You're in my road there.'

She knew about the chauffeur, because the mistress had warned her that they would have to entertain him in the kitchen. It had caused a moderate stir. Any visitor was a welcome interruption, and there was always the chance that he would be young, handsome and lively – or at least one of those things.

In the event he turned out to be slightly deaf, with a lower lip like a spoon, which made him look disagreeable. And elderly. 'At least the Oliphants won't lose him to that conscription,' Cook philosophised.

'He can't help how he looks,' said Ada.

And in fact, apart from the deafness, Craven proved perfectly pleasant. He was polite to everyone, praised the supper he shared with the servants, and had some interesting anecdotes about the family. He even went so far as to say, 'Our miss is lucky to get your young gentleman, in my view.'

Cook demurred politely. 'Oh, no,' she said. 'She's a very pretty young lady – and pretty-behaved, too, which is more than you can say for every girl these days.'

'I don't say she's not a picture,' said Craven, 'but she's a regular feather-head. Nothing up top at all.'

Cook was slightly taken aback by such frankness. She rallied. 'Well, Mr Craven, you know and I know that gentlemen generally prefer a pretty girl to a clever one.'

'Chosen right, then, hasn't he?' said Craven, shortly. 'I've had the driving of her all these years, to one thing and another. Dancing lessons, tennis lessons – and that's another thing. No sticking power. One week it's all macramé, next week that's forgotten, and it's watercolours or Swedish drill.' He shook his head. 'Never sticks at nothing, that one,' he said, with a sad lapse from gentility.

'Oh, well, she's young,' Cook said generously. 'She'll learn.'

★　★　★

In the drawing-room, Sadie was remembering how amusing Hank Bowers was. She was also discovering that he was still in love with Diana, which was sad. It made her want to take him to one side and say, 'It's no use, you know.'

There was much talk over dinner of his imminent departure for France. He had joined the Sherwood Foresters, a line regiment of distinguished history. 'That's the benefit of volunteering instead of waiting to be called up,' he said, with a covert glance at Diana, hoping she was impressed. 'You get to choose the best regiment.'

Diana listened, or at least appeared to listen, and looked beautiful and sad. It was very affecting. Sadie could never do that. It occurred to her that if she had been in Diana's shoes she probably would have had to 'snap out of it' long before this: if you weren't beautiful, people had less patience with you. She wouldn't have been any less sad than Diana, but plain people had to hide it better.

After dinner, Hank followed the women straight into the drawing-room, saying apologetically that in America people didn't divide and, if it was all the same to them, he'd sooner be with the ladies.

He meant, of course, with Diana, the poor goop, thought Sadie. So, since the three matriarchs made a natural grouping, she decided to take pity on him and occupy Sophy's attention so that he could have Diana to himself.

It was easy to cut Sophy out and start her talking, and from the corner of her eye Sadie saw that Hank and Diana soon had their heads together. It was hard to find common ground with Sophy, though. She didn't like horses (too dangerous) or dogs (dirty paws, loose hairs). Walking was nice, she allowed, when it was fine and the paths were not either muddy or dusty, but she preferred having shops to look in. She said she loved the countryside for its pretty flowers and dear little birds, but could not name a single one of the latter, and when asked about her favourite flowers said roses, then ran out of ideas.

Favourite books were a wash-out – she said she never had time for reading. She did, however, go to the cinema sometimes, and had a tenacious memory for every moving picture she had ever seen. Having started her off, Sadie was able to sit back and listen as Sophy told her the title and plot of each, plus a surprising amount about the lives and careers of the actors in them. Sadie had been to the pictures only twice. She'd have liked to go more often, but she was too busy with war work. Anyway, she couldn't have gone alone, and Diana had never cared for the pictures.

Sophy also spoke modestly but extensively about the various beaux she had turned down for David. She would be astonished, Sadie reflected, had she known that not a single chap had ever taken that sort of interest in *her*. She thought briefly of John Courcy, the veterinary officer, now out in France tending the army's horses, and put the thought quickly away. She couldn't think of Courcy in that way. Had no right to.

Early February had been mild and wet, with winds from the south-east; now they had gone round to the north-west and strengthened, and it had turned very cold. On a dark day, with snow blowing in, there were worse places than the drawing-room of Lady Frances Webber's house in Bedford Square, with a good fire, and a fine fug that seemed somehow equal parts ceaseless conversation and cigarettes.

'I think about poor Sam, though,' said Louisa, as they shed their coats, scarves, hats and gloves. Her brother, who had been a shipping clerk in peacetime, had volunteered for the navy, and was serving aboard a Devonshire class armoured cruiser on convoy duty, protecting merchant shipping in the White Sea. 'Imagine what it must be like for him. In his letter he said it was so cold on deck, the tears froze on his cheeks!'

Laura and Louisa had been semi-detached members of the Bedfordite circle for some time now. Laura really went for Louisa's sake: the Bedfordites had been her friends back in suffragette days, and the high-flown intellectual argument satisfied something in her character, where Laura would always sooner be *doing* than *talking*.

But at least Lady Frances's food and drink were better than average. 'Bohemian' parties tended towards undergraduate fare, like cocoa and sausages.

A sensation was caused during the evening by the arrival of Rupert Wroughton (now, of course, Lord Dene, though Laura kept forgetting his title), resplendent in a very new army uniform.

'My God, Rupert!' The voice of Freddy Fawcett rose above the welcoming babble. 'They got you!'

'Not a bit,' Rupert returned blithely. 'I got myself.' His eyes, dancing gleefully round the company, paused on Laura a moment, and he gave her a nod, which seemed somehow significant, though she could not imagine on what account. She didn't mind Rupert, thinking him a conceited ass who would one day engineer his own downfall, but she didn't like his friend Erskine Ballantine, who was creeping in sulkily in his wake. She thought him an unhealthy little beast.

'Rupert, sweetie, what can you mean?' chirruped 'Baby' Melville. 'And what are those darling little red bits on your tunic? They're awfully jolly. Why hasn't my brother got some?'

'Don't tell me Boy has been called up!' Grace Lattery interrupted. She had long harboured a not-very-secret passion for Baby's brother, Boy, otherwise the novelist Tom Melville. 'I wondered why I'd not seen him for a while. How positively gruesome!'

'Yes, poor Boy!' Baby trilled. 'But he's looking on the bright side, the darling – you know how brave he is. He's thinking how many wonderful plots and characters he'll get out of it.'

Since Melville's eight novels so far had all concerned

fiercely intellectual romances between artists of one sort or another, Laura wondered how much help the war and soldiering would really be to him.

Rupert retrieved the conversation. 'The little red bits are gorget tabs, you positive ignoramus,' he said loudly to Baby, 'and they demonstrate to anyone with half a brain that I am on the Staff.'

'How divinely rude you are, darling,' said Baby, imperturbably. 'And what staff is that? The staff of Derry & Toms?' Hilary Ogden, her closest friend, gave a little shriek of admiring laughter.

'No, my pet,' said Rupert, with a poisonous smile. 'Not "a" staff but *The* Staff, with great big capital letters. The advantage of having a papa with influence in the right places. Since it seemed inevitable that I would get called up sooner or later, the pater and I decided the best thing was to get it over with as quickly as possible and secure me a billet at Headquarters, where my particular talents will be best used.'

'And what *are* your particular talents?' asked Sylvia Partridge, drily.

Rupert darted her an impudent look. 'Nothing *you* need enquire about, dear child.'

'It's all right for him,' Erskine moaned. 'What's going to happen to *me*? That's what I want to know. I can't go off to war. Suppose it's France and the trenches? I just *can't*.'

'You'll have to be a conscientious objector, then,' said Grace Lattery. 'How romantic!'

'I must say I'm finding myself not terribly keen on that any more,' said Freddy Fawcett, slowly. 'I can't help feeling it's not quite the thing.'

'My dear Freddy,' said Lady Frances, 'you've always been the most implacable opponent of war. You can't apostasise now.'

'I'm *still* opposed to war,' Freddy said. 'Never more so.

It's *ugly*, and I've devoted my whole life to beauty. But it's one thing to stand against it on principle, another to refuse to do one's bit when the country's up against it.'

There was an outcry, five or six different arguments advanced by five or six different speakers at once. Above it, Freddy raised his reedy voice. 'I know, I know, but don't you see how it *looks*?'

'One must follow one's conscience,' said Leland Brandt.

'Well, my conscience tells me I don't want to go,' Erskine said.

'Then you must stand by it, and refuse,' said Brandt. 'And go to prison.'

Erskine's eyes opened wide and he gave a squeak of horror. 'Prison!'

'Oh, how wonderful!' Grace Lattery said admiringly. 'You'll be a hero.'

'I don't want to be a hero,' Erskine cried.

'No, no, we can't have poor Erskine in prison,' said Rupert, merrily. 'It wouldn't be his thing at all. Shaving in cold water with a blunt razor? Wearing a suit with horrid arrows all over it? Unthinkable! No, I've told him, he'll have to become gainfully employed and indispensable.'

'In a starred occupation, you mean?' said someone, doubtfully.

'Quite. He might become an engine-driver. Or a coal-miner.' Rupert's eye roved round to Laura again. 'Or a policeman, like Miss Hunter.'

'You mean police*woman*,' said Grace Lattery.

'No, he's right,' said Laura, amused. '"Man" in that context doesn't connote gender. It means "member of the human race", of mankind.' Louisa gave her a look of respect. Laura didn't usually join in with the abstract conversations that occupied so much of their energy – but that didn't mean she couldn't.

Grace Lattery took it up. 'But there you are, you see –

*man*kind. Why is the whole species named after the male creature? Why are women a sub-division of "man"?'

'Anthropologically speaking,' said Leland Brandt, 'given that most ancient societies were matriarchal, it's more likely that the species was originally named "woman", and that "man" came afterwards. "Man", in fact, is probably short for "woman".'

Rupert hooted with laughter. 'Short for woman! I love it! I'm short for woman! Erskine, on the other hand, is rather tall for one – though put him in a dress, with some lip-rouge and a little kohl round the eyes, and he'd pass delightfully. Indeed, *has* on occasion.'

'Shut up, Rupe,' Erskine muttered sulkily.

'Oh, Rupert, you're so frivolous,' complained Freddy. 'We were discussing something important, the nature of duty and the role of conscience.'

Other voices jumped in, eager to prove themselves *not* frivolous by taking up Freddy's subject. Rupert slid away from it and eased himself up to Laura.

'Mr Ballantine, a coal-miner?' she opened. 'That takes more imagination than I can muster.'

'I'm sure there must be starred occupations that are less physically demanding,' Rupert said. 'But I don't despair of getting him a cushy billet somehow. Really, making Erskine a soldier would be a sure way to lose the war. I'd ask my father to help, but the trouble is, the mater doesn't exactly love poor Erskine. And the Guv'nor tends to do what she wants.'

'So it was she who secured your staff appointment, was it?' Laura said.

'Well, the pater did the actual bizney, of course,' said Rupert, 'but she was behind it, the way gunpowder is behind a rocket.'

'She didn't want you to go to France?'

He shook his head. 'With Charles gone, you see, all their

hopes rest on me.' He met her eye. 'For an heir, and all that sort of thing.'

'I see,' she said.

'It would be a disaster if I went to France and got myself killed, like Charles, before producing the next generation. Of course, I'm not as clumsy as Charles, poor fellow, but they say there's no arguing with a German shell and – well, getting an heir takes time.'

'Particularly when you're not even married,' Laura suggested.

'Quite. So the idea is to keep me safely at home until I can get the thing done and the inheritance secured, because otherwise some ghastly colonial cousin gets the lot.'

'I expect your mother has a list of suitable young women,' said Laura.

'Yes,' said Rupert. He was silent a moment, thinking, which struck Laura as remarkable, she not having believed he could do either, let alone both at once. He roused himself. 'Of course, the mater *could* produce someone at the drop of a hat. But not necessarily someone I could consider.'

He stared at her so long and thoughtfully, she half wondered if he was going to propose to *her*. She smiled at the thought, and he seemed to find the smile encouraging.

'Your niece,' he said. 'Miss Hunter – Miss Diana Hunter. How is she? I haven't seen her since I came up to Town. Is she – over it?'

'I can't speak to the state of her heart,' Laura said, 'but she's carrying on, as women do. She's not locking herself in a darkened room or starving herself to death.'

'No, I suppose she wouldn't,' he said thoughtfully. 'I believe she was always very popular.'

'It's a little early for her to be thinking of replacing your brother in her affections,' Laura said drily. 'But when she does, I imagine there will be plenty of candidates.'

'Does she ever come up to Town?' Rupert asked.

'As it happens, I believe she has been invited to stay with her cousin Beth for a week or so – the wife of my nephew Jack who's at the front.'

'Oh, yes, I know Mrs Jack Hunter of Ebury Street. We met last year,' said Rupert. 'When will that be?'

'I really don't know,' Laura said. 'Soon, I believe.'

Lady Frances came up to claim Rupert's attention, and soon he was in the centre of a lively group. Laura turned away and joined a conversation with Sylvia Partridge. She pondered, in the back of her mind, on Rupert's questions about Diana. Had it just been idle curiosity? Or was it possible he was thinking of her in a romantic context? It seemed unlikely, given that Charles's fancy for Diana had been so out of the usual. And Rupert had always seemed so much more wedded to his rank than his brother. Probably just idle curiosity, then. Nothing for her to do about it, anyway.

CHAPTER FIVE

On Wednesdays, Edward worked late at the office, then went to dine with one of his clients. What he didn't tell them at home was that it was always the same client, and that he dined with her at her home. He wasn't sure why he kept this a secret. But it could, he supposed, be misunderstood. There really was no business need for him to see Élise de Rouveroy *every* week.

But it wasn't as if there was anything vicious in his relationship with her. He liked talking to her, that was all. She interested him – and was interested in him. It reminded him of the early years with Beattie, when she had loved his company, and had told him all her little concerns when he came home at the end of the day.

But as time had gone on – and particularly in recent years – Beattie had become more silent, more withdrawn from him. He felt, often, like a visitor in his own home. He worked long and hard in Town every day to maintain his wife, his home, his family, but did any of them care how he felt, wonder what he was thinking?

Élise made him feel welcome. For those few hours in her company, he was not lonely. So it pleased him to keep her as his secret – his harmless, but pleasant, secret.

He arrived on this particular evening to find her poring over the newspaper. 'It is very bad, this business at Verdun,' she greeted him. 'My poor country! They say the Boche are bringing in hundreds of heavy guns and thousands of men.'

'It looks like a major offensive,' he agreed. 'And they hold the high ground. Counter-attacking would be very costly.'

'But they shall never have Verdun!' she said fiercely. 'It shall never fall!'

Verdun held a particular place in French hearts – a ring of defensive forts built by the great Vauban in the French hinterland, on the banks of the Meuse, and recently modernised and made more formidable. The Région Fortifiée de Verdun had been regarded as the guarantee that Germany should never enter France by the back door. Edward was aware of the passion and pride with which the French believed in Verdun. They would never accept defeat there. The worry was that the Germans knew that, and would keep attacking, from their position of strength on the high ground, until the French wore themselves out, or bled to death.

He talked to her about most things, but some aspects of the war he wished he could keep from her. He felt protective of her. To distract her on this occasion, he said, 'I had an interesting meeting today with a rather important person.'

She was instantly engaged. 'But why should you sound surprised that important people wish to see you? Who was this fellow?'

'The home secretary.'

She made that little puff of the lips that was so French and dismissive. 'He does not sound so very much. Secretary of the home. Like Solange – she is my home secretary.'

'It's one of the great offices of state,' Edward said. 'In England, we like our titles to be smaller than the men who wear them.'

'I know, you are a modest people, *jamais le gasconade*,' she said. '*Voyons*, who is this housekeeper of state? What is he like?'

'His name is Herbert Samuel, and he's a fine, handsome man – with a large moustache,' he added, since he knew she liked moustaches and thought a man incomplete without one. 'And he dresses very well.'

'Oh, I am not so shallow,' she said, though in fact she had an intense interest in appearance, and made shrewd judgements from the way people dressed. 'What is he *like*?'

'He was at Balliol at the same time as me,' Edward said. 'I was a year ahead of him, but we became friends all the same. You see, he was born to Jewish parents, and there were some who didn't approve of that.'

'But you defended him,' Élise concluded.

'He is a fine person with a good mind. Very able,' Edward said. 'I've never cared for that sort of prejudice. In fact, he abandoned his religious beliefs when we were still at Oxford – I don't think he had ever held them deeply. Though I understand he still keeps up some of the practices, for his wife's sake. He's devoted to her.'

Élise nodded. 'That is as it should be. I like this house-keeper of yours. And how did you meet him again? Was it a "bumping in"?' She had learned the expression recently and found it intensely amusing, for reasons Edward couldn't quite fathom.

'No, in fact he sent me round a note asking if I could find it convenient to have a drink with him at the club before dinner.'

'And what did you talk of?'

'Shortage of manpower – his particular responsibility. It's the biggest worry for the government. It's hard to conduct a war without men.'

'Without ammunition, too,' she said. They had discussed on more than one occasion the shell shortage, which she had gleaned from the newspapers and quizzed him about on their evenings together.

'They're dealing with that – munitions factories being

built at a tremendous rate. They think they'll have the problem solved by the summer. But it's comparatively easy to make shells and bullets – harder to conjure up soldiers.'

'But now you have conscription,' said Élise. 'Is it not enough?'

'That's what I asked Samuel. He said it would be enough if everyone who was called up actually served. But one in two is refusing.'

She laughed. 'That is what you get for being so *gentil*! In France, in Germany, they do not *ask*, they *command*.'

'That is why there are revolutions abroad, and not here,' Edward countered. 'It's called democracy.'

She said *pfft* again. It was a very useful sound, he thought. 'But how is this problem relating to you?' she asked. Her gaze sharpened. 'You will not have to go, will you?'

'No. I told you, the upper age limit is forty-one.'

He did not tell her that Lord Forbesson had told him the conscription age limit was bound to be raised sooner or later.

'So, then, did Mr Housekeeper want only to sip sherry and gaze at your *beaux yeux*?' she teased, with a tight, amused look.

'I'll explain. You understand that when a man is called up he has the right to appeal?'

'*Bien sûr.*'

'Very well. The appeals are heard by a town or district board made up of local worthies – tradesmen, clergymen, retired gentlemen, and so on.'

'*Les gens du monde,*' she said.

'Well, whoever they can get, really,' Edward amended. 'The quality of the individuals is variable, and so is the quality of their decisions. There's no consistency across the country, and of course it causes resentment. So there has to be a system of appeal.'

'Ah! Now we come to you, I think,' she said.

'You are very quick. Yes, the Appeals Tribunal for Middlesex—'

He stopped as she gave her customary snort of laughter. She thought the word 'Middlesex' very funny. She said that when she had been a ballet girl in Paris, she had known many Middlesex people.

'– for Middlesex sits in Westminster, and he has asked me if I will serve on it.'

'How often would you be wanted?'

'Once or twice a week, from two in the afternoon until eight at night. I said I thought that was possible. It would mean I could get my work done in the morning—'

'And afterwards take a late supper with your friend Élise, and tell her all that has happened,' she said gleefully. 'I am sure there will be much you will want to talk about.'

'Samuel warned me that it will be a thankless task. After all, one may be sending a man to his death.'

'God decides,' she said. 'You need not think of it.'

'I'm bound to think of it,' he said. 'I have a son and a nephew in France.' He paused a moment, then went on, 'Samuel also warned that whatever one decides will upset someone. If you let a man off, you're encouraging scrimshankers. If you don't, you're robbing some poor widow of her only son.'

'Then there is no reason not to be impartial,' she said briskly. 'But, attend, I have a most important question.'

'Which is?'

'What,' she asked, screwing up her face, 'are *scrimshankers*?' She said it with an exaggerated French accent, which made it sound ludicrously funny.

A disconsolate group of young men stood at the edge of the airfield with their hands in their pockets. It was nearly two weeks since there had been any flying – the weather

68

had been 'unfavourable'. Today, one of the machines had been wheeled out of the sheds, but their hopes did not rise. If anyone *was* going to fly, it would be one of the senior pupils. The weather would not be good enough for instructional flying.

The machine before them, they now knew, was an MF.7, a Maurice Farman biplane known as a Longhorn. It had puzzled them mightily when they had first seen it. It had an elevator sticking out in front on long, curving outriggers, and a double set of elevators projecting behind on wooden spars, so it was hard to tell which way it was facing. Somewhere in the middle was what appeared to be the sort of old-fashioned bathtub in which Marat had been murdered. They had learned that this was called the nacelle – *not* the cockpit, gentlemen. All around it was a forest of struts and spars, with floppy white canvas drooping from various surfaces, and what seemed an impenetrable tangle of piano wire. It did not look at all the sort of thing that might ever leave the earth – and yet on this strange creature their future as flyers depended.

So far, all they'd had was talk. Instruction on the ground was not much thought of at flying school, and occupied only a couple of hours a day, even when there was no flying. What they learned in the classroom did not seem to be very helpful, and was usually appended with the words, 'You'll see when you get up there.'

They learned that the two fatal errors in flight were 'spinning' and 'stalling', and that remaining alive and aloft was a matter of maintaining a foothold on the narrow ledge between the two. The Longhorn, for instance, left the ground at around thirty-six miles an hour, and her top speed was around forty-six, giving you ten miles per hour to play with. Try to fly too fast, and the engine would overheat and die; lose too much speed and you would stall. Try to dive too fast, and something would snap off, or the wings would be ripped from the body. Bank too steeply and you would fall into a spin.

Then there was the mystery of 'lift': the combined favourability of the air, the wind, the clouds. An instructor captain took them outside and tried to get them to sniff the air and develop a 'nose' for what conditions aloft would be like. His lectures invariably ended with 'You'll see when you get up there.'

They learned a few 'golden rules' – never turn downwind at low altitude; if in difficulties after take-off, go straight on, don't try to turn back – but otherwise they had nothing to do but get up late, wander down to the sheds and stare at the machines, speculate on when they might fly and which of them would fail the course.

Bobby found himself remembering Braithwaite's words, that a lot of officers gave up and went back to their regiments. He was determined to stick it. He was becoming firm friends with Farringdon and Porteous – whom Farringdon called Porker because of his wholesome pinkness. Despite his innocent appearance, Farringdon said, Porker was a devil with the females. 'They all want to mother him,' he complained. 'They all want to press him to their bosoms.'

'I have to force myself,' Porteous said sadly. 'It's only polite.'

Bobby thought it more likely that Farringdon, with his faintly piratical air, was the greater lure to womankind, but whichever was the ringleader, the only thing they thought about besides aeroplanes was women. Several nights a week they abandoned the mess, begged a lift from a transport and went into Brighton to pick up girls. 'You should come too,' Farringdon urged.

But Bobby said, 'There's time for all that later.' He wanted only to fly.

He spent his leisure time curled up in an armchair in the mess, or on his railway-carriage bed, reading everything he

70

could find on aeronautics, meteorology and aero-engineering, and studying maps of the area so that if he ever did get aloft, he would know where he was.

On this damp grey morning there was at least no rain, and the clouds were quite high. Bobby sniffed the air and said, 'I make the wind speed about ten miles an hour – what do you think?'

'I'll take your word for it, old hound,' said Farringdon.

'Seems about right to me,' said Porteous. 'P'raps a bit more.'

'Maybe they'll let one of us go up,' Bobby said wistfully.

'Incurable optimist,' said Farringdon.

'I say, something's happening,' said Porteous. A moment later he slumped as the mechanics wheeled out one of the single-seater machines, which were rumoured to be capable of ninety miles an hour. 'Not for us, then,' he said.

But they followed anyway, to see which lucky pup might be taking off today, and saw one of the instructors, Captain Andrews, walking across from the main hut with a pupil at his heels.

'It's Braithwaite,' Porteous said. 'He must be soloing.'

'Does he look a bit green to you?' Farringdon suggested.

'It's just the morning light,' said Bobby.

'No, I tell you he's in a funk,' Farringdon said, lowering his voice. 'What a chump! I wonder if *that*'s why he wants an admin job?'

The cadets had been encouraged to watch any flight and learn from it, so they gathered along the edge of the airfield, and the instructors stood nearby to point out anything they might need to know. Braithwaite mounted the machine and the propellor was swung. The engine caught and roared. They heard Andrews shout, 'Get well out across the aerodrome before you take off,' and saw Braithwaite, unrecognisable now in flying cap and goggles, put up his thumb in acknowledgement. Then he was bumping away over the long

71

grass and the instructor was walking back to stand with the others.

They watched as the machine taxied to the far side of the aerodrome and turned. After a short pause, they heard Braithwaite give it full throttle, and the aeroplane surged forwards into the wind and lifted off the ground, climbing steeply towards the sheds.

A dozen heads turned with it, filled with the longing to be the one up there. They shaded their eyes against the light to keep the small machine in view as it passed above the line of sheds, as it cleared the telegraph poles lining the road on the far side of the field and climbed on. And every one of them heard the sputtering noise of an engine in trouble. The roar of the exhaust faded, the nose dipped, and a hand clutched each heart.

Braithwaite had reached about a hundred and fifty feet. Ahead of him, as Bobby knew, having studied the terrain during his hours of idleness, there was a series of small fields divided by hedges and intersected with drainage ditches. 'He's going to have a rough landing,' he said. 'Broken undercarriage, at least.'

'Poor devil!' said Farringdon. 'D'you think they dock your pay?'

'No, by God, he's turning back,' said Porteous.

'He must be a better pilot than we took him for,' Bobby said, but with doubt in his voice. Hadn't they been told never to turn downwind at low altitude? That was exactly what Braithwaite had done. He must be losing airspeed. The machine had reached the sheds, and he tried to bank, but the nose jerked downwards in a stall.

'He's going to spin,' Farringdon said, and there was no excitement in his voice, just dead calculation.

'No, he'll make it,' Porteous said, his voice cracking.

The aeroplane seemed to fall sideways in the first turn of a spin. The starboard wing tip caught the end of the shed roof and flipped the machine, like a balsa-wood toy. It disappeared behind the end shed and a second later there was the appalling sound of a crash.

No-one said anything, but as one man they began to run.

'Pupils, stand still!' one of the instructors shouted. 'Stay where you are!'

But he had as much chance of success as Canute. Every man was running, pupils, instructors and mechanics. The latter, Bobby saw, were carrying axes and fire-extinguishers, and a strange-looking hook on a coiled rope. Two of them had a folded-together stretcher. The realisation struck him graphically, as things do at such tense moments, that it was not the first crash they had attended. They knew what to do.

Beyond the last shed, the aeroplane lay like a dead bird, flightless, ruined – a mess of wreckage. Braithwaite was sitting motionless in the smashed cockpit. Bobby thought he was dead, but all at once he seemed to shake himself, and started fumbling with his safety-belt. The first of the mechanics had reached the wreckage when one of the others shouted, 'Fire!'

Bobby saw it, a flicker of flames below the fuselage, red and hungry like tongues.

'Look out!' someone else shouted, and the mechanics jumped back as a gout of flame leaped up from the burst petrol tank. It roared over the whole wreck, engulfing the pilot. For an instant he disappeared, and then, as he managed to free himself at last, he came struggling and tumbling out, his clothes alight. One of the mechanics knocked him to the ground, Andrews grabbed a blanket from the stretcher and threw it over him, and between them they rolled and beat at him. Coats and a sack were brought into play by two more mechanics, while the others were trying hopelessly to quell with extinguishers a fire generated by thirty gallons of petrol.

Captain Cardoon limped towards the little knot of horrified pupils, his arms slightly out as if he could shield the view from them with his meagre body.

'Go on back,' he said. 'You can't help here.' And when they hesitated, 'Go away, damn you! Get out of here!'

They went, silent and shaken.

It was quiet in the mess. No-one wanted to leave until everything was known, but no-one much wanted to talk. They drank beer, avoiding each other's eyes, and smoked, and waited. At last one of the instructors, Captain Peterson, came in, walked up to the bar, and was given, without even asking for it, a large brandy.

When it was nearly gone, one of the senior pupils, a lean fellow called Ampleforth, said, 'What news, sir? How's Braithwaite?'

Peterson turned. His face was dirty with soot, but quite expressionless. 'Didn't make it,' he said. 'Doc says he had a fractured skull, so he probably didn't know much about it. Andrews has some bad burns on his hands. That's all.' He finished the rest of the brandy with a convulsive jerk of the wrist, and walked out.

A little while later the squadron commander, Major Corning, walked in. They jumped to their feet, but he said, 'Sit down. I want to talk to you.' They'd had little to do with him so far, and it was obviously a serious matter for him to address them in the mess.

He clasped his hands behind him, subjected each face to a lengthy scrutiny, and finally began, quite abruptly, 'You have witnessed an unhappy accident. The first and only thing to do in such an event is to see what caused it, what the pilot did wrong, and to learn the lessons. This crash was stupid and unnecessary, but perhaps some good will come of it, if none of you ever does the same thing.'

Bobby felt obscurely comforted by the bracing words.

74

Flying was not, after all, an unnatural act, irrationally dangerous, horrible and cruel: it was something they could learn to do safely. He sat up straighter.

'The engine failed,' said the major. 'That was not the pilot's fault. But what happened afterwards *was*. He need not have died.' He paused a beat to allow them to digest that. Then he resumed: 'The pilot turned downwind at low altitude and lost flying speed. What should he have done?'

He looked straight at Bobby, who answered without thinking. 'Carried on, sir, not tried to turn back.'

'Correct,' said the major, unsmiling. 'Aeroplanes are designed to glide, gentlemen. If you have no engine, keep going until you find a place to land. Maintain flying speed. Do not attempt to turn. Put down as best you can, even if it's a rough landing. Better smash your wheels than your skull. Have you got that?'

'Yes, sir,' they murmured.

'Now get to bed. The weather's improving. We're hoping for some flying tomorrow.'

He strode out.

'Flying tomorrow,' Farringdon said, in a voice between doubt and hope.

'It's what we're here for,' said Porteous.

'We'd best get some sleep,' said Bobby.

'The old man didn't say we couldn't have a nightcap,' said Farringdon, and beckoned to the mess steward.

None of them mentioned Braithwaite's name again.

Frank Hussey, who had once been Munt's boy, and was now second gardener at Mandeville Hall, had a pleasant habit of turning up every now and then for Sunday dinner. Cook would have been glad for him to come every week. He was welcome to all of them, as a source of new conversation and news from a wider world. Servants didn't mind hard work – they were used to it – but boredom was a trial to them.

It was quite a gala Sunday when Frank arrived on the same day that Ada had invited Corporal Armstrong. The two men greeted each other cordially, and Cook proudly brought in the vast joint of pork, its crackling gleaming, bronzed roast onions sitting round it on the dish, while Emily and Ethel followed with the dishes of baked potatoes, cabbage and parsnips. Cook loved to feed people, but most of all she loved to feed men. Corporal Armstrong looked as though he could do with feeding up, and Frank, fine figure of a man that he was, had a physique to maintain. They were both good eaters, she observed. She hated people who picked at their food. She only hoped Ethel wouldn't say something sour and spoil things, but Ethel was deep in her own thoughts again.

The two guests entertained with anecdotes about their very different lives. Len Armstrong made them all laugh about goings-on at the camp. Frank told them how Mrs Oliver had asked him, via Mrs Hunter, if he would come round and advise her about a new asparagus bed, and how Mrs Hunter had written to his employer, and how proud he had been to be able to help. And Mrs Oliver had given him a very fine tea, the details of which they were eager to hear, food being always of intense interest to them.

They had finished their pudding (bottled-plum pie and custard) when Len spoke about a camp concert that was coming up, and hoped they would all attend it. It should be very good, he said, and added modestly that he was singing a solo, and would be glad of their support.

'What are you singing, then?' Ada asked.

'"Memories",' said Armstrong.

'Ooh, I love that one,' said Cook. 'Won't you oblige us with a rendition now, Mr Armstrong? Do!'

He demurred politely, but was soon persuaded to stand

up, clasp his hands before him, and sing the popular ballad. He had a very pleasant, true voice.

'Round me at twilight come stealing
Shadows of days that are gone
Dreams of the old days revealing
Mem'ries of love's golden dawn . . .'

It was an affecting song, with the sweet melancholy that had replaced the excitement and bullishness of the wartime songs of the early days. The chorus had them all swaying gently in their seats.

'Childhood days, wild wood days
Among the birds and bees
You left me alone, but still you're my own
In my beautiful memories . . .'

'Ooh, that was lovely,' Cook said at the end, dabbing the corner of her eye with her apron. 'And very nicely sung, too, I'm sure. Thank you, Mr Armstrong.'

Ethel got up from the table abruptly and said, 'I'll make the tea,' and whisked away into the kitchen. It was unusual for her to volunteer for any task, but Cook was busy begging Len Armstrong for another song. Only Frank Hussey had noticed Ethel's face while 'Memories' was being sung.

'I'll help,' he said, getting up.

'No need,' said Cook, automatically. 'Emily'll do it.'

'No,' said Frank, laying a heavy hand on Emily's shoulder as he passed to stop her. 'I'm up now. Leave it to me.'

In the kitchen Ethel's back was towards him as, standing at the stove, she finished blowing her nose and stuffed her handkerchief back into her pocket. 'I've got a clean one, if you need it,' he said.

She flicked him an angry glance. Her eyes and the end

77

of her nose were pink, but she had shoved the tears back down. 'Why should I want your hanky?' she said. 'I got one of my own.'

He came closer. 'It's no sin to cry, you know. It can even help. Like a good clear-out.'

'Fat lot you know about it,' Ethel said, with a reasonable attempt at her old spirit.

'I saw you crying when Mr Armstrong was singing.'

'Wasn't crying. I got something in my eye.' She looked into the awful tenderness of his face, and hit back. 'How come you've not been called up, anyway? Don't tell me they swallered that old eyewash about being needed to grow vegetables.'

'Maybe they don't think it's eyewash,' Frank said calmly. 'I didn't come in here to talk about me. Here, put the kettle on, so's we don't get disturbed.'

Ethel watched him dully as he filled the big black kettle and heaved it onto the stove. Once, his following her out would have given her a thrill, but she had long ago decided he was not interested in her in *that* way. She didn't know what his game was – it was something outside her experience. Men were always trying to get something from her or she was trying to get something from them. Disinterested kindness had never come her way.

In any case, something inside her had closed down when Eric was killed. She couldn't seem to care about things the way she had. It was as if the Ethel inside her head, who had always looked out for her and fought her corner, had died like him.

Frank turned from the kettle and stood square before her, a big, strong man with a strong man's gentleness. He was so blamed sure of himself, she thought, with a distant ghost of old resentment. She'd called him a coward and a shirker for not volunteering, but all her barbed remarks had simply bounced off him. Now he took hold of both her hands in his big work-scarred ones. Her own, hard with housework, simply disappeared in them.

'I'm worried about you, Ethel,' he said.

'Worry about yourself,' she retorted. She looked up at him, and fought the desire to lean against him and bury her face in his chest.

'I saw you the other night, coming out of the Red Lion. That's not a nice place.'

'What was *you* doing there, then?'

'I was passing by on my bicycle, going back from Mrs Oliver's to the station. I see you come out. You weren't alone.'

'I don't have to ask *your* permission to go out of an evening.'

'Listen,' he said. 'We don't have much time. Someone could come in any minute. That man you were with – Sergeant Wood. I know about him. You're not seeing him regular, are you?'

'What if I am?'

'He's a bad lot. You know he's married?'

She was ashamed to answer that. She freed her hands with a violent jerk, and said, 'Leave me alone. It's none of your business.'

'Maybe not, but I'm fond of you, and I don't want to see you get into trouble. I know you had a rotten break, losing that nice chap you were seeing, but don't let it knock you off the rails. You'll get over him one day, and find someone else, and when you do, you don't want no Sergeant Wood in your background. You don't want anything you have to keep a secret.'

'Oh, lay off me!' Ethel cried desperately. She grabbed the tea caddy from the mantelpiece and banged it down violently on the table.

'I won't say any more. Just keep in mind, that man means you harm, whatever he might say to flatter you.'

'I know what I'm doing,' Ethel said, spooning tea into the pot with ferocious gestures.

'Dunno that you do,' he said, with gentle humour. 'You've not warmed that.'

She looked up at him, about to say something searing, but at the last moment the words dissolved, and she stared at him speechlessly, with such sadness that Frank almost took her there and then into his arms. He said, desperately, 'I'll always be your friend, you know. If you're ever in trouble, come to me, and I'll help you. Promise me, if you need help, you'll come to me.'

She looked a moment longer, then turned her back. When she spoke her voice was dull again. 'If you want to help, don't just stand there, get the cups and saucers from the dresser and take 'em in.'

So he got the cups and left her.

In bed that night, Ethel lay listening to the soft, rhythmic snoring of Ada in the next bed, and thought about Frank, and his words. Was Andy Wood's reputation so bad it had become a matter of common knowledge? Well, it hardly mattered. She didn't care any more. No-one had ever wanted her, except Eric, and as soon as God saw how she and Eric were getting on, He took him away. No, nice things were not for Ethel, things other people had. Even that daft cow Ada had a bloke (scrawny little corporal nobody – but he was hers; and he had a nice voice, it had to be said).

She sighed, turned over on her side and stared at the wall instead of the ceiling. She was sick of this life. She was sick of everything. She had a restless urge to get away (and there was in the back of her mind something – she wouldn't even openly acknowledge to herself that it was there – that she wanted more than anything to get away from). Then the idea came to her. There was one thing she could do. One thing that, in the greyness of indifference, she wanted.

80

Quietly she slipped out of bed, and picked up the electric torch on the chair beside it. When the blackout had started, the master had bought each of them an electric torch in case they had to walk home in the dark with no streetlights. She listened a moment to check that Ada was still snoring, then got down on her knees and lifted the square of lino under the sink in the corner, and carefully pulled up the half-floorboard below it. In the cavity between the floor and the joists was a tin box. She took it out, and sat on the floor, reaching inside her nightdress for the key that hung on a piece of string round her neck. Not that she didn't trust Ada, but that Emily was a thief if ever she saw one, and there was no harm in being careful.

Inside the box was the money she had been saving from her wages, and the three envelopes. She had moved them from her drawer to the box because Emily had known where they were. She had never read the contents. Now she touched them warily with her fingertip as though they might bite. Finally, winding up her courage, she opened one.

There was an address at the top: 2 Potters Row, Northampton. She shuddered slightly, as though she had been dealt a blow, painless now, but which might take her life.

It was written in pencil, in a scrawl that was hard to make sense of, especially in the wavering light of a torch. *Hopeing this finds you as it leves me in the pink,* it began. Ethel rolled her eyes and read on, reluctantly. *Well, Ma, I am in the fambly way agen but Sneb have gon he went Munday week pars. He say he going for milk but he never come back. Can you send munny. The baby has a cold. I get sick mornings but all rite else. Love from Edie.*

Ethel put the note back into its envelope with hands that trembled slightly. She didn't open the other two. She didn't want any more evidence of how stupid and illiterate her sister was. She had run away with a tinker, for God's sake!

81

As far as she remembered, the tinker's name had been Joe, not Sneb, so presumably she had parted ways with him at some point.

And yet this hopeless woman had something Ethel wanted. Ethel had struggled against wanting to know the answer to a certain question, but now the restlessness was on her again, and in the emptiness of her life, since Eric had been killed and her spirit had been broken, it seemed like something to hold on to. A quest. A reason to go in one direction rather than another.

She had money, her life's savings. She had been saving to provide herself with a trousseau when the right man asked her to marry him. She wouldn't need it for that now. Why not spend it finding the answer to the question that nagged at the back of her mind?

She decided. Tomorrow, first thing, she would give the mistress her week's warning. In a week, she would be off. The thought was both terrifying and invigorating. She returned the box to its hiding place and climbed, shivering, back into bed. It was a while before her feet warmed up enough for her to fall asleep.

CHAPTER SIX

Ada was in tears as she watched Ethel pack her few belongings.

'But where will you go?' she asked, for the fifth time.

Ethel hadn't answered the four preceding times. Now, to stop Ada repeating herself, she said, 'I got a plan. There's something I got to do. Someone I got to see.'

Ada almost asked *what* and *who*, but thought better of it. 'Why've you got to give your notice to do it? Can't you do it on your day off? Oh, Ethel, don't go! It's not safe.'

'Safe?' Ethel actually looked at her for a moment.

Ada blushed. But she said, 'There's more things than Zeppelins.'

'Oh, don't you worry about me,' Ethel said sourly. 'You just cuddle up with your Corporal Armstrong and sing in your silly choir. *I*'ve got better things to do.'

'But *what*?' Ada asked. 'Where'll you go?'

'Why do you mind?' Ethel asked, exasperated. 'You've never liked me.'

'We've been friends,' Ada said pleadingly, though aware this was not strictly true. It had never been possible to be friends with Ethel – she wouldn't allow it. She tried to be more exact. 'You been here a long time. We share a room. *Course* I mind.'

'Well, good for you. You'll have someone new in this bed, and I hope you'll be very happy together.'

Ada was silent, hurt by the rebuff. Emily sidled up to the door, her eyes wide with interest, excitement and a certain degree of apprehension. She wished she had the courage just to *go*, like that. 'I think you're ever so brave,' she ventured.

'Who asked you?' Ethel said. Then she gave her a malicious look. 'Making calf's eyes at Con Meyer. Think no-one's noticed?'

Emily blushed deeply. Her passion for the bread man, who delivered for Hetherton's Hygienic Bakery, was fairly new and very painful. 'I don't know what you're talking about,' she said. She adored him from afar, knowing he would never notice the likes of her. The two-wheeled bread cart was drawn by a wall-eyed vanner, and Con liked to drive standing up. In her mind he was a sort of Roman charioteer, and entirely god-like.

'You'll be all right,' said Ethel. 'They won't call him up. He's deaf as a post.'

Blond, blue-eyed Con had once shown interest in Ethel. He wasn't bad-looking, but he had adenoids, which gave him a strange, toneless voice, and she had rejected him. Maybe he wasn't deaf, she thought, but he *sounded* deaf.

Ada went to the door and took Emily's arm. 'Come on, we'd better leave her to it,' she said, with as much dignity as she could muster. Ethel was obviously in a mood, and would lash out at anyone. She propelled Emily before her, but turned back to say quietly, 'All the same, I wish you wasn't going. I shall miss you. But I wish you good luck.'

Ethel didn't turn her head. She pushed the last things into her bag, and fought down second thoughts. Here she was known, she was safe, she had at least the semblance of friendship. Out there, all was dark and unknown.

But she had burned her boats. She couldn't stay now, so there was no point in moaning about it. Done was done.

★　★　★

84

'Just like that,' said Beattie. 'It's *most* inconvenient. I always thought we'd have trouble with her sooner or later, but she'd quietened down a lot since that terrible Zeppelin incident. And one does feel a responsibility towards them – I hope it didn't unbalance her mind. It seems such a sudden decision.'

'You can only do so much,' said Sonia. 'I mean, if they want to go, you can't stop them. You don't know that she hasn't been planning it for months.'

'True,' said Beattie. Who knew what went on inside servants' heads?

'Have you found a replacement?' Sonia asked.

'Fanny Oliver's recommended a girl to me – some relation of her cook, I believe. She's a local girl, which I prefer – London maids could be *anyone*.'

'Don't speak of it!' Sonia said, rolling her eyes. 'The stories I could tell.'

'She's very young,' Beattie pursued, 'but in some ways that's better – get them before they develop bad habits and train them properly. And the girls can help a bit until things settle down – or Sadie can.'

Sonia poured more tea. 'How long is Diana staying with Beth?' she asked.

'Two or three weeks was spoken of,' Beattie said. She had handed Diana over in Ebury Street before coming on to Kensington. 'But I think it could be more. I'm so glad Beth asked her. I do hope it cheers her up.'

'Poor Diana – is she very low?'

Beattie hesitated, seeking the right word. 'Serious. She used to be quite different, and it's sad to see her like this. It's as though she's suddenly ten years older.'

'I hope it hasn't spoiled her looks,' said Sonia.

'I don't mean that,' said Beattie. Sonia, Edward's younger sister, was not of the very brightest. All the brains in the family had gone to Edward and Laura. 'Beth said she's just the same when Jack goes away. She feels the years settling on her. And I feel like that with David. By the time this war ends we'll all be ancient ruins.'

Sonia felt around for an end of meaning to get hold of. 'Well, at least everyone will be in the same boat from now on. Conscription will even everything out.'

'Except that Edward says a lot of people are trying to get out of it.'

'How shocking! We all have to do our bit,' said Sonia, placidly, inspecting a biscuit with a frown that suggested it might have been planted on her by a German spy. 'I wanted to have the hall and stairs redecorated – the paper's awfully rubbed. People will brush up against it as they go up and down, especially the servants, no matter how often one speaks to them. But our decorating firm, which has always been so reliable, has had three people called up, and they're closing down until after the war.'

They were interrupted by the entry of Sonia's eldest daughter, Mary.

'Hello, Mumsy, hello, Aunt Beattie. Is there any tea left in the pot? I had some at the WVR meeting, but I'm parched again.'

Beattie said, 'Don't pretend insouciance, dear. You know I'm all agog about your uniform.'

Mary was sporting a khaki tunic, with four large pockets, over a khaki blouse and green tie, and a tough-looking, sensible skirt. 'It *is* rather smart, isn't it? I must say, I do love it, though it did cost two pounds – and that's without the boots. But I needed a new pair of those anyway. We can wear stockings and shoes in the summer. If the war's not over by then.'

Mary sat down, helped herself to a large piece of cake, and was handed a cup of tea by her mother. 'I just felt I wanted to do something,' she said. 'I mean, something solid and useful, for the war effort. It's all very well knitting things, but somehow that doesn't feel enough.'

86

'Especially as there's no uniform involved,' Beattie murmured.

'I suppose it was Aunt Laura started it off, but I couldn't quite see myself doing what she does – and, frankly, Mumsy and Poppa would have had a pair of heart attacks.'

'We certainly should have,' said Sonia.

'Oh, did you hear about that dreadful court case she was supposed to be giving evidence in?'

'Mary!' Sonia said, in sharp warning.

'Oh, it's all right, Mumsy, I'm not going to give any of the details – not that I actually know them, of course, but I know it was something shocking. Well, it turns out that she and Louisa won't have to give evidence after all, because the men pleaded guilty rather than go to the Crown Court, so there'll be no trial. Poppa says it's because their solicitor told them that the fact there were female witnesses made it certain they'd get convicted, so they owned up in the hope of a lighter sentence. The funny thing is,' she concluded, 'I believe Aunt Laura's actually disappointed not to be going to court.'

'So tell me, what does the Women's Volunteer Reserve do?' Beattie asked, to get her onto safer ground.

'Oh, well, I can't tell you much yet, because this was only the second meeting. The first one was for taking down our names and addresses, and today we just did an awful lot of drill – lining up and marching and about-turning and so on. Of course, nobody'd done anything like that before, so we got into awful muddles.' She giggled. 'A lot of people don't know their left from their right. And some of the ladies are quite old, and one or two are *very* stout.'

'You shouldn't make fun of people, dear,' said Sonia, taking another biscuit.

'I know, but if you'd been there . . . At any rate, our *purpose*, according to the handbook, is to render efficient service to the state in case of National Emergency.' Her

87

voice made clear that those two words had capital letters. 'Because if there were a National Emergency, with so many of the men away at the Front, it would be essential to have a trained and disciplined force to help out.'

'Help out with what?' Beattie asked.

'Oh, whatever was needed. Help the police or the army, direct traffic, carry messages, tend the wounded, organise evacuations, set up camp kitchens and so on. Anything, really. Mrs Britton, who's our commandant, says there's no knowing what we might be called on to do, so we have to be ready for every eventuality.'

'That's a large responsibility for young ladies.'

'Well, I'm sure you'll do it very nicely, dear,' Sonia said. 'It's a pity Audrey doesn't get involved in something like that, instead of reading and studying all day until her eyes give out. I've told her she'll give herself hunched shoulders and a squint, and then she'll—'

'Never find a husband,' Mary finished the sentence for her briskly. 'Mumsy, all Audrey wants is to go to university. She doesn't want a husband.'

'She will do one day,' Sonia said firmly. 'And then it will be just as well if she doesn't have a squint and round shoulders.'

'How's Diana?' Mary asked, to turn the subject.

'Well enough, but I'm hoping staying with Beth will cheer her up,' said Beattie.

'I must go over and see her,' said Mary. 'We could do a little shopping together and perhaps see a matinée.' She stood up energetically. 'Yes, Mumsy dear, I'm feminine enough still to like shopping, even if I have been marching all afternoon. And now I must go up and have a bath because it was *very* dusty in that hall. Old floorboards, you know. Have we got any books on first aid in the house?'

'I think so, dear. Wasn't there one put in the cellar with the air-raid things?'

'Oh, yes, probably. I'll have a look later. We're starting first aid next week, and I'd like to be ahead if I can.'

'Very wise,' said Beattie. 'When Sadie did her class, the brighter pupils got to do the bandaging, while the duller ones had to be the patients.'

'I'm well warned, Auntie. Me for bandag*er*, not bandag*ee*, every time!'

When Mary went over to Ebury Street, she wore her uniform so that Diana could see it – and was secretly hoping that some emergency would arise on the way so she could prove her worth. Not a really *bad* emergency, of course, but the sort of thing for which a Boy Scout in uniform might be turned to. But the world did not require her services that morning.

She found Diana and Beth lingering over their breakfast coffee, Beth reading letters and Diana glancing through the newspaper. 'Shockingly late, I know,' Beth apologised, 'but we had rather a late night. Theatre, followed by supper at the Trocadero.'

'No, it's me,' Mary said cheerfully. 'I'm too early. Mumsy says I have *no* social sense.'

'You're welcome any time, dear,' said Beth. 'So that's the uniform, is it? I must say, you look ready for anything. Tell us all about it.'

Mary obliged, and finished with an appeal to Diana: 'Why don't you think of joining too? We all have to have our war work, and it would be something to interest yourself in.'

Diana eyed the uniform without enthusiasm. 'Mm, no thanks. I don't think it's me. And I have plenty of war work at home.'

'Oh, knitting and suchlike,' Mary said. 'That's not enough for an energetic, intelligent woman.'

Diana wasn't feeling either intelligent or energetic, these days, but she was a month older than Mary so wasn't going to be upstaged by her. 'I have my hospital visiting, too.'

Mary wandered over to the mantelpiece and said, 'Goodness, you do have a lot of cards!' She examined one. 'Tea with Lady Smith-Dorrien? I didn't know you knew her.'

'I don't,' said Beth. 'I'm sure the tea-party will be an excuse to collect donations for her Hospital Bag Fund. Not that I mind giving. Jack tells me the men really appreciate the bags.' Mary was taking up invitations in turn and inspecting them. 'A great many of those invitations will be war work in disguise.'

'But not all?'

'By no means,' said Beth. 'They've only started arriving since Diana's been staying here. I'm asked for her sake, you see.'

'Oh, that's not true,' Diana protested.

'It is, darling. Tonight,' she told Mary, 'we go to dance at Lady Teesborough's house. I don't deny there might be a collection taken up for some project or other, but the interesting thing is why Lady Teesborough thought of us in the first place.'

'Why did she?' Mary asked obediently.

'She's Rupert Wroughton's godmother,' said Beth.

'I met her once, when I was staying with Lady Wroughton,' Diana countered. 'No need to bring Rupert into it.'

'Ah, but how did she know you were in Town, staying with me?' said Beth. 'Rupert arrived on the doorstep promptly the day after you got here, and since then there's been a flood of invitations.'

'Oh,' said Mary. 'So he told all his people to invite you to things?'

'They can't want us for our money, because we haven't any,' said Beth.

'I don't even like him,' said Diana.

'But does he like you?' Mary asked.

'I don't know,' said Diana. 'I didn't think so. He was very

90

unpleasant to me when I was engaged to Charles. Then he seemed to change. Last time I saw him – before I came here, I mean – he seemed to want to be friends.'

'When he called, he couldn't have been nicer,' Beth concluded. 'I'd say he definitely wants to be friends.'

Diana looked at her seriously. 'But why would he?' she said quietly.

Beth saw that Diana was not begging for compliments. Yes, she was beautiful – but Rupert was now heir to an earldom and a large estate. People like that looked to their own circle for wives. Charles had been the exception – but Charles had been different in many ways.

Beth said, with equal seriousness, 'We don't have to accept any of the invitations, if it makes you uncomfortable. I just thought it would be diverting for you. Rupert is good company – at least, he always has been when I've met him.'

'You should go,' Mary said, having thought about it. 'You never know who you might meet, or what good you might be able to do.'

'What good can I do dancing?' Diana said.

'There are bound to be soldiers home from the Front, and keeping up their morale is important war work,' said Mary. 'I'm sure they'd all love to dance with someone like you. Your looks are a gift from God – you should use them to help our brave soldiers.'

Beth almost laughed. 'That's a very ingenious argument, Mary dear.'

'Dancing with soldiers, war work?' Diana said. But there was an element of truth in it. When she visited the wounded officers in hospital back home, she wasn't providing medical help, she was just cheering them up. Yet it *was* worthwhile. And she knew, without vanity, that they liked looking at a pretty face. 'But what about the theatre and the ballet? Rupert is arranging parties for both.'

'The labourer is worthy of his hire,' said Mary.

91

'*I* have no conscience about it,' said Beth. 'If Fate wants to invite me to all the best balls, dinners and so on – so be it!'

Diana said, 'All right, I'll go along with it. I wouldn't want to rob you of your share of the fun.' Despite herself, she was glad to give in. It *would* be fun. And it was true, Rupert *was* good company – when he wanted to be.

After the death of Braithwaite, a period of fine weather set in, and there was instructional flying every day. Bobby got airborne at last, and the moment the earth first unpeeled itself from beneath him, he knew he had found true bliss. After that, he ate and drank and dreamed flying. It was all he cared for. The Longhorns could not cope with much in the way of wind, so most flying was done in the stillness of early morning or the calm of late afternoon. There were still too many cadets for too few machines, so flights were short, no more than twenty minutes.

But when he found himself up in the air, with the engine behind him, ticking like a giant alarm clock, the forward elevator out in front of him like a comforting tea-tray, he felt a great sense of peace mingled with intense awareness, as though he were twice as alive. England, hundreds of feet below him, looked so beautiful and perfect, like an exquisite jewelled artefact. He gazed at it from this new angle enraptured, and a stirring in his heart whispered that this land was worth every sacrifice. He felt sorry for anyone who never saw it like this, who never reached the upper air. This was where he wanted to be. The air was his home, and this big, gentle, strange-looking bird, the Longhorn, was his means to get there.

He learned all about her, learned the sounds she made, began to understand what the forest of struts and spars and the tangle of piano wire meant – and how to find his way through them to take his place in the nacelle. He had his hands and feet resting lightly on the controls while the instructor flew the aeroplane to try to deduce the effect each movement had on the machine.

Once they had had a dozen or so flights, the cadets were allowed to land and take off with the instructor just touching the controls. After that, lessons became a succession of take-offs and landings – they were, after all, the trickiest part of the business. There were many crashes – the wrong speed, 'flattening out' too early, a gust of wind at the wrong moment – but no-one was badly hurt. The instructors were sanguine about them. 'Just don't kill yourself, or bust the machine to bits. That's all we ask,' Cardoon said, in the mess one night, when Farringdon was limping from a jar got when 'pancaking'.

One day, a flyer arrived from the squadron at Gosport in a Shorthorn, bringing the major a message from their squadron commander. The Maurice Farman 11 differed in many ways from the older Longhorn, but the most imme-diately noticeable was the absence of the forward elevator with its long, curving booms – hence the nickname. The cadets crowded round, fascinated, never having seen one in the flesh before. The pilot had been a cadet at Shoreham only a few weeks earlier, and knew some of the older pupils, and while they quizzed him, Bobby walked round the Shorthorn, examining every detail and gazing at the ungainly craft with longing.

He didn't notice Cardoon behind him until he spoke. 'Like to go up in her?'

Bobby turned. 'God! Yes, please, sir!'

'All right. Fetch your cap and goggles.'

Bobby ran so fast he was gasping for breath when he got back.

'That's what I like about you, Hunter,' Cardoon drawled. 'Your enthusiasm. Right-oh. Up you get. Once around the lighthouse in the Saucy Sue.'

The bathtub nacelle was mounted halfway up the inter-plane struts, so the front seat was well ahead of the wings. This, plus the absence of the comforting tea-tray, made Bobby feel as if he was leaning perilously out of a theatre box. The engine seemed noisier, and in flight the Shorthorn felt much less stable. It was only a ten-minute spin, but afterwards Cardoon said, 'There, now your log-book will say you've been up in a Shorthorn. It all helps. Beast of a bus,' he added, turning to stare at her. 'Underpowered, too much drag, and stalls at the drop of a hat. But you need experience of as many different machines as possible.'

'Thanks for taking me up, sir,' Bobby said.

Cardoon gave him a nod, and a look-over. 'You're going to be a good pilot, Hunter. I can tell. You'll go far. How much dual control have you done?'

'Three hours and ten minutes,' Bobby said, aware of how little it was. 'Twenty minutes now.' He hoped Cardoon might offer him some more. But he only nodded again and walked away.

The next day, the cadets went out before breakfast to stand by the sheds, wondering whether there would be any early-morning flying. The mechanics had wheeled out a couple of Longhorns, and were idly leaning against the struts.

'Looks as though someone will be lucky,' said Porteous.

'You can have my share,' said Farringdon. 'Damned uncivilised, flying before brekker, when a man's all hollow inside.' But Bobby knew he was as keen as anyone to be chosen. They watched with painful hope as the instructors came out of the office, chatting. Andrews peeled himself away from the group and walked briskly over to the cadets. His eye came to rest on Bobby, whose heart gave a little, happy squeeze.

Andrews said, 'Like to go solo this morning?'

There was a muted gasp from the group. Bobby was too

surprised to join in. Normally you were told in the mess the night before: 'You'll go solo at dawn tomorrow.' They had heard older pupils being given this sentence: it might as well have been 'You'll be shot at dawn tomorrow', for it usually caused consternation.

Bobby heard himself say, 'Yes, sir,' before his brain had properly caught up. And then a fierce joy joined the trepidation inside him. He wasn't afraid of being killed or even injured. Not only was he twenty and therefore immortal, but the Longhorn was his faithful friend and the air was his home: it could never hurt him. He was only afraid that he would make a hash of it, and a monumental fool of himself, and that everyone would laugh at him.

But this was what he had been longing for, what he was born to do. The joy was much stronger than the trepidation.

'All right. Take this one,' said Andrews. 'Remember, maintain level flight, keep your airspeed at about forty-two, don't try any sharp manoeuvres – nice gradual movements. Don't stay up more than twenty minutes. Off you go.'

Gently the Longhorn rose into the air; delicately Bobby held the handlebars between forefinger and thumb; tenderly he trod the rudder pedals as though they were unbroken eggs. Keeping the tea-tray on or just below the horizon gave you level flight. Air speed – forty-three. Just right. He risked a glance down. How green everything looked! To the other side, rows of bungalows, the long line of shingle, the dark blue of the sea. He felt the air holding him up kindly, heard the engine ticking away reliably, like the nursery clock that keeps watch over the sleeping child. His heart was so full of peace and happiness, he never wanted to go down. He moved the controls delicately, without even thinking about it: it seemed natural to him, as though the old Longhorn's shabby wings were his own; and she responded as naturally as his own limbs.

Ahead and below he saw Brighton coming up, the stately pleasure domes of the Pavilion, the pier poking out into the sea, with little dots of seagulls drifting around the end. He had better get back. Make a turn: bank gently, nose down just a little to increase air speed – but not too much! Left rudder; level off; nose up just a trifle. Flying into the wind now, quite a different feel. There was Shoreham again, there was the airfield up ahead. Oh, Lord, he didn't want to go in! But he was flying solo and, so far, hadn't made a mess of it! Nose down, throttle back. Air speed, forty-two. The airfield was green, coming closer, the long grass rippling in the breeze, a group of people standing by the sheds, looking up – looking at him! Gently the Longhorn glided towards the earth. He used the rudder to straighten her, pointed her dead into the wind. Now, now was the moment – he felt it. He flattened out, heard from beneath the hollow rumble of the wheels and the scrape of the tail boom behind. She gave a little lurch, and it was all over.

He taxied back towards the sheds, seeing Andrews waiting for him there, arms folded over his chest, ready to deliver his criticism. All Bobby could think was, *I want to go back up!* Already, he missed it.

There was a letter for him next to his plate at breakfast, in Dobbin's thick, stubby hand.

I'm sorry to have to tell you that Lord Kitchener didn't want me. I failed the beastly medical examination. I'm sure the mater is secretly pleased, but I felt no end of a failure. But, though not passed for active service, I will still be in uniform. The major who interviewed me quizzed me closely and asked a lot of questions I didn't see the point of, but no doubt he had his method, because at the end of it he asked how I would feel about joining the Intelligence Corps. So I am to go to some secret location for three months to learn about signalling, and after that will be sent to the War Office.

The good thing about it is that, being settled in London, I felt able to ask Mary Talbot to marry me, and to my astonishment she said 'yes'. I am almost as bewildered as I am happy – I really, truly don't deserve her. Well, you've met her, so you know! We are planning to get married some time next year, and hope very much that you are in the country when it comes off, as I'd really like to have you at my side to hold me up. I'm sure to need it!

Bobby was very happy for dear old Dob. He remembered Mary Talbot with faint wistfulness: if there was any woman who could rival an aeroplane for his affections, he thought it would be her. But even if someone like her should come along and take a fancy to him, he couldn't think of that sort of thing for the foreseeable future. Flying was everything – and it was all he wanted.

CHAPTER SEVEN

There was consternation at Highclere. Biggs had been conscripted in February, and then in March Baker was called up. This left only the stable boys, Bent and Oxer, and the head man, Podrick, to do the work – apart from the army's presence in the form of Private Higgins.

'And he's not much help,' said Mrs Cuthbert. 'Always sloping off to have a cigarette, never around when you need him.'

Sadie was glad when he *wasn't* around. She had seen the way the horses started nervously when he came near them, and suspected that he hit them when no-one was watching. She thought he was one of those hard sorts who believed kindness was wasted unless there was a tangible return – and that kindness to animals was for mugs and 'wimmin'.

But there was no doubt that, even if she came for longer hours, those who were left couldn't manage.

'*You* won't leave us, will you?' she asked Podrick. She couldn't guess how old he was, and was too polite to ask.

'They won't take me, miss,' Podrick said, with certainty, but when she asked him why, he wouldn't say any more.

Sadie and Mrs Cuthbert were strapping a bay gelding out in the yard, working one on each side. Nailer was snuffling happily at a hole beside a drainpipe under the end box. He had followed her from the house one morning, and she had finally heard him toiling along behind her when

98

she was too far from home to take him back, so she had put him in the front basket and taken him with her. She'd intended to tie him up somewhere until she cycled home again, but Mrs Cuthbert had welcomed him and given him the run of the yard. She loved dogs, especially terriers; and they certainly had a rat problem.

Nailer had demonstrated that he understood the terms of the bargain, for he had caught two beauties that first day. Highclere was paradise to him, full of the most exquisite and sometimes unexpected smells, all the rats his heart could desire, plus comfortable places to lie when he was not working, and more than his fair share of lunchtime sandwiches in the tack room. He had a high opinion of horsy people – so much more likely to throw a piece of cold sausage *to* him than a missile *at* him. In addition, he spent more time with Sadie, who knew the exact spot behind his ears he loved to have scratched; and he got rides in the bicycle basket, which he adored. He still had his other responsibilities to see to around Northcote, but more often than not the sound of Sadie wheeling the bicycle down the side passage would have him waiting for her at the gate.

'I think there's a nest under that corner,' she said now. 'He seems to be very interested in that hole.'

'I might get Podrick to have a dig later,' Mrs Cuthbert said.

'Podrick won't get called up, will he?' Sadie asked. 'He says not, but I don't know how he knows.'

'I'm not sure if it's because he's Irish, or over the age,' said Mrs Cuthbert, 'but he seems sure he won't be – thank God. We certainly couldn't do without him.' She stopped working, and leaned on the bay's rump, looking at Sadie across it. 'I had a letter yesterday from the head of the Remount Service.'

Sadie's heart sank. She remembered Munt telling her that the army would take the horses away from them sooner or later. They would not like civilians – especially women – running part of their empire. Tidy-minded, Munt said they were, in the army. Liked everything in nice, straight lines.

'They're closing us down!' Sadie cried. 'I was afraid they would,'

Mrs Cuthbert laughed. 'No, dear, on the contrary! They want us to expand.'

Sadie looked her astonishment. 'But – how?'

'They say the way we've been working so far, taking a batch of six or ten, working them up, sending them off, has been fine as far as it goes. But now, with conscription, they're getting new soldiers all the time, and they need horses in a steady stream, rather than fits and starts.'

'But how would it work?'

'They'd send us new horses just as they got them, a few at a time, and we'd send them back when they were ready. They come on at different rates anyway, as you know, and it's wasteful to keep the quick learners here, waiting for their fellows to catch up.'

'Not wasteful,' Sadie said. 'We go on teaching them.'

'There won't be time for refinements. The army's going to be expanding at a huge rate this year. What they need is an efficient machine, raw horses in one end, rideable horses out at the other. Like a conveyor-belt.'

'You'd need a lot more grooms,' Sadie said.

'A lot more of everything,' said Mrs Cuthbert. 'They've said they'll build us a new stable block – there's plenty of room behind the loose-boxes – and any other buildings we need. Another barn, at any rate, to keep the hay and straw in. And they'd send us another soldier to help out. But from the numbers they're thinking of, we'd still need more hands. Boys will only last until they're called up – Bent and Oxer will be taken next year. So I've thought out a plan to deal with that.'

'Tell me,' said Sadie.

'It's you who've given me the idea,' said Mrs Cuthbert. 'You work so hard and so willingly, and you're so good with the horses. Now, there must be a lot of girls up and down the country like you, girls who love horses and who'd be glad to have a chance to do war work.'

'How would you find them, if they're up and down the country?' Sadie asked.

'Advertise,' said Mrs Cuthbert. '*Horse & Hound, Country Life* and so on.'

'But – would their mothers let them come? And where would they live?'

'I'd kill those two birds with the same stone. They'd live here, under my strict supervision, so their mothers would know they'd be taken care of. I've talked about it with Horace, and he thinks it's a fine idea. Our house is enormous, and we rattle around in it. We could easily take a dozen girls – more, perhaps, if we make a dormitory in the attic. The army would provide beds and blankets and so on, and rations. We'd need to take on an extra cook, but the dining-room is big enough to seat twenty, and there's the sitting-room and the garden room, which could be turned over to their use, so that Horace and I can have the drawing-room and library to ourselves.'

Sadie was surprised at the scale. 'Twenty girls?'

'Oh, we'd start small, until we see how it works. Perhaps with half a dozen. But we have to plan ahead. They're predicting at least two more years of war, and the demand for horses will only increase. There's room for us to run a large establishment here. The army will cover all the expenses and do the building work. For instance, the old kennels have a big copper, and we could turn that into a laundry, and a shower block for the girls. Horace is all for it – he loves the idea of having the place seething with horses and bright young women. What do you think?'

Sadie was reeling from the flood of information. She drew breath to answer, but Mrs Cuthbert, her eyes alight with excitement, was off again.

'There's only one problem I can think of. What do we call the young ladies? Girl grooms? Pupils? Residents? Perhaps novices would strike the right sort of monastic tone to reassure the mothers!' She laughed, then stopped. 'Sadie, you haven't said a thing. Do you think it's a terrible idea?'

Sadie got to the end of a strenuous piece of imagining, and looked up into the bright but anxious face opposite. 'I think,' she said, with emphasis, 'that it's a simply *topping* idea! It will make us so big, they'll never take it away from us.'

'Who – take what away?' Mrs Cuthbert asked, puzzled.

'The army – take the horses away, because we're civilians. And females.'

'The more men they call up,' said Mrs Cuthbert, seriously, 'the more they'll have to rely on women. They won't be able to dismiss us any more. But now, my dear, you really think it's a good idea? Because I can't manage it without you.'

'What do you want me to do?'

'These girls will be enthusiastic, but we don't know how much experience they'll have. They'll need to be instructed, guided, supervised. Many of them won't be used to regular work. You'll be my head girl, my right hand. What do you think?'

'I'd love to do it,' said Sadie.

'It'll be a lot more work.'

'I like work,' Sadie said.

Mrs Cuthbert laughed. 'I know you do. I'll write back, then, and tell them we're willing.'

'When do you think it will happen?'

'The army won't want to wait. They'll get the buildings

up within the month, and the horses are already in the system. We have to get on and find the girls.'

'Shall I ask around Northcote? There may be some local girls who'd want to come.'

'Yes, do, and I'll sound out Rustington. The sooner we get them here and bedded in, the better.'

The new maid, Ethel's replacement, was called Lilian, and came from Hendorp, a village two miles away to the south, in hay country. Her father was a hedger and ditcher and lived in a tied cottage. She'd been to Hendorp village school, where she'd learned reading, writing, reckoning and needle-work, and had been at home for two years 'helping Mother'. But her next sister had reached the age of twelve and could take over the role, so Mother wanted Lilian out of the way and earning a bit.

She was a thin, pale girl with a slightly pink nose, like a white mouse; her eyes were a faint blue and her hair was so fair it was almost silver. Emily fell instantly in love with her, thinking she was so beautiful she must have been swapped in the cradle by the elves – she must really be a fairy princess. Lilian found Emily bewildering, and couldn't understand most of what she said.

But Lilian found everything about The Elms bewildering. The house was so big, she was afraid of losing her way in it. She didn't understand the work – didn't even understand the names of things. There were so many people, and they all talked so quick and said so *many* things – at home, nobody spoke much, and then it was short: 'Lil, put the kettle on.'

'Pass the bread.'

'Poke that fire up.'

'Pick up Baby.'

'Go to bed.'

She was terrified out of her wits by Mrs Hunter. She'd

never had to do with posh people. When Mrs Hunter had interviewed her, Lilian had been too frightened to speak, or even to understand what was being said to her. She had been brought along by Mother's cousin Maud, who was cook to a Mrs Oliver, and *she*'d had to do the talking. Since then, if she caught sight of 'the mistress' Lilian tried to hide, or at least flattened herself against the wall until she'd passed. When the mistress smiled and said, 'Good morning, Lilian. Are you settling in?' she could feel all the blood rushing from her head.

The first day, she was told to clear the breakfast table. She had crept into the morning room, peering round the door first to check that it was empty of people, then picked up a plate and a cup and saucer and trotted back to the kitchen with them. Everyone seemed too busy to tell her what to do next, so she put them down on the kitchen table and went back for some more. This time, Cook (oh, so frightening, so fierce!) turned and saw her, and said irritably, 'Don't put 'em there, take 'em into the scullery!' And then, realising what Lilian was doing, exclaimed, 'Are you bringing 'em in one at a time? What in the world— Use a tray, girl! Whatever next?'

Lilian stood quivering, until Cook pulled out a tray from their place between the larder and the broom cupboard, shoved it into her hands, and said, 'Pile everything on that and bring it back all at the one go. My Lord, save us, she doesn't know what a tray is!'

'Never had one at home,' Lilian whispered in shame.

'Well, you know now. Go on, get on with it, or it'll be dinner time 'fore you're done. And don't drop it!' she shouted after her, as Lilian slunk away.

After that, Cook assumed the child knew nothing, and gave her more detailed orders, when she remembered, so it was a little better, but Lilian went on being afraid, and wasn't helped by hearing Cook grumble, 'Half-witted, that's what she is. I never knew the like. Fell down with the last rain, that one.'

There was also a terrible old man, like a goblin, who came into the kitchen sometimes and looked at her as if he was casting bad spells on her, and said sudden loud things at her that made her jump. And a ginger boy who liked to pinch her or pull her apron strings undone. And all the people 'upstairs', who multiplied in her fevered mind into a throng of beautiful, cruel gods eight feet tall, able to confer life or death at the raising of a finger.

She cried in her bed every night – though not for long, because she was so tired she fell asleep pretty soon from sheer exhaustion. She didn't exactly miss home – it had never been a place of comfort or affection – but she missed the familiarity of it, the knowing-what-to-do of it. She felt as if she was drowning in a sea of words and orders and objects she didn't understand or recognise.

'I don't know, ma'am,' Cook said, after a week, when Beattie asked her how the new maid was fitting in. 'I never thought I'd miss Ethel, but you didn't have to tell her things. This one – it's like trying to teach a dog or a cat that don't understand what you're talking about.'

'Is it really that bad?' Beattie asked. 'Do you want to get rid of her?'

Cook hesitated. 'Well, ma'am . . .' she said, thinking. There was nothing bad or vicious about the girl, and when she'd learned something, she remembered it. You just had to take it slow, and remember to tell her *everything* when you gave her something new to do because, Lord save us, she didn't know what a duster was, or how to tuck a sheet, or clean a bath! If only she wasn't so scared of everyone . . . When Cook spoke to her, she looked like someone going to the scaffold. It was disconcerting, because Cook had always thought of herself as a particularly kind and warm-hearted person – motherly, almost.

'We can give her her week's warning, if you think she's no good,' Beattie pressed her, thinking what a nuisance it was, and how she hated trying to find new servants.

'No, ma'am,' Cook said at last. 'I think we should give her a bit longer, see how she goes. She's got a lot to learn all right, but she's a good girl underneath. I must say, it's refreshing not to be talked back to, after Ethel. I think we should persevere with her for a week or two. We'll train her up all right.'

Cook's tried and trusted method of training involved a lot of sharp rebukes, tellings-off, and a sprinkling of broad insults ('Call that clean? Where was you brought up? In the pigsty?') She believed that kindness only encouraged people to be lazy, and that understanding positively begged them to take advantage. Lilian had no idea that she had the power to leave, so she crept about in misery, trying to learn enough not to be snapped at, aware that her very timidity got on Cook's nerves, but unable to do anything about it.

It was Ada who saved her. Lilian had inherited Ethel's bed, in the room shared with Ada, which was another source of anguish to her, for Ada was nearly as frightening as Cook. When she wept at night, she did it silently, afraid of provoking her unpredictable room mate.

But one night Ada heard her. She didn't say anything at the time, but listened, feeling rather uncomfortable, until the tiny sounds died away into the steady breathing of sleep. The next morning, when she roused the child, she did it with a little more kindness. 'Come on, Lilian, time to get up.' The girl opened her eyes and looked up apprehensively. 'Don't be so scared. I know it's all new to you, but I'm going to help you. You'll soon learn. If there's anything you want to know, you ask me – I promise I won't be cross. Understand?'

'Yes,' Lilian whispered, but without great conviction.

106

'You're doing all right,' Ada said. 'It takes time to learn a new job, but you've not done anything wrong yet, so cheer up. And don't you mind about Cook. She only tells you off for your own good, so's you'll learn proper. She doesn't mean anything by it. Come on, girl, get your face washed and get dressed, and I'll do the fires with you.'

After that, things got better. Ada showed her what to do, and spoke kindly to her, and sometimes, when she was doing a job she knew how to do, she would find herself actually enjoying it. The food was better than at home – so much better, there ought to've been a different word for it – and her bed was a couch fit for a queen, compared with the one she'd shared with three sisters. They had a bath every week, and once she got used to it, she liked being clean and wearing clean clothes. The work was hard, but work always had been and always would be, so that didn't bother her.

And one Sunday, at church, when she dared join in for the first time with the hymn, Ada discovered she could sing. Later that day, they were having dinner and Frank Hussey was there (he was frighteningly tall and male, but when she dared look at it, he had a kind face) and Ada made her sing for everybody. She thought she would die, but Ada started her off (she had a nice voice too) and she sang 'The Lass of Richmond Hill', which she'd learned in school, and everyone applauded afterwards, surprising her. Frank Hussey said, 'That was beautiful,' and even Cook said, 'Well done, dear.' Then Lilian thought she would die of pleasure. No-one had ever praised her before.

In bed that night, she said softly, 'Ada?'

Ada had been drifting into a nice reverie about Len Armstrong and the little cottage they had been planning to live in when the war ended, but she came back patiently and said, 'Yes?'

'I liked singing today,' Lilian said.

'Singing's good,' said Ada. 'It always makes you feel better.'

'I wish I knew more songs.'

'I'll learn you some.' She was drifting off, when the little voice spoke again.

'Ada?'

'What is it this time?'

'Thanks for . . .' Lilian didn't have words for it. *Being my friend* wasn't in her vocabulary. And Ada was a grown-up – you couldn't have a grown-up as a friend.

Ada smiled as she turned over. 'Go to sleep,' she said kindly. 'You've to get up in seven hours.'

Mrs Oliver was a catalyst for many of the things that happened in Northcote, and in Beattie's life. She always remembered afterwards that it was Mrs Oliver who introduced her to Mrs Dawson. It was at a tea-party at Manor Grange, ostensibly about Lady Smith-Dorrien's Hospital Bags, but really because Mrs Oliver loved having tea-parties – parties of any sort, but particularly tea-parties.

And she had an old school friend staying with her – always a good excuse to entertain. Mrs Dawson's brother, Humphrey Crane, had married Mrs Oliver's sister, Della. Della was mother to Mrs Oliver's favourite nephew, Aldis, who had been killed in 1915 at Bellewaarde. It made another bond between them.

Mrs Oliver called the ladies to order and addressed them over the teacups.

'Now that the Hospital Bag Fund has been registered by the government as an approved voluntary organisation, all requests for the bags will be sent via the War Office. They calculate that at least sixty thousand a month will be needed by casualty-clearing stations and the like. It really is time Northcote did its bit.'

'Sixty thousand a month?' Beattie said wonderingly.

'I'm not sure it's the most pressing use of our time,' said

Mrs Fitzgerald, the rector's wife. She didn't like schemes she hadn't initiated herself.

Mrs Dawson drew herself up. Fanny Oliver had warned her in advance about Mrs Fitzgerald. 'Not *pressing*? Dear lady, Hospital Bags are *quite essential*. You can have no idea how important they are to our dear men at the Front.'

'I'm not sure I know what they are,' said Mrs Lattery. 'Is it something medical? Don't tell me,' she added hastily, 'if it's – you know – something *intimate*.'

'No, dear, it's not medical,' Mrs Oliver explained. 'When a man is wounded, he's sent to a casualty-clearing station, and the first thing they do is remove his uniform, and take everything out of his pockets. All his personal possessions, all the little things that are precious to *him*, well, they're put on the floor or under his pillow or somewhere, and of course they soon get scattered and lost unless the nurses have a bag to put them in. The poor man often gets sent to three or four different hospitals before getting back to England, so you can imagine, the hospital bag is the only thing that keeps his little bits and pieces together, and with him, through the journey.'

'Oh, yes, I see,' said Mrs Lattery. 'What a good idea.'

'It's *terribly* important for morale,' Mrs Dawson said. 'Lady Smith-Dorrien gets letters by the hundred from the dear fellows, all telling her how grateful they were for them, and from generals saying how much their men appreciate them.'

'It does sound like a useful scheme,' said Mrs Carruthers. 'Especially now, with conscription. I mean, it's all of our sons, isn't it? And I know if my Ronnie got wounded, which God forbid—'

'I should think you'd be more keen that there were bandages for him than bags,' said Mrs Fitzgerald.

'Nobody is suggesting that the two are mutually exclusive,' said Mrs Oliver, knowing the rector's wife could be subdued by vocabulary. 'Bandage-making and -rolling will go on as before. This will be something extra – something for the spirit of the men, not just for their bodies.'

Mrs Fitzgerald found herself cornered: it would have been odd for *her* to plead the body over the spirit.

'Well, I'm for it,' said Mrs Carruthers. 'I'd like to know Ronnie's things are safe. His father gave him a beautiful leather pocket-book when he went away. With his initials on it in gold.'

'Oh, was that the one in Rice's window?' asked Mrs Frobisher, eagerly. 'I was going to get one for Eric.'

'No, Mr Carruthers got it in London,' she answered proudly. 'At the Army & Navy. It was—'

Beattie caught Mrs Oliver's eye and retrieved the ball. 'What are these bags like?' she asked. 'I've heard of them, but never seen one.'

Mrs Dawson answered: 'They're made of cretonne, about ten inches by twelve, with a tape drawstring, and a strip of glazed calico about two inches from the bottom for a label. They write the man's name and other information on it in ink. Lady Smith-Dorrien has a large quantity of cretonne that she bought wholesale and sells to anyone who wants to make bags at fourpence-ha'penny a yard. You can get three bags out of a yard. And you can buy the label strips from her at fourpence a hundred.'

'Ah. But where does the money come from?' Mrs Fitzgerald asked, in a last attempt to scupper the idea.

'Where it always comes from,' Mrs Oliver said. 'Donations. We'll start it off and, if necessary, we have a sale of work or a flag day or something to raise more.'

'*Another* flag day?' Mrs Fitzgerald said scathingly. Since someone had first thought them up, they had proliferated like black beetles in a basement. In London you couldn't walk down a street without being accosted by two or three ladies with a collecting tin and a tray of tiny paper flags on pins.

110

'The sums aren't large,' Beattie said. 'We can raise enough just between us to get things started. Thirteen shillings will pay for a hundred bags, and I'm sure we could manage two shillings each.'

'I could certainly spare two shillings to know that Ronnie's things would be safe,' said Mrs Carruthers. 'That pocket-book was expensive, with the embossing. I know for a fact—'

'Leather's awfully expensive,' said Mrs Frobisher. 'Eric's boots—'

'My nephew Adolphus, who's out in Malta—' said Mrs Fitzgerald, determined not to be left out.

Mrs Oliver poured more tea and her maid went round with cake. Conversation veered away onto various topics.

Mrs Dawson changed seats to sit by Beattie, and said, 'How quick you were to work out the cost of a hundred bags.'

'I've always been good with figures,' Beattie said. 'I feel sorry for the poor women who find household accounts a trial.'

'Are you one of those prodigies who can add up a column of shillings and pence in a single glance?' Mrs Dawson asked.

'Not quite,' Beattie said, 'but there is a pleasure in it, don't you find? One can be quite sure with numbers that the answer is correct. That doesn't happen with much else.'

'That's true,' said Mrs Dawson. 'It's unusual to find a lady who has a grasp of money – oh dear, that didn't sound quite the way I meant it to.'

Beattie laughed. 'The word "grasp" perhaps shouldn't be used near the word "money".'

'Leaving that aside, I wonder if I could interest you in another scheme of mine. It is so hard to find suitable ladies, and particularly those one gets along with.'

'I have rather a lot on my plate at the moment,' Beattie

111

said cautiously. One was always being asked to do this or that, and it was better not to be sucked in until one had discovered what was entailed.

'That's what *I* always say when anyone asks me to join something,' said Mrs Dawson. 'Fanny said I would like you – and she was right.'

'Are you flattering me to force me to say yes?' Beattie asked, enjoying this refreshingly open conversation.

'Would that work? I'm happy to try it.'

'Just tell me what the scheme is. You can flatter me later.'

Mrs Dawson smiled. 'I'll bear that in mind. It's quite simple, really. I help to run a canteen in Waterloo station, for the servicemen. We like to keep it open long hours, so we need a lot of volunteers so as not to put too much strain on any one of them. Willing volunteers aren't *too* hard to find, but I have terrible trouble recruiting ladies who can give the right change. So many of them haven't handled actual money since they got married, if ever – their husbands write cheques, and the servants deal with the tradespeople at the back door. And there is, I'm sorry to say, a certain sort of serviceman who wouldn't shrink from cheating them if he thought he could get away with it. It's almost like a game.'

'You make it sound most alarming.'

'Oh, no! You mustn't think that! Most of them are dear chaps, and so grateful for any attention. But there is the odd "fly" fellow, and it's important to be able to spot them. Won't you *please* think about helping? It needn't be too many hours, if you really are busy, but I would like to have someone I can rely on to watch the money side of it. It's just serving tea and buns and so on. The standing is rather hard on the feet to begin with,' she added honestly, 'but as long as you wear sensible shoes . . .'

'I think it sounds rather fun,' Beattie said. 'I'll do it.'

'My dear! Don't you want time to think about it?'

112

'No need. I'll be happy to help.' To do something directly for the men would be more satisfying than rolling bandages or sitting on committees.

'Thank you so much,' said Mrs Dawson. 'I'll get out my schedule before you leave and we'll see when you can fit yourself in. I'm so glad – I'm sure we'll get on.'

Mrs Oliver came over. 'Did she say yes, Milly?'

'She said yes,' said Mrs Dawson.

'I thought she would.'

CHAPTER EIGHT

Porteous went up on a solo flight early one morning, and didn't come back. It was not an unprecedented occurrence. Engine failure was common, and if a pilot had to put down somewhere, it could take time for him to find someone to tell; then it was ten to one against that person having a telephone. More usually a boy had to be found to be dispatched to the nearest post office, which might be miles away.

But as hours passed without news, there began to be apprehension that Porteous might have been hurt, or be otherwise unable to go for help. Andrews went up in the little Martynside scout to search for him, and the major rang round the other local airfields to ask them to keep a look-out. But Andrews came back at dusk, shaking his head. It was not until after dark that the news came in.

Porteous had put down in a field too small for the job and had run headlong into a tree. A farmhand working some distance away had seen him go over and had heard the engine cut out. He had heard the crash, but having no-one with him, and being some distance from civilisation, he hadn't known what to do except walk in the same direction and see if he could find the young 'flying man'.

He had found Porteous, at last, sitting in the crushed nacelle with struts, spars, wires and drooping white fabric spread around him in a train of destruction. He looked unhurt but unconscious, until the farmhand had given him a gentle shake, and then the angle at which his head had flopped over proved his neck to be broken. The labourer had then had another long walk to find someone to tell, and when the police, in the form of a village bobby, had finally been informed, the officer knew nothing of airfields and had to conduct enquiries by telephone to find which authority to inform.

Porteous seemed to have gone far out of his way, and there was no way of knowing why he had done so, whether he had been lost, or struggling with a faltering engine, or had himself been suffering in some way that impaired his judgement. Whatever it was, the news was finally brought to the waiting cadets, idling about in the mess, that their colleague was dead.

Bobby and Farringdon drank rather a lot that evening. Later, in his narrow bed in the railway carriage, Bobby found the alcohol perversely prevented him from sleeping. His mind revolved annoyingly round the same few thoughts until, at the very first peep of first light, he got up and dressed, and went out to clear his head.

He walked for a bit along the shingle, but the breeze was cold, and the sea looked unfriendly, grey under a grey sky, so he turned inland. His steps took him without his volition to the sheds, his favourite place to be. Here there was always comfort. The sight of aeroplanes made him feel alive, and strangely safe, because they were his natural home – and one was always safe at home.

Poor old Porker hadn't been either safe or at home – the one depending, he supposed, on the other.

He stood with his hands shoved into his pockets, trying to think profound thoughts about life and death, but wondering instead about the chances of flying that day. One of the mechanics, Ricks, came out of the shed, wiping his hands on an oily rag. He was a wrinkled and scrawny man with so few teeth he would never have been accepted into the army, except that he had expertise hard to replace. He kept an unlit, battered roll-up always between his lips, ready for when he'd be far enough from aircraft fuel to light up.

He saw Bobby and tacked over to him, removed the roll-up, and examined him sympathetically. 'Don't you fret, sir,' he said kindly. 'He wouldn't never have made no pilot, not nohow.'

What an epitaph, Bobby thought. 'Wish I knew what happened,' he said.

'You don't never really know what's going on,' said Ricks. 'Don't do no good to brood over it.' He put the roll-up back between his lips, and felt about for a match. 'Better get off to breakfast, sir, hadn't you?'

Breakfast was always the high point of the day. They did you well at brekker, Bobby thought, and the coffee was surprisingly good. He was on his second cup, feeling the reliable comfort of good food, when the major came in and said, without preamble, 'Hunter, Farringdon – you're being transferred to Gosport.'

'Gosport, sir?' Bobby said, in surprise.

'You'll complete your training there,' said the major, 'and once you're qualified you'll be attached to a new squadron they're forming. There'll be transport for you at nine.' He glanced at his watch. 'Better finish up quickly.'

It was a quarter to. 'We'll never get our kit packed in time, sir,' Farringdon objected.

'Well, the tender can't wait. Just grab what you need immediately and someone'll pack up the rest and send it on. Good luck, chaps.'

He left. They stared at each other for a moment, Bobby with a piece of toast and marmalade in his hand, Farringdon cradling his third cup of coffee, until Cardoon said sharply, 'You heard the major. What are you waiting for? If you miss that tender . . .'

They both jumped up. Bobby crammed the toast into his mouth as he shoved his chair back, Farringdon abandoned his cup to say pleadingly to Cardoon, 'Why the short notice?'

'The army moves in mysterious ways,' said Cardoon. 'You should be pleased. They have a lot more machines at Gosport. It's a step up for you. Now *double*!'

As the Crossley tender bumped its way gently along winding country lanes beginning to burst into spring green, Farringdon passed Bobby a cigarette and said, 'It's to do with Porker, you know. I bet it is. Why us two and nobody else? They're moving us to a place where we won't be reminded of him.'

Bobby stared at him in amazement. 'This is the *army*,' he said.

Farringdon nodded. 'You're right. Of course they don't care how we feel. I don't know what I was thinking.'

'Cardoon said it was a step up, and that's how I'm going to think of it. I want to get my wings as soon as possible so I can get out to France, and if this is the way forward . . .'

'All the same,' Farringdon said, after a moment, 'I wish I knew how it happened, poor old Porker.'

'You don't never really know what's going on,' Bobby quoted wisely.

'You are tired,' said Élise, as Edward was shown into her sitting-room. 'Come, sit down, have some sherry before supper.'

'Thank you,' said Edward. 'Sherry would be welcome. I'm not sure I have much appetite for supper.'

'That is because you are tired. I remember when I was dancing, sometimes I was too tired to eat, but that is always a mistake. One becomes weakened, and sickness follows.' She brought him a glass, and sat down beside him on the sofa.

117

It had indeed been a long day. He had gone into the office early, knowing that he would be leaving early to sit on the Appeal Tribunal, so that by the time he took his seat there at two o'clock, he had already done a day's work.

'And I miss Warren,' he said. 'I always knew he was an invaluable young man, but I'm now discovering how much he did to save me work.'

'Is your new man not good?' she asked. 'What is this his name is?'

'Murchison.'

'*Murrr*chis*oon*,' said Élise, with much rolling of the *r*. She knew about Murchison and his shortcomings, and also that Edward needed to talk about it. *Get it off his chest*, as the strange English saying was. Off the stomach, she considered, would have been a better phrase. Troubles sat down there, in her experience, and churned about and made nuisance. 'What has he done wrong?'

'Oh, it isn't that he does anything wrong. He's a decent fellow, honest and hard-working. But he's so slow. And he has to have everything explained. I know some of the work is complicated, but I was used to Warren, who picked up everything on a hint. Murchison has to have every sentence completed. Sometimes, when he gives me that *look*, over the top of his glasses, and says, "I beg your pardon, sir, but I don't quite understand" – well, sometimes I just want to strike him!'

Élise laughed. 'You cannot beat your employees, Édouard. Even I know that. In England this is not allowed.'

He smiled a little. 'Don't tell me it's allowed in France.'

'Why not? You know, we are barbarians, we foreigners!'

'I've never said that,' he said gallantly. 'I think you're a beacon of civilised behaviour.'

'Do you mean me, or *tous les français*?'

'You in particular and the French in general. Why do you think we are fighting this war, if not to save France?'

118

'Ah, who knows?' she said lightly. 'I think men like wars, or why would they have so many of them? But drink your sherry a little more and tell me about the tribunal. Did you have any interesting cases?'

'There was a rather touching one – a fellow who ran a grocery store. He'd built up the business himself, and he was so proud of the place. He even brought us a photograph of it, with him standing in the doorway, so that we could admire it. Now all his assistants have been called up and he's running it single-handed. If he had to go, he'd have to close down and risk losing his life savings. He's not married and has no family, so he has no one to leave in charge.'

'And what did you decide?'

'We gave him a postponement of one month to put his affairs in order,' said Edward. 'The poor man broke down in tears. I think the shop was wife, family and everything to him.'

'You are too sensitive for this job, Édouard,' Élise said sternly. 'You see the thing from his side, when you are supposed to see it from the army's.'

'I do see both sides,' Edward protested, 'but I don't let it affect me.'

'Not affect your judgement. But, *voyons*, it does affect *you*. Tell me another one.'

He smiled at her indulgently. 'A really sad one?' he asked.

'Of course. I like *les histoires*, me.'

'Very well. We had a young fellow, the son of Germans who had fled from Germany to escape military service. He'd been brought up in England and taught that all warfare was wrong.'

'Ah, the conscientious objector, *n'est-ce pas*? Do you find them difficult?'

'Not generally,' said Edward. 'When it's a genuine, deeply held belief and not just squeamishness, we try to put them into non-combatant service.'

'*Squeam* – what is this word?'

He thought a moment. '*Délicatesse*,' he offered her. 'But this case was slightly different. The parents had opened a butcher's shop, as so many German migrants did, and had been a happy part of the community until the war started. After that they were attacked several times, the shop was wrecked and looted, and they were intimidated and insulted in various ways. It convinced him all over again that violence was wrong.'

'So you excused him?'

'We couldn't do that. The others were inclined to dismiss his appeal entirely. But I pointed out that he would be fighting in France against men of his own nationality – or, at least, his parents' – and one couldn't be sure he would do his best in those circumstances. He might have ended up being more trouble than he was worth to some commander in the line. The others saw my point, and we sent him to a labour battalion to serve in this country.'

'Was it a good ending for him?' said Élise.

'It was a practical solution,' he said, and sighed. 'You are kind to let me maunder on like this about my day. I don't know why you're so kind to me.'

'You don't?' she said, looking straight into his eyes. 'Édouard, you are so innocent! It is *très gentil*.'

For a moment the room seemed very quiet and warm. She was so close he could catch her perfume, and her soft lips seemed to part as though inviting him – inviting him to—

He drew back, turned his head away. 'I'm sorry,' he said. 'I think I must have come over a little dizzy just then. The sherry must have gone to my head.'

'Oh, Édouard,' she said, shaking her head, 'it is not faintness or sherry. *Tiens*, men are very good at not seeing what is *sous le nez*. What are we doing here? Tell me that.'

He groped after acceptable words. 'You are my client. I

have your welfare at heart. I – I feel a responsibility. And, perhaps I dare add, I regard you as a friend.'

'And is that all? A *friend*?'

He could not pretend not to understand her. 'I am a married man,' he said desperately.

She gave a little nod, as though to herself. '*Eh, bien.* We shall be friends. It will do for now.'

'I think perhaps I ought to go,' he said awkwardly. 'It was probably not wise – that is, I think I ought not to visit you at home any more. We can discuss your business affairs in the office in future.'

'But I do not like to come to your office,' she said firmly. 'It is more convenient here. And you visit other clients in their homes, this I know.'

'Yes, but—'

'Oh, Mr Hunter, please sit down,' she said, laughing. 'You are quite safe from me. Supper is ready, I can smell it, and you are hungry. We shall be as proper as you like. You do nothing wrong here.'

He was silent, wondering about that very point. He was attracted to her, of course he was, but he had never meant . . . He loved his wife, he would never betray her . . . And yet he was here, and she did not know about it . . . *I must not come here again*, he thought. But when he viewed the future without these suppers, it seemed bleak. Beattie had been withdrawing from him for some time, and David going to war had accelerated the process. Here, he was welcomed, he was listened to, he was important. Surely if they were just friends – if he *did* nothing wrong, *intended* nothing wrong . . .

The smell of cooking intensified as Solange opened the kitchen door, and a moment later she appeared in the doorway with an enquiring look, silently announcing supper.

'Please stay and eat,' Élise said, in a normal and serious voice. 'It would be sinful to waste good food, would it not?'

'It would,' he said. 'And I do have some matters I want to raise with you, about your investments.'

'Of course you do,' she said. There was nothing in her expression, but he couldn't help feeling she was laughing at him all the same.

Lilian came back from her first day off a changed girl. She had gone home, and had been welcomed. Her mother was pleased because she had brought home her wages, her father with her improved looks. Whatever Emily thought, she was not beautiful, having rabbity teeth and an insufficiency of chin, but good food and regular bathing had given her a healthy glow that suited her. She had things to tell her siblings, and being the centre of attention roused her spirits.

She had liked seeing her family again, but the deficiencies of her old home seemed stark by contrast with what she had become used to at The Elms. She was not sorry to catch her bus back to Northcote, bearing the thing that would most endear her to her fellow workers: news.

Hendorp was humming with it: 'They're building a munitions factory,' she told the kitchen breathlessly.

It had started with extending the railway lines from Hendorp Halt into an area of open fields, which had naturally fuelled wild rumours among the locals as to what they could be for. One of Lilian's brothers, Noah, had got work as a labourer with the railway-layers, at 'really good wages'. Before, he had only been able to get intermittent day labour on the local farms, which paid a pittance, so he was very happy.

'Won't he be called up in the army?' Ada queried.

'He hasn't got enough teeth,' Lilian said, forgetting, in the excitement of being the news-bearer, to be shy. 'He got kicked in the head by a bullock years ago. Knocked his teeth out and broke his jaw. It didn't mend straight, so he talks funny, too. We can understand him, but strangers think he's

122

simple, so he doesn't like going far from home. But he's a good worker, and they took him on the railway – there's work for loads of our local boys, doing the railway lines, and then a whole lot of buildings are going up.'

On the far side of the open fields was a small sweets factory, which had been built beside the Grand Junction Canal and had its own loading wharf. This, Lilian had learned, would be the offices, and the railway lines would go over the whole site and link up with the wharf as well, so that materials could be brought in by boat as well as train.

'There's twenty buildings already up,' Lilian went on. 'Pa said he'd never seen people work so fast.'

'Are you sure it's munitions?' Cook asked.

'Filling shells, Noah says, and cartridges, and making fuses and the like. He says they'll be starting work next week, and they're going to be taking on hundreds of people – women, even. And paying ever such high wages.'

'Oh, wouldn't it be fine to work there,' said Emily, 'knowing you were helping to win the war? Knowing you'd made a shell that was going to blow a Hun to bits?'

'That's enough of that talk,' Cook said sharply.

Emily looked stubborn. 'Anyone's got a right to get a job, haven't they?'

'You've got a job.'

'And ever such high wages, Lilian says.'

'Yes, and you'd have to spend 'em all on board and lodging, think of that,' said Cook. 'You get it all for nothing here. Girls that go and live in lodgings are no better than they ought. I've heard about 'em. I'm not letting you get yourself into trouble, not if I can help it. What would your mother say?'

'It's dirty work, Em,' Ada said, 'and dangerous, so my Len says. You'd much better stay here.'

'That's right – and there's supper dishes out in that

scullery that won't wash themselves,' said Cook. 'So get to it, or you'll still be at it at bedtime. Lilian, seeing you're back, you can make the cocoa.'

'Can you believe it?' Sadie exclaimed, coming home from Highclere one day. 'They're building an extra siding at Rustington station especially for us!'

'I'm not sure why you're sounding so pleased about it.' Beattie said, sitting at the morning-room table darning socks.

'Because it means they're taking us seriously,' Sadie said.

Beattie looked up. 'I thought you knew that already.'

'But there's something more solid about a railway line,' said Sadie. 'They won't close us down once they've put in actual *rails*.'

'I suppose it *is* a commitment,' Beattie allowed, trying to engage with her strange child's enthusiasm. She snipped the wool, laid the sock aside, and picked up another. 'I don't know what William *does*,' she murmured, sliding the mush-room under a gaping hole. 'He goes through the heels in a week.'

'Apparently,' said Sadie, 'Captain Casimir pointed out to his superiors that the Office of Works was already in the area, putting in rails at Hendorp for the filling factory, so they might as well tack us on. They sent the workmen up with some spare rails and sleepers and it was done in no time.'

'Is everyone talking about the filling factory? Your father said he knew about it weeks ago but that it was supposed to be a secret.'

'I don't see how you can keep something like that secret. Mr Cuthbert heard from the railway foreman that the site covers two hundred acres and will probably have four hundred buildings in the long run. There'll be no hiding *that*.'

'Well, talking about it ought to be discouraged, in case

of German spies,' said Beattie. '*And* for the sake of my sanity. I had Mrs Fitzgerald here this afternoon in a state of agitation.'

'Oh dear,' said Sadie. 'I thought you were looking a bit tired. Did she go on and on?'

'She did rather. She's seen a recruitment poster – apparently they're all over Harrow, and there was one in Westleigh station. She's sure they'll be here next. It said, "Women workers urgently wanted for Government work in Middlesex", and it had "GOOD WAGES" in huge capitals.'

'And that's for Hendorp, is it?'

'It said "Munition Workers" at the top, and Hendorp's the only munitions factory in Middlesex, according to Mrs Fitzgerald.'

'But why is she upset about it? I don't see what it's got to do with the Church,' Sadie said, puzzled. 'I mean, the rector's never denounced the war or anything, has he? And if you have a war you have to have munitions.'

'It wasn't a religious objection,' Beattie said. 'She thinks the high wages will tempt all our servants away – apparently, there's a real servant problem in other places where they have them.'

'Really?'

'She thinks so, at any rate. And she says girls will be coming in from all over the place to work there – flighty, unreliable girls. They'll be living in lodgings without supervision, and they'll get into trouble.'

Sadie had a sudden image of the entire population of the army camp on Paget's Piece clashing with an army of flighty, unsupervised girls in a wild carnival of the sort of thing Mrs Fitzgerald called 'trouble', and had to suppress a giggle. 'But what does she want *you* to do about it?' she managed to say.

'I think it was a general warning,' said Beattie, wearily, 'to keep an eye on my servants. I'm not sure. I think mostly she wanted someone to complain to.' She looked up. 'She's heard about *your* girls, somehow. She was hinting about them. Something about the general movement of young women away from their homes and into unsuitable situations.'

'Well, our girls won't be causing trouble,' said Sadie. 'You can't think how strict Mrs Cuthbert can be! Anyway, by the time they've done a day's work on the horses, they'll be too tired to gallivant.'

'I'm afraid *you*'re going to be too tired, with all this extra work,' Beattie said, realising that she hadn't properly thought through the changes that were coming to Highclere. Sadie would be up there for much longer hours, and supervising other girls, when she was hardly more than a girl herself. She looked at Sadie properly for the first time in months, and saw the changes in her. There was firmness in her face, decision in her voice and movements. But what sort of a life was it for her up there, messing about with horses – even in a good cause? She would never find a husband that way.

And then she halted that line of thought. The war was going to change the marriage prospects of every girl. Look at Diana – engaged in triumph, and widowed before she had ever married. What hope was there for any of them, with the men all away? Even the feared and hated Sophy – she was engaged to David, but she would barely even see him until the war was over.

Instead of any of the things she might have said, what actually came out was, 'I'll hardly see anything of you.'

Sadie was touched. She had never been a favourite with her mother, she knew, but everything was changing. And Diana had been away in London for weeks – perhaps Mother was lonely. 'The girls don't come for two more days,' she said. 'I don't need to go to Highclere tomorrow. If you like I could stay at home. We could – do something, perhaps. Go shopping or something?'

126

Beattie raised an eyebrow. 'What a curious suggestion,' she said. 'You've always hated shopping. Besides, I'm going up to London tomorrow. It's one of my canteen days.'

'Ah,' said Sadie, rebuffed. 'Well, I'm sure there'll be something for me to do at the stables.'

CHAPTER NINE

Six girls had arrived at Highclere, and Sadie had spent the day helping them settle in. Five had come in answer to advertisements. There was Catherine, who was from a working-class family and, loving horses, had helped out at a riding stable in return for lessons. Now at fifteen she had to find employment and the advertisement had seemed the answer to her prayers. Her father was against it, wanting her to get a job in a shop and help the family budget, but her mother had pointed out that she would get her bed and board at Highclere so would cease to be a drain on her parents, which was almost as good.

Catherine was shy, and small for her age, and Sadie wondered whether she really was fifteen. There was already a fine tradition of lying about your age for patriotic reasons – Victor Sowden, a local ruffian, had managed to get taken into the army at fourteen.

Jennifer and Jane were sixteen, friends, and rather giggly. They'd had ponies all their lives, but with grooms to look after them, they'd never done stable work, though they claimed to have 'watched it all'. Sadie was going to have to teach them everything, as she was Winifred, who'd never even had a pony, but 'loved animals' and was 'willing to learn'. She was a tall, plain girl of seventeen. Her letter of application had said she was passionately eager to do something for the war effort, though to Sadie she didn't seem to have enough spirit to be passionate about anything.

Monica was uncommunicative and aloof, but it was soon clear she knew what she was doing. She had been a girl groom at a racing stables in Yorkshire, but the war had taken away most of the horses, and as the lone female she had been the first to be let go. Sensationally, she had short hair, cut off at jaw level all round, like a medieval page boy. When she was working, she wore a round knitted hat, like a tea cosy, pulled down over it, so that from the back, in her breeches and puttees, she looked like a boy.

The sixth girl was from the Rustington area, and Mrs Cuthbert had found her. Mary was tall, and at eighteen the oldest of them. She had large-knuckled hands and a plain, sensible face. She came from an upper-class family, had ridden all her life, hunted and point-to-pointed. Her family had also kept grooms, but her mother, who was a hard woman to hounds, had insisted that Mary know how to do everything in the stable, for otherwise how could she tell if the grooms were doing it properly? And until the army had requisitioned her last horse, she had preferred to groom and feed him herself, though she left the mucking out, pulling and clipping to others. Bereft of horses, she had jumped at Mrs Cuthbert's suggestion. 'I'd love to do some schooling – I've always wanted to, but Daddy bought me made horses, so I never had the chance.'

At the end of a very busy day – much of it spent rounding up Jennifer and Jane, who had no idea of application to a task and tended to wander off after a few moments unless they were kept at it – Sadie left them up at the house planning to bathe before dinner, which was already smelling delicious in the background. The sitting-room that had been made over to their use had a big fire crackling and a comfortable sofa and armchairs drawn up before it. Sadie could imagine the six of them gathered in that cosy room, laughing and chatting together. As she cycled home, she wished she could have stayed. She'd never really had friends like that. Perhaps that was why she had always loved horses.

'You can never be lonely with a horse,' she said to Nailer, who was sitting in the basket, facing forward, his eyes closed in bliss against the breeze of passage.

What about us dogs? Nailer said, in the growly country voice she imagined for him. *Here I am, risking life and limb to keep you company . . .*

'Oh, I'm never lonely with you either. But sometimes it would be nice to have a conversation where I didn't have to provide both sides.'

To which Nailer could only reply with a sniff.

Mr Weston picked up the post from the hall table and carried it into the breakfast-room. Antonia was already seated, and tilted up her head to smile at him as he laid a hand on her shoulder in passing.

'One for you here, my dear,' he said. 'From our own correspondent at the Front.'

He passed it to her and went on to the sideboard to help himself to bacon and eggs. It was not usual for a young woman to correspond with a young man to whom she was not engaged, but Mr Weston had had no qualms about giving his permission. Young Hunter hadn't a dishonest bone in his body, and it was obvious that his friendship was entirely platonic. He'd had boys like David Hunter through his hands while he was the headmaster of St Hugh's: serious boys, whose minds were set so high they seemed to float a little above the earth. Sometimes life brought them down with a bump, but he hoped that would not happen to David – he was very fond of the lad. Antonia was, too, but he trusted her good taste not to offer more affection than was wanted. Having been brought up inside a boys' boarding-school, she'd

130

had plenty of practice at being a big sister, and had developed, besides, an almost masculine cast of mind. And now, of course, there was a fiancée in the background, at whose feet the parfit, gentil David was to lay his feats of arms, so the correspondence couldn't have been more innocent.

He took his plate to his place, and looked indulgently down the table at his daughter. 'Read it aloud to me, dear.' She glanced up enquiringly. 'It will be interesting to see how what he says fits with what General Wolfram was telling me the other day.'

Mr Weston had a large acquaintance among parents of former pupils, many of them people of influence or retired military men, who passed him interesting snippets of information about the war that were not in general circulation.

'He doesn't say much. It's quite a short letter,' Antonia replied, and obediently began reading.

My dear Antonia,
I'm sorry I have taken so long to reply to your last, but we have been very busy. We were sent on exercise to a pretend battlefield, all marked out with tape and signposts, where we had to advance and capture positions over and over again. And we officers had lectures at night, with maps and strategies to learn. All very interesting but exhausting! Did I mention my friend Jumbo, brother to the Divine Sophy, has been made captain? So we are now commanding sister companies. After exercises it was our turn in the trenches, and now we are out again, behind the line.

Thank you for the dried fruit you sent with your last – the food here can be so monotonous. Please also thank your father for the Horace, which I am still enjoying. I'd write to him myself but this is my last sheet of paper. The hardest things to get here are soap, razor blades and writing paper!

We are moving next week to another part of the line – I can't tell you where. The rumours are of a big push coming, but I doubt if that is divulging a secret. Everyone has always said something would happen this summer. The French are catching toco at Verdun and we have to do something to help them. The men are pleased and excited at the thought of getting to grips with Fritz and bringing things to an end.

I have enjoyed the experience of being a part of this great endeavour, and in many ways will be sorry when it's over. I longed to do something worthwhile, and what could be more important than defending the glorious land I love so much from barbarity? I think often of your gentle corner of it – so green, so beautiful, so worth every strained sinew to protect. I wish I had more paper so I could express all my thoughts. Please send me a long letter filled with yours. My adored Sophy is no great correspondent. God willing it will all be over this summer, and I can come home and marry her, so letters will no longer be necessary. But yours I shall always value.

Your sincere friend,
David.

'Hmm,' said Mr Weston, when she finished. 'You're right. He doesn't say much. Except about the Divine Sophy!' he added, with a chuckle. 'When serious boys like him come a cropper over a girl, they fall hard and painfully.'

'Yes, Daddy,' said Antonia, absently.

'Cheer up,' said Mr Weston. 'She may not be his equal, but the chances are that he'll never notice. He'll invest her with his own qualities, and if she's the wit to keep her mouth shut, she'll do very well. They'll be very happy together.'

'Oh, I know,' Antonia said. 'I was just thinking that we ought to see if we can send him some writing paper in the next parcel.'

'Good thinking,' said Mr Weston. 'Then we might get a more interesting letter next time.'

Beattie would not have thought of her experience at the canteen as being in any way similar to Sadie's at Highclere – in truth, she hardly ever thought about Sadie at all – but she had found in the various ladies a similar disparity of ability, intelligence and purpose. Milly Dawson was a delight to work with, not only efficient, but an amusing companion. She handled the customers with a skill that looked easy until you tried to copy it. The canteen was always thronged, with soldiers going off to war, some excited, some anxious, some not knowing what was ahead of them, others knowing only too well. In the general churning of emotions they were sometimes too forward, and to welcome and restrain them at the same time needed delicate judgement.

Those coming back from the Front yearned for contact with the female half of humanity, of which they had been starved. Some could still be bumptious, but most were just grateful, and the danger was of being too touched by them.

The women she worked with were mostly middle class and married, like herself, and she quickly discovered the truth of Milly's complaints about their financial abilities. Mrs Parling couldn't subtract sevenpence from a shilling, and got a different answer every time. Mrs Eade couldn't subtract anything from anything, and begged the soldiers to give her the right money, so that her customers were often to be found rummaging for pennies, and entering complicated financial contracts along the lines of 'If I give you tuppence and Jim thruppence and he gives you a shillin' and you pay for my tea and bun, we'll come out even.'

Lady Betty Frampton coped by pointing at Beattie and saying, 'Please pay that lady, there's a good fellow.'

But Beattie liked working with her. She was brisk and jolly and, like Milly Dawson, had exactly the right touch with the soldiers. Oddly enough, she disliked serving officers – unlike Mrs Eade and Mrs Parling, who would elbow each other out of the way if an officer came up to the counter. Beattie asked Milly Dawson why, and Milly said she didn't know, but perhaps it was because her brother had been killed at St Quentin, and they reminded her of him.

Beattie liked it when she had an officer to serve. It made a change, and she could ask them how the war was going – it was no use asking the men, whose perspective was always intensely personal. Sometimes the officers told her interesting things. And she was hopeful that one day one of them would turn out to know David.

She went home from her canteen duties exhausted. In part it was the noise and movement: spending most of her life in a quiet backwater, the sheer volume of humanity was enervating. It was hard, as Milly Dawson had warned, to be on her feet for so long together. And it was hard to have her emotions so constantly engaged. Until she could develop a shell against them, the soldiers made her feel too much.

Edward expressed concern when he saw how tired she was. 'It's too much for you,' he said, more than once. But she would not give it up. She felt she was making a direct difference to the lives of the men, however small. And it made her feel more in touch with the war, and therefore more in touch with David.

The army sent Highclere more uniformed help in the shape of Private Stanhill. Sadie was glad to find him as different as could be from Higgins. He was in his thirties, a quiet man with a strong, pleasant face and an educated voice. The reason for his presence was obvious: his right hand lacked the top two joints of the first and second fingers, though it didn't seem to hamper him: he managed everything very well with the stumps.

134

'But I've nothing to pull a trigger with, you see,' he explained to the girls, on his arrival, 'so I'm no use in combat.'

'Couldn't you use your left hand?' asked Jennifer, staring at the wounded one with unseemly interest.

He pretended to be shocked. 'You can't fire left-handed in the army! It'd spoil the symmetry of the ranks.'

To Sadie, when they first worked together, he admitted that he was also partly deaf in his right ear. 'A shell exploded on that side of me. The shrapnel took my fingers, and the concussion deafened me. Once I recovered I was sent to a labour unit. They wanted agricultural workers, so I volunteered, and when this came up I volunteered again.'

'You've worked with horses before?' she asked. 'You're a country man?'

'Not before the army. Do I come across that way? No, I'm from a very industrial background really – born and brought up in Bradford. Trained as a teacher, and taught at a boys' boarding-school, Hawksworth Hall. That *was* out in the country, though I didn't have much chance to enjoy it, teacher by day and housemaster by night. Boys take a lot of watching.'

'Hawksworth,' Sadie said. 'That's a nice name.'

'Do you know it?' She shook her head. 'It's just a country village. Most famous thing about it is that it was the basis for the novel *Windyridge*, by Willie Riley. Have you read it?'

'No, I'm sorry.'

'It's not bad. I've got a copy – I'll lend it to you, if you like. Willie Riley was a Bradford man too. We went to the same school – he was before my time, though.'

'I'd like to read it,' she said. 'How did you come to join the army?'

'I volunteered right off, in 1914.' He gave a deprecating smile. 'Tell the truth, I wanted a change from boys and teaching. Thought it'd be an adventure.'

'Like in the *Magnet*,' said Sadie.

'You read comics?'

'I have brothers,' she said.

'Ah, that explains why you're so easy to talk to,' he said.

Perhaps teaching and house-mastering boys was a good training for taking care of horses, for he proved very good at it, displaying endless patience and the quiet firmness that gave horses confidence. He didn't shirk, but was always ready for a chin-wag, too, and Sadie found herself drawn to him by the ease of his conversation. He talked to her so straightforwardly, as if they knew all the same things – almost as if he was talking to himself. He treated the other girls rather as she imagined he must have treated his boys – with amused but patient kindness – but from the first he seemed to see Sadie as a fellow-soul. It made working at Highclere even more agreeable.

He concurred with her about Higgins. 'I don't like the cut of him,' he confided one day. 'Maybe you could arrange it so that he does the work that doesn't involve handling the horses. There's plenty of that. But I'll keep an eye on him.' He gave Sadie a frank look. 'If there's one thing I can't abide it's cruelty, to animals or those weaker than ourselves. I never allowed any bullying in my house, nor boys tormenting cats, or pulling the legs off spiders.'

He proved himself to Sadie one day when he was grooming Crumbs, a blue roan with a distinctive scatter of brown and black freckles over his quarters. Stanhill had named him: he had a fertile imagination when it came to names. Crumbs was a decent horse but skittish in the stable. Sadie was in the next stall when there was a high snort and a thud, and Stanhill came flying out backwards to land on his seat in the gully, his cap several feet away and his fair hair madly ruffled.

Sadie hurried out. 'Are you all right?'

He was rubbing his thigh and grimacing. 'He got the

meat, not the bone. But I shall have an interesting bruise tomorrow.'

'What happened?'

'He's ticklish about having his belly brushed. But I'll fettle him.'

Sadie watched in faint alarm as he scrambled to his feet, restored his cap, looked around, and grabbed a length of thin rope that was hanging from a nail in the wall. Crumbs laid his ears back and rolled a suspicious eye, but Stanhill went up to his head and stroked his neck and nose kindly, murmuring soothing words. Then he stooped, slipped the rope round a fetlock, and in a neat movement drew the foreleg up tight under the horse's chest and secured it by the haynet hook.

'He can stand on three legs and kick me with the fourth,' said Stanhill, 'but I reckon he can't stand on two.'

Sadie was impressed. 'Where did you learn that?'

'Worked it out from first principles,' he said, taking up the body-brush and bending to his task. Crumbs jerked about a bit, trying to free his foreleg, but he was trussed firmly, and could only lash with his tail. Sadie took hold of it so it shouldn't smack Stanhill in the face.

'I'm glad you think he's a good horse,' she said.

'They're all good horses. I dare say I shouldn't like a scratchy old brush across my belly.'

Sadie laughed, mostly in pleasant shock that a man should feel so comfortable with her that he could say the word 'belly' – which was perfectly correct in horse terms, but not something that often smote the ear of a young lady, even in a stable.

'Diana? Is that you?'

Walking along the corridor on the way back to the ball-room from the ladies' room, Diana turned at the sound of the voice, and saw Olive Marlowe sitting on a velvet bench

137

in one of the alcoves. She was the only one of Charles's circle Diana had really liked – the only one who had treated her kindly from the start.

'Obby,' she said. 'How nice to see you.'

They shook hands. 'Are you staying in Town with Cousin Violet?' To Diana's slightly blank look, Obby amplified. 'Lady Wroughton.'

Diana remembered that Charles had called Obby's mother 'Cousin Maud'. She had never really come to grips with the complicated relationships that connected the upper classes like a sticky web. 'No,' she said. 'I'm staying with my cousin Beth. I haven't seen or heard from Lady Wroughton since before Christmas.'

'Ah,' said Obby, as if all was now clear. Then she said kindly, 'You mustn't mind her. She's like that with everyone. She takes someone up for a while, then drops them. She was nice to me for a bit when I first came out but then . . .' She shrugged. 'And it must be a terrible blow for her, Charles being killed. Won't you stay for a bit and talk? I must sit down – my feet are throbbing.' She sank back onto the bench and patted it for Diana to join her. 'I see you're looking at my terrible red hands,' she said ruefully.

'I'm not,' said Diana, who wasn't.

'You can always tell a nurse by her red hands and swollen ankles,' said Obby. 'I didn't really want to come to this ball, but it was for a good cause and I was persuaded. By Ellen de Vries – do you know her? She nurses with me. We came with her brother, and her brother's friend, who's home on leave and Ellen is sweet on. She said nursing makes you too introspective if you don't get out now and then. I'm afraid the brother is getting short weight with me. I've only danced twice. Who are you here with?'

'Rupert – Lord Dene,' Diana corrected herself.

'Oh, the ineffable Rupert! Don't you find it really *odd* calling him Lord Dene? That name is so much Charles's.'

138

'Yes,' said Diana.

'Sorry – clumsy of me. Of course you must think so. How *is* Rupert? I heard a rumour that he'd been called up, but if he's here, that can't be so, can it?'

'He was, but his father got him a billet in Horse Guards,' Diana explained. 'I don't know exactly what he does, but he seems to have lots of free time.'

Obby laughed. 'That sounds like Rupert. But it's nice that he's being attentive to you. Perhaps the war's making him grow up. He used to be beastly to me when I was younger – pulling my hair and putting spiders in my pencil box. He tore the head off my doll once, just to see what was inside. It made me cry.'

'He called me a suburban vamp,' Diana said. It was nice to get that off her chest at last – she had never told anyone, and it still rankled.

'Oh dear!' said Obby. 'Yes, I can imagine him saying it. All I can say is, he hardly ever means what he says. I don't think he's cruel underneath. He does things to see what will happen, without thinking about the consequences.' She looked down at her feet, wriggling her toes thoughtfully inside her dancing shoes.

Diana followed the direction of her gaze. 'What made you become a nurse?' she asked.

'It was to get away from home, mostly,' Obby said frankly. 'It was really deadly after Rolo volunteered last year.' That was her brother. 'He's in France now. Did you worry all the time about Charles? I worry about Rolo. I keep waiting for a letter, then when one comes, I'm so relieved for about one day, and then I start worrying again until the next one.'

Diana was ashamed to remember that she hadn't worried about Charles. It had never occurred to her that he could be killed. How naïve she had been! Rather than answer the question, she said, 'I have two brothers serving. One's in France, the other's in the RFC, training as a pilot.'

'You must be proud of them,' Obby said. 'I'm fiercely proud of Rolo. That was another reason I became a nurse. I kept thinking, If he should be hurt, I'd want to know someone was taking really good care of him. So it was up to me to take good care of someone else's brother. A sort of ethereal balance, if you see what I mean. So I joined a VAD.'

'What's it like?' Diana asked. When she visited wounded officers back home, their wounds were all tidily hidden away. She couldn't imagine seeing them without the bandages, all raw and terrifying.

'At first, like being a housemaid,' Obby said. 'Except that any servant treated the way we were would leave instantly. Even now, a lot of it is washing things and scrubbing things and cleaning things. Hence the red hands. But now I've got my first-year pip, I'm allowed to do proper nursing. So it's much more interesting.'

'Isn't it – horrible?' Diana asked awkwardly.

'Oh, yes,' Obby said seriously. 'I still feel faint when I see some of the wounds for the first time. But you have to think what it's like for *them*, and that helps you get past the faint-ness and concentrate on what you have to do.'

'Yes, I see,' Diana said.

'The men are amazingly stoical,' Obby went on. 'And terribly grateful for anything one does. At first, all us VADs were only allowed on the officers' wards – they thought the men would be too rough for us. And a lot of the girls I started with have chosen to nurse in convalescent hospitals for officers. But I felt it was important for the men to get just as good care, so I asked to go to a war hospital, and that's where I am now, at the 2nd London General.'

'I think,' Diana began, intending to say, 'I think you're terribly brave,' but at that moment Rupert appeared.

'There you are! I thought you'd run away, or got lost, or something,' he said, then spotted her companion. 'Obby!

What are you doing here? I didn't see you dancing, or I'd have asked for one.'

'I'm resting my feet,' she said, 'but I ought to go and find my party. I've behaved frightfully badly by them. My poor partner will think me heartless.'

'All you girls are heartless,' he said. 'Here I am, ready, willing and able to dance, the most eligible *parti* in the building, and you prefer to sit and talk to each other.'

'Rupert, darling, since when were you ever a *parti*?' Obby laughed.

'Since I came in for the title,' he said, and then, to Diana, 'Oops! Sorry. Treading on toes. And, speaking of which, you must come and dance. I must be seen with you. My reputation is suffering.'

'We'll both come,' said Obby, climbing gingerly to her feet. Rupert offered Diana his arm, then the other to Obby, who took it, with a curious look at Diana that she couldn't quite fathom.

In the taxi, on the way home, Rupert was quiet, until he suddenly asked Diana, 'What were you and Obby talking about?'

Diana came back from a reverie. 'Oh – nursing, mostly.'

'You're not going to become a nurse?' Rupert said, sounding alarmed.

'I hadn't thought of it,' Diana said. 'Why?'

He didn't answer at once. Then he said, 'It would be such a waste.'

She didn't pursue his meaning. She felt tired, and rather dispirited. Talking to Obby had made her think about Charles all over again.

When they reached Ebury Street, Rupert jumped out and ran up the steps to ring the bell, then came back to help Diana out, so that by the time she reached the door, it had been opened by Mrs Beales, Beth's housekeeper. Beth was out with friends of her own that evening.

Rupert had been so punctilious, she thought she should ask him in. 'Would you like a nightcap?'

She expected him to decline, but he said, 'Thank you,' promptly, as if he had been expecting it. She nodded to Mrs Beales, and led the way up to the drawing-room.

The fire had been banked, but it took only a few prods to stir it into life, and there was a tray of decanters and glasses on the table in the corner. 'What would you like?'

'Brandy, thanks,' said Rupert. She brought it over, with the siphon. He looked at the glass and grinned. 'You have a delightfully amateur hand in pouring brandy – or are you trying to get me drunk?' She blushed and said nothing, proffering the siphon. He added only a token splash. She didn't normally drink before bedtime, but she didn't want to provoke his mirth by ringing for cocoa, so she poured herself a small sherry.

When she turned back, he was sitting on the chesterfield, and patted the seat beside him for her, so she felt obliged to go and sit beside him.

'Ghastly dance, wasn't it?' he said. 'Why does one put oneself through these things? But one must do something, I suppose.'

'You're a serving officer,' she reminded him. 'You must have duties to occupy you.'

'Hm? Yes, I suppose I have,' he said vaguely, his mind obviously on other things.

'What exactly *do* you do?' she asked.

He didn't answer. Instead he said, 'You might have noticed that I've been – well, very *attentive* towards you lately.'

'I don't know why,' Diana said bluntly. 'You don't even like me.'

'What a terrible thing to say! It's not true,' he protested.

'You called me a suburban vamp.' It was the second time in one night she had vented that terrible poison from her system. It felt good.

He seemed surprised. 'Did I? I don't remember. Well, I suppose that might give you the idea . . .' He thought for a moment, and said, 'I loved my brother. You might not think it, but I did. I was afraid you were marrying him for his fortune. But now I've come to believe . . . well, that you really did love him.' There was a faint question mark at the end of the sentence, but she said nothing. She stared into the fire, feeling his eyes on her.

'Look here,' he began again, 'we're in the same boat, you and I. Or a similar one, at any rate,' he added.

Now she examined him curiously. The firelight was flickering on his face, marking his features, lighting gold glints in his hair, and reddish ones. He was handsome, in a way Charles never had been. And yet he seemed to her somehow less real. There had been something overwhelmingly solid about Charles, something undeniably *there*. He had seemed to draw all the life out of the air into himself, so that sometimes it had been hard to breathe beside him. Rooms had seemed too small when he was in them; only the outdoors had been big enough to accommodate him.

Whereas Rupert was slim and flexible, handsome and charming, a social creature, a man of interiors, of society, of parties and dinners and conversations, tall, as Charles had been, but lacking his bulk. She felt that if she blinked he might disappear in a little puff of fragrant smoke. He was insubstantial. 'I don't know what you mean,' she said.

'I've given you enough hints,' he said restlessly. 'I hoped you might acknowledge . . . Well, perhaps not. But it's dashed difficult to tell what you're thinking. I suppose I had better put my cards on the table. I'm asking you to marry me.'

It was utterly unexpected. She could only stare. Eventually she said, 'You told me – back at Dene Park – that you had a plan.'

'This is it,' he said. 'My plan was to marry you. Did you

really not suspect it? Have I been wasting my time being charming to you all these weeks?'

'I didn't think you *were* being,' she said awkwardly.

'My God! That was below the belt! You didn't even *notice*?'

'I thought . . .' Yes, what *had* she thought? That it was some trick, that he was working up to a dénouement where he humiliated her? Perhaps, at first – but lately, no, she hadn't thought that, had she? She hadn't really known what to think, but she had begun to enjoy it. It was somehow easier being with Charles's brother than with an unrelated man. It didn't feel so much like a betrayal. 'I didn't think you meant it,' she said at last.

'I suppose I deserve that,' he said. 'I know I'm a byword for insincerity. The truth is, I'd sacrifice anything for the *bon mot*. I like being clever. But I'm telling the truth now. Will you do me the favour of believing me?'

She looked at him unhappily, and nodded, unsure of what was going on.

'I am asking you to marry me,' he said. 'I think our time together lately has been – well, not *un*pleasant to you. And while I know you didn't want to marry Charles for his fortune, you must regret the loss of it. But it can all still be yours – think of that! Dene Park, the house, the land – everything. You can still be Lady Dene, and Lady Wroughton one day, with all that goes with it. The house in Town. The patronage. The position in society. Everything *Charles* wanted you to have.'

She had listened to this without reaction, still unsure of his motives. But she remembered how Charles had loved the estate, how his whole desire was to serve it. He had told her his schemes for improvement, and she had begun to share his enthusiasm. If she married Rupert, she could see them carried out after all – she didn't believe Rupert would do it. She saw herself, the chatelaine of Dene Park, taking care of it as Charles would have: creating the land of his dreams.

She thought of Sadie. After the war, there would be balls and weekend parties: she would make sure Sadie met the right people. She could help the boys' careers. She could do good in hundreds of ways. And one day she would be a great lady, and would pass on the estate and the values to her children—

Ah. That made her pull up short. She came back from the dream and looked at Rupert. 'Marry *you*?' she said faintly.

He was silent a moment, looking at her seriously. 'I know what you're thinking. We're not in love. But your heart is buried with Charles, so love doesn't come into it for you. The way it seems to me, I'm pretty much the only man you could marry now. And you're the only woman I could marry. So why not combine forces and do each other some good?' She didn't answer. 'You needn't worry about the intimate side of it. I shouldn't bother you in that way – as *you* very well know,' he added, with a short laugh.

'Do I?' she said, puzzled.

'Don't pretend,' he said. 'As long as we had an heir, and perhaps a spare if you didn't mind too much, you'd be free to live your own life. As to *getting* the heir, well, I can promise you I know how to do it pleasantly enough. It won't be a horrible experience.'

Diana ought to have been blushing at these references to something so unmentionable, but she wasn't. There was something very *odd* about this conversation. She felt slightly drunk, though she hadn't touched the sherry. It was the oddest proposal she had ever heard of, and it was hard to believe it was actually happening. She felt as though there was something very, very important she hadn't grasped, but she couldn't work out what it was.

'What do you say?' Rupert urged her at last. 'Will you do it?'

'I – I need to think,' she said.

145

'You do believe I mean it? I promise you, this is not one of my jokes. It's a genuine proposal of marriage, and I'm as keen to have you accept as any man could possibly be.'

'I believe you,' she said, from what felt like a long distance away. 'But I still need to think about it. It – it's a big step.'

'Not so very big. You were going to do it with Charles. Now you can do it anyway – same surname, same title, everything. *I Diana take thee, Rupert.* Just one word different.'

She fumbled mentally after reason. 'I just wish I knew why you wanted to.'

'I've told you,' he said impatiently. 'I *have* to marry – and you're the only woman I possibly could. So think about it, if you must, but please don't take long.' He gave her a rather pathetic look. 'They could still send me abroad, you know. Papa's settlement might not be as permanent as he thinks. And if I went—' He gave a little shudder. 'Well, there's no knowing what may happen.' He stood up. 'You look tired. I'll leave you now, but please let me know as soon as possible.'

She saw him out, then hurried to bed, not wanting to be up when Beth got home. She didn't think she could take any more talk tonight, about anything. In bed she lay staring at the ceiling, her mind in a turmoil. She didn't want to fall asleep, because she was sure in the morning she would think this had all been a dream.

CHAPTER TEN

Gosport was uncomfortable for the first few days. Bobby had got used to Shoreham, had liked the other pupils, the instructors, had been doing well. He had even liked his idiosyncratic quarters in the railway carriage. At Gosport they were quartered in a large warehouse, all in one huge industrial room with wooden partitions creating cubicles giving them their only privacy. There was not enough hot water in the bathrooms, their kit did not arrive for two days, and the mess was too small for the number using it. There were not only too many pupils for the instructors, but there were also a number of older cadets, who already had their wings and were waiting to be assigned to a squadron. They created competition not only for space in the mess – and, of course, they had first claim on the armchairs and the stewards' attentions – but for flying time.

There was only one Longhorn in the sheds, which meant a long queue for her. There were also a couple of Shorthorns, and Bobby blessed Captain Cardoon, for since his logbook showed he had already been up in one, they gave him an extra resource. All the same, progress looked like being distressingly slow. He hung about the sheds all day and pestered everyone who came along to take him up.

There were other machines in the sheds, which Bobby looked at with interest and longing – Martynside scouts; frail-looking Blériot monoplanes, both single and double-seaters;

147

tough little Caudrons with the powerful 80 h.p. Gnome engines; a Morane-Saulnier N; BEs of various sorts – they were becoming the standard workhorses of the RFC. His persistence began to pay off. At first to stop him annoying them, and later almost out of habit, the instructors took him up in the various different aeroplanes, and he began to accumulate both experience and solo flying hours in his logbook. Most of these machines were 'tractors' rather than 'pushers', and at first he found it disconcerting to have the noisy, spark-spitting engine in front of him instead of safely behind. He couldn't help thinking that a crash of any sort would throw him into a deadly, whirling incinerator.

But he was learning: the different controls, the different noises, the different stall speeds, climb rates, landing glides. The Blériot relied on wing-warping for lateral control; the Caudron's rotary engine had a powerful torque that made turning one way much faster than the other, and threatened the unwary pilot with a spin. He was careful, and managed not to blot his copy-book. More importantly, flying was becoming instinctive to him. He did not need to think about stick and rudder: his body became part of the aeroplane and he flew with as little thought for the mechanics of it as when he walked on his own two legs. It was glorious!

He began to feel that he was looked on with some favour by the instructors – though they would not have dreamed of praising him to his face. But Farringdon complained a little sourly that he did not get as much time in the air as Bobby. One of the winged seniors offered him a cigarette one day and asked him what school he'd been to; and the mess stewards saw him when he tried to attract their attention.

His suspicion that he was doing all right was confirmed one day when he was called into the office and given an urgent letter that had to be delivered to a senior officer at Shoreham.

'There's a BE free at the moment,' said the squadron commander. 'You've soloed in a 2c, haven't you?'

'Yes, sir. Twice.'

'All right, you can take that. Go straight there – the letter has to catch him before he leaves. But don't take any risks. Watch your flying speed. Don't break anything.'

'Yes, sir,' Bobby said, trying to sound sober and sensible when he really wanted to turn cartwheels.

'You lucky pup!' Farringdon said, when he met Bobby outside and heard the news. 'I made sure you were getting the sack when you were sent for. What do you *say* to these types to get them to love you so much? Let me in on the secret, old man. I'm never going to get my wings if you hog all the flying time.'

'I'm good, that's all,' said Bobby.

'You're bound to get lost,' Farringdon told him. 'We'll have to come out in the Crossley to fetch you. I reckon the Old Man would have done better to trust the post office.'

'Ass,' said Bobby, punching his shoulder.

'What bus are you taking?'

'BE2c,' Bobby said, with some pride.

'Really? Oh, well, you know they're the devil for spinning.' Farringdon offered his hand with a grave look. 'Probably better say goodbye now.'

But nothing could shake Bobby's happiness. The 2c was a little heavy in the controls after some of the other machines, but she was stable, strongly built, and easy to fly. Bobby flew along the coast, navigating by the towns he now recognised from the air, though he probably would not have known them on the ground: Fareham, Chichester, Arundel, Lancing. It was a fine day, with wisps of white cloud high up; he climbed to four thousand feet, and had the sky to himself; below him, England was greening up, woods were filling in, and there were sheep with lambs, white dots against the sward.

149

At Shoreham, he could see Longhorns, like big drag-onflies, slowly circling the aerodrome, and felt a thrill of superiority in his workmanlike aeroplane. Some of the pupils he had known were still there, and as he came in to land, he saw them assembled in front of the sheds to welcome him, or to witness his shame if he bungled.

He delivered the letter, and the major congratulated him on a 'very nice landing'. Outside, his former acquaintances were waiting to slap his back, carry him off to lunch, and quiz him about every aspect of Gosport, his training there, and the 2c in particular. It was altogether a delightful experience, and he flew home through a surprisingly warm afternoon with a sense of well-being he thought would be hard to top.

Two weeks later, he, Farringdon and four other cadets were driven by Crossley to the Central Flying School at Upavon to be examined for their wings. On the journey they revised feverishly, sometimes in their heads and some-times together. The accumulated knowledge they had on aerodynamics, engine fitting, aeroplane rigging, wireless operation and navigation seemed pitifully inadequate.

'I can't remember a thing about Gnome engines,' Dent wailed.

'And they test you on Morse code,' Abbott said gloomily. 'I know I'll be too slow.'

'I don't think I've got enough flying hours,' said Moore. '*You*'ll be all right, Hunter. Your logbook looks like a cat's cradle.'

'If you fail,' Heard said anxiously, 'it sets you back weeks – months, even. I want to get out to France before the fun's all over.'

'We all want that,' said Farringdon. 'I don't hold out much hope for myself. My brain's a complete blank. I can't remember *anything*.'

However, on the way home in the dusk, the sheer relief

that it was over had them in good spirits, whatever they thought of their chances. They sang as they bumped along the country lanes, and persuaded the driver, without much difficulty, to stop at a pleasant wayside pub so that they could drink to their success.

Two days later the results came in. The six of them were summoned one by one into the squadron office. The squadron commander congratulated Bobby, told him he was now a qualified pilot, a full member of the Royal Flying Corps, entitled to wear its uniform rather than that of his old battalion, to sport the badge with its motto of *sic itur ad astra*. 'We're proud of you, Hunter, and I hope you will always live up to our expectations, and remember the honour of the Corps in everything you do.'

Outside, Bobby waited as each of them came out, beaming and triumphant.

'Next stop, France!' said Farringdon.

'No,' said Bobby, 'next stop the tailor's shop. I want my wings sewn onto my jacket.'

'Good idea,' said Heard. 'I can't wait to show them off!' In the end, all six of them went.

That evening, Bobby wrote home. He had written three days earlier to say he was taking the examination; now, intensely conscious of his new wings, he could tell his father that he had passed.

The following day a parcel arrived from home. Inside was a small box containing a wrist-watch. Before the war, wrist-watches had been almost unknown (and were considered rather caddish), but it was becoming the mark of a serious flyer to have one. A pilot could not be fumbling his watch out of his pocket whenever he needed it. Like many of the cadets, Bobby had had a leather device made so that he could hang his pocket watch where he could see it from some useful promontory in the cockpit.

Now he had the real thing; but the best of it was that he

realised, after a moment, that his father must have posted it before he'd heard the results of the examination. He had been sure Bobby would pass.

The most shocking thing about the shocking events in Dublin over Easter was that the Irish rebels, bent on forming a republic, had been depending on help from the Germans, who had sent a shipload of arms to them. The idea that Ireland might provide a back door to German invasion had long been a worry to the government, but the Easter rebellion brought it home to the British public at large. In the event, the German arms had been intercepted by the Royal Navy after failing to rendezvous with the rebels, but the pro-German sentiment among republicans remained an anxiety.

For Beattie, the fear was for her sister, Addie, her husband and sons, who lived in Kildare, only twenty-odd miles from Dublin. It was known that there were republican cells in many places near the city, and Addie's husband Jock – Sir John Carbury – was a magistrate and therefore could be considered a target. It was an anxious week for her until she received a telegram from Addie to say that they were all well; a letter came several days later.

There was trouble in Wexford [Addie wrote], where they blockaded the barracks, but Kildare was quiet. The worst we saw here was a parade of Volunteers on Easter Sunday, which we'd been expecting anyway, and Jock had given permission for. They had a band, and some of the villagers turned out and waved tricolours, but it went off peacefully enough. But with the news coming out of Dublin getting worse every day I didn't sleep a wink until the surrender on Saturday. The idea of shells and machine-guns in Dublin, and the streets running with blood – most of the people who were killed or wounded were civilians, isn't that dreadful? I can't believe it's the same Dublin where we were girls, and went to dances and rode home in cabs in our finery. They say Sackville Street is in ruins – the Metropole Hotel is just a shell, where we went to that May dance, do you remember? And the GPO, where the rebels had their headquarters, was burned to the ground. And now they'll be executing the ringleaders, which I know is necessary, but shocking all the same, as they were our own people until this republican madness got into their heads. Jock says there'll never be peace here until the whole thing is sorted out, but I don't see what we can do. Except that we have decided to send the boys to America, at least until the war's over. Jock's cousin Bernard in New York has been inviting all of us for years. Jock won't go and I won't leave him, but at least the boys will be away from this poison that seems to make nice men go mad. They are keen to go, and I'll feel easier about them, though I'll miss them dreadfully. It's a pity the conscription didn't apply over here because they were wild to go and fight and at least they'd have been safe in the army.

Safe in the army? Beattie wondered. It seemed an odd expression. And not long afterwards it was learned that Mrs Oliver's nephew, Hank Bowers, was one of the 116 British soldiers killed in the uprising. Sherwood Foresters had been among the reinforcements hastily sent to Dublin. Landing at Kingstown on Wednesday, the 26th of April, and advancing towards Dublin, they had encountered heavy fighting at the rebel-held positions around the Grand Canal. They were repeatedly caught in cross-fire while trying to cross the canal at Mount Street, and 240 of them were killed or wounded, including Hank Bowers, who was shot in the neck.

Sadie went with her mother on the visit of condolence.

She had wept for Hank, remembering his kindness and high spirits, and his hopeless fancy for Diana. It seemed to her such a pitiful death, not nobly facing the foreign foe but in a skirmish against one's own people. Civil wars, she concluded, were the worst of all conflicts.

Mrs Oliver was grey-faced and shadowed about the eyes, but was never less than in control. When Beattie remarked on her stoicism, she said, 'My dear, people are losing their sons and husbands. What right have I to make a fuss about a nephew?'

But Mrs Oliver had no children, and Beattie knew her nephews were as sons to her – and particularly Hank, who had been staying with her since he was stranded in Germany on holiday when the war broke out. He was a young man of whom it was very easy to become fond. Beattie had noticed his preference for Diana, and had frequently wished that she had chosen him instead of Charles Wroughton. Now the folly of such a wish came home to her. None of their young men was safe while the war lasted.

And Mrs Oliver, hearing the echo of what she had just said, laid a hand on Beattie's and said, 'I'm sorry, my dear. I'd like to tell you your sons will be all right, but you're too intelligent to take false comfort. We can only pray, and trust in God.' She looked at Sadie. 'And do our best to help here at home. Our land is worth fighting for – and we are all warriors, in our small ways.'

It didn't seem odd just then that Mrs Oliver, who had lost someone, should be comforting someone who hadn't.

Lady Betty Frampton touched Beattie's arm. 'Oh, my dear, there's an officer at the end of the counter. Would you serve him? I have to refill the urns.'

Beattie might have said that she'd refilled them herself not ten minutes ago, but she was used to Lady Betty's foibles now. She put down the cloth with which she'd been drying mugs (Who'd have thought, a part of her mind wondered, that she'd ever have to do washing-up?) and walked down to the end of the counter, towards the tall figure in the khaki tunic transsected by the Sam Browne, with a major's crown on his cuff flap.

As she approached, some sense deep inside her began sounding an alarm – the animal sense that recognises significant shapes, that allows the prey to distinguish the predator among the leaves. But it was when he courteously removed his cap at her approach that her stomach seemed to fall away from her, the blood leave her heart so that for a moment she thought she would faint.

Her lips formed a word soundlessly – the two syllables of his name, which they had known all too well when she was young and passionate, which they had formed in tempests of tears for so many years afterwards; the syllables that meant *him*, and all she had lost. He looked at her without recognition for a moment, and then she saw his eyes widen, his lips part.

'Beattie? Is it – is it really you?'

She put her hands to her cheeks in a defensive gesture, expecting them to be hot, but they were cool, and her hands icy cold. 'Louis,' she said, making the sound aloud for the first time in – she didn't know how many – years. 'How – what are you doing here? I thought you were in Kenya.'

'I came back,' he said, as though it were that simple. As though anything that had happened between them had ever been simple.

Major Louis David Rathvilly Plunkett. He had been Lieutenant Plunkett back then, back in Dublin, when the world was young and innocent and wars only happened in far-flung places.

Beattie and her circle – girls of an age to fall in love, to be looking for husbands – had noticed him, had talked

155

about him, in whispers, heads together, in powder-rooms, behind fans in the corners of ballrooms. Not all of them had thought him handsome. He was tall and broad-shouldered – good! – but there was something hawk-like about his face, something too marked and unusual about his features to sit well with the drawing-room ambitions of untutored girls. He looked somehow wild, unpredictable. Such a man might do anything. He would be dangerous. That head, with its dark reddish hair and proud carriage, those high cheekbones, that jutting nose and strong chin spoke of some alien blood. Alice Mulholland, shuddering, said he looked like a Red Indian.

Beattie thought him utterly beautiful – more beautiful than she had ever believed a man could be. She was thrilled by the sense of danger that came from him. To receive gentleness – and she was sure from his eyes and his mouth he could be gentle – to receive gentleness from such a wild, powerful creature would be worth so much more than from the domestic dogs than ran tame about the fine houses of Dublin Society. She developed a sensitivity towards him that meant she knew when she entered a room if he was there. She could pick him out in any throng. She could identify the shape of him, from the back, in a crowded street or a military parade. Her eye would go straight to him, without search or hesitation, wherever he was.

And when he noticed her, she fell instantly – without stumbling, without struggling – absolutely in love.

He asked her to dance one evening, at a ball up at the Castle. He danced well, with the control of an athlete. For such a big man he moved lightly, and he held her as though she were an eggshell he had sworn not to break. She adored the sense of power that came from him, from his long, muscled arms and legs, his broad chest, his strong neck. But what she loved even more was that he talked to her.

From the very first moment, he addressed her as though

she were an equal – and not only an equal, but someone he had known for years. There was none of that preliminary conversational fumbling: *who are you, what are you interested in, have we anything in common, how far can I go?* He began talking to her without preamble, as he might talk to his long-term companion in arms. It was intoxicating. Girls were never spoken to like that. They were treated, she always thought, like imbeciles, or invalids, too fragile to be exposed to the real world, or even to ideas, lest the delicate bloom, which was all they had to sell, should be rubbed off.

He talked of military matters and, as a soldier's daughter, she had enough vocabulary to understand and encourage him. He talked of politics. He talked of Dublin as if he supposed she knew it as he did. He talked of books. Through each of their subsequent meetings he talked, and she listened, and felt herself expanding – no, *unfurling*, spreading damp, crumpled wings in the sunlight of his notice. She felt she might become something she had never imagined – not a wife-and-mother and dispenser of teacups, but a whole person, as full-fledged and real as a man.

Through the summer of 1893 she came to know him and to love him; little by little she gained the confidence to talk to him as he talked to her. She hadn't a great deal of knowledge, but she was not completely ignorant. She had read widely; she had lived in India and Malta; she had listened to many male conversations and absorbed more from them than she had realised. Little by little, she came to feel that he was falling in love with her, too.

Passion was something she had been aware of from the beginning, without entirely understanding it. When she looked at him, her eyes were the outposts of her fingers, which longed to touch where she looked. She wanted to stroke the lean brown of his cheek, to cup the strong lift of muscle at the back of his neck, to dig into the thick spring of his hair. When they danced, she wanted to press the

157

whole length of herself against him. When they talked, she watched his lips, and sometimes felt dizzy at the thought of what they might feel like against hers.

One warm night, as he helped her on with her wrap, his fingers brushed her bare arm, and for a moment fastened round it with a fierce grip that just stopped itself hurting her. The next night, at Lady Dalrymple's ball, they stepped out onto the terrace for a breath of air, and found themselves alone. He moved with her to the side of the windows, where they would not be seen, looked down at her, and said gravely, 'May I?'

She said yes; would have said yes to anything. She had given her whole being into his charge. He bent and laid his lips on hers, passing his arm round her at the same moment to support her. Something inside her loosed, and a torrent raged upwards, like a spring from which the rock had been rolled away. She kissed him for her life; drinking the furious sweetness that passed from him to her, growing drunk on it. It was as well that he broke the contact – she could not have.

After that, things were different. She knew better, now, what she loved. She wanted him, all of him, always. She began to wonder if they might marry. She knew he was not rich. To marry him she would have to follow the drum. She was not sure her father would approve of that. He had mentioned Lieutenant Plunkett only twice, and then coolly. After that evening, he had said to her at breakfast, when she sat in a reverie, 'Don't dance with the same man too often – it doesn't do. And this Plunkett fellow – don't encourage him. No prospects.' Then he had returned to his newspaper, dismissing her from his thoughts.

But she had thought she had time. Her father was not a harsh man, and she knew he was fond of her. She could work on him. He would get used to Louis being around, and come to accept him.

But it turned out that there was no time after all. One day, when the trees on St Stephen's Green were gently weeping gold onto the grass, and the air was full of the smell of ending, he came to the house at morning calling time, and told her that his battalion was being sent to India. They would be stationed there for several years – perhaps as much as ten. Tours of garrison duty were long before the war. She would be middle-aged when it ended.

She had looked achingly into his face, waiting to hear him ask her to marry him, longing for it, expecting it. Instead, he had asked if she could slip out of the house that evening and meet him.

She was supposed to be going to a *soirée* with her father and sister. But it was not difficult for her to pretend an indisposition. In truth, she felt sick and feverish all day with a mixture of anxiety and hope. They had left her behind that evening, tucked up in bed with the light left on low. When they were gone and the servants were settled, she had got up, dressed and slipped out to meet her fate. She had looked back as she left the house, part of her thinking she might never see it again, thinking he might ask her there and then to elope with him.

Two days later he was gone. She never heard from him again, though occasionally she had news of his battalion. It had fought in the South African War; had taken part in the relief of Ladysmith. She had wondered, with an agonised part of her mind, if he had been killed, or wounded. But a long time later she had learned, in part of an overheard conversation, that he had survived the war, left the army, and was growing tea in the Aberdare Mountains in Kenya. And that was the last she had heard of him.

He had never known about David. She had had no way to contact him once he was gone. She'd had to grow up very quickly. When she discovered her condition, she had no-one she could confide in. Social ruin faced her, but even worse would have been the anger, disappointment and, perhaps, contempt of her father.

There was a constant suitor in her background, a nice-looking, gentle, kindly man, who had been pursuing her in a mild but persistent way since before she had first danced with Louis. Marriage to him seemed the only possible solution – if she could induce him to propose to her, and to do it quickly, before her shame was known. Part of her felt bad about tricking him, but that voice was drowned in the sheer blind terror that had seized her. She assuaged the guilty part by promising it she would be a good wife and make him happy – if only he would rescue her.

It was as desperate a campaign as any that would follow for the army in South Africa. Afterwards she suspected, uncomfortably, that Edward had known all along what she was doing, but was too much of a gentleman ever to speak of it to her. He accepted her favour with gratitude, followed her leads, proposed to her within a week, allowed her eagerness to marry him to seem like a compliment. She didn't know what was said in the serious talk he had with her father, but she knew, with deep certainty, that if he *did* know, he would not have betrayed her. He would never do that.

He had a steady employment and a decent, if unremarkable salary, enough to support her in moderate comfort. She hoped her father gave his consent believing it was a case of unstoppable love. He had never mentioned Louis to her between then and the day he had died.

And she had been happy with Edward – as happy as she could have been with anyone who was not Louis. She knew the thanks for that lay with Edward. They had never talked about where David came from, and Edward had always treated him as his own son, had always loved him, perhaps, more than the others, which was, she thought – sometimes with exasperation – so like Edward. But though never expressed, the suspicion that he *knew* had gradually filtered into her consciousness and into their relationship. It had changed things.

Once she had become pregnant with Diana, she had made a vow never to think of Louis again, had shut him firmly out of her thoughts. She had been pretty successful, on the whole. She thought – she hoped – that Edward was happy. She had given him the large family he wanted. She had moved from London without objection when he proposed it. She had loved him as much as she could. In the early days, before childbearing had taken its toll, they had had a good physical relationship. She was passionate by nature, and he took care of that. It really had felt like love, for much of the time.

But the war had churned things up. The thought of losing David gripped her with unreasoning terror. Locked in a silent struggle with her fear, she had had nothing to give Edward. She knew she had been neglecting him. He had tried on several occasions to touch her in bed, and she had turned away from him, unable even to be held by him, far less to give him what she knew he wanted from her. David was everything. *She must not lose him*, or she could not live.

The sight of officers passing through the station, on their way out or on their way back, had been an exquisite torture. Every one of them was David; and when she saw one coming back wounded, it was agony.

Every officer was David. How well she understood Lady Betty's reluctance to serve them.

What she had never expected – never, *never* expected – was that one of them would be Louis.

'I came back,' he said. 'My father died in 1914 and I came back to England to deal with his estate. Then the war started, and they were desperate for experienced line officers, so I volunteered. My old regiment took me back, and I've been in France ever since.'

161

'What . . .' Her mouth was dry. His voice was deeper than it had been twenty-two years ago, but it was still his voice. She tried again. 'What about your farm in Kenya?' 'The plantation? I have a good manager. He'll keep things going. I was more needed here.' He was examining her as he spoke. 'And you? You live in London.' It seemed to be a statement, not a question. He went on searching her face, and something changed in his eyes. 'You're married? Of course you're married.'

She nodded. A great avalanche of words was building up inside her head and she was afraid of opening her lips and letting it out. 'A cup of tea?' was what she managed at last to say.

'Tea,' he agreed, though she thought it was at random.

That gave her a few moments to turn her back to him, busy herself with mug and urn, and compose herself. *Louis! Louis was here!* Her love, the love of her life, lost for ever, torn from her heart in pain and blood so long ago – here, in the flesh, inches away from her, to be spoken to and looked at and – oh, God, forgive me! – even perhaps touched. She wanted to touch him, to be sure it was not a dream. Just to touch his hand – just that, forgive me, Lord.

She turned back with the mug – thick, serviceable earthenware, comical in the context – placed it before him, and said automatically, 'That will be twopence, please.'

He laid his hand over hers. The turning world slowed and stopped, as though a gigantic brake had been applied. She could feel it creaking, pushing against it, even as, in the stillness, she felt the warmth of his skin against hers, felt his fingers fold round hers and press them. They were alone in a little white space, a bubble in time. She looked at their hands – his so brown and strong, hers white and smooth – and then up into his face, and was lost.

Beattie, he whispered. She saw the word but didn't hear it. *I love you*, she replied, but that was only inside her head.

But he heard it, she thought he heard it. He said – quietly, but the words were in the real world, spoken aloud, 'I'd love to talk to you. Properly. Can we meet somewhere, later? When are you off duty?'

'Ten o'clock,' she heard herself say.

'I'll wait for you,' he said. 'Under the clock. We'll have a little supper, and talk.'

And then, perhaps with some instinct for how much she could bear, he pressed her hand again and walked away, losing himself in the khaki masses.

The brake slipped, the world jerked forward and rolled on again, mighty and inevitable. Reality settled over her, like a smothering weight. She was not Beattie Cazalet on the brink of life, she was Mrs Edward Hunter, almost forty-four years old, wife and mother of six, someone for whom life contained no more surprises, no more possibilities, only ageing and ending.

But he had said he would wait for her. She could not, *could not*, let him walk away again, out of her life, without at least learning what had happened to him in between. She knew at ten o'clock she would go and see if he was there. She had to.

'Didn't he want that tea?' Lady Betty's voice said from behind her.

She made her face blank, and turned. 'I suppose not.'

'Poor fellow,' Lady Betty sighed. 'So many of them are confused when they first come back. Oh, two chaps down there – will you see to them, dear? I think I might drink this tea – he didn't touch it, did he?'

'No, he didn't touch it.'

CHAPTER ELEVEN

Bobby came home on leave, looking healthy and handsome, and very proud of the wings on his tunic.

After Gosport, he had been sent for Higher Training at Upavon. Here cadets were encouraged to fly every day, to undertake cross-country flights, to climb above eight thousand feet. They learned the elements of formation flying, trained in observation, aerial navigation, the interpretation of ground-based signals from the air, and aerial gunnery, which largely consisted of firing a Lewis gun at a target being pulled by a tow-plane (it could be identified on the ground by the bullet-holes in its rudder).

Now the Corps evidently felt he was ready for the theatre of war, for this was his embarkation leave.

'You look so brown,' Sadie said admiringly.

'Never mind that,' William said impatiently. 'Tell us about the aeroplanes!'

'Tell us about the training,' Edward countered. It was Saturday afternoon – he was very glad the forty-eight had been given over a weekend or he'd have seen little of his son.

'Oh, there isn't a great deal of that,' Bobby said. 'After the basic instructions for taking off, landing and turning, it's rather up to you to work things out for yourself in the air. They always say, "You'll find out when you're up there."'

'But isn't that rather dangerous?' Beattie asked, frowning.

'There *are* lots of crashes,' Bobby said, without concern. 'Quite a few deaths, too. They say you're more likely to be killed during training than in combat. I suppose it weeds out the chaps who'll never make flyers.'

'The Darwinian principle,' Edward said, with twinkling eyes.

Beattie didn't twinkle. 'It sounds brutal,' she objected.

'Well,' said Bobby, apologetically, 'we have to be able to think for ourselves when we're flying. There's no-one to ask when the engine cuts out at five thousand feet. But,' he added, for the sake of a mother's sensibilities, 'all the buses glide beautifully, so you can generally get down in one piece. We practised emergency landings at Higher Training.'

'It's not really *dangerous*, Mother – is it, Bobby?' William said anxiously. 'I mean to join the RFC as soon as I'm old enough. I wish you could come and give a talk at our school. We had a man from the horse artillery a couple of weeks ago, but he was really dull.'

'Sorry, old man,' said Bobby. 'Perhaps next leave.'

'I wish you *had* given us more notice,' Beattie said.

'None to give, Mum. It was very sudden. "You're off to France, take a forty-eight," they said, and that was that.'

'But – going to *France*!' William said rapturously.

Bobby gave him a sympathetic look. 'Yes, we are pleased. Some chaps seem to hang around for weeks waiting for orders. They're forming a new squadron and we thought we'd be attached to that. But apparently they're short of pilots over there, so they picked a dozen of us to go out and fill in. The Old Man says we should look on it as a compliment, because they want the best chaps in the pilots' pool. But when the squadron goes, they'll fly out, while we're only going by boat and train.'

At William's insistence, Bobby embarked on a description of the various machines, which now included Avros and Morane-Saulniers. After a bit, he broke off, looking at his

165

mother, and said, 'Am I going on too much? You look as though you're falling asleep!'

'Not asleep – she's miles away,' Sadie said.

Beattie came back with a jerk and said briskly, 'I was just wondering whether the leg of lamb this evening will go round.'

'Which reminds me,' Bobby said. 'I must go and see Cook and Ada.'

Everyone loved Bobby, but while Ada was most dedicated to David and Nula, who had nursed them all, loved Diana best, Cook had a soft spot for the second son, who was 'such a charmer' and so very appreciative of her cooking.

'Roast leg of lamb,' she confirmed. 'O' course it'll go round. D'you think my dinners can't stand one person extra?'

'I never thought any such thing,' said Bobby. 'Lots of garlic with it?'

'Not *too* much,' Cook said firmly. 'And there's asparagus, and little roast onions, like you like 'em. New potatoes – I wish there was some peas for you, but Munt says they'll be a couple of weeks yet. But there's some lovely forced rhubarb – I know you like my rhubarb tart.'

'I like everything about you,' Bobby said, throwing his arms round her and squeezing, making her shriek and hit him – but not too hard – with the wooden spoon she was holding.

Nula was there when he visited, having brought some hand-sewing down to the servants' hall for the company while she worked. Having begun as Beattie's personal maid and then become nursery maid, she was now married and came in to do sewing and alterations as required. She came over to inspect his wings. 'That's some nice stitching,' she conferred her blessing. 'Professional.'

'It's the Corps tailor,' Bobby said. 'And he's quick, too. You never saw such whizzing fingers. He had six of us to do, and we'd hardly had time to sit down and light a fag when he was done.'

'Hmm,' said Nula, but couldn't find anything to complain about. Instead she said, 'Now, have you anything that needs mending before you go? I know what you boys are like for tearing things. Shirts? Pyjamas? Anything that wants washing, while I'm at it? And if you let me have that uniform, I'll sponge it for you.'

'Can't do that,' he said. 'Mum wants to show me off around the neighbourhood this afternoon.'

'Well, just give me the jacket, then, and I'll have it back to you in half an hour. Can't go showing yourself to people looking like that.'

'I do have a shirt with a tiny tear in the sleeve,' he admitted, to keep her happy. 'Caught it on a nail in the mess when we were playing waste-paper-basket polo.'

'Ooh, whatever is that?' Emily asked. She and Lilian had been in the background, their eyes huge as they admired this handsome Hero of the Skies.

Bobby made himself comfortable and told them.

Edward wondered what Beattie had really been thinking of. When she had spoken of the lamb, she had looked at him quickly, then away again. If it had been anyone but Beattie, he'd have thought it a glance of guilt. As it was, he wondered what *he* had done that merited her disapproval.

His conscience prodded him again about Élise. Of course he didn't tell Beattie everything he did at work, and certainly didn't itemise his client visits, but all the same . . . He resolved to introduce Madame de Rouveroy's name into the conversation at some convenient point, and mention that she was one of the clients he visited when he stayed late in Town. It would be good to have a clear conscience again.

Bobby's short visit was shared with as many people as

possible. Beattie took him round to various acquaintances that afternoon, and on Sunday morning after church he was the centre of attention. Edward noticed with an inward smile how the young ladies of the neighbourhood, starved these days of nice young men, were all a-swoon before his handsome brown face, fair hair and blue eyes, his officer's uniform and, especially, the magical wings.

Bobby was universally charming and attentive, answered their questions, admired their costumes, revived little jokes with girls he had known all his life and laughed at theirs, and managed, Edward had no doubt, to make each of them think he had paid her the most attention. But he was not interested in any of them, as his father could well see. For Bobby, there was only one passion at the moment. He had married the sky, and whatever his smiling words and merry eyes suggested to the contrary, he had no heart for anyone else. And no young lady, however perfect her face and figure, could rival the struts and spars, wire, wood and canvas of the RFC's aeroplanes.

The hours of his leave flew by, and before they had got used to having him at home, he was off, with his kitbag on his shoulder and a packet of sandwiches from Cook in his pocket, to catch his train to Victoria. He had orders to report to the Flying Corps headquarters at St Omer, and who knew what adventures lay beyond? Edward walked with him to the station, and said goodbye there. He received a shyly emotional thank-you for the watch and the faith it had shown in him. He gave Bobby ten pounds ('You're bound to have unforeseen expenses over there'), exchanged a hearty handshake, and watched him walk briskly away, just another khaki uniform among the many. From the back, of course, you couldn't see the wings.

'I shall be working late this evening,' Beattie said at breakfast, a few days later.

Edward looked up from the newspaper. 'I wish you wouldn't,' he said.

'Someone has to do it,' Beattie said. 'We simply don't have enough volunteers.'

'It's too much for you. You're always so tired the next day.'

'One has to do one's duty,' she said, turning her head away and staring at the window as she sipped her coffee.

Sadie spoke up. 'Would it be all right if I stayed at Highclere tonight? The girls are planning a supper party with games, and Mrs Cuthbert says I can have the spare room, so I don't have to cycle home afterwards.'

'Of course,' said Beattie, absently.

Edward was dismayed. Diana had gone back to Town to stay with the Palfreys for a couple of days. The family seemed to be thinning out alarmingly. 'It will be a rather dull dinner for me tonight,' he said.

William looked at his father with quick sympathy. 'We'll be here, Dad,' he said, and Peter looked up from removing the spine of his kipper and nodded agreement.

Edward smiled at the son who looked most like him – the long, oval face, round chin, dark hair and solemn dark eyes owed little to Beattie – and said, 'We'll have a special evening together, then. You shall dine with me, and we'll play some games afterwards. How would that be?'

'Topping!' said William, and Peter chimed, 'Super!'

Edward folded the newspaper and stood up. 'I must be off,' he said. 'You'll tell Cook, will you, my dear?'

'I'll tell her,' Sadie said, jumping to her feet. 'I've got to tell her I won't be here either. And I should be going too.' She paused and looked at her father. 'I'm sorry I'll be leaving you alone,' she said uncertainly.

'That's all right,' Edward said. 'We don't want girls around, do we, boys? Girls only spoil things.'

Sadie was startled for an instant, before she realised he was joking, and laughed. 'Dad-*dee*!' she protested.

All the same, she thought, as she lifted the waiting Nailer into her bicycle basket, it must be rather sad for him to be abandoned by everyone like that. He worked such long hours, and ought to have the comfort of the family he supported in the evening. She resolved to be extra nice to him at the weekend – and then remembered, with a slightly sinking heart, that they had been invited to Dene Park for a Saturday-to-Monday – Mother, Father, Diana and her. It would be odd, she thought, sleeping at Dene Park when they had their own perfectly good beds only two miles away, but Diana had said it wouldn't be fair on the chauffeur to make him turn out late at night to take them home; and it would break up the party.

The oddest thing, though, was Rupert Wroughton, the new Lord Dene, proposing to Diana. No, the *really* oddest thing was her accepting. Sadie had summoned all her reserves of tact not to say anything that might hurt Diana's feelings, but she had been unable to stop herself saying, just once, 'I thought you didn't like him. You said he was rude to you.'

'He's different now,' was all Diana had said.

Sadie had seen other girls gush about their fiancés, but Diana didn't glow and blush, talk endlessly about him, continually flourish her ring. Rupert had bought her a new and very large diamond (so different from the old-fashioned ruby ring, a family heirloom, that Charles had given her).

You think the fanciness of a ring makes it right? Nailer enquired.

'Of course I don't,' Sadie said, free-wheeling down the hill towards Rustington. 'Besides, it doesn't need making right,' she added, catching up with her own thoughts. 'Who says it's wrong?'

You do.

'I don't think it's wrong,' she said stoutly. 'Just – odd.'

Man picks a beautiful girl to marry, and you think it's odd?

'Because he could have had anyone. And,' she forestalled

170

Nailer, 'I know Charles could have, too, but Charles was different. Charles was – Charles was—'

She couldn't define the difference, and for once Nailer, usually so useful in clarifying her thoughts for her, had nothing to say. He yawned hugely, and then coughed as a fly shot into his open mouth.

'Rupert belongs to the London set,' she said at last. 'The smart, titled young people, who go to all those balls and dinners and so on.'

Maybe Diana does too, said Nailer.

'But I didn't think she did.'

Maybe she wants to.

That seemed to make a kind of sense. At least, it was an answer of sorts. Diana, more beautiful than any of them, would fit in with that set all right. And a 'good marriage' for her was what everyone had always hoped for. Sadie just hoped she would be happy.

Why shouldn't she be? said Nailer, with an air of finality.

Lady Wroughton had *not* been happy. 'It's completely out of the question!' she said, when Rupert told her.

'It had better not be that,' said Rupert calmly, 'because I've asked her now.' His mother didn't frighten him. He was over age, and had inherited the competence that was due to him as second son, a legacy from an uncle, when he was twenty-one. There was the allowance paid to him now he was heir, which could be stopped, and it was useful to be able to stay at Dene Park and Wroughton House without expense, but he didn't really think his mother would cut him off, now there was only him. He had never been so much in awe of her as Charles had. Bolder by nature, and with nothing to lose anyway, he had grown up in his brother's safe shadow, unregarded by his parents, left to go his own way.

So he faced his mother down with a coolly raised eyebrow.

She scowled. 'Are you trying to make this family a laughing stock? It was bad enough for Charles to pick that girl when he could have had *anyone*, but for you now to take her over like a cast-off coat! Respectable men don't marry their dead brothers' fiancées!'

'You'd better tell that to the King,' Rupert said, lounging against the windowsill in his mother's writing-room at Wroughton House in Belgrave Square. 'As I remember, Queen Mary was engaged to his older brother, and he took her over when Prince Eddy died.'

'Don't be impertinent!' snapped Lady Wroughton. 'What happens in royal circles is not to be *our* template. Stand up straight! Take your hands out of your pockets when you're talking to me!'

He did as she commanded, but lingeringly, to prove he did it because he wanted to, not because she ordered him. He drawled, 'I thought you'd taken a fancy to her, after Charles died. You invited her up to the Park often enough. Cosy little tête-à-têtes over the teacups. You and your pretty daughter-in-law-that-wasn't.'

The countess opened her mouth to snarl, but then a puzzled look came over her face. When she spoke, she sounded almost pathetic. 'What *is* it about that girl? First Charles, now you. I don't understand, Rupert. Haven't we suffered enough? You will make us a mockery. Whispers behind hands. Have you no family pride?' He didn't reply, gazing at her with his most inscrutable – and annoying – smile. She hardened. 'You will be earl one day. It is your *duty* to choose a suitable wife, one who will take my place. You cannot marry a banker's daughter – a girl from the *middle classes*!'

Rupert grinned impudently. 'I almost think you'd prefer it if I married a housemaid.'

'It would be more understandable,' Lady Wroughton snapped.

'Well, Mater, I'm sorry if it upsets you, but it's Diana

Hunter or nothing. I've chosen her, and I categorically refuse to marry anyone else, so unless you want the line to die out with me and the estate to go to the Canadian cousins, you'd best grit your teeth and swallow it.'

'Blackmail,' said Lady Wroughton, with a savage look.

'Pre*cisely*,' he said, with satisfaction.

Her nostrils flared, and she got up from her desk and walked up and down the room, clenching and unclenching her hands. Rupert watched the hands, knowing that she longed to slap him, if only it were something a countess could ever do. Finally, she had control of herself again. 'Very well,' she said coldly. 'I will do what is necessary. I just wish,' a tremble in her voice betrayed that she was close to breaking, 'that I knew why. Why *her*?'

Rupert pretended to consider. But when he spoke, it was to be annoying. 'It is my whim,' he said.

'Oh, get out!' cried the countess, and he went.

Beth had been puzzled, and worried. 'Are you sure?' she had asked.

'Why should I not be?' Diana had answered. She had surprised herself by saying 'yes' to Rupert, but she didn't like anyone – not even Beth, of whom she was very fond – questioning her judgement.

'Well, it seems awfully quick,' she said. 'Why the hurry? Wouldn't it be better to wait for a while, get to know each other?'

'He might be sent abroad at any time,' she said.

'But, darling, you mustn't let the war make a decision of this importance for you. The war won't last for ever, but marriage does. You'll be with Rupert for the rest of your life. You must be sure.'

'I'd have been with Charles for the rest of my life,' Diana said, 'and I hardly knew him. I know Rupert much better, by comparison.'

Beth said, even more tentatively, 'Is it the estate? The title and Dene Park and everything?'

She feared Diana might take offence, but she said seriously, 'It's part of it. It's what Charles wanted me to have. That's what Rupert says. I ought to have it, for Charles's sake. And I can do the things he wanted to do – the improvements and so on. I can do a lot of good, you know, helping people. Taking care of the tenants, doing things for the village. Charities.'

'Yes,' said Beth. It all sounded rather dreary – not that there was anything wrong with helping people, but this lovely girl, trembling on the brink of life, had not spoken one word about love. Had she really 'buried her heart'? But she was so young! It was too soon to be giving up. Beth knew that if anything happened to Jack, she would not be able to contemplate marrying again. He was the love of her life. But she was twenty years older than Diana, and had been married blissfully for most of those. Diana had tasted nothing of the feast, had barely smelt it cooking.

Did Rupert love her? He must do, surely, if he wanted to marry her, when he could, literally, have anyone. And he played the part. He lavished her with attention, compliments, gifts. She looked at the large, glittering diamond on Diana's finger, catching the firelight and splitting it like lightning. She could not know if he had spoken of love to Diana, but he did and looked all the right things. But she felt uneasy. There was something *about* him – something that always made her feel he was acting a part, or playing a game. Though what on earth the game could be, she had no idea. He *had* proposed, he *had* bought the ring – there could be nothing wrong with that.

She dismissed her fears, telling herself firmly that she had nothing to accuse him of, and really ought to do him the courtesy of believing in him. He had always been as

174

nice as could be to her. Anyway, the announcement had been in the papers now, so it was too late to withdraw.

Everything would be all right. She just wished Diana looked more *glowing*.

Nula removed the pins from her mouth and said, 'Penny for them?'

'Hmm?' Beattie said, from far away.

'You're in an absolute reverie,' Nula said. 'Thinking about the wedding, maybe. Well, it's a nice ending, after all. Bit of a fairy-tale. And our lovely Diana will still be a countess. I call that justice. When she goes up to the Palace to get crowned, or whatever they do, the Queen will think she's never seen a more beautiful one.'

'Mmm,' said Beattie.

'You're tired,' said Nula. 'Working in that canteen is wearing you out. You ought to tell them you can't do it any more.'

'We all have to do our duty,' said Beattie, automatically.

'Maybe so, but there are always other things you can do that don't wear you to a shadow.'

'I'm not worn to a shadow,' said Beattie, patiently.

'Then why am I taking in this dress?' Nula said triumphantly. 'You've lost weight, so you have.'

'I could afford to,' Beattie said.

'Not at your age. You don't want to get scrawny, now, do you? You were just right as you were. It's too much for you, standing about serving tea to God knows who, washing up and everything – look at your hands! Ada says you've been hardly touching your food – too tired to eat, that's what it is!'

Too happy to eat, Beattie thought, but she didn't say so, of course. It was good that she had learned long ago the skill of hiding her feelings, had developed over the years an ability to present a serene and unchanging face to the world.

It served her well now, when inside she was filled tight with a joy that must never be revealed. And especially not to Nula, who had been there, who had been the only one who knew then, and must never, never guess now.

That first night, when she had left Lady Betty at the canteen, the station had still been reassuringly full of to-ing and fro-ing, which she hoped would baffle any curious eye. She had half wondered if he would be there – half thought it had all been a dream. But her heart jumped painfully as she picked out the shape of him, standing under the clock, one hand behind his back, the other holding a cigarette. It was the usual meeting place at the station, and there were others there, waiting; no-one gave them a second look.

He smiled. 'I wasn't sure you'd come.'

'I wasn't sure you'd be here.'

It was enough for now. They walked to the exit, side by side, not touching – but she was intensely aware of him, as though he radiated like a stove. He led the way to a small back-street restaurant, a Bohemian sort of place with check tablecloths and candles in bottles. 'It's quiet, and the food's good,' he said. 'I've eaten here a few times. My father had a house near here, where I've been living when I've been in London. That's how I happened to see you tonight. I'd just come up from the Tube and decided on a whim to have a cup of tea before going home.'

'I didn't know your father had property,' she said, as they settled into the seats at a small corner table. Around them there was a low murmur of conversation, and in the dim lighting you could not properly make out those at neighbouring tables. The idea came to her that it was a place of assignation, and it caused her a momentary qualm, on two fronts. Was *this* an assignation? And had he come here with other women?

He leaned forward a little so that his face came into the

candlelight, and all other thoughts fled from her but that she was here with him. With *him*! A low paean of joy and triumph sang in her guts, where the beast of loneliness had lived these twenty-two years, crying to be relieved.

'It's not much of a house. Just a little slice of a thing for him to stay in when he had to come to Town. I got rid of the rest of his effects when I came back in 'fourteen, but I kept the house until last so I'd have somewhere to stay, rather than the expense of an hotel. And when it came to it, I didn't need to sell it – the rest of his estate just covered his debts. By then, I'd decided to volunteer and kept it, so I'd have a pied-à-terre.'

'Your father was in debt? I didn't know.'

He looked rueful. 'It was a matter of great shame to my mother, and she preferred it not to be talked of. He was a gamester, you see. That was partly why I went into the army – to relieve them of the cost of me.'

'I knew you were not well off,' she said faintly, remembering her wild hopes of marriage that had perished when he went away.

'It was worse than that,' he said. 'I had to send my mother my salary so she could pay the tradesmen. If things had been otherwise . . .'

There was a world of regret in those words.

'Yes,' she said. They were silent a moment. Then she said, with an effort, 'Did you ever . . . Are you married?'

'No,' he said. 'I never married. There was only one woman I ever loved.' Too painful to talk about that yet. 'I chose a life of adventure instead. I managed to accumulate a little money in India, and when I left the army, I went to Kenya where I picked up a neglected plantation cheaply. I've improved it over the years, and now it's doing well. It was hard work, but it paid off.'

'A lonely life,' she said.

'Yes, at first. But there's a lot of society in the area,

177

wealthy white people – English and Anglo-Irish mostly. Dinners, card parties, polo and so on. It kept me occupied when I wasn't working.'

Women, she thought. There must have been women, some of them much younger than their husbands, and bored. She had seen as a child – though not understanding it until later – what had gone on in India among the army families. He was wildly attractive and unmarried. There must have been temptations. Had he had a mistress? Her mind shied away from the thought, and yet it did not hurt as much as if he had been married. The fact that he had not married soothed something in her that had been hurting all these years. *He had not preferred anyone else to her.*

'But you gave it all up to volunteer,' she said.

'My country needed me,' he said. She saw in him then the same simple faith that David had: that to be good was the important thing; the noble ambition, to do one's duty.

The tiny regular army of ninety thousand had held off the mighty German machine, but by Christmas of 1914 had been reduced to a handful. The reservists and Territorials had been called in, but there had still been a desperate shortage of men, and particularly of experienced officers. By Christmas, he had completed the work on his father's estate and was free to do as he wished.

She was glad he had not gone in at the beginning – the ninety thousand had suffered terrible casualties. Still, he had been serving at the Front ever since, and had somehow escaped death and injury.

'And now I'm at the War Office, advising and training. You know there's going to be a big push this summer?'

'I've heard it said.'

'I can't tell you where or when, but it was considered I had experience that would be useful in the planning stages, so I was attached to the War Office for a few months. Thank God I was, and thank God I kept my father's house, or I might not have met you again.' He reached across the table and laid his hand over hers.

Her fingers curled round his automatically, but her mind had seized on some particular words.

'Attached?' she said. 'For a few months?'

'Yes, it's a temporary assignment,' he said. 'When the push comes, I'll go back to my battalion.'

Their eyes locked. *He'll go back to the war*, she thought.

He said, in a low voice, 'I'm so glad you're here. All these years . . . I thought of you so often. Those few months in Dublin – they seemed more real than anything since. I never forgot you.' A breath. 'You married.'

'It's different for women,' she said.

'Yes,' he said, in justice, 'I suppose it is.'

And then they talked of other things, talked through the meal and so long afterwards that she forgot the time, and only became aware of it in a panic when she realised she was in danger of missing the last train. He took her in a taxi to Baker Street, offering the driver a large tip if she caught her train, and she made it, by the skin of her teeth. When they parted there was nothing said about another meeting. But he knew where to find her. She knew she would see him again.

CHAPTER TWELVE

In May the Season got into full swing, and Diana was at the heart of it. Rupert took her everywhere, from polo matches to gallery openings, from tea-parties to opera premières. They were received with enthusiasm: if hostesses mourned the loss of an attractive bachelor, they were at least gracious about the presence of Diana, glad he was marrying a beauty.

And if there was unkind whispering about her change of allegiance, she was unable to hear it, being always at the centre of a lively, noisy group.

It was fun, being engaged to Rupert. It was so different from her experience with Charles. Of course, Charles had been absent for most of the time, but had there been no war, she didn't think he'd have enjoyed the Season as Rupert did. He had been shy and diffident. Rupert, with his high spirits, charm, wit and quick repartee, was a different animal.

'You see,' he said to her, on one occasion, 'this is what it will be like to be Lady Dene. You'll get invited to everything. We don't have to live in that dreary little house in Clarges Street, you know. I have my own quarters in Wroughton House, big enough for two, and we needn't ever bump into the Aged Ps – I manage to avoid them all right. Or we can let Clarges Street and rent a nicer place of our own – Brook Street, Albemarle Street, somewhere jolly like that.'

'You don't mean to be much in the country?' she asked.

'Oh, we'll have the occasional Saturday-to-Monday, and the odd house party in the summer when London becomes intolerable. But I'm not Charles, you know – I'm a Town bird, through and through.' He studied her expression. 'You aren't pining for the country, are you? You can go any time you like. Not yet – I need to show you off – but once we're married. I don't mean to come the heavy with you and order you about, you know.'

'I just wondered about the estate – the land,' she began.

'If it doesn't bother me, I won't bother it,' he said promptly.

'You don't have any plans for improvement – once you're the earl, I mean?'

He cocked his head. 'Is this old Charles's ideas? Did he convince you of them? My dear girl, if you want to have a go at improvement, by all means do. As long as I have you at my side when I need you, the rest of your life's your own. I thought you understood that.'

There were many things she didn't entirely understand. She was enjoying herself, and had got over her suspicion of Rupert: he treated her with every attention, brought her flowers and chocolates, introduced her everywhere with pride and invited praise on her behalf ('Isn't she lovely? Did you ever see such a beautiful girl? Am I not the luckiest man on earth?'). But he had never kissed her, other than the occasional chaste peck on the cheek in farewell. He didn't even hold her hand in taxis. They were almost more like brother and sister. It seemed odd that a man so forthcoming in other fields should be so shy in that one, but she supposed it *must* be shyness.

For herself, she felt no physical yearning towards him, as she had felt towards Charles. And yet she was aware of a restlessness that longed for intimacy. Something had awoken in her with Charles that could not now be denied. The trouble was, she found it impossible to imagine what it would be like with Rupert. He was handsome, and she

181

had seen other girls flirting with him, but whenever she tried to envisage their wedding night, her imagination shied away.

He didn't help, his attitude to that side of marriage being extremely unromantic. 'I think we should have two children, if that's all right with you,' he said one day.

'I should like children,' she replied.

He raised an eyebrow. 'I should hope so, that being the whole point.' She didn't know what he meant by that, but before she could ask, he went on, 'I think we ought to get it over with right away. I know it will mean a dull couple of years while you're having them, but then we'll be free to have fun.'

She had always thought having children was supposed to be fulfilling, but perhaps men didn't feel the same way. She asked tentatively, 'What if I wanted more than two?'

He looked surprised, then shrugged. 'Well, if that's what you want, so be it. *I* shan't get in your way. But it doesn't sound like fun to me.'

She didn't understand that. But she quite often didn't understand the things he said. Once, when he told her he was going to Paris for a few days with Erskine Ballantine, she mentioned that she would like to see Paris too.

'So you shall, my dear, when we're married,' he answered, and added, with a laugh, 'But not when Erskine goes, Madame de Trop!'

She wanted very much to like Erskine, but somehow she couldn't. He seemed for some reason to dislike her. He was never rude, but he hardly spoke to her, and when she initiated conversation, his replies were brief. And she caught him looking at her sidelong sometimes, with a cross, even sulky expression. He was embroiled at the moment in an appeal against conscription, which made him even less attractive to her. She felt it wasn't manly to try to avoid service.

But Rupert was devoted to him, and whenever he told

her he couldn't see her on a particular day, it was because he was doing something with Erskine.

From time to time she went home to rest and refresh herself after the social whirl. Home seemed very quiet, and surprisingly small after her London experiences, but she made and received visits from old friends, who wanted to know what she'd been up to, and who admired her ring much more than they'd ever admired Charles's ruby. Alicia Harding was full of wonder that, after having lost Lord Dene, she was going to be Lady Dene after all. Lizzie Drake thought Rupert much more attractive than Charles and hinted that everything had worked out for the best. And everyone wanted to talk about the wedding.

It was to be at St Margaret's in July, a full Society affair this time, and Diana had no qualms about allowing Lady Wroughton to arrange it. (Her mother had raised no objection – she seemed more than usually distracted, these days, and hardly seemed interested in the wedding at all.) Lady Wroughton was not warm towards Diana, but after their teas together, Diana was not afraid of her. A sign of the improvement in their relationship was that she had agreed to sponsor Diana when she was presented at Buckingham Palace. And Diana was to have Wroughton family jewels to wear with the wedding dress – a diamond necklace and tiara. She was to wear the dress Nula had made for her for Charles, but Nula was sewing on some extra trimming: floral figures in crystal beads. 'The diamonds'll make it look too plain otherwise.'

Strangely, the thing that troubled Diana most was Sadie's lack of excitement. Diana had never been close to her sister, but Sadie was older now and a sister of eighteen could be a real confidante, where a child of sixteen was simply annoying. But Sadie was always busy with her horses up at Highclere, and when she had a spare moment she visited wounded soldiers at Mount Olive. She begrudged taking time from her war work to be fitted for the bridesmaid's dress, and was reluctant to accept the loan of any jewellery to go with it.

'I'm not a jewellery sort of person,' she said. 'I'd feel silly in it.'

'That's not the point,' Diana said.

'What is, then?'

'The point is that it's *my* wedding, and it should be the way I want it. If it was your wedding, I'd go along with what *you* wanted.'

Sadie sighed. 'I'm sorry. You're quite right. I'll wear anything you choose.'

Diana was not appeased. 'Why are you being *like* this?' she asked crossly. Sadie didn't answer. 'Is it jealousy?'

'Jealousy? Goodness, no! I'm very glad for you, if it's what you want. But it's not what I'd want. Except for the horses. You'll be able to have horses after the war. But I suppose you won't want them.'

'I've already told you, you shall have horses at Dene Park,' Diana said.

'Yes, I know. And thank you,' Sadie said.

'You don't sound very grateful,' said Diana.

'I am.' Sadie frowned in thought. 'It's just—'

'What? It's just what?' Diana prompted irritably.

'I don't know,' Sadie said, seeming to struggle with her thoughts. 'I don't really know what it is, except that – well, Rupert somehow doesn't seem quite real to me. The war is real, Highclere is real, David and Bobby are real, but Rupert . . . I know he's in uniform, but what does he actually *do* at the War Office?'

Diana had asked herself the same question, but she said, with a touch of loftiness, 'It's obviously something important, and probably too difficult for us to understand.'

'Well, I'm glad for your sake he's there, not at the Front.' Sadie made an effort and smiled. 'I'm happy for you, really

I am. And you'll make a wonderful queen of Dene Park one day.'

Then she went on to ask Diana more questions about the wedding plans, and Diana was mollified. Afterwards she suspected she had been being 'handled', but it had made things all right between her and Sadie, so that was good.

There was another letter from David, for Antonia to read aloud to her father. 'There seems to be a little more meat to it this time,' she said.

'Carry on, my dear,' said Mr Weston.

She read:

My dear Antonia,

First, belated thanks for the Easter gifts. Please thank your father for the chocolate and Mrs Bates for the splendid cake, which delighted more hearts than one. We officers share our good things. And thank you for the book of poetry (which I didn't share). With food for the mind and for the body, and a modicum of tobacco, I had everything a man needs for a civilised interlude. You will wonder why I didn't thank you sooner, given that I had told you we would be out on rest, but this is how it was. The adj called a sudden meeting of company commanders and said orders had come in for a forced march up to the line. Apparently the higher powers had been thoroughly shaken by the Irish rebellion, and were afraid that an Irish division in the line might "cut up rough" and go over to the Germans. So we had to get up as fast as possible and relieve them. It was a very hot day, not pleasant for forced-marching, and the men were tired anyway, not having long come out of the line.

Once we got through Doullens we called a halt in

an orchard and the men got a rest under the trees and had a meal, and then it was on again through the sultry afternoon and dusk, arriving after eight at night. We took over the position, and as there were two Irish battalions in the line and we were only one, we were stretched to our limit. Only one man to a firing bay where there should have been three, and two in three bays unmanned. The hardest thing was for the men out at listening posts. Usually you have two together, to keep each other alert, but we had to send them in alone, and they were bone weary from the march. I spent all night going round to make sure they were awake. To fall asleep at your post attracts the death penalty, but these men didn't deserve that. It was hard duty for a couple of days, but the colonel appealed to Brigade for more men and they finally sent us up another two companies from a half-battalion, so we managed. It was an unexpected consequence of the Rising, which caused me much alarm anyway as – I think I told you – we have relatives near Dublin.

But a letter from home says they were all right. Awful to think of them being helped by the Germans. But the Irish troops I've met over here have been splendid fellows, and of course they were all volunteers, so I think the high-ups might have overreacted. I had a letter from the Divine Sophy. She is with her family in London, enjoying the Season, which I believe is rather sparkling this year. I hope she isn't enjoying it too much – or is that selfishness? As a woman, perhaps you can enlighten me on how much pleasure is appropriate for an engaged lady when her fiancé is absent. On the subject of which, have you met any handsome officers lately, who are vying for your heart? It does seem extraordinary that someone didn't snap you up

186

long ago. My brother is apparently now over in France with the RFC, but I don't suppose we will meet, the Front being such a big place. I'm told he is somewhere near Armentières, no doubt getting a fine bird's-eye view of us toiling fools in the trenches. What it is to be an airman!

Your firm friend, David.

Louisa was overjoyed when her brother's ship, having been detached from the 7th Cruiser Squadron, put into Chatham for repairs. She and Laura travelled down by train to be on hand when shore leave was given.

'We'll be here for three days,' Jim said, gazing at his sister and her friend in a starved sort of way. 'Gosh, it's good to see females again! My shipmates are all good fellows, but you get awfully sick of nothing but men! How's Aunty?'

'Much the same,' said Louisa. 'A bit older, a bit more crotchety.'

'Does she worry about me?'

'No, not at all,' said Louisa. 'She's so busy worrying about me, it never crosses her mind you might be in danger. I'm so glad you're back from the White Sea. Was it awful?'

'Awfully cold.' He looked around. 'I can't get over this warmth. And all the trees. So green! Oh, and look, the pigeons, and the sparrows!'

'What odd things to be glad of,' Louisa said.

'You notice what you haven't had,' he replied. 'Can we get something to eat? I'm starving.'

They took him to an hotel for lunch. Laura and Louisa did most of the talking as he tucked away leek soup, roast beef with Yorkshire pudding, potatoes, carrots and cabbage, plum duff with custard sauce, and a good part of a ripe Stilton cheese. He was a broad-shouldered, healthy-looking young man, not tall, but muscular, with frank blue eyes and Louisa's fair curly hair, bleached almost white by the weather.

His skin was weathered to mahogany, which made him look older, but when he spoke, he had the same engaging naturalness that Laura liked in his sister.

He told them a little about his recent cruise, but seemed disinclined to say much about it – or perhaps couldn't think of any details that would make sense to them. He was much more interested in their experiences as women police officers, and listened round-eyed, surprised but not disapproving. 'You always were a tomboy,' he said to Louisa. 'I suppose it's no wonder you've got into something like this. Well, good for you! I'm sure the streets of London are safer for it. What does Aunty think?'

'She doesn't know the half of it,' Louisa said.

'You don't tell her lies?'

'Of course not. I just don't tell her everything. She'd only worry. And it really isn't dangerous, you know. Laura takes care of me,' she added, with a smile. 'It'd be a foolish villain who tackled Laura.'

His round eyes moved to Laura and assessed her gravely. 'Now I know you're joking,' he said. 'I can see she's a lady through and through. But what about those old Zeppelins? We hear about 'em, you know.'

'We haven't seen much of them this year,' said Laura. 'I believe there've been some attempted raids, but they've been foiled by bad weather. At any rate, London hasn't been hit, though there've been some bombs further north.'

'You can't rely on bad weather for ever,' said Jim. 'And one thing we know about the Hun – he keeps on going until you smash him completely.'

Louisa asked him, 'Do you know where you're going next?'

'We're being attached to the 2nd Cruiser Squadron,' he said. 'When the repairs are done, we'll be steaming up to Scapa Flow to join them. Don't know exactly what's going on, but rumour is we're going to give the German U-boats a pasting. Causing us a lot of trouble in the North Sea. Can't let 'em have it all their own way.'

'Oh, well, that doesn't sound too bad,' Louisa said. 'The North Sea's not as rough as the White Sea, is it? Not as cold either.'

He gave her an affectionate smile. 'I'll be all right,' he said. 'Aunty always said I was born to be hanged, and if I'm to be hanged, I can't drown, can I? Remember that day trip we had to Henley when we were kids? And you fell in the river?'

'I was feeding the ducks,' she said.

'Trying to make sure the shy ones at the back got some,' Jim agreed, 'which was just like you. Only you leaned out too far.'

'And you jumped in to save me,' said Louisa.

'But that chap with the rowing-boat pulled you out before I got to you,' Jim said, 'so all I got was wet. Lord! Aunty was cross. My best suit was all over green slime.'

'But you were still my hero,' Louisa said, laying a hand on his arm.

Laura watched them fondly. 'I wonder if my brother would have jumped in to save me,' she said.

'You wouldn't have fallen in in the first place,' said Jim, 'if I'm any judge of character.'

The Hunters always enjoyed making a Sunday visit to the Palfreys, Edward's other sister's family. They were greeted at the door with news before they had even got their coats off, the youngest son, Douglas – known as Duck – competing with the maid, Leah, for the telling of it.

'Donald's been called up!' Duck cried. 'Poppa's been in absolute fits!'

'The missus had hysterics,' Leah chimed in simultaneously. 'Doris had to burn a feather under her nose –'

'– letter came yesterday. Donald says he was expecting it –'

'– that white, she was almost green –'

'– says everyone's got to do their duty –'

'– master sent for the brandy –'

'– time it's my turn, the war'll be over, worse luck –'

'– can't abide the taste of spirits –'

In the drawing-room, Sonia was still the centre of attention, having got to the weeping stage now, and was having her hands patted on one side by Audrey and her tears mopped from the other by Mary, while the menfolk stood by the fireplace looking on, Aeneas glumly and Donald with a restless face that squirmed from excitement to concern and back again.

Everyone was glad of the interruption. Sonia flung out her hands to Beattie. 'Oh, at least *you*'ll understand! A mother's heart, a mother's tears!'

Aeneas said, 'Edward! What on earth am I to do? Donald's been called up! I can't possibly cope without him. How am I to run the business? Look here, you know more about it than anyone: what are the chances of having him exempted?'

'But I don't *want* to be exempted,' Donald cried, going red in the face. 'I *want* to do my duty. Everyone would say I was the most frightful slacker – they'd think I was a coward—'

'Don't contradict your father!' Sonia recovered enough to rebuke him.

'But, Pa, Donald's right,' Duck said urgently.

'Yes, Uncle,' William added his support. 'I can't wait to be old enough to go.'

Beattie sat down next to Sonia and took over the hand-patting. Sonia raised drowned eyes to her. 'How shall I bear it? How do *you* bear it, Beattie dear? Suppose they send him to the Front? It's so *dangerous*. One hears all the time of people being wounded – even *killed*.'

'Oh, Mumsy!' Donald cried, exasperated.

'Statistically,' Duck told her seriously, 'it isn't so very dangerous – far more people *don't* get wounded than do.'

'Shut up, Duck,' Audrey said. 'Not helping.'

'Edward!' Aeneas called back his attention. 'Can I get him exempted?'

All eyes were on Edward now. 'I'm afraid not,' he said. 'Starred occupations are strictly defined. The view would be that anyone could do Donald's job – it is only clerical and managerial, after all.'

'Making biscuit for the army is government work,' Aeneas said.

'Doesn't help,' Edward said. 'We heard an appeal the other day from a baker, who said the nation had to be supplied with bread. But he also made cakes and pasties, so it was decided he couldn't claim his work was essential. We turned him down.'

Sonia gave him a reproachful look. 'Poor fellow! He must have been someone's son.'

'Everyone is someone's son,' Edward said. 'Very few people are given an absolute exemption. The exemptions my tribunal has given have been for a few weeks, for the applicant to make necessary arrangements. Everyone owes a duty to the state in a time of emergency.'

'Well,' said Aeneas, 'I suppose if you say so, it must be. Not worth my appealing, then?' Edward shook his head. 'Then I shan't waste my time. My dear, you'll have to make up your mind to it.'

'Oh dear!' Sonia said tremulously, on the brink of another flood.

But Mary said, 'Think how proud you'll be to see him in uniform, Mumsy. He'll look so handsome! He's got the build for it – not like Tom Amberley down the road.'

It worked. She sat up straighter, took the handkerchief from Mary and wiped her eyes almost impatiently. 'Tom Amberley is pigeon-chested, I've always said so. Mrs

Amberley was so ridiculous, bringing that photograph of him in uniform round to all the neighbours to admire. I'm sure I should have better taste than to do something like that.'

'Of course you would, my dear,' Aeneas said soothingly. Then, to Edward, 'But it doesn't solve my problem. How on earth am I to replace him? You know what I'm talking about, Edward. You were devastated when young Warren went. It's not a matter of replacing a clerk. It's the knowledge of the business, and the dedication.'

Edward nodded agreement. 'I can't get used to Murchison,' he sighed. 'Warren was like a part of myself. I didn't have to tell him things.'

'Quite so – Donald's the same. No-one else can do what he does.'

'I can,' said Audrey.

Aeneas gave her a small smile, acknowledging she had spoken without really listening to what she had said. 'Perhaps we could apply for a temporary exemption, while Donald trains someone.'

'I said, I can do it, Poppa,' Audrey said more loudly.

Aeneas attended at last. 'Do what, dear?'

'I can do Donald's job.' He looked at her blankly. 'I know a great deal about the firm,' she said, 'and I care about it as much as he does. I'm very good at arithmetic – much better than him – and I've been studying book-keeping.'

'The dickens you have!'

'I have!' she said defiantly. 'When it was obvious that you were never going to let me go to university, I decided I'd better have some skills so that I could have a career. I talked to Miss Tomlinson at school. She doesn't think women ought to have to get married, as if there's nothing else they can do. She got me books on book-keeping and office duties and I studied them in prep, when I'd done my homework. And Aunt Laura's helped me as well. She was the one who said it was obvious Donald would have to go sooner or later, and that it would be my chance to show what I can do. I've even been to the factory a couple of times to look around.'

'I'll be damned,' sad Aeneas. 'I never saw you.'

'I chose days when you weren't there. A very nice foreman was only too glad to show me round. I think he was flattered I was taking an interest.'

Aeneas and Donald exchanged a look. 'I'll bet that was Barrett,' said Donald. 'Soft-hearted idiot.'

'The point is,' said Audrey, firmly, 'that I'm ready for it. I'm capable, and I'm the best person you could have for the job. I've the company's interests at heart – and I'll never be called up.'

'It's out of the question,' Aeneas said.

'Why?' said Audrey.

'Because you're a female,' Aeneas answered promptly.

'But what does that matter?'

'It's not just clerical duties,' Donald said, but kindly – he was fond of his sisters. 'It's managerial, too. The men wouldn't obey you.'

'Why ever not?' said Audrey. Donald didn't have an answer to that.

Aeneas said, 'It's a step too far.'

Mary said, 'But why, Poppa? Things are changing – they *have* to change. Look at me, in the WVR. Look at Aunt Laura. Look at Sadie – she's doing work for the *army*. That's a much further step than doing something for your own father's firm.'

Aeneas looked an appeal at Edward. 'You tell them. You're with me on this.'

Before he could answer, there was an unexpected intervention from Sonia. 'I think you should try her out,' she said. Everyone looked at her in varying degrees of astonishment. 'She's far and away the brainiest of the family –

you've always said so. If Donald could learn the work, I'm sure she could. You ought to give her a chance.'

'Well done, Mumsy,' said Mary. 'That's very modern of you.'

'As Edward said, everyone owes a duty to the state in a time of emergency.' She was clearly enjoying the attention this novel stance was bringing her. 'There's a war on. Things are bound to be different, and we must make the best of them.'

Donald turned to his father. 'I don't see why not, Poppa,' he said. 'I've got a couple of days before I have to report. I could spend them showing Audrey the ropes.'

'But then if she doesn't frame up, we've no time to find someone else before you go,' said Aeneas.

'I'll frame up,' said Audrey. 'Don't worry, Poppa. I won't let you down.'

At this interesting moment, Laura and Louisa were ushered in. 'What's this I hear?' said Laura. 'Donald called up, and Audrey taking his place?'

'Leah's been listening at doors again,' said Mary. 'You can't keep anything secret in this house.'

'Oh, was it a secret?' Laura said innocently. 'I think it's splendid!'

'Of course *you* would,' said Aeneas.

'Are you wavering?' Laura asked him, with an amused look. 'But, my dear, I thought it was frightfully canny of you! Not only is she as bright as a button, and a tremendous resource, but she's your daughter, so you'll only have to pay her pocket money. Think what you'll save on wages!'

'Aunty!' Mary protested.

But Aeneas smiled. 'I had already decided to give it a try, but your intervention is well taken. Audrey, we'll start tomorrow, sharp at seven at the factory, and see how you do. With Donald and me both teaching you, it'll be a test of character, if nothing else.'

Audrey ran to him, wound her arms round his neck and kissed him. '*Thank* you, Poppa! I won't let you down. You'll see.'

He patted her back kindly. 'There, there. We'll see how you feel in a week. You'll never want to eat another biscuit, I give you my word.'

'I don't eat them anyway,' said Audrey.

CHAPTER THIRTEEN

After lunch, back in the drawing-room, Edward and Aeneas talked business. 'Donald leaving could hardly have come at a worse time,' Aeneas said. 'I'm negotiating a government contract for jam. It will mean a big expansion.'

'You'll need larger premises,' said Edward. 'Have you somewhere in mind?'

'There's a closed-down factory in the next street, which more or less backs onto my yard. We can move the whole of the jam business into the new factory, and expand on the bottling plant in the old one. Bottled fruit is going to be important if the war goes on long. It's hard for them to get fresh fruit over there, and we can't have the men getting scurvy, can we?'

'You're a philanthropist,' Edward smiled. 'So, with all this expansion, I assume you'll want a loan?'

'I was coming to that. What a thing it is to have a banker for a brother-in-law! I suppose you'll be able to do something for me?'

'Certainly,' said Edward. 'In fact, I've been looking for investments along those lines. With the army growing so rapidly, food for the troops is going to be a lucrative field. I went to see Lord Walsham last week. He's got a place in Suffolk, open fields and dry sandy soil, perfect for pigs. He simply hadn't thought about it – hardly knew what a pig was. I pointed out how much pork the army consumes, and gave him some figures for the returns he could hope to get, and now he's as keen as mustard.'

'Walsham – wasn't he with the Admiralty?' Aeneas said.

Laura joined them at that moment. 'Did I hear the word "Admiralty"?'

'We were talking about Lord Walsham. He was one of the sea lords,' Edward said. 'He's a client of mine. I visited him last week.'

'Ah, then perhaps you have some current information on what the navy's up to,' Laura said. 'Louisa's brother's ship is joining the Grand Fleet at Scapa Flow and she wonders where he'll be sent next.'

'Well, I don't mind telling you,' said Edward, 'that the Germans are up to something pretty big in the North Sea. They've been massing ships in the Skagerrak, and it doesn't take much naval intelligence to guess that they're intending to attack the east coast. The Grand Fleet will be sent out to counter them.'

Laura was concerned. 'So you think there'll be a battle?'

'It's common knowledge that the navy's been agitating for a show-down with the German fleet for some time,' said Edward. 'They're harrying our merchant ships, and the U-boats are becoming a big problem. I understand the naval brass feel it would be better to deal with it sooner rather than later. So I think you can take it that something big is in the offing.'

'Oh dear, poor Louisa. It was bad enough when her brother was only on convoy duty, but if his ship actually goes into battle . . .'

'Perhaps you'd better not tell her,' Aeneas suggested.

'Oh, no, I couldn't keep it from her,' Laura said. 'That wouldn't be fair.'

'You mean, she has the right to be worried?' Edward said.

'Of course,' said Laura. 'Friends treat each other with

197

respect. I should have thought you men would understand that.'

'Yes, but we *are* men,' said Aeneas. 'Women are delicate. They should be protected from harsh reality.'

'My goodness, if this war doesn't rid you of that sort of thinking—' Laura began hotly.

Edward laughed. 'He was teasing you. I should think you and Louisa have seen plenty of harsh reality on the streets by now.'

Ethel walked slowly along the grimy street, uncomfortable in the sunshine. A sunny day in Northcote had been a blessing; here it only emphasised the dirt and shabbiness in its cruel brightness. And the evening decline of the sun had brought little relief: the glare had faded a little, but the stifling heat remained. It was like being smothered by a dusty carpet.

She was weary of her task, no longer had any great belief that it would succeed, but she had been engaged in it for so long now that she couldn't quite bring herself to give up and call all those months wasted. She had used up nearly all her savings, but she'd got a job as a chambermaid – fortunately, there were always hotels, and they always needed chambermaids. It meant she could only search in her time off, so she had no choice but to trudge the streets with her feet throbbing and her back aching from work, when all she wanted was to lie down and rest.

Lately at least she had had a defined area to search, a web of streets lined with Victorian terraced two-up-two-downs, but even so it was laborious to knock on every door, and dispiriting to get the same blank look and impatient denial. Every now and then she had been met with kindness. One woman had offered her a drink of water; another had let her sit down inside for a few minutes. But she was very tired, and decided she would do to the end of this side of the street – three more houses – then give it up for the day.

Another door. Paint peeling from it. The number missing, but visible in ghostly outline: 23. She knocked. Cracked doorstep, unscrubbed. One square of the downstairs window had lost its glass and had been filled in with brown paper. A poor household in a street of poor households. Behind her, dirty, ill-dressed children were playing in the road, boys kicking a can in place of a football, girls playing some game that involved chanting: their high rhythmic voices sounded to Ethel's weary ears like the cries of seagulls.

She knocked again, and the door was opened. A slatternly woman with a child of about two on her hip gave her the blank, unfriendly stare she had grown used to. But before she could begin her enquiry, a different look seeped into the face – it was recognition, but not the welcoming sort. 'Well, well. Look what's turned up, like a bad penny.'

'Edie?' Ethel queried. Yes, now she could see the strong resemblance to Ma. 'Is it you?'

'What do *you* want?' said Edie, sourly.

Ethel couldn't frame an answer, after all these months of searching. There was a horrid pressure in her ears, and black spots before her eyes. Unwillingly, but quite gracefully, she fainted.

She had thought at the beginning it would be so easy. She had the address: all it needed was the determination to knock at the door and face the consequences. But Edie no longer lived there, and the new people had never heard of her.

Fortunately, the next-door neighbours, an old couple, the Feeneys, had known her, and were willing to tell what they knew. Edie had lived there with her husband, not the tinker, Mulroney, with whom she had fled Gosford, but a man called George Cloutsham, and two small children. Cloutsham was a bus conductor, a decent sort, except when he'd had a few too many. Because of the drinking, his wages weren't enough for the small family, and Edie had got a job at one of the shoe factories. The Feeneys had looked after the children when she was working.

But one night Cloutsham, walking home from the pub the worse for wear, had been knocked down and killed by a motor-van. After that, Edie had taken up with a bad lot, a labourer called Sneb Cranston, who was in and out of work, a waster and ready with his fists into the bargain. The Feeneys hadn't liked him, but did their best to protect the children, who were as often in their house as at home.

Between them, Cranston and Edie couldn't afford the rent of the house, and had got into debt, living in the twilight world of loans and pawnshops and the dread of the bailiffs. Then one day, Sneb had disappeared, leaving Edie in the family way again. She had been forced to move to a poorer area and a house with a lower rent. The Feeneys had given Ethel the new address; but when she went there, she found Edie had long since moved on again.

After that, Ethel had been following ever more tenuous clues. She couldn't even be sure she was following the right name any more. Was Edie calling herself Lusby, Mulroney, Cloutsham, Cranston, or something else entirely? Ethel had no idea if she had married any of the men, or how many more there might have been since Cranston.

But Cloutsham was at least an unusual name, and three weeks ago, Ethel had been told by someone answering one of the doors that she remembered a Mrs Cloutsham, and believed she was now living in one of the streets off St Andrew's Road. It had given her fresh hope, for a while. But there were a lot of streets and a lot of houses, and she was tired to death. Only an inability to think of anything else to do had made her go out every time she was off duty. She had stopped thinking about what she would say to Edie if she ever did find her. Or whether, indeed, Edie would be glad to be found.

It wasn't a complete faint, only sufficient dizziness to bring her to the ground, where the blood soon returned to her head. It did, however, put the onus on Edie to let her in. 'I s'pose you better come in the kitchen,' she grumbled. 'I'll get you a drink o' water.'

The door opened straight into the front room, which was taken up with an unmade bed, a wooden chair and little else. 'Lucky for you Kettel's not in,' she said, with a glance at the bed. 'He sleeps here when his back's bad and it don't put him in a good temper, I can tell you.'

She led the way through the further door. A steep, narrow staircase went up between the front and back rooms. The back room was a tiny kitchen with a door into the back yard, off which was the privy and a coalshed. Edie put the child, which was naked, apart from a sagging and odiferous nappy, on the floor, went over to the sink and ran water into a cup, which she handed to Ethel. Ethel looked at it doubtfully. It was much stained inside, the rim was chipped, and the water seemed to have bits floating in it.

Edie said impatiently, 'Sit down if you want. Shove them things on the floor.' There was a wooden table covered in dirty crockery and old newspapers, and a wooden chair either side of it littered with clothes. Ethel was still feeling dizzy, and needed to sit down, but she didn't like to put the clothes on the floor, which was filthy – even though the clothes didn't look clean. Edie made a sound of exasperation and cleared the seat with one shove. 'Dainty, ain't you? Sit down, for God's sake, 'fore you fall down. You're white as a sheet.'

Ethel sat, putting the cup on the table without regret. Edie folded her arms under her bosom aggressively. 'Well?' she said. She was examining Ethel with sharp, raking eyes, taking in everything about her, her clean hair, hands and face, moderately decent coat and hat, worn shoes and dusty stockings. 'What've you come here for? If you want money you've come to the wrong place.'

Ethel said the first thing that came into her head. 'Ma's dead.'

'Oh?' said Edie, without interest.

'She died January last year. Lungs.'

'You took your time telling me, then.'

'Didn't know where you were. It's taken me four months to find you.'

'Could've saved yourself the trouble.'

Ethel didn't wonder at the lack of emotion. Ma had never been the motherly sort, and Edie had left a long time ago. Instead, she said, 'You knew who I was. How'd you recognise me?'

'You look like me at the same age. Anyway, who else'd come knocking at my door?'

'Cyril's gone too,' Ethel said. 'Died a long time ago, of gangrene when he cut his foot.'

'I know. Ma writ me that.'

'She kept some of your letters. I got 'em when she died. That's how I found you.'

Edie tossed her head, like an irritable horse. 'So what *do* you want?'

Ethel swallowed, summoned her courage. 'Ma said you was my real mother.'

Edie didn't blink. 'Well, she's a rotten liar, then, ain't she?'

Ethel kept staring at her. Eventually Edie glanced away, and sighed. The child was sitting in a puddle on the floor, playing with a bent spoon. She stared at it a moment, with a look of profound weariness, then turned back to Ethel. 'All right,' she said. 'What about it?'

'You *are* my mother?' Ethel pressed.

'I *had* you. That's all. I wasn't never your mother. For God's sake, I was just a kid myself. Ma took you, soon as I was out of bed, and I never thought another thing about you. So don't come looking to me for mothering, or whatever it is you want.'

'I don't want anything from you,' Ethel said, nettled. 'I've done all right for myself.'

'Yeah, Ma writ me you'd gone to school an' all. And you talk all la-di-dah.' A gleam of malice came into her eyes. 'In the fambly way, aren't you?'

Ethel blushed with distress. She had lost a lot of weight since leaving Northcote, so her clothes hung loose on her, except where they didn't. She didn't think anyone had yet twigged to her condition – but perhaps Edie was an expert. 'What if I am?' she said defiantly.

'And you ain't wearing a wedding ring. You've got nothing to give yourself airs about, have you?'

'It was an accident,' Ethel said.

'Ain't it always?' said Edie. There was a very slight softening of her expression. 'You in trouble? Scarpered, has he?'

'He doesn't know. He's no-one.' She thought briefly of Sergeant Andy Wood, and quickly hauled her thoughts away. '*I* didn't know when I came down here.'

'Well, it's no use looking to me for help,' said Edie. 'I got three to feed, with this one, and Kettel's in and out of work, with his back. And when he does get any wages, it's a toss-up whether I get 'em or the landlord of the Bird in Hand, useless sot that he is.'

'He's your – husband, is he?'

Edie gave a short laugh. 'Husband! That'll be the day.'

'What happened to Mulroney?'

'Good Gawd, you want to go back in history, do you?' She shrugged. 'All right.' She sat down on the other chair, planted her elbows, and told her story.

Mulroney, the tinker, had been good to her, but she'd

tired of life on the road. She wanted a house that stayed in one place. 'And I was mug enough to think I could have a better life that way.'

She'd met George Cloutsham at a wayside pub one day. He was on an outing with some pals from work. He'd taken a fancy to her, and she'd abandoned Mulroney and the baby she'd had with him without regret, and gone home to Northampton with her new man. He'd got a decent job as a bus conductor, and had rented a house for them, and they'd been happy at first, until the children came along. 'Kids ruin everything,' she said shortly. 'Don't seem to be no way of stopping 'em.'

Cloutsham had started staying out late because of the children, and drinking more, and things had gone downhill. Then he'd fallen under the wheels of the motor-van when he was dead drunk. 'And that was the end of him.'

Then she'd taken up with Cranston. She'd had two children with him; her two from Cloutsham had died of the whooping cough when they were nine and ten years old. He'd rubbed off when she fell pregnant with a third. She'd lost that one. Then she'd been on her own for a bit with Cranston's two, until she got in with Ezra Kettel, who wasn't a bad bloke really, only lazy, milking his bad back every time he didn't fancy going to work. So he was always losing jobs and having to find new ones. And like all men, he was fond of his beer. So it was a struggle. Cranston's two kids were at school now; this one was Kettel's. Fortunately Kettel's bad back prevented him pursuing 'the old how's-your-father' very often, so she was hopeful that this little snotter would be her last.

She looked dispassionately at the child as she said it. Ethel looked too. It had to be said it was unprepossessing.

'Good thing about the war,' Edie said more briskly, 'the boot factories are all on extra time, so there's good work to be had. I got my plan. Find someone to mind the kid,

204

get myself a job, hide the money from Kettel somehow. I suppose I'm stuck with *him*, now, useless article. They called him up, but he got rejected at the medical.' She came back from contemplation of her own life, and regarded Ethel curiously again. 'So, what's *your* plan? Not going to marry this bloke of yours?'

'He's married already.'

'Oh, one o' *those*. You're a mug, you know that? If you'd asked my advice, I'd've said keep away from men, but I see it's too late. So what you going to do?'

'Work as long as I can. Save as much as I can. Have the baby. Then . . .' Her imagination failed. 'Get another job, I s'pose.'

'Good luck to you,' Edie said sourly, 'with a kid in tow.'

'I've been a fool,' Ethel said bitterly.

'You have,' Edie agreed. 'And don't think you can dump it on me, because *I* won't have it. You'd best try one of them churchy types, the do-gooders that takes care o' fallen women.'

Ethel's heart failed. She had come to the end of her quest, which had buoyed her up, helped her to forget the trouble she was in. There was nothing to take her mind from it now. How long would the hotel let her carry on, once they knew she was pregnant? There was good work at the factories, but the same problem applied. And where would she live? And when the baby came, who would look after her?

She half wished she had stayed in Northcote, never started this – but Mrs Hunter wouldn't have kept her once she found out. They were always the most disapproving: those who'd never been in trouble were harshest on those who were. It would have been all high and mighty finger-wagging, and never darken my door again . . .

Edie was watching her while these thoughts struggled through her mind. Now she stood up and said, 'Well, you've made your bed so you must lie on it. And now you'd better go. Don't want you here when Kettel gets back. He'll take any excuse to thump someone, whether it makes sense or not.'

Ethel rose wearily, buttoned her coat, and walked back through the other room to the front door. There was nothing for her here, not even any sympathy. She was on her own – and even in a lifetime of always knowing she was on her own, she had never felt more lonely.

Edie followed her, and at the door, she said, 'I still don't get what you came here for. All this way, just to tell me Ma was dead?'

'It wasn't that. I wanted to ask you—'

'What? Whether I really was your mother? Well, I hope it was worth it,' Edie sniffed.

'No,' said Ethel. 'I sort of knew that. What I wanted to know, given you *were* my mother, was who –'

'Don't,' said Edie sharply. 'Don't ask that.'

'– who was my father?'

Edie stared at her in exasperation mixed with pity. 'Questions, questions. That's what going to school gets you. Who was your father? You bloody little idiot, who'd you think?'

'Was it Mulroney?' Ethel asked falteringly. She didn't want to be a tinker's daughter. She didn't know what difference it would make, really, but she didn't want—

Edie sucked in an impatient breath. 'Never met him till you was five years old. Use your brains, if you got any. Who was the only man around?'

Ethel stared at her, the horrible thought being born, and growing rapidly into full, ugly certainty. 'Cyril?' she whispered. Their older brother Cyril?

Edie's answer was a grimace, as she shoved Ethel unceremoniously across the threshold. 'Bloody Cyril. Right. Much good may it do you, knowing about it,' were her last words, cut off by the slam of the door.

* * *

206

The bridesmaids' luncheon at the Ritz was a pleasant affair. There were to be eight this time. As well as Sadie, Mary and Audrey, Diana had asked – at her mother's suggestion – Sophy to make a fourth. With David away, it was important to show proper attention to Sophy. She had also asked Obby Marlowe, who had been flatteringly pleased about it, and the other three were Lady Wroughton's choice from the last time, Wroughton cousins who, Rupert said, would add tone to the affair, as well as putting his mother in a good mood. Lady Lolly Harcourt, Galatea Blandish, and the Honourable Erica Stannerburn had been a little stand-offish at first, but Rupert assured Diana it was just shyness, and by the bottom of the first glass of champagne, the atmosphere was more relaxed.

It could have been an awkward group, divided into the middle class and the upper class, but Obby and Rupert kept everything going. Rupert's best man, Lord Teesborough, was also a thoroughly good sort. He was an airman, who had volunteered at the beginning of the war; he had been shot down and now, owing to a stiff leg, was no longer fit for combat duty and was an instructor at Upavon. He had plenty of amusing anecdotes, and hadn't the slightest 'side' to him. He also remembered Bobby, which helped unite the party.

Lord Teesborough was the son of Rupert's godmother and in all ways well qualified for the job of best man, but Diana was surprised Erskine Ballantine hadn't been chosen. But when she asked, Rupert had said that Erskine would be too awkward and, besides, his appeal against conscription hadn't yet been allowed. 'No point in choosing someone who might not turn up.'

A year ago, the thought of the ceremony, with its grandeur and all the possible pitfalls, would have terrified her. Now she was rather thrilled by the idea. Rupert seemed as eager as anyone for everything to be done in the most lavish style

– he had almost a feminine eye for detail, Diana thought. The wedding breakfast would be at Wroughton House, then she and Rupert would 'go away' to a suite at the Ritz. Abroad was out of the question because of the war, and he didn't want to go to the house at Clarges Street – 'Too dreary. And I don't want you to be bothered with house-keeping. The Ritz will make us comfortable, neither of us will have to lift a finger, and we'll have all the restaurants and theatres at our doorstep.'

Diana was glad. She was afraid Clarges Street would always be haunted for her by thoughts of Charles. Perhaps Rupert felt the same way, because by his decree Clarges Street was to be let, and they were to take a house in Park Place after the honeymoon. She had seen it from the outside and liked it. There were tenants in there until the end of June; then it was being altered and redecorated, and it would be ready in the autumn. Rupert was handling everything. He had explained to her that, in his world, it was for the man to make a home for his bride, not the other way around.

Diana was happy with the arrangement. She was not, by nature, a nest-builder – not for her the brooding over soft furnishings and fussing over the precise arrangement of ornaments. Her bridesmaids found her attitude quite normal. Mary and Audrey had too much else to think about; Sadie couldn't care less about home comforts, though she'd have planned a stable to the last manger; and the upper-class girls had the same expectations as Rupert.

Only Sophy thought it odd. She said *sotto voce* to Sadie, 'I shouldn't want anyone else to choose for me. I know the dinner service I want, and Mummy and I have already picked out the linens in Selfridges. Your sister doesn't even seem interested in silver patterns.'

'Everyone's different,' Sadie said vaguely.

'I'm looking forward to making a lovely home for David,'

Sophy said. 'Of course, it's a long way off yet,' she added, with a sigh. 'I do wish this war would end.'

Sadie summoned her sympathy. 'It must be hard for you.'

'Diana's so lucky her fiancé is serving at home,' Sophy said. 'Everyone seems to be going. Even Humphrey Hobart's been called up. And all Freddie's friends who used to visit. There won't be anyone left to dance with.'

'I expect David will get leave soon,' Sadie said soothingly.

'But we still can't get married until the war's over.'

Darvell's factory, on the road between Northcote and Westleigh, had used to make brass door furniture, decorative horse brasses, fire irons, and so on. Now it had closed. William brought the news that there were obviously serious building works going on.

'It's being turned into a munitions factory,' he told Sadie. 'Jack Chaplin told me. To make shell casings. It's got all the foundry equipment already there, so it makes sense.'

'I suppose they'll send them to Hendorp to be filled,' said Sadie. 'This area will really be contributing to the war effort.'

'Jack Chaplin says it'll mean a lot more jobs for men, which'll be good for Northcote.'

'Yes,' said Sadie. 'I suppose men working in a munitions factory won't get called up.'

'But I expect there'll be jobs for women as well,' William said. 'I say, I saw some munitionettes down in the station yard. They'd just got off the Hendorp bus. I suppose it was the end of their shift and they were going home.'

'How did you know they were munitionettes?'

'Their hands and faces looked sort of yellow. That's from the sulphur in the powder and everything.'

'I know,' said Sadie. 'They put cornflour on their faces when they get to the factory to protect them.'

'And they had trousers on,' said William. 'It was funny

209

seeing people turn their heads and stare. Some looked terribly disapproving.'

'I hope Mrs Fitzgerald wasn't there,' said Sadie.

'No, but I heard two girls at the bus stop talking, and they were dying to go and be munitionettes themselves, so Mrs F wasn't far wrong. I'd have thought going yellow would put them off.'

'They wear trousers, have money in their pockets, smoke, and go into pubs,' said Sadie. 'A bit of yellow'd be a small price to pay for all that freedom.'

CHAPTER FOURTEEN

In the evening of the 2nd of June, the first news arrived of a great sea battle between the British and German fleets off Jutland. The source was an official German news release, which claimed the battle as a victory for Germany, with the destruction of a battleship, two battlecruisers, two armoured cruisers, a light cruiser, a submarine and several destroyers. The Kaiser proclaimed a new world order and German children were given a school holiday.

On the 3rd of June, the newspapers were reporting the British defeat, and though the Admiralty countered with a report of German losses, the nation was shocked that the mighty Royal Navy could have been anything but victorious. Ships from the encounter were beginning to make port, and their crews were sending messages to friends and relatives, so the news could not be suppressed. Some coming ashore found rumours that were much worse than the reality had been, saying the whole fleet was feared lost; in other places they were jeered for showing their faces after allowing themselves to be beaten.

Six thousand seamen had perished, it was said. Louisa was sick with anxiety, for Jim's ship, the *Hampshire*, was reported to have been in the engagement. Laura went straight to Edward's office, begging him for news. A few discreet telephone calls enabled him to tell her that *Hampshire* was already on her way back to Scapa Flow, and was completely unscathed.

'I can't tell you specifically about Jim, but I can tell you *Hampshire* suffered no casualties – she wasn't even fully engaged in the battle,' he told her. 'She was on the fringes of it, and I'm told only fired four salvoes at distant targets the whole time.'

'Oh, thank God,' Laura said. 'Jim's all Louisa has, apart from her old aunt. They're very close. Well, if you're orphaned at a young age, you would cling together, wouldn't you?'

'I expect he'll send her a message of some sort from Scapa,' Edward said. 'That'll be the first time he touches port.'

'I'll tell her. She'll be so relieved. I don't suppose you have any idea where *Hampshire* will be going next?'

'None,' said Edward, 'but I don't imagine there'll be any more set battles for a long time, if that's any comfort. She'll probably go back on convoy duty.'

'Of course the sea is never completely safe,' Laura said, 'but Louisa will be glad to hear that.'

On the 6th of June, there was a letter from Jim in the first post. Louisa devoured it over the breakfast coffee, reading out bits to Laura. 'They didn't do anything but take pot shots at what they thought were submarine periscopes. They missed all the action.' And, 'They were detached before they even heard the full news about the outcome – sent back to Scapa.' And, 'Oh, now they're taking Lord Kitchener to Russia, to persuade the Tsar to stay in the war.'

'Thank goodness it's June,' Laura said. 'Imagine that voyage in the depth of winter. I suppose they'll go up round the top of Norway – how cold it will be!'

It was then that the telephone rang. It was Edward, calling from his office. 'I wonder if he's got some more news,' Laura said, as she waited for the connection.

Edward's voice came on. 'Are you both up?' he asked.

'Yes, we're just finishing breakfast. What is it?'

'I'm afraid it's bad news.'

'My dear, you do sound grim. What's happened?' A thought came to her. 'Oh, God, it isn't David, is it?'

'No, I'm afraid it's Louisa's brother,' Edward said. 'I think I'd better tell you, and let you break it to her. It will be in the papers this evening, or tomorrow at the latest, but I had a call from my chap at the Admiralty, seeing I'd been asking about *Hampshire* so recently. She's gone down.'

'*What?*'

'Hit a mine, apparently – or possibly was torpedoed, they can't be sure,' said Edward. 'People watching from the shore saw an explosion around half past seven on Monday night. She sank by the head about fifteen minutes later. In heavy seas. No lifeboats have been found – it's thought it was impossible to launch them.'

'Are there – no survivors?' Laura asked, her mouth dry.

'They're saying a handful of sailors got to shore on two Carly floats, but what condition they'll be in . . . The seas are icy, even in June, and a gale was blowing. There are no names at the moment. They'll issue a list when they have it. They think about twelve men survived. None of the passengers.'

'Oh, God, Lord Kitchener – I'd forgotten,' said Laura.

'He's lost, I'm afraid,' said Edward. 'It will be a terrible blow to the nation. The people adored him.'

'But there's still a chance,' Laura began – though she knew what sort of a chance it was: twelve out of six hundred or more.

'Chance of what?' came Louisa's voice from behind her. Laura turned, the telephone still to her ear. Louisa's face whitened. She reached behind her for a chair. 'It's Jim, isn't it?' she said.

The next morning every newspaper bore huge black head-lines: KITCHENER DROWNED, and LORD KITCHENER LOST AT

SEA. Photographs of him were on every page, formal portraits in full uniform on the front page, others inside taken from news stories, of the great man on his horse reviewing troops, speaking to soldiers at the Front, conferring with generals. As much of the story as could be verified was printed, along with a number of unsubstantiated rumours in the more popular papers, and theories about conspiracies. It was widely held that German spies had got on board the ship and blown her up to kill Lord Kitchener and demoralise the British. Much was made of the fact that only about a hundred bodies had been recovered – though in such seas it was hardly surprising.

The nation mourned. Nothing else was spoken of. Ever more bizarre theories expanded on the summer air: one said that Kitchener had shot himself in his office, and the sinking had been arranged to cover up the shame; he had never been on *Hampshire*, and she had not sunk but been sent to join the Russian fleet under another name. Louisa suffered silently, not really believing, but tormented with hope all the same that Jim would be one of the few survivors. But the list came out, and his name was not on it. And eventually came the official letter, declaring him lost at sea. By then Louisa had gone back to Wimbledon, to be with her aunt, who had taken to her bed with the shock of it.

Laura carried on her policing duties glumly, missing Louisa, and feeling more than ever that she was ready for a change.

Diana had had a week at home, and had gone back to London to stay with Beth again to do some final bits of shopping. The wedding day was suddenly close, and she was feeling nervous for the first time. It soothed her more to be in London than in Northcote, which only emphasised the difference between her old life and what would be the new. At home the news about Lord Kitchener occupied

214

every mind and conversation, to the exclusion of her wedding – even Nula talked about the Great Man while making a last-minute adjustment to her train.

She was alone at the flat one afternoon, while Beth was out visiting a friend, when Rupert arrived in a state of agitation. For a horrible moment she thought he had bad news about David or Jack – death was rather on her mind with Aunt Laura's friend Louisa losing her brother, and the newspapers full of the planned memorial service at St Paul's for Lord Kitchener. Her fears seemed justified when he drew her down to sit on the sofa with him, holding her hands too tightly and looking at her with agitation. 'It's too awful!' he said. 'It's Erskine! His appeal has been refused.'

It was so far from her fears it was almost bathetic, but she tried to find some sympathy. 'Oh dear. I'm sorry. Did he tell them he had moral objections to killing?'

'Of course he did. But they don't care. One of them asked what he would do if a German attacked his mother, and the only way to save her was to kill the German. When he said he still wouldn't kill the German, the fellow said he deserved to be shot.'

'How unkind,' Diana said.

'What a choice he's got before him!' Rupert cried. 'Either he'll have to join the Non-Combatant Corps, where they'll force him to do physical work beyond his strength, or they'll send him to prison where he'll get hard labour. Either way, he'll be worked to death like a wretched cab horse. And if he joins the Non-Combatant Corps, he might get sent to France anyway.'

'Perhaps he ought to give in and join up after all,' Diana said. 'He might not ever have to kill anyone. I mean, he'd be an officer, wouldn't he? Perhaps it would just never come up.'

'He doesn't really have objections,' Rupert said impatiently. 'He's just terrified of going to the Front, poor lamb – and, really, who wouldn't be? Oh, it's a wretched business alto-gether! I'd suggest he ran away, but he'd have to go abroad, and even if he could manage to get away, he'd never be able to come back and I'd never see him again.'

'You mean,' said Diana, digesting what he'd said, 'that he's just a plain coward?'

'Oh, don't look like that! We can't all be heroes. He can't help being afraid.'

'I expect most of the men at the Front are afraid, but they still do their duty.'

He withdrew his hands. 'Now don't lecture,' he said crossly. 'You're supposed to be my loving support when I'm upset.'

'I'll try to be,' Diana said, 'but I don't understand why you care so much about Erskine. He doesn't seem a very admirable character.'

'Well, I didn't choose him for his warlike qualities, dear,' Rupert said wryly. 'One can't help who one falls in love with. You ought to know that.'

'What do you mean?'

'You and Charles were an unlikely enough match,' said Rupert. 'Much more unlikely than Erskine and me, if it comes to it.'

'But you and Erskine – it's different, surely, with friends.'

'Now, don't play coy with me,' Rupert said, looking at her with arched eyebrows. 'I know you know about me and Erskine. That's why you're the only woman I can marry, as I've so often told you.'

'Know *what* about Erskine and you?' Diana pursued.

'Oh dear, don't be tiresome. I know you know, because of your aunt Laura – she told me you and she are very close, so you must be in on her secrets.'

Diana looked at him in bewilderment. 'What's Aunt Laura got to do with it?'

He stared back, doubt beginning to impinge on him. 'Your aunt Laura and her little friend Louisa. They're – like

216

me and Erskine. Louisa's her wife, and Erskine's mine. *Don't tell me you really don't know.*'

'I really don't know what you're talking about,' Diana said, growing impatient. 'How can Erskine be your *wife* when he's a man? I think you're trying to be horrid to me.' She stood up abruptly. Had he reverted to his insulting behaviour? Had his niceness all these months been only an act? Had he tricked her into agreeing to marry him, only to humiliate her? 'I don't know what's going on,' she said angrily, staring down at him, 'but if you *don't* want to marry me, I assure you I will release you right away. You don't have to insult me to make me do it.'

'*Insult* you?' Rupert cried. 'It's the farthest thing from my thoughts.' And then suddenly he was on his knees before her, clutching her hands, and, shockingly, there were tears in his eyes. 'Please, please, don't chuck me! Don't even think about it for a second. Oh, please – I can't lose you! Darling, beautiful Diana – you *must* marry me! Swear you will! Swear it.'

'You're hurting my hands,' Diana said, trying to pull away. It was horrible to see him like this. She would sooner he was arrogant than grovelling.

'I'm sorry,' he said, lessening his grip, but not releasing her. 'I never want to hurt you – you do believe me? I know I was horrid to you when I first met you, but I didn't know you then. It's different now. I *want* to marry you – I *have* to marry you. I'll make you happy, I swear it, only don't, *don't* leave me!'

He really was crying now. He let her go at last to put his hands over his face and, doubtfully, she touched his head, then stroked his hair. He nuzzled into her stomach and put his arms round her.

'Don't cry,' she said. 'Of course I'll marry you, if you want me to.'

'I *do*,' he exclaimed, muffled by her dress.

'Please get up,' she said, after a bit. 'Let me get you a brandy and soda, and we'll sit on the sofa and talk.'

The programme seemed to appeal to him. He unwound himself and got up, turned his back to her while he plied his handkerchief, and by the time she was back with a brandy and soda, he was sitting on the sofa, a little ruffled, but otherwise back to normal.

'I don't know what came over me,' he said cheerfully, downing half the drink. 'Wedding nerves, or something. I assure you I'm not usually a cry-baby. Please forgive me. I promise it will never happen again.'

'There's nothing to forgive,' she said, still puzzled. 'But what was all that about Erskine and my aunt Laura?'

'Nothing, nothing at all. Sheer nonsense. The babbling of a blinking idiot. It didn't mean anything. Please, if you have any pity, don't repeat what I said to a soul. Will you do that for me?'

'Of course I won't repeat it,' she said. Why would she repeat nonsense? 'But I wish I knew why you said those things.'

'I suppose I was just upset about Erskine losing his appeal, and had a sort of fit. I didn't mean any of it. Look here, I've behaved like a complete oaf, and I must make it up to you. Let's go and have a little supper at the Ritz, and afterwards if you like we can walk round to Park Place and see how the house is getting on. Would you like that?'

Diana did like it. He was on his best form for the rest of the evening, and she put the incident out of her mind. She had heard of wedding nerves, and though she had never heard of a man suffering from them, she supposed it must be possible, so she decided it was best to put it down to that. The wedding was too close now to cancel. And her reasons for accepting him hadn't changed. She could never fall in love again, but she felt she had a better chance of being happy with Rupert than with anyone else.

The next day he met her and Beth after shopping and took them to luncheon at Wroughton House with the earl and countess and sundry guests. In the taxi on the way there, he told them in a subdued voice that Erskine had decided submitting to conscription was the lesser of the evils open to him, and he would be off in two days' time to an initial training camp in Hampshire. 'And I suppose he'll go for officer training when he's finished the basic. So it will be the autumn at least before he has to go to France.'

And then he changed the subject and was lively, cheerful and extra charming for the rest of the day.

It *wasn't* much of a house, as he had said – just a narrow, dusty three-storeyed slice in an early-Victorian terrace. The furniture was shabby, the wallpaper rubbed and the carpets worn; in winter, Beattie guessed, it would be both cold and damp. But now, in summer, it was cool and dim, like a cave to retreat to from the midday sun. Most of all, it was private. No-one Beattie knew would ever be passing down the street to see her get out of a taxi and wonder why she was there.

Louis had a servant who took care of him, kept the house in moderate order, and left them food – cold suppers and picnic fare, but it was all they wanted. Waites was never there when Beattie was. He was, as Louis said, 'discretion itself'.

'Does he know about me, then?' Beattie asked.

'He knows *who* you are, but not your name. And he's been with me for eighteen years – he would never betray me.'

It was safe in the house, and if the rooms were poky and the furniture uncomfortable, it didn't matter. They didn't want to go out, even if they could have. What they mostly did was to make love, and talk. After love-making they would lie entwined together in the bed and their murmuring voices would rise and fall like the peacefulness of bees in a border.

They talked about the past, in Dublin – though the time they had been together had been short, it was precious, and they never tired of revisiting it. They talked of things that interested them, and of each other, as lovers do.

And they talked about their present occupations, though it was mostly Louis talking and Beattie listening. Being on the inside at Headquarters, he had information that mattered to her, with two sons at the Front. He told her that the Germans had made a surprise approach to the French to discuss terms for a peace. 'It's not widely known – the public mustn't be let in on it, of course,' he said. 'The Huns are bleeding the French white at Verdun, and *we* haven't made any progress against them since last autumn, so they must think they have the upper hand. If they negotiate now, they'll get more favourable terms. And, for exactly the same reason, we don't want to negotiate until we've given them a good thrashing.'

'The Big Push?' Beattie said.

'Exactly. The original plan was for a joint offensive in the autumn, with the French veterans steadying the new British troops. But the French have said they can't hold out until then. So it has to be this summer. And they're withdrawing more and more men to Verdun every day, so it looks as though it will be a mainly British action.'

'Do you know when?'

He hesitated a moment, then said, 'The end of the month. I daren't say more.'

She was lying with her head on his chest, tracing idle circles with her fingers on his skin. She said, 'Will that be an end of it?'

'Of the war? I'm afraid not. With so little help from the French, and largely untried troops, we can't roll up the Germans all at once. Haig is talking about victory next year. The object of the Picardy campaign is to weaken the Germans and position us for that. And to relieve the French at Verdun, of course. There'll be a bombardment before the battle, the heaviest barrage ever. And there'll be diversionary attacks. The plans are well made, and Haig's the steadiest hand since Wellington. The Germans will take a beating.'

'The end of the month,' she said. 'I suppose, then, you'll have to go?'

'You always knew I would,' he said. He stroked her hair. 'I told you that I would have to go back to France when the action started.'

She lifted her head to look at him. 'When?'

'I'll be leaving on the twenty-third,' he said.

'So little time,' she said.

'We must make the most of it, then.' He drew her closer to him, raising her face to kiss her lips. After a while, he said, 'Can I write to you?'

Not 'May I?' but 'Can I?' She thought about it. 'You could send letters to Nula. She could bring them to me.'

'I thought you said Nula would disapprove if she knew about us?'

'She would – she will. But she's loyal. She was the one who helped me – before.' She caught herself up in time.

'Helped you?'

'After you went, and I was so unhappy.'

'Oh, my darling, I hate to think of you suffering! But what could I do? I couldn't marry you – your father would never have entertained it for a second. I had no money, not even my salary. I had to play cards for money to pay my mess bills.'

'I didn't know.' She was faintly shocked. 'You were a gamester?'

'Oh, not that,' he said. 'I don't have my father's taint – to tell you the truth, I wouldn't care if I never saw another pack of cards in my life. But there was a set of senior officers at the Castle who liked to play whist for money, and I made up their tables. At whist, you see, a good player will always win in the long run, and I was a good player. So it wasn't really gaming, it was earning a living.'

'A precarious one.'

'I hated being the shabby junior hanging on their gilded coat-tails. But what else could I do? At least the army provided a job and a roof over my head. And the chance of something better in the future. But my only happiness was the time I spent with you, and the greatest grief of my life was leaving you. My one hope was that you wouldn't suffer as much as I did, that you would understand and get over it and make a life for yourself with someone else. And so you did. I can't tell you what a comfort it is to me to know that.'

She closed her eyes and forced herself to breathe slowly. He wanted to think she hadn't suffered as much as he did, and she had to let him. He didn't know about David, and she couldn't tell him.

'But I never loved anyone but you,' he went on, in a low voice.

'It's the same for me,' she said. She felt a pang of disloyalty. Edward had been good to her. But here, in Louis's arms, a different universe held sway. 'I've never – never stopped loving you.'

He turned over on his side, moving her so that he could see her face. 'We have two weeks left,' he said. 'And I'll come back on leave. I'll write to you. Promise you'll write back?'

'I promise.'

'It isn't everything,' he said, 'but it's something.'

She folded herself against him, pressed her face into his neck, revelling in the smell of his skin, more familiar to her than her own. After such long famine, for her it was everything.

Sadie was tired. It was a hot day – even Nailer had declined to accompany her, looking out from the deep shadow of the laurels when she called him that morning. She had been lungeing horses under the relentless sun, their hoofs beating up a dust from the dry ground that seemed to have coated her not only outside but inside, so that she could taste it and smell it. The hedges were full of the wild roses and honeysuckle of June, but she had dust in her nostrils. And now she had Rustington Hill up which to push the bicycle, which was not growing any better-tempered with age: it delighted in biting her ankles with its pedals, stubbing itself on stones, and if possible plunging down the drainage runnels that cut through the grass verge. These days, there was so much traffic on the road, it was safer to push the bicycle on the verge, in spite of the difficulties. Some of the army lorries were fast and careless.

When she was halfway up the hill, she stopped to rest a moment, and a motor-car slowed and stopped beside her, just as had happened on another occasion. This time, to her surprise, it was Mrs Cuthbert's small tourer, with its hood down, but the driver was the same: her heart jumped as she saw John Courcy behind the wheel.

'We seem to make a habit of this,' he said, proving he remembered too. 'Can I give you a lift?'

She didn't hesitate. She knew Mrs Cuthbert didn't mind a bicycle on the back seat. He lifted it in for her, then held the door open courteously for her to get in, as if she were a lady. 'No Nailer?' he asked.

'Too hot. He's spending the day in the shade.'

'Wise dog.' He went round and got in beside her. 'I expect you're wondering about the car. I got back on leave today, and went straight to Highclere, and when Mrs Cuthbert said you were cycling home, I borrowed her motor to see if I could catch you before you hit the hill. I'm sorry I was only half successful. And the first bit's the steepest.'

'I'm glad to be saved any of it, on a day like this,' she said, squinting up into the flawless sky.

An army lorry roared past, going too fast down the hill. Several soldiers looking out of the back shouted, 'Oy oy!' and whistled.

'Friends of yours?' Courcy asked.

'I don't know them,' she said. 'They seem to do that a lot, though – shout and whistle. I think they're just being friendly.'

He smiled at her innocence. Did she really not know? 'They do it whenever they see a pretty girl,' he said. 'Soldiers the world over.' She blushed a little and didn't say anything. He wasn't sure if the implied compliment pleased her or not, so he dropped it, and said, 'Are you in a hurry to get home? I thought of going and having some tea somewhere. Some nice little place with a garden. Seems a shame to waste the car and a lovely day.'

'I'd love that,' she said. 'I've been eating dust all day.'

'They won't miss you at home?'

'There's never anyone there, these days. David and Bobby are in France, Diana's in London, the boys are at school and then off with the Scouts. Father works late, and Mother – well, she's always busy with war work.'

'Then I shan't feel guilty about stealing you away,' he said. He turned the car across the road and drove back down the hill. 'I know a little place about three or four miles past Rustington. Village called Chartley. I've driven through it several times, and there's a café there I've always wanted to stop at.'

Down in the valley they swung across the river and up the other side, out into the deep green country. 'Mrs Cuthbert tells me your sister's getting married,' he said. 'To her late fiancé's brother.'

'Yes,' said Sadie.

'Do you think that's odd?' he asked.

She thought about it for a moment. Loyalty to Diana struggled with her desire to talk to Courcy, and talking to him would always require the truth. 'It *does* seem odd – a bit. To be going through all the same things again – the wedding and everything. Only it's better this time. She's more confident, and Lady Wroughton's got used to the idea. And Rupert's *here*, not at the Front. That's the biggest difference.'

Courcy forbore to probe any further. He suspected a girl used to being the local beauty would find life intolerable with all the men away at the Front, and would be glad to secure such an eligible match. But he didn't know Diana Hunter, and didn't want to belittle her, especially not to her sister. He knew Sadie was loyal – even to the little mongrel dog. It was one of her most endearing features.

'And you'll be a bridesmaid again?' he asked instead.

'Not so much *again*, as I wasn't really one before,' she said. 'I like the dress better this time. It's pale yellow, which suits me better than pink.'

'Describe it to me,' he said.

She looked sideways at him. 'You're not really interested in dresses. You're just humouring me.'

Diana wasn't the only one who had gained in confidence, he thought. 'You've changed quite a bit since I last saw you,' he said.

'Have I?'

'You've grown up at least two years in six months.'

'Everyone said I was young for my age before,' she said easily, 'so I expect I'm just catching up.'

She smiled, but didn't look at him, as if she was smiling to herself, which was intriguing. If she hadn't been such a straightforward person, he might almost have thought she'd learned to coquette.

She said, 'I have to supervise all those girls now, so I have to be serious and responsible.'

'It suits you,' he said. 'But don't change too much. Keep room for a little of the old Sadie.'

'I don't know who that is,' she said. 'I suppose I'm different on the outside. But inside I feel pretty much the same as before. I *think*.'

Incurably honest, and unselfconscious. No, she was not coquetting. He said, 'I think I knew that, really. That's the Sadie I like.'

They went on in silence after that, Sadie gazing around her at the countryside with innocent enjoyment, and John Courcy looking sidelong at her whenever he could. She intrigued him. She always had, but the change in her had made her even more interesting.

The café was a little thatched cottage whose garden rioted with traditional flowers, so much like a painting on a chocolate box it was almost absurd. At the back was a lawn where wrought-iron tables and chairs were set up. Only one was occupied, by an elderly motoring couple. Courcy led the way to a table on the opposite side, and ordered afternoon tea, and he and Sadie exchanged small-talk until it came.

'Gosh, it looks good,' she said. 'I'm starved.'

'So am I. Dig in!'

When the sandwiches and teacakes were gone and the second cups of tea drained, they slowed down and talked again.

'You've changed, too,' Sadie said.

'How so?' he asked.

'You look thinner. And . . .' She had to think for the words. 'As though you'd seen bad things.' He didn't reply. 'Is it the horses?'

'Yes, of course,' he said. 'Even though there've been no major battles, there are wounded and sick horses all the time. I dread to think what it will be like when the Big Push starts.'

'They're saying the end of the month – is that right?'

'As far as I know. The actual date's supposed to be a

secret, in case it gets back to the Germans. But when the artillery bombardment starts, they'll know anyway.'

'I hate it,' she said, 'that we're training all these horses to go out there and get hurt. Sometimes I wonder why I do it. But I suppose if I didn't, someone else would. At least *you*'re only doing them good.'

'What little I can. Some of the wounds are so terrible, there's no alternative but to shoot them. Some are breaking down under the strain of overwork. Then there are those suffering from what, I suppose, we would call shell-shock in humans. Their nerves are all in pieces. It's pitiful.'

'What can you do for them?'

'Very little. The facilities are often so primitive, there's not much we can do for any of them.' Then he seemed to make an effort to cheer up. 'But the army's building a big new horse hospital at Le Touquet, with all the latest equipment. It should be finished by the end of the month.'

'Will you be working there?'

'Yes – they've asked me to be second in command. I'll be made up to major.'

'Oh, but that's wonderful! Congratulations.'

'Thanks. I wish you could see it. You'd be so interested. There'll be a swimming-pool, for instance, to give them water therapy when they're convalescing. And wonderful operating theatres with tilting tables and slings and hoists – rather different from a table made of hay bales. Or a flat piece of grass – sometimes that's all we have.'

She saw his enthusiasm suddenly flag. The strain came back into his face, and he stirred his tea absently. 'You mustn't mind so much,' she said. 'Everything you do helps. If you weren't there, it would be so much worse for them.'

He looked at her. 'What troubles me most is that I care so much more about the horses than the men. There are men being killed and wounded all the time, but I haven't any compassion to spare for them. It makes me feel horribly guilty that what happens to the horses seems so much worse.'

'But it *is*,' she said. 'Because they don't understand. They trust us, and let us guide them, and then we put them where terrible things happen to them.' She paused a moment. 'And *still* they trust us,' she added quietly. 'That's the worst thing of all.'

He found he had reached across the table and taken her hand. 'You understand,' he said, with a shake of relief in his voice. Her eyes were bright, and her hand – hard-palmed and calloused, *not* a young lady's hand – pressed his in return. 'Thank God for you,' he said.

Feelings were too close to the surface. He released her hand, coughed, and said in a normal voice, 'Any more tea in that pot? I could do with another.'

She lifted it and gave it a swirl. 'Might get another cup out of it,' she said, in a voice matching his.

And they talked about Highclere until it was time to go.

CHAPTER FIFTEEN

As many as possible were being given leave before the Big Push, and David's coincided with the wedding, and with his birthday, which was on the day before. The family was staying in Kensington for the wedding, which was convenient as it meant David could stay there too (the influx of extra guests never upset the Palfrey household) and still be near the Oliphants.

Beattie's joy in seeing him again was so intense it was barely distinguishable from pain. At the wedding, she sat where she could continue to look at him while appearing to watch the ceremonials. How like Louis he was! The resemblance was astonishing. There seemed to be nothing of her in his looks, as if the power of love had burned away all other traces. She longed for Louis to see him, but knew it must not happen – the dangers for everyone were too great. But David would be like Louis in more than looks. It was fitting that he was a soldier – an officer. He would be a great one. She doubted he would remain in the army afterwards, but two or three years of war would provide as much opportunity for noble, heroic achievement as a whole career in peacetime.

The wedding. Yes, Diana looked beautiful. One would have expected nothing less. The diamonds suited her now, where perhaps she would have been too young for them a year ago. Rupert cut a fine figure in dress uniform. The

229

bridesmaids looked elegant and behaved perfectly. Beattie felt a moment of relief when the words 'I pronounce they be man and wife together' were spoken. Nothing had occurred to prevent it this time.

The wedding breakfast at Wroughton House. She was aware of food being put in front of her, but she was not aware of having eaten or drunk anything. Perhaps she had not. She supposed there had been conversation, but she remembered nothing of it. She was seated next to the earl, splendid in military full dress, but her eyes were for David in his khaki number twos, seated at a distant table, but to her standing out as though rimmed with light; his dark reddish hair, his hawk-like profile, his smile that could light a room.

Afterwards the guests mingled while the couple went to change. She found David again. He was standing with Sophy, but she found her corrosive jealousy of Sophy had gone, washed away by the joy of seeing her son. Sophy looked at David with big, adoring eyes, and that was fitting. The analytical part of her brain told her that he had risen in Sophy's estimation by association with this Society wedding. But she couldn't hate Sophy. No-one would have been good enough for David, and the child was harmless enough. They would make pretty babies. Above all, she was determined that David should never know the pain of loss she suffered. If he wanted Sophy, he must have her, and she would do all in her power to secure their happiness together.

Much later, after the couple had departed, the Hunter contingent retired to the Palfreys' house, where the celebrations went on until the early hours. Someone put on a gramophone record; the carpet was rolled back. She danced with David, resting her cheek against his shoulder, simply happy to be with him, to be touching him.

And now she was in bed, with Edward beside her, staring into the darkness and reliving her memories. She thought he was asleep, but after a while he said, 'It was a happy day, wasn't it? You were happy, I think?'

'Yes,' she said. She roused herself for him. 'Everything went very well.'

After a pause, he said, 'I'm glad David was able to be here.'

'Yes,' she said again. She could not trust herself to say more.

And after another long pause, he said, very quietly, 'I love you, Beattie.'

He said it as though he did not expect an answer; and in thinking what hers ought to be, she left it too long. To say anything now would sound insincere, so she said nothing.

'And that's it,' said Rupert.

He carefully eased his weight from Diana, and moved to her side. Diana appreciated the tact with which he had turned out all the lights, so that she had the comforting privacy of darkness in which to consider matters.

'It wasn't too bad, was it?' he said.

Diana wanted to say, *It was horrible!* But she didn't want to hurt his feelings. And it wasn't exactly that it was horrible, rather that it seemed so – *unecstatic*. Was that what all those poems and songs had been about, all that *literature*? So much writing and agonising and yearning about love, and it came down to *that*? How could God have arranged matters so awkwardly?

She had left it too long to answer him – not that she knew what to say. She knew that he was looking at her. She felt his breath on the side of her face. Now in the dark he reached out and gently touched her face. 'Don't cry,' he said. 'Please don't cry.'

'I'm not crying,' she said.

His fingers wiped tears from under her eyes. 'I'm sorry if I hurt you,' he said, 'but it's only because it's the first time. It won't hurt like that again, I promise.'

She had to say something. 'So now I'm going to have a baby?' she asked.

'We hope so,' he said. He sounded as if he was smiling. 'We may have to do it a few more times to be sure.'

'Oh,' she said.

'Come here, let me make you comfortable,' he said. He drew down her nightdress and straightened it, brushed the hair from her forehead with a kind hand, turned her on her side and settled her with her back to his front. 'Better?' he asked.

'Mm,' she said. It really was rather nice – comfortable. The warm pressure of his body all down her spine and his arms around her made her feel safe and cherished.

'This is your reward,' he said. 'Women always like this bit – being cuddled. And talking. Would you like to talk? What shall we do tomorrow?'

'I don't know,' she said. 'Anything you like.'

'All right, then. We'll go shopping first. I don't like that pink shantung of yours – the colour's vile and the shape's hideous. Everything about it's wrong. I've seen the most delicious little two-piece at Aldiss's in Bond Street. The jacket is sort of cape-like, with points at the front and such pretty tassels. I'll show it to you, and if you like it, we'll get it made for you at Bertil's. He can copy anything – he's a genius! We'll choose the material from his swatches. French crêpe or shantung. Pink, yes, but it has to be a more *bluey* shade – towards lavender – for your colouring.'

'It sounds nice,' she said sleepily.

'And then we'll go to the Wallace and look at the Watteaus and Bouchers, because there's always someone there, and I want to show off my pretty wife to everyone. You can wear the dove-grey tailor-made with that sea-green silk shirt. We're bound to find someone agreeable there to lunch with. I expect it will turn into a party – because, frankly, Lady Dene, everyone wants to look at you as much as I want them to! And in the evening we'll go to the Four Hundred or the Bon Anchois for dinner and have some dancing. And then . . .'

She was drifting to sleep on the gentle swell of his voice. Really, this was rather agreeable. And he was *very* sweet. It seemed as though being married would be easier than she had expected.

Laura had enjoyed the wedding. She'd had misgivings about the marriage – she was afraid Diana was rushing into it, not giving her broken heart time to heal. A lot of girls, seeing the men disappearing from their world, were dashing into marriage while there was still a chance. Two years of war must seem like an eternity when you were eighteen. She had met David's fiancée Sophy a few times, and thought she recognised the symptoms of impatience. Laura wagered that if Sophy could marry David at once, she would, whatever the practical disadvantages.

Well, Diana wouldn't have to face those, at least. Even if Rupert had to go to the Front at some point, she would have a house of her own and an income. Edward had confided in a relaxed moment what Diana's allowance from the cadet estate would be, and it was extremely generous. Rupert was handsome and popular, and if Laura had sometimes suspected something a little unwholesome about him, he seemed to have changed since he had started courting Diana. There seemed no reason they should not be happy together.

Diana had looked radiant – Laura had even seen surprised approval on the countess's face – and had behaved beautifully. The breakfast had been delicious and elegant, and there had been almost a superfluity of champagne. Her neighbour across the table had leaned forward and whispered, with a twinkling look, that it must have been Rupert's influence. The earl had a good cellar but only got the best out for his close cronies, and Lady Wroughton cared nothing for wine.

The neighbour was one of the large contingent of Wroughton 'cousins', a designation that covered a wide spread of relationship. Lady Agnes Daubeney was a duke's daughter, so the distance of her connection to the Wroughtons was mitigated by her social position. She had a large private income, and lived in London, alone except for a lady-companion who, as she explained to Laura when they met the next day for luncheon, 'never troubled' her.

'Papa almost had a fit when I told him what I wanted to do. I was twenty-five, yet he wouldn't countenance my living anywhere but in the family home unless I had a respectable older woman with me. Even wringing that concession out of him took six months. I had to make his life a misery at home, poor pet, so that in the end he thought getting rid of me was the lesser evil. He's got used to it now, but I think it still makes him a little uneasy, when he thinks about it.'

'What about your mother?'

'Oh, she gave up on me long ago. When I reached thirty without marrying, she knew I was a hopeless case.'

'Did you never want to?'

'I wouldn't have minded it if I'd found the right man, but I never did. What about you?'

'Much the same, I suppose. Except that I thought the right man didn't exist – the sort of man who would let me be *me*, and do what I wanted to do. I had no aversion to the married state in itself, and I would rather have liked some babies. But too much else seemed to come along with them – too much curtailment of freedom.'

'I know what you mean,' Lady Agnes sighed. She had already told Laura to call her Annie. They seemed to have become fast friends from that first whisper and complicit smile. Sometimes it was like that, Laura thought – the best times.

The lunch was Annie's idea. 'The day after a wedding

234

can seem so flat. Have luncheon with me, and we can cheer each other up.'

So they met in Selfridge's restaurant, and picked up the conversation, as old friends do, as though there had been no hiatus.

The talk came round to the war, and war work. Annie was on a great many committees, and was fascinated by Laura's more practical experience, first in driving Belgian refugees, and then in joining the Women Police Service.

'I'd have thought it was fascinating,' said Annie, 'but do I detect a note of discontent in your voice?'

'I am beginning to feel restless,' Laura admitted. 'It's rather limiting, you know. Most of the time we're dealing with lost children and confused mothers, or moving prostitutes along. The real police are glad to have us take the women off their hands – isn't it strange how much men hate tears? – but they don't really want us on the streets with them. I thought it would set me free, but it's just backed me into a different corner.'

'I know exactly what you mean. I am so tired of committees! Half the women on them seem only to want an excuse to get out of their own houses and chat and drink tea in someone else's! Oh,' she corrected herself, 'I'm being unfair. Most of them are really dedicated, and it's impossible to overestimate the good they do. But we never really see the results of our work.' She looked at Laura almost speculatively. 'You said you're ready for a change?'

'Have you something in mind?'

Annie leaned forward. 'I've bought an ambulance,' she said. 'Well, it wasn't an ambulance when I bought it. I've had to have it converted, but it's ready now, and all I have to do is assemble the equipment and the staff, and then – off to France!'

'France?' Laura exclaimed. It was a bolder step than any she'd contemplated.

Annie laughed with sheer excitement. She was a tall woman with a pleasant, lightly freckled face, smooth brown hair and hazel eyes. She must have been approaching forty, but when she laughed like that, she looked young and almost impish. 'There's a terrible shortage of army ambulances. Even adding in the FANY, there simply isn't enough transport to get the men back to the hospitals. I know several people who have taken a private one over, and I'm going to do the same. I've got a young doctor, Elsie Murray, who's longing to go. She's with the Women's Hospital Corps at their hospital in Endell Street – have you heard of it?'

'It was started up by Louisa Garrett Anderson, wasn't it?'

'Yes, and it's completely staffed and administered by women. I'm acquainted with Louisa, and she's happy for Elsie to go – in fact, it was she who introduced her to me. I've got another young woman, Flora Hazlitt, who's been nursing in a VAD hospital, and I've done first-aid training. What we don't have is a driver. But you can drive. Will you join us?'

Laura made herself consider, rather than simply jump in. 'A team of four?'

'Yes, we think that will be enough. The ambulance will carry four stretchers and two walking wounded. Conditions may be primitive – we may have to sleep in the ambulance at times. And it may be dangerous. We'll be going up close to the line. There'll be shelling, perhaps aeroplanes dropping bombs. It won't be for the faint-hearted.'

'Faint-hearted I'm not,' Laura said, 'and I'm not afraid of primitive conditions. And I've done first aid – it was part of the police training. Also, when I did my driving course, I learned how to do simple repairs and change a tyre.'

'Better and better,' said Annie. 'I was worried about how we'd manage if Bessie broke down.'

'Bessie?'

236

'That's what I've called the ambulance. After my first horse, a dear, good brown mare – not a great deal of speed, but awfully willing.'

'Good name. Well, if we do break down and I can't fix it, there are bound to be soldiers about who can help.'

'Does that mean you'll come?'

'I'll come.' Laura grinned. 'You couldn't keep me away. There's just one thing – my friend Louisa Cotton. She and I joined the Women Police together, and I'd like to ask her to come as well. We did the same driving course, and a second driver could be useful, supposing I got hurt, or ill.'

Annie thought for a moment. 'You're right about that. I'm sure we could work with five instead of four. Yes, do ask her.'

'By the way, who's putting up the money for this?'

'Me mostly. Elsie and Flora don't come from wealthy backgrounds, but I've wheedled donations out of some of my friends.'

'Well, I have a decent income, and I'm happy to help,' said Laura. 'It will be wonderful to feel one's actively helping, that one's money is doing a useful job.'

'I couldn't possibly,' said Louisa. 'I can't leave Aunty. She's much too frail. I can't leave her alone, when Jim—' She swallowed. 'It was a terrible shock to her. I don't know if she'll ever get over it.'

She looked to Laura somehow diminished, as though some of her substance had rubbed away. She was pale from being indoors, and the suburban villa, full of overstuffed furniture and quietly ticking clocks, had the air of closing round her, like a tomb. It was a place where nothing could ever happen, voices were never raised, and expectations were so low that they were never disappointed. Laura didn't want to leave her there. She thought she might simply fade into transparency, like an ant's discarded wings.

'Couldn't you get her a nurse, or a companion? I really want you to come. You must *want* to come?'

'I don't,' said Louisa. 'I think you're quite mad. Living in squalor, eating bad food, being dirty all the time – where's the pleasure in that?'

'This isn't like you,' Laura said, 'worrying about home comforts.'

'And have you thought how dangerous it would be?'

'It's dangerous for the soldiers.'

'They have to be there. You don't. It's not just the bombs and shells, either, though God knows that ought to be enough. But soldiers are not all saints. What if one tried to rape you?'

'I can take care of myself. I know ju-jitsu.'

'It wouldn't help you if he had a gun. If there were several of them with guns.' Louisa got up and walked over to the window. 'What if they were Germans?'

Laura got the impression that a slow dust was falling through the air, a dust of centuries, quietly covering her up. She said, 'You can't worry about everything that might happen, or you'd never do anything.'

'I think,' Louisa went on, still with her back turned, 'that you've been mesmerised by this Lady Agnes person. For some reason you feel you have to go along with her, or you *want* to go along with her, whatever she says.' She turned back, and her look was grim. 'Well, if that's what you want, good luck to you. Go off with her to France, leave me behind. I just hope you don't regret it.'

Laura tilted her head, puzzled. 'Lou, why are you being like this?'

'I'm not being like anything. I don't want to go to France, that's all. You do as you like.' There was a thump on the ceiling from the floor above. 'That's Aunty. I have to go to her,' she said. 'Can you see yourself out?'

Laura walked back to the Underground station, trying to

puzzle it out. Why had Louisa been so cold? Could it be jealousy? Did she feel Laura had been neglecting her since she went back to Wimbledon? Was it a symptom of grief over Jim? Was it dog-in-the-manger, resenting Laura's greater freedom?

Laura hoped that, whatever her circumstances, she would have been happy for Louisa to do something she really wanted to. She was sorry, and disappointed in her friend. But it wouldn't change her mind. She was going to France. This might be the greatest adventure life would ever offer her, and she wasn't going to turn it down.

'I suppose,' said Edward, 'there's nothing I can say to change your mind?'

'How well you know me,' said Laura. 'Now, dear Edward, be glad for me. Look on the bright side – this may cure my itch for adventure for good.'

'I somehow doubt that. But as I can't stop you—'

'You can hinder me,' Laura said. 'I want to realise some capital.'

Edward raised an eyebrow. 'I thought Lady Agnes was paying for everything.'

'Not quite everything. I have to buy my own kit and pay for my food and keep. And I've told her I would like to make a contribution towards the medical supplies.'

'You ought to have some cash available, too, in case of emergencies,' Edward said. 'I can realise some of your securities and make the money available through a French bank. How long will you be over there?'

'I have absolutely no idea,' Laura said, 'but let's plan on a year, shall we?'

They talked about finance for a while, and then Edward said, 'There's one thing I'd like you to do before you go. I'll arrange it – you can call it my present to you, my contribution to your crazy scheme.'

239

'You don't think it's crazy,' she said, studying him. 'You half wish you were going yourself.' He shook his head, smiling, but he didn't deny it. 'So what do you want me to do?'

'Take a lesson in shooting. There's a private gallery in St James's – they don't usually teach women, but I can arrange it. I'd like you at least to know how to load and fire a pistol and a rifle – just as a precaution.'

'Edward! How advanced of you!'

'Don't joke. You're going into a war zone,' he said seriously. 'God forbid you should stumble into the enemy, but if you did—'

'Knowing how to shoot won't help me, without a gun.'

'That's the other part of my gift to you. I'll buy you a suitable small rifle. Just having it may be enough to drive off trouble – you might never have to use it. And it will make me feel better.'

She was touched, and went to kiss his cheek. 'Dear Edward. There never was a better brother. And I promise I will be careful over there. I'm not going with the express intent of courting danger. I just want to *help*.'

'I know,' he said. 'And, while we're on the subject, there never was a better sister.'

Bobby's leave overlapped only one day with David's. The brothers sat up late on that evening and talked as only men who had been at the Front could do. It did them both good. With the rest of the family, Bobby's way was to be cheery and devil-may-care, David's to be grave and economical with words. To be able to talk freely relieved some of the pressure inside them.

David departed to catch the train to London, where the Oliphants would have the privilege of seeing him off from Victoria. The morning after that, Bobby was down so early that only Sadie was there, and the coffee pot hadn't yet come in.

'I thought you'd be staying late in bed, while you could,' she said.

'So did I. But I've got used to getting up early,' he said. 'We have to go out on dawn patrols, and I've developed a sort of instinct for when dawn's coming. I can't seem to switch it off.'

Sadie was inspecting her brother. His face was tanned and his mouse-brown hair, cut very short, was sun-bleached at the front. His smile was the familiar old Bobby smile, but she saw that he had grown up. He had been twenty in February, but he looked more like twenty-five to her. The roundness of his cheeks had flattened; his neck was muscled; his shoulders were stronger. It was not difficult to imagine him behind the controls of an aeroplane: his blue eyes already had that long focus. 'You've changed,' she said.

'You have too,' he replied. 'You were just my horse-mad little sister at Christmas. Now . . .' He waved a hand over her.

'I'm a woman,' she said gravely.

For some reason, it sounded very funny the way it came out, and they both burst into giggles, which broke the slight ice they had discovered between them

Lilian came in with the coffee pot and gave Bobby a shy, adoring look. 'Breakfast will be ten minutes,' she whispered. 'Cook didn't know you were down.'

'No hurry,' Bobby said. 'A lot's changed,' he said, when she'd gone out. 'A new maid, for a start. What happened to Ethel?'

'She left. I don't know where she went. She was different after that Zeppelin bomb.'

'I'm not surprised.'

'I thought she might have gone to work at the munitions filling factory, but I haven't seen her around anywhere. That's another thing that's changed – the factory at Hendorp. A lot of girls have left domestic service and gone to work there, because the wages are so high. Mrs Fitzgerald gets incensed about it. She thinks all girls do immoral things as soon as they live in lodgings instead of respectable people's houses. And now that Darvell's is going to make shell casings, the filling factory's going to be expanded. They're saying there's eighty more buildings already at some stage of construction, and there'll be three hundred by Christmas. And you see the munitionettes waiting at the bus stops, and going into the shops. Some of them,' she added with wide eyes, 'wear trousers *even when they're not working*.'

He laughed. 'That was Mrs Fitz again, wasn't it? You've been wearing trousers for years.'

'Jodhpurs and riding breeches are different. Although she never approved of those either. She thought females ought to ride side-saddle and that was that. But you can't school a horse for the army riding side-saddle.'

'I don't know if I've mentioned how proud I am of you,' Bobby said. 'Your war work is really important.'

She shrugged it off. 'I love horses, so it isn't hard for me.'

'I love flying, so it isn't hard for me, either.'

'Tell me about what you do.'

'You really want to know?'

'I really do.'

'Well, the two main jobs are reconnaissance and artillery spotting. They're tremendously important, but of course the Germans want to do exactly the same thing, and they want to stop us doing it, and we want to stop them doing it. Which is where the fighters come in. You see, nearly all the service aircraft – the ones doing the photographing and spotting – are BE2cs. They're marvellously steady buses. They *want* to fly level and straight – so much so that they'll self-correct if you don't have your hands on the controls. They literally fly themselves, and since the pilot is the one who has to take the photographs, that's a very useful trait.'

'I'm sensing there's a "but" on its way.'

'The "but" is that it's hard to make them do anything *but* fly level and straight, so you can't manoeuvre quickly. And they're very slow. Which means they fall easy prey to the German fighters.'

'Can't they defend themselves?'

'Not easily – not against Fokkers. The Fokkers have interrupter gear – that means they can fire straight ahead through the propellor. So the pilot can aim the whole aeroplane at the target and just stick his thumb on the firing button. In a BE the observer has a machine-gun, but his field of fire is very small. He can't fire forward because of the propellor, and he can't fire backwards because of the planes. Last year the Fokkers had it all their own way. They downed so many of our buses, they're calling it the Fokker Scourge.'

'But why don't you have interrupter gear?' Sadie demanded, indignant on his behalf.

'Ask the government that – I can't tell you! We're told they're developing it, but there's no knowing when it will come. It takes a long time to design an aeroplane, build the prototype, test it, and start manufacturing it. I don't know why – the Germans seem to manage it quickly enough.'

Ada and Lilian came in with the trays. 'Cook's done you kidneys,' Ada told Bobby. 'I hope you're hungry. She'll be ever so upset if you don't eat 'em.'

'Don't worry about that. I could eat a horse – sorry, Sadie!'

When the maids had left, Bobby went to inspect the dishes. 'Kidneys, bacon, sausages – and what's this? Tomatoes? Good old Munt! I love a grilled tomato. Come on, Sadie, or I'll eat the lot.'

Back at the table, Sadie dabbed mustard on the edge of her plate, and resumed. 'Go on about what you do.'

He obliged. 'We go out on escort duty – usually three of us, escorting up to three service aircraft – and if the

Fokkers try to attack, we drive 'em off, and down them if we can.'

'But if you can't fire through the propellor like they do—'

'Ah, we have a new secret weapon,' Bobby said. 'The DH2. It's a pusher, you see. That means—'

'That the engine's behind. Goodness, I know *that.*'

'Clever, aren't you? All right, then – it's the most comical-looking machine, but it does the job. It's a single-seater, and the nacelle is slung well forward of the planes, so it's got a clear field of fire. The gun's mounted on a swivel, but in fact it's better to fix it to fire straight ahead, rather than try to manoeuvre the aeroplane and aim at the same time. It means we can point the old bus at the target and shoot, just like the Germans do. And here's the thing – once you learn how to handle it, it's a much better flyer than the Fokker. All right, it's slower, but it'll do eighty-five in level flight, which is pretty good, and it can turn like the dickens. You can out-manoeuvre the Hun every time.'

'You said, "when you learn how to handle it",' Sadie queried.

'Well, it has a rotary engine, which gives it tremendous torque in a turn, and if you don't have light hands, you can easily go into a spin. A lot of chaps crash when they first try them.'

'But not you?'

'Not me,' Bobby said, with a grin. 'I'm the golden boy. Just as you can ride any horse, I can fly any aeroplane. You just get a feeling for it – don't you think?'

'I know what you mean,' said Sadie. She had never doubted she could ride any horse she got astride. 'Have you shot down lots of Germans, then?'

'Oh, one or two,' he said modestly. 'Our boss, Boom Trenchard, has given the order that we're never to leave a Jerry unmolested, so it's what we do every day.'

'Tell me one,' Sadie begged.

'All right, just one. I don't want to be a bore. I was escorting a BE2c on a reconnaissance mission over the line, flying along at about nine thousand feet, when a Fokker came at me from above and behind. He was shooting from about five hundred feet above me, and one of the bullets went through my top plane, which made me mad. So I did an upward spiral to spoil his aim, and when I was about a hundred feet below him, I pulled the nose right up and climbed straight at him, firing my gun into his belly. The old bus didn't like it much – you can't climb like that without stalling – and the engine started to miss, but I held on, emptied half a drum into Jerry, and managed to reach his height. Then I twisted and turned about until I got behind him, right on his tail, about two lengths away, and I put the rest of the first drum into him. I was trying to change drums when he started flying erratically, with smoke pouring out of him, so I knew I must have hit him badly. The next thing he side-slipped about five hundred feet. The side-slip turned into a nose dive, and down he went. Bye-bye, Jerry. So I picked up the BE2c again and went on with the escort.'

Sadie sighed with satisfaction. 'You've got to tell the boys your stories. They'll be mad for them.'

'I already have,' Bobby said. 'You don't think we were really playing cricket yesterday when we went up to the common? William wants to join the Corps as soon as he's old enough. Peter was more interested in gory tales about crashes. Why are little boys such ghouls?'

'You won't crash, will you?' Sadie said, knowing it was a foolish question.

But he smiled reassuringly. 'It's the novices who come to grief. The more flying hours you have, the less likely you are to get into trouble. It's funny,' he reflected, 'it seems like only yesterday I was hanging around the sheds at Shoreham, longing to get up in an old Longhorn. Now I'm regarded as one of the seniors. When the new cadets come in, they gaze at me as if I was the oracle, and I have to pass on my wisdom and helpful tips.' He reflected a moment. 'Like yesterday, and at the same time like years ago. It's as if all I've ever done is what I do now.'

'Home doesn't completely seem real to you, does it?' she said.

'No,' he said. 'All the time I'm seeing the patchwork of France and the zigzags of the trenches below, and the distant dots of approaching HA's. And hearing the wind singing in the wires, and seeing the wisps of cloud whipping past. I miss the sky. I miss it all the time.' He paused. His focus changed, and he smiled at her. 'How did you know? You're a clever girl,' he said.

'Woman,' she corrected, and after a second they both started laughing again.

My dear Antonia,

I'm sorry that I didn't have time to see you while I was on leave, but with my sister's wedding – oh, what a grand affair! I'll have to wait until I do see you to tell you all about it. I couldn't do it justice on paper. Suffice to say, it feels very odd to have a sister who is Lady Dene and will be a countess one day. I feel it ought to change me, this contact with the *haut monde*. But twenty-four hours back here and nothing but this seems real at all. I took a working party into the trenches yesterday, zigzagging up the communication trench for a mile and a half or more. At this time of year it is a thing of beauty – on either side, the piled earth has cloaked itself with fresh thick grass, bunched white daisies and blood-red poppies, and this wonderful garden is colonised by bees and butterflies and all manner of flying insects. Through this corridor of beauty

246

we make our way into the line, and back to rest for a short spell of peace. And through the daisies and poppies are carried the wounded, their white bandages splashed with scarlet.

We are preparing now for the Big Push, and if success depends on planning, it will be the greatest success. No detail is left to chance. We have moved into our attack area, and I am busy ensuring all my men have the right equipment for the battle itself. The list is long – besides the normal equipment and rifle, each man will have to carry two days' rations, a bomb, a pick or shovel, an Ayston fan (for clearing gas out of the dugouts), Verey lights, flags, and a triangular piece of tin to be fixed on the back to show the position of our advanced line to aeroplanes when the men lie down. We have rehearsed the attack until everyone knows his part. We've even studied clay models of the area so as to have an idea of the terrain.

We are all exhilarated that the moment is coming, and confident that this time we will break through, and hurt the enemy so badly the end will be brought within touching distance. I feel proud and honoured to be part of the generation that is given the chance to do this for our country. Our fathers were never so blessed, and our sons will not be. This is the noblest passage in our national life, and I am humbly grateful to be at the beating heart of it. I won't have time to write again before we go into battle, but I will send you a letter when it's all over. Pray for our victory.

Yours in friendship
David

CHAPTER SIXTEEN

He was gone. They had said their tender farewells at the house, before walking together to the main road, where he put her into the first taxi, and waited for another for himself. Her last sight of him was through the tiny rear window: with his back to her as he looked down the road for a taxi, he was just another figure in anonymous khaki. She realised then the full force of the word 'uniform'.

She didn't want to go home, but his house was no haven any more, just a drab terraced cottage smelling of dust. She felt lost, undirected, like a loose feather picked up by the wind. She considered alternatives: she could call on Beth, go to the Palfreys' house and visit Sonia. She could – extraordinary thought – go to a news cinema. She had never been to a picture palace alone. But the newsreels would be all about the war, and she didn't want to think about that now. She could call on Diana – yes, that was better. She rapped on the glass, and when the cabbie opened it, gave the change of destination. He brightened, no doubt anticipating a better tip from a Wroughton House fare than a Baker Street fare.

It was strange to say, 'Mrs Hunter for Lady Dene,' to the elderly manservant who opened the door. He admitted her at once, and showed her into a small sitting-room on the first floor. She waited only five minutes before Diana came in, looking lovely in a dress of apple-green linen. There was about her already an extra polish that came, Beattie guessed, from having a good ladies' maid.

'How lovely to see you!' she cried. 'But I'm just about to go out. I wish I'd known you were coming.'

'I was just passing, and thought I'd drop in,' Beattie said vaguely.

'Just passing?' Diana said. 'Where were you going, then?'

It was too much of an effort to think of a lie. Beattie left the question unanswered and said, 'How are you, darling? You look well. Are you happy?'

'Oh, yes,' Diana said at once. 'Rupert's busy at the War Office, but we still have our evenings together. I know how lucky that makes me. And in the daytime there's so much to do – I have more invitations than I can accept.'

'That's good,' said Beattie.

Diana glanced at the little French clock on the mantel-piece. 'Oh dear, the taxi will be here for me any moment. I wish we had time to talk.'

'It's all right,' Beattie said. 'I only dropped in on a whim to see how you were getting on. I'm glad you're happy.'

Diana looked at her intently for a moment, then said, 'Mummy, can I ask you something?'

The appeal touched her. Beattie said, 'Of course – anything.'

Diana bit her lip, searching for words. 'You see, I find—' she began, then tried again. 'I think a lot about Charles. Do you think – is that being disloyal to Rupert?'

Beattie felt all the irony of such a question to her. What to say? But she must ease her daughter's path if she could. 'You miss him?'

'Yes – no – I don't know. It's just . . . being Lady Dene,' she looked shy as she said the name, 'it was always Charles's name.'

'I think it's natural that you think about him sometimes,' Beattie said. 'That will pass as time goes on. But it's best that you try to control your thoughts.'

'*Can* you control thoughts?'

'With practice. If Charles comes into your mind, think of something you like particularly about Rupert, or something nice he's done for you.'

'So you *do* think it's wrong?'

'Not wrong – but perhaps inadvisable.'

Diana nodded slowly. 'I see. Well, I'll try.' She let out a shaky sigh. 'I'm glad you called in. I needed to ask you. I – I miss home, you know.'

'There's no need to. You can visit any time. But I expect when you get your own home – instead of living in someone else's like this – you'll never want to leave it.'

The door opened and a smart lady's maid stepped in. 'The taxi, my lady,' she said.

My lady, Beattie thought.

'I have to go,' said Diana.

'It's all right,' said Beattie, 'so have I.'

As she settled herself in the train at Baker Street, her thoughts went back to Diana's question. Can you control thoughts? Yes, she had had a lot of practice in controlling hers, and her face. She had trained herself to give nothing away, to maintain a serene look at all times, no matter what went on inside. And over the years, the pretence had become a reality. It would be easier for Diana, she thought. Charles was dead, irrevocably gone. For Beattie, the first few years had contained, like a thorn deep in the flesh, the thought that he might come back. It was only when she had truly accepted that she would never see him again that the thorn had ceased tormenting her.

Apply your own nostrum to yourself, Beatrice Eugenie Cazalet! Think of something nice about Edward: but everything was nice about Edward. Think of something nice he had done: he was always doing nice things for her. Perhaps he'd been less at home lately, because of the war, less attentive. He hadn't brought her flowers in a long time. But the other day he had said, 'You look tired. Let me brush your hair for you.' He had learned once, long ago, from Nula, that having her hair brushed soothed her. She didn't think it did any more, but he offered because he wanted to be kind to her.

Edward was everything a husband should be, and she was very lucky. He was everything a man should be – except that he wasn't Louis.

She wanted to put her face into her hands in a mixture of shame, anguish and despair, but she had trained herself never to show any emotion. She sat straight, looking out of the window, and none of her fellow passengers would have known that the respectable middle-aged lady in the corner seat was a cauldron of passions, longings and unshriven sins.

The Great Bombardment had started, and the newspapers were full of it. 'Now we'll give Jerry what-for!' Cook exclaimed in satisfaction. 'Serve him right, the dirty blighter!'

Lilian, setting down the teapot, made round eyes. She had never heard Cook use strong language before. 'My dad says—'

Cook had no intention of letting Lilian become a second Ethel, full of opinions. 'Never mind what your dad says, go and tell Mr Munt that lunch is on the table.' Lilian scuttled away. 'Go on reading,' she said to Ada, who was patiently waiting with her finger against the place where she had stopped.

It was an eye-witness account in the *Daily Mirror*. '"The concentration of artillery is literally appalling,"' she read laboriously, '"every species of weapon, from the gigantic fifteen-inch howitzer to the quick-rattling Stokes trench mortar, pouring thunderous avalanches upon the enemy positions."'

'Coo!' said Ginger, appreciatively. 'They say it's three times more'n what they chucked at Jerry at Loos. Thundering avalanches! Wish I could see it.'

'Mr Meyer said this morning that the Huns'll probably surrender,' Emily said, bringing in the plate of bread and butter. Con Meyer, the bread man, was the source of all wisdom to her. 'He says they can't stand bein' shelled.'

'Them as dishes it out 'as to take it,' Ginger pronounced.

'Am I reading this out or not?' Ada asked.

'What jam shall I bring?' Emily asked Cook at the same moment.

'The gooseberry, of course. Same as we had yesterday.'

'Ah, no, I don't like gooseberry. Can't we have something else?'

'If you don't like gooseberry you don't have to have it,' Cook told her. 'You can have your bread plain. I'm keeping that last blackcurrant for the master, and the strawberry's only for upstairs. Go on, Ada, read us some more.'

Ada obliged. '"This morning I stood upon the brow of a ridge, overlooking the much 'strafed' town of Albert. I do not think I exaggerate in the least when I state that the shell bursts often reached five hundred in one minute along the length of front commanded from the vantage-point upon which I stood. As far as I can gather, the German batteries made virtually no reply to this opening bombardment."'

Lilian hurried back in with Munt behind her. 'What'd I miss?' she asked.

'I'm not reading it again,' said Ada. 'This bloke uses too many long words. He says the Germans aren't firing back, I think.'

'Saving their shells,' said Munt. 'Waiting till there's something to fire at.'

'What do you know about it?' Cook said impatiently.

'My Len says the bombardment's to cut the German wire

and break down their defences, then our boys'll just walk through.'

'We'll see,' said Munt. 'Didn't walk through at Loos, did they?'

'This'n's three times more'n what they had at Loos,' Ginger informed him. 'The Jerries won't know what hit 'em!'

'And to think,' Ada added, 'that some of those shells might've been made in our own factory at Hendorp. Makes you feel proud, doesn't it?'

Emily piped up: 'Mr Meyer says one of his lady customers knows someone who lives in Kent, and they can *hear* the guns, all the way from over France. My God, that must be loud!'

'No need to blaspheme,' Cook said automatically. 'I wonder if my sister in Folkestone can hear 'em? I must ask her when I write next.'

'France is only twenty mile across the Channel,' Munt said, taking his usual seat. 'That's no distance. You can hear thunder twenty mile away, can't you?' He rolled his eyes at the ignorance of women, and lifted two slices of bread onto his plate. 'Twenty mile o' water, that's all 'at keeps the Kaiser from settin' up house at But'nam Palace. You remember that. If the Jerries took the Channel ports, it'd be all over.'

'Well, they're not going to,' Cook snapped. 'We don't want none of that sort of talk in this house.'

Munt said those things only to provoke. He knew the BEF would prevail over the slack-twisted foreigners – though it'd be a longer job than these daft women supposed. He changed the subject. 'Gooseberry jam *again*? I don't know why I bothers growing soft fruit when all I get given is gooseberry.'

'You can have your bread plain if you don't like it,' Emily advised him.

Cook saw Munt about to explode at such cheek, and said hastily, 'Read us some more, Ada. Emily, pour the tea.'

On the 26th and 27th of June, there were violent summer storms in France, and in the early hours of the 28th it was still raining heavily. Such a quantity of rain had fallen that there were lakes of standing water, and the ground everywhere was sodden. By mid-morning the sun was shining again, but it would take time for everything to dry out. Word came down from Headquarters that the attack would be delayed by forty-eight hours. Instead of the 29th of June, as planned, it would go in on the 1st of July.

It meant a huge amount of reorganising. Two hundred battalions and their support units had already been got into position. The first wave, uncomfortably settled in the front-line trenches, had to be marched out, the second wave moved back to make room for them; new orders had to be drawn up, and the artillery ordered to keep firing for another two days. Meanwhile, night raids had to be continued so that the Germans would not suspect anything unusual was afoot.

Back at their new position in the reserve trenches, life was Spartan. All their personal effects had been packed up and sent back, so they were squatting on the ground and eating basic rations. Everything had been completed for the off – equipment issued and checked, pay books made up, letters home written and sealed, will forms, for those who wanted them, filled in and filed. The men had been keyed up to a peak of readiness, and somehow they had to be got through two days of anticlimax. But it was the new Kitchener units who were worst off in that respect. David and most of his men had already been through battle, and regarded themselves as old hands. They adopted whatever poses of relaxation they could manage in the space, and smoked, and drank tea, and waited with blank minds. A soldier's life,

David had learned, consisted of periods of intense activity interrupting long stretches of boredom. He read Sophy's latest letter a seventh time, then on a whim left his lieutenants in charge and went along the line to find Jumbo, who might have something to eat about him (he had never known Jumbo not to have a slab of chocolate somewhere about his person), and to whom at least he could talk about Sophy.

The rain made for bad flying conditions, even after it stopped, for when the sun started to evaporate the standing water, it created layers of steam, like low clouds, and a general murkiness that killed the 'lift' in the air. Bobby's squadron was out on dawn patrol each day, but it was too misty to see much of what was going on on the ground. The mist lay like continuous cloud, grey-white, the surface trembling and rippling with the concussion of the guns firing beneath it. At least they had the skies to themselves at that early hour. Later, when the mist cleared, the HAs – their shorthand for hostile aircraft – would emerge, and the game would become lively again.

At four a.m. on the 1st of July, there was a little patchy drizzle here and there, but by six thirty it had stopped and the sky was a fine, cloudless blue, with a light south-westerly wind and the promise of a hot day. The barrage was thundering below. It would intensify at seven twenty, and then at seven thirty it would cease and the men in the first wave would go over the top. The job of the flyers would be to make sure no HAs got the chance to harass the men on the ground; and there would be reconnaissance flights – more vital than ever, of course – and bombing raids, targeting ammunition dumps, stations and railways, troop trains, and any large bodies of reserves marching up.

There was the danger of Archie – anti-aircraft fire – and of being attacked by HAs, but that was all part of the fun. There were ways of avoiding Archie, provided you kept your wits about you. There was a lag of about fifteen seconds between seeing the muzzle flash and the shot reaching you, so as long as you made a quick change of course after about ten seconds, you had the satisfaction of seeing the missile whistle through the spot where you would have been, and of imagining the frustration of the gun crews below.

As for the HAs – the Fokkers and Albatroses and such – that was what the game was all about! It was the most exhilarating thing in the world to dodge and twist away from the Hun who believed he had you cold, and re-emerge on his tail to give him a blast and, one hoped, watch him spin down to the unwelcoming ground. Their boss, Officer Commanding the RFC in France, Brigadier General 'Boom' Trenchard, was a snorting warhorse if ever there was one, and had issued the simple order ATTACK EVERYTHING. It was extremely satisfying.

'I'm so glad I'm not one of the Poor Bloody Infantry down below,' he said to Farringdon that morning, as they hurried through first light towards their DH2s.

'Every day they must wake up and think, "This is Hell, nor am I out of it."' said Farringdon. 'I tell you, if I couldn't fly, I wouldn't touch this war with a bargepole.'

'The Old Man says we'll be doing some bombing raids this afternoon,' said Bobby. 'Lay a few eggs on Jerry's head.'

'Good-oh! I like seeing 'em go up. Especially if you hit an ammo store.'

There was still an hour before the first attack went in. When Bobby's patrol had made their height, they could see the landscape below, torn by so many shells – thousands of them – that it was impossible to tell which shot had been fired from which battery. The air trembled with the concussion.

Bobby was at the rear of the patrol when he saw an HA trying to sneak back across the line behind him: probably a reconnaissance flight keen to get back with information.

Bobby peeled off and attacked, firing half a drum at about 150 yards, but the aircraft dived and hurried eastwards towards Bapaume.

Bobby was following, when he saw two German fighters coming west from the same direction. The rest of his patrol was some distance ahead of him now, so it was up to him. He turned and dived at the rearmost machine, firing the rest of the drum at him. He saw the observer slump over and, with the excitement of the chase tingling in all his nerves, he broke off and spiralled upwards to make some height while he quickly changed drums. Then he went after the other.

With the speed of his dive he was able to come up behind him, and fired off half a drum from close range. He saw a piece of the tail stabiliser disappear in a shower of debris, and at the same moment the machine side-slipped and went spinning downwards out of control, to crash on the ground far below. Bobby was leaning out watching when a hail of bullets whistled past him, one of them ricocheting off a propellor blade with a ting and a whine, while several small holes appeared in the left upper plane. A third aircraft had sneaked up on him from behind.

He banked in automatic reaction, his heart clenching. It was a Fokker, he saw, and he got a glimpse of a grim mouth snarling below goggles as the airman fired again. He didn't know where those bullets went. He made a rapid turn, and the enemy followed, firing. A shot went through the nacelle's body close to his foot and another through the lower plane. He turned again, twisting round with the DH2's famous torque, on the borderline of spinning. The Fokker was faster, but he turned like an elderly elephant. Bobby went round again, climbing until he had enough height, and dived at him, this time from the rear. The pilot looked over his shoulder as Bobby opened up – he saw the same snarl of teeth and blank goggles – and fled, heading eastwards towards his own territory. Bobby pursued, firing, but in level flight he could not catch the Fokker, and none of his shots did anything fatal to the machine. Some grey puffs of Archie began to appear around him, and he realised he was being lured too far over the line for a lone scout. He turned away, climbing again.

The sky was a deep, rich blue, the temperature rising into the seventies. The warm air from the ground was giving him lift, a glorious feeling. He had downed one HA, driven off another and knocked out an observer. And it wasn't even seven thirty yet. His brother, he thought, was probably crouched in a muddy trench somewhere down there, with someone's elbow in his back, and shells whistling overhead, waiting for the signal to heave himself out and run on his own two legs across the pitted ground. God, who'd be an infantryman! He began to whistle as he headed to join his patrol.

A figure appeared in the kitchen doorway, a thin woman in a coat and hat that had seen better days, with a carpet bag in her hand, and a white, weary face.

'Oh!' said Cook, in surprise. Then she recognised the woman. 'Oh, it's you,' she said unwelcomingly. And then she took in the shape beneath the coat, and her face reddened with indignation. 'Oh, you wicked girl! I see what you've been up to! How dare you come here in that condition? You clear off this minute!'

Ethel looked at her, beyond being afraid of her, beyond almost any feeling. 'Help me,' she said.

'Help you? I should think not! The very idea! You get out this minute, before one of the girls sees you. There's nothing here for you. Now get out! Get out!' She hurried towards her, grabbing the broom as she passed the better to drive her off.

'I've nowhere to go,' Ethel said despairingly.

'That's your concern, not mine. Coming here in that state, you shameless hussy! I don't doubt you got somewhere to go – your sort always has. But you're not coming in here. Now go. Go. Go!' Each 'Go' was accompanied by a jab of the broom's head.

'Haven't you got no pity?' Ethel said quietly, retreating from the attack step by step.

'Not for the likes of you!'

'Would you give me something to eat then – just a bit of bread or something?'

'I'll give you the flat of my hand if I get near you. And I'm calling the police. If I see you round here again, I give you fair warning, you'll get taken up and put inside, and we'll see if that mends your ways!'

She drove Ethel all the way to the gate, and waited, panting from the exertion, to see that she walked away, before returning indignantly to her work.

Ada came in. 'What was all that palaver?' she asked. 'I could hear you upstairs.'

Cook hesitated. But Ada was walking out with a soldier now, and ought to know what was what. 'That Ethel turned up – begging, she was. She was . . .' she pursed her lips, searching for a word, and lowered her voice to say urgently '. . . in a *condition*.'

'What sort of a condition?' Ada asked. And then two red spots appeared in her cheeks as she gathered, from Cook's expression, what she was talking about. 'Oh!' She thought a moment. 'Why'd she come here?'

'Begging, like I said.'

'But who's the father?'

'D'you think I had a friendly chat with her? I don't know and I don't care – don't suppose she knows either, and that's the last I want to hear of it! Her name's not to be mentioned, d'you hear? Emily and Lilian's too young to know about things like that.'

Ada said, 'All right, I was just asking.' And she went back to her work, thinking about Len and the concert at the camp he'd invited her to. He was singing a solo: 'If You Were the Only Girl in the World'. It was lovely to think the words were meant for her.

Beattie came home from a bandage-rolling session at Mount Olive, to see a figure lurking in the side passage in the shadow of the laurels. It was obviously a female figure, so she was not alarmed, but she wondered why, if it was a friend of one of the servants, she didn't go straight to the back door. The figure detached itself from the shadow as she approached, and came to the gate to meet her, and Beattie saw with surprise that it was Ethel. She looked pale, almost ill, and very thin, though her face was clean and she was wearing a hat and gloves, so she was still making an effort. She was clutching her coat around her in an awkward way – as though she had a stomach-ache, Beattie thought. 'Ethel? What are you doing here?' she asked.

'Oh, ma'am,' Ethel said urgently. 'I'm in trouble. I know I got no right to bother you, but I don't know what else to do. Cook sent me away, but I've no place to sleep and no money, and I haven't eaten since Thursday. Please, ma'am – I know you're a charitable lady. Please won't you help me?'

'What's got you into this state?' Beattie asked. 'I thought when you gave your notice you were going to another job.'

'I *have* been working,' Ethel said. 'I'm no beggar, but I can't help it now. They won't let me work. You see—' She unwrapped her arms and let her coat fall open.

Beattie saw the shape of her with a cold little shock that ran across her scalp. Perhaps every mistress feared the complication of a pregnant maid. But Ethel had left her employ and was no concern of hers now. 'Haven't you got a family

260

you can go to?' she asked. She tried not to see the impact of her words in the girl's eyes.

'There's only me,' she said, her voice trembling. 'I've got no family – no-one. I didn't know where else to go, only here.' Her head went down, as if defeated.

Beattie did not ask the question about the father. She knew it would be useless. Many people had predicted Ethel would come to a bad end, and here it was. Well, there were church organisations that dealt with this sort of thing. The prudent thing would be to send her away, go indoors and forget about her. It was not her business.

But Beattie's sensibilities were closer to the surface, these days, and they were tingling now. It was the words 'I didn't know where else to go' that got through her guard. She had been in that state once, and someone had come to her aid. She had survived, and remained respectable, because when she had prayed for help, help had arrived. *Let him who is without sin cast the first stone.* The words etched themselves in her mind in lines of pain. Homeless, friendless and pregnant. Had she loved the man? Was she grieving for him? No matter. Ethel had come home, to the only home she could think of.

'Let's get you inside,' Beattie said. Not via the kitchen, if Cook had already turned her away. She took her through the front door and into the drawing-room, though Ethel's thin body cringed in reluctance, and Beattie had to push her to make her sit down in there. She rang the bell. 'We'll get you some food, and arrange a bedroom for you. There's the old nursery, the nanny's bed. You'll be quiet up there.' Ethel looked at her with wide eyes, like a calf looking at the butcher's knife, not knowing what was to come, but dreading it. 'Don't be afraid,' Beattie said briskly – she guessed that the girl would trust matter-of-factness more than softness. 'I won't send you away. You can stay here until the baby's born, and then we'll arrange something.'

Ada came in, and her shocked eyes went straight to Ethel.

Before Ada could speak, Beattie said, 'Bring some food in here on a tray – bread and cheese and milk will do for now – then go and make up the bed in the old nursery. Ethel will be staying here for a while.' Ada hesitated, her lips moving soundlessly. Beattie said harshly, 'Straight away, please.' Ada flinched, and went.

Ethel said, in a low voice, 'They won't like it.'

'They'll do as they're told,' Beattie said. 'How far along are you?'

'About six months,' Ethel said.

Beattie considered. 'If I remember rightly, you're quite good at needlework?' Ethel assented. 'Very well. There's plenty of sewing to do, and we'll find you other little jobs. I'm sure you'd sooner feel you were earning your keep.'

'Yes, madam. Thank you, madam.'

'I'll make sure the others leave you alone,' Beattie added kindly.

Ethel's eyes filled with tears. 'I'm sorry to make trouble for you,' she began, but Beattie held up her hand.

'What I do, I do for my own reasons. Now, when you've had something to eat, I expect you'd like a bath. Have you a clean nightdress? I'll have one put in your room for you, and then I think you'd better go straight to bed. I'll have some supper sent up later. I expect you're tired anyway, but it might be best to stay out of sight for a while.'

Cook was quivering with indignation, the meat of her cheeks trembling with the effort of containing her wrath. 'It's not right, madam! Playing up to that hussy only encourages that sort of behaviour. What will people think? And the girls – Emily and Lilian – they're only young. What sort of example is that to put before them?'

'Those are all my worries, not yours,' said Beattie.

'It's a disgrace, that's what it is. A girl like that, mixing with decent, respectable folks. I won't have her in my kitchen!'

'She'll work mostly upstairs, and she can eat in the nursery, if the sight of her offends you,' Beattie said.

'And that's another thing! If you think I'm going to prepare food for her, let alone traipse upstairs to serve her—'

'Your job is to prepare food for whomever I choose to entertain,' Beattie said, in the voice servants didn't argue with. 'If you don't wish to continue in my employment, that is your choice, but in my house, I make the decisions.' She let that sink in for a moment, and added, 'And no-one expects you to carry trays upstairs. One of the maids will do it, if you're sure you don't want to save them the trouble and have Ethel eat with you all.'

Cook's face was pale now. Her lips moved, but she saw the chasm that had opened up. Not that she couldn't get another job – a good cook could always find a place – but she was comfortable here, and had no desire to move. A new mistress, a new kitchen, new companions were not things she wanted to have to get used to at her time of life. And who knew whether any change would be a change for the better? She had a good place here – or it had been good until that hussy Ethel came and ruined it. But if she was kept upstairs, perhaps it wouldn't be too bad – if only it didn't get out! She could imagine what the neighbours' servants would say if they knew. They'd be looked down on – sneered at. How would they hold their heads up again? Oh, that Ethel! She could kill her! She'd always known she'd be trouble.

'We'll have to see, madam,' Cook said as distantly as she could. 'If them's your orders—'

'I have taken Ethel in, and she will stay until I decide what to do with her.'

'Very well, madam,' Cook said. She began to turn away,

but internal convulsions turned her back to say pleadingly, 'I just wish I knew *why*.'

Charity, compassion, fellow-feeling. Cook would have felt them all for almost any creature down on its luck, hurt and needy. But when sex reared its ugly head, Beattie thought, Christian feelings seemed to fly out of the window. Mrs Fitzgerald was the same (Oh, God, Mrs Fitzgerald! What would she say when she found out, which inevitably she would?) The fallen woman fell outside the circle of pity. It made Beattie angry, and all the more determined to keep Ethel against all protests.

Cook was waiting for an answer. And she couldn't tell her what was underneath it all – Louis, David, Edward, casting the first stone. Shared pain. She said, 'God knows where every sparrow falls.'

She saw Cook trying to digest that. 'Very well, madam,' she said, evidently no wiser, and went away, head high – a short, wide receptacle of self-righteousness.

God may know where every sparrow falls, Beattie thought, but it doesn't mean He puts out a hand to catch them. That seems to be left for us.

'I hope the master understands,' she heard Cook mutter, as she went out.

The FE2bs took off in pairs and patrolled their section of the line until relieved by the next pair, so that observation was continuous. The DH2s went out in flights of three, relieved in the same way, but ranged further.

Down below, Hell seemed to have been unleashed. Along the Front for a stretch of eighteen or twenty miles, wave after wave went in, company following company in remorseless attack until, in places where no man's land was wide, as many as twenty waves might be in the open at the same time. And they were cut down like corn by the enemy machine-guns. The bombardment hadn't destroyed the

264

enemy's trenches, or their fire-power, as well as expected. In places, it hadn't even cut the wire: those places could be recognised from above, for the British dead lay in heaps where the wire had stopped them.

In other places the first-line trenches were taken, and the attackers scrambled on to the second. Fierce battles were fought to small local victories. But as the day ripened, the German artillery opened up, laying down fire across no man's land, which would severely hamper the bringing up of reserves, and isolate men in forward positions.

At least, Bobby thought, he and his colleagues had ensured that the German air force had been unable to interfere in the battleground. They came in waves from the east, and were driven off, some brought down, some damaged, some turning back, no doubt to try again later. Bobby's machine picked up several more battle scars, but he had the satisfaction of fatally injuring an Albatros, which managed to make it back across the line before crash-landing. On the debit side, he saw one of his squadron hit by Fokker fire, knocking out the engine, and go down, though later in the day word came through that Tudor, the pilot, had survived, with a broken ankle, collar bone and rib. If you could avoid spinning, it was generally possible to land more or less safely: the DH2, like all aeroplanes, was built to glide.

Bobby came back from that patrol and found Farringdon just having landed. They walked together towards the huts, where the squadron commander was standing, watching the sky for returning flights. They made their reports, and the Old Man said, 'Get some grub, the two of you, and wash your faces. You've got half an hour, then I want you to go out on a bombing raid. Lay some eggs on Bapaume, see if we can't give the Jerries something else to think about. There've been some reports of large numbers of reinforcements coming up. Target those if you see them, otherwise use your wits. Bapaume is the enemy headquarters, so disrupt whatever you can, get away, come back and reload.'

'Yes, sir,' Bobby said. 'How is it going, do we know?'

'Curate's egg,' said the major. 'Good in parts. Broken through in some places, knocked back in others. Not our business – we've got our own job to do.'

Bobby and Farringdon went on to the mess, where half a dozen others were being fed and revived. They joined the group, sitting around the big table, and discussed their experiences of the day, the successes, and the word on those who'd been knocked out. All of them were going out on bombing raids that afternoon. It was hard to hit a target with a hand-thrown bomb, but as Farringdon said cheerfully, 'Wherever it lands, it'll be unwelcome.'

'I'm going to look for a nice railway train,' said Hollinshead. 'So satisfying if you get a hit on one of those. When I was a kid I had a train set, and I was always trying to crash it. Made my father mad.'

'What a horrid boy you must have been,' said Bobby, grinning. 'I bet you kicked down sandcastles, too.'

'Always was a destructive beggar,' Hollinshead agreed. 'Suppose war's the right place for me. Fag, anyone?' The cigarettes were passed round, and they smoked comfortably until Bobby, looking at his wrist-watch (*Thanks, Dad!*) said, 'It's about time. Think I'll just pop along and clean my teeth before we go.'

Farringdon shook his head in amusement. 'Think you might dazzle old Fritz into crashing?'

'You never know,' said Bobby.

David and the remains of his company had reached a German reserve trench after fierce fighting, driving the enemy before them. But now they were being shelled, and were pinned down. The trench was growing more battered as shells nibbled away at the defences. Sweating, swearing, mired in chalk and blood, they toiled to rebuild them, firing in the pauses in the direction of the enemy, so they should not have it all their own way. Sometimes a shell landed actually in the trench, with devastating results. After one such blast. David had to dig himself out from a heap of rubble, soil and slimy chalk, debris and human parts. He scrabbled frantically, in desperate, nauseated panic: his greatest dread, he discovered now, was being buried alive. Any death was preferable to that.

'Sir,' said a voice, and hands came to help tug him free. It was one of his own men, Diffley. He was filthy, and looked exhausted, his eyes red-rimmed from the irritation of dust and bitter smoke. 'Sir, Eddoes copped it that time. He's bad, sir.' He looked frightened.

David followed him to the stricken Eddoes's side, and saw why. His right arm and leg had been torn off by the blast. David helped clear the rubble off him, and prop him up on the firing-step. He was awake and rational, and looked at David with clear blue eyes from under gingery eyebrows clogged with white dust. 'Is it bad, sir?' he asked. Before David could answer, he moved his hand across his chest, feeling for damage, until it contacted the pulp where his right shoulder had been. 'My God,' he said, almost calmly. 'I've lost my arm.' He felt on, down towards the stump of his thigh. 'Is that off too?' he asked.

David couldn't speak. He nodded.

'I could really go a fag, sir,' Eddoes said.

There was nothing else they could do for him. Someone produced a squashed packet of cigarettes, and David lit it for him, then put it between his lips. He sucked in, and then, after too long a pause, lifted his left hand to it. David knew, with a cold, sick certainty, that he had tried automatically to take it with his right hand.

The shelling went on. Until it lifted they couldn't move forward, and were cut off from reinforcement from the rear.

They could only huddle, wait and hope. Eddoes remained conscious, smoking cigarettes, uncomplaining. Later when David crawled over to him, he said he was thirsty. David had water in his canteen, and put it into his left hand, but he seemed too weak to lift it. David held it to his lips, and he sipped feebly. Then he yawned. 'Sorry, sir,' he said faintly. 'Sleeping on duty.'

'Don't worry about it,' David said.

'I knew a bloke once called Campbell,' Eddoes said quite clearly. His eyes closed, and he said no more.

David was called away by his sergeant, and when he returned five minutes later, Eddoes was dead. All he felt was huge relief.

CHAPTER SEVENTEEN

The evening paper gave the first news of the Big Push, which everyone had been expecting, though no-one had known exactly when it would happen. The headlines were bold.

GREAT BRITISH OFFENSIVE
ATTACK ON A TWENTY MILE FRONT
GERMAN TRENCHES OCCUPIED
MANY PRISONERS TAKEN
OUR CASUALTIES NOT HEAVY

The text was equally cheering: 'Attacks were launched at 7.30 this morning on the north of the River Somme in conjunction with the French. British troops have broken into the German forward system of defences on a front of sixteen miles. Fighting continues.'

And: 'Many prisoners have already fallen into our hands, and as far as can be ascertained our casualties have not been heavy.'

Edward was doing his best to absorb the details of the report, but his household was, for the time being, much more interested in the immediate invasion by Ethel. On his arrival home – he had worked late at the office – he had, at Beattie's request, gone up to see her in the nursery, though he had demurred at first: domestic servants were the business of the mistress of the house, not the master.

'But I want her to know you agree to it, or she might be afraid you will overrule me and turn her out.'

'Very well, I'll go and reassure her,' Edward said. He did not go immediately, however, but stood looking at Beattie, troubled. 'Are you all right?' he asked at last.

Her head went up, in the defensive movement that always reminded him of a deer scenting danger. 'Why should I not be?' she asked sharply.

'My dear,' he began gently, but saw the warning in her eyes. She could not at the moment bear him to get closer to her thoughts. He said, 'Whatever you decide, I will support you, of course. But would it not be better . . . There are, I believe, homes for—'

'She came here,' Beattie forestalled him. 'This was the only place she could think of. She has no home.'

'She's not your responsibility,' he tried.

But she said, 'She is now,' and he knew there was no more point in arguing. 'There's plenty she can do to earn her keep. The porcelain figures all need washing. They can be taken to her upstairs and she can do them. Darning and household mending – I haven't time for it any more. And—'

'Whatever you want,' Edward said. He went upstairs to reassure Ethel, and found her so changed – a miserable, apprehensive shadow of her former bold self – that he pitied her. On his way downstairs he was accosted, much to his surprise, by Cook, whom he never saw out of her kitchen. But the reason was in her belligerent eye. He got his shots off first. 'No use in making a fuss,' he said firmly. 'Your mistress has decided and I agree with her. Are we not bidden to help our fellow creatures in distress?'

'Hmph!' said Cook. Not when they brought it on themselves, said her expression, by wicked, wanton, *sinful* behaviour.

'Please don't raise this again,' said Edward. 'I have more important things on my mind. There's a war on, you know – and I have two sons at the Front.'

Cook wilted. 'I'm sure they'll be all right, sir.'

'I'm sure they'll do their duty, whatever it is,' Edward said. 'I suggest we all do the same.'

Sadie wandered down the garden, with Nailer at her heels – he had become much more attached to her, now he spent most days with her. The long twilight of the English summer lay, like a soft, lambent fog, over the garden, while the red of Munt's dahlias and the blue of his delphiniums seemed to glow preternaturally in the golden light. England was so beautiful at this time of year; so peaceful. It was hard to believe that less than a hundred miles away guns were being fired, and men killed, and horses – she didn't want to think about the horses. Why couldn't all mankind enjoy the loveliness of the world without hurting each other? Why did the Germans want to take other people's lands and kill and destroy?

She found Munt sitting on an orange box outside the door of his shed, enjoying a last cigarette before going home. She stopped before him, feeling an urge to communicate, and searching for a subject.

He puffed out smoke, like an old bee-bellows, and chose it for her. 'Gotter visitor up at the house, seemin'ly.'

'Yes,' she said. 'It's rather odd. You know who it is?'

'Ar. That baggage. Allus knew she'd come to a bad end.'

'Is it a bad end? I suppose it must be, but I can't help thinking of the poor little baby – oughtn't all new life be a happy thing? It's not *its* fault.'

He eyed her through the fumes. 'You're a queer one,' he said. 'That ain't the way the world wags, you know that 's well as me.'

'I know,' she said. 'I do know, but when you think of all the death everywhere, especially in France, well, life starts to look a bit more precious. I mean, Charles – Lord Dene—'

She stopped there. She had brought him up as an example

271

because she knew Munt had approved of him – sort of – as much as he approved of anyone. But it seemed odd to mention Lord Dene in the same sentence as Ethel's bastard baby.

'Devil takes care of his own,' Munt said, examining the end of his cigarette and pinching out a bit of loose tobacco. Large, soft moths were flitting about now, their wings rimmed with light from the declining sun.

'Oh, but poor Ethel, she doesn't belong to the Devil,' Sadie said. Munt gave her a cynical, squinty look through a new plume of smoke. Sadie changed tack. 'What I don't understand is why Mother took her in. I mean, I'd have thought she'd agree with you – you know, about Ethel being a bad lot. And Mrs Fitzgerald's going to make the most *awful* fuss, and Mother hates stirring her up. I'm surprised she did it.'

Munt removed the cigarette from his lips and screwed it out carefully in the old tobacco-tin lid in his lap. The sun dipped below the trees, and the garden took on a soft blueness. 'There's stuff in everyone's life you don't know the what and why of,' he said. 'People has their reasons.' He stood up. 'Well, I better be gettin'.' He regarded her a moment. 'Big battle goin' on in France, could be a decider. Worry your head about that, if you want to fret. That baggage'll land on her feet, mark my words.'

'I hope she does,' Sadie said defiantly.

Munt looked past her. 'Bat,' he said. 'See it? Little mouser!'

She turned and saw the pipistrelle flickering back and forth like a fragment of charred paper tossed in the wind. 'I like bat time,' she said. 'Everything looks so mysterious and interesting in this light, as though it's about to change into something else and hasn't made up its mind what.'

Munt shook his head at her fancies. But he said, 'Whole world's like that – on the edge of bein' otherwise. *Chance* you get born at all.'

Sadie smiled. 'I thought it was God decided that,' she teased.

'Same thing,' said Munt.

He disappeared into his hut. Nailer came back from investigating a heap of flower pots, and looked at her hopefully, wagging his tail. A walk in the twilight was more fun with company, he suggested.

'I have to go in,' Sadie said, turning back.

Nailer went off on his own. No sense wasting good smelling time.

The Sunday papers were full of reports, most of them vague and general, but some with details that Edward absorbed hungrily. There was a map in one, with lines and arrows adding more to confusion than illumination. He longed for an informed source; tomorrow, he thought, he would telephone Lord Forbesson – he'd be bound to know something.

There was an unpleasant incident at church, when Mrs Fitzgerald waylaid them and took Beattie to task over Ethel; but Edward stepped to her side and took her hand through his arm, and told Mrs F that he supported his wife's decision entirely and that it was a matter of Christian charity. He thought he had her there, but she was of the view that in a clear case of sinful behaviour, it was for God to provide the charity, and for man to make an example, *pour encourager les autres.*

'How are we to keep our local girls straight if they see such wickedness being rewarded? We already have munitionettes striding around in trousers, smoking cigarettes in public! We'll have every decent maid running off to join them and sinking into degradation if we don't make a stand.'

'You paint an apocalyptic picture,' Edward said, 'but I must stand by our decision. Ethel will be kept out of sight at home, so there's no reason anyone else should learn about her position.'

'People always find things out,' said Mrs Fitzgerald, grimly.

Edward tipped his hat and walked Beattie away. 'And I know who generally tells them,' he murmured, as they went to catch up with Sadie and the boys, who had gone ahead to avoid the contretemps.

'Thank you for supporting me,' Beattie said after a moment.

'You're my wife,' Edward said simply.

Beattie's mouth turned down, but he was looking at the children and didn't see it. *Coals of fire*, she thought. She tried for a normal tone. 'I hope Cook's annoyance doesn't affect her Yorkshire pudding. It's a very nice piece of beef and it deserves the best.'

They caught up with Sadie, who heard her. 'And there are raspberries,' she said. 'I saw them last night. I do think raspberries are nicer than strawberries.'

Later, William went down to the village to fetch the special late bulletin newspaper, and Edward was able to read:

> Heavy fighting has taken place today in the area between the Ancre and the Somme, especially about Fricourt and La Boisselle. Fricourt, which was captured by our troops about 2 p.m., remains in our hands, and some progress has been made east of the village.
>
> In the neighbourhood of La Boisselle the enemy is offering a stubborn resistance, but our troops are making satisfactory progress. A considerable quantity of war material has fallen into our hands, but details are not at present available.
>
> On the other side of the valley, on the Ancre, the situation is unchanged. The general situation may be regarded as favourable.
>
> Up to noon today some 800 more

> prisoners have been taken in the
> operations between the Ancre and
> the Somme, bringing the total up to
> 3,500 including those captured on
> other parts of the front last night.

With the aid of the map he had saved from Saturday's paper, he was able to identify the areas. He was still comparing the bulletin with the map when a telegram came.

He joined Beattie in the hall. Her face was white, but expressionless. Her hands were folded in front of her like a nun's. He wanted to say, 'It could be good news,' but he knew that was nonsensical. Nobody sent good news by telegram in a war. It was David, he thought, with a sick emptiness in his heart. He thought of the German shells and machine-gun bullets, and the casualty figures from other battles. They had been just numbers – but each of the numbers must have had a name. *David – dead, or wounded?*

Ada took it from the boy and brought it to him with a frightened look. In the background he was aware of the other servants hovering in the kitchen passage. The boys were hanging back in the drawing-room doorway, but Sadie came up to his other side, as though ready to catch him, and he thought, confusedly, *She's a good son to me.*

He seemed to have stepped outside his body, to be looking down on himself as he opened the telegram. He could not feel his hands, though he saw them draw out the sheet and open it, and for a moment he could not read the words, as one cannot read words in a dream, though one can see them.

Sadie had read it over his arm, and gave a little cry, which seemed to cut him to the heart. His fingers clenched, he was back in his body, and the words were all too clear now.

He read aloud, rather than have to say it more than once.

'Deeply regret to inform you 2nd Lieutenant R. D. Hunter, RFC, killed in action in France July 1st.'

Someone behind him – probably Cook – moaned, but there was no other sound.

It was Sadie who moved. 'No answer,' she said to the boy, and went to close the front door. There was a vase of delphiniums on the hall table, and she noticed their intense colour, the colour of the deepest part of a summer sky. *Bobby*, her mind said. She saw him, in his aeroplane, skimming through the blue, like a swift, utterly at one with his element.

No-one else had spoken. Edward took Beattie's elbow and turned her back towards the drawing-room. The boys dissolved out of the way, and at his look oozed upstairs, afraid and disconsolate, but half glad to be away from such emotion. Sadie hesitated at the door. But when she saw her father put his arm round her mother, she went away too.

In the drawing-room, the touch of Edward's arm was the last straw. Beattie shuddered, pulled away from him, sat down blindly on the nearest chair, and buried her face in her hands. She could not let him touch her, or look at her. She wished him, at that moment, at the farthest end of the earth. She wished she were alone in the universe to contemplate without witness the horror in her soul.

Because when he had read out the telegram, for an instant, just for an instant, what she had felt was relief that it was not David.

Lilian brought Ethel's meals up to her. Ethel was glad it was her, because Emily would have chattered and Ada would have sermonised. She was glad to be isolated from the household. She had come here in desperation, not really thinking they would take her in; and now that they had, she was riven with shame, and wanted to limit her contamination of their lives.

It was not the baby. She had been a fool, and careless,

but in other circumstances the baby would not have been a problem. Lots of girls – perhaps most of them – got pregnant before they married. The only difference for her was that there was no marriage in the offing. She didn't see that as sin or degradation. She had been unlucky. Besides, despite her growing bulk and its movements within her, she hardly believed in the baby. It didn't seem real at all.

It was the other thing that set her apart from decent people, and it was a thing she could never be free of. No-one must ever know. She could hardly bear to think about it, and yet she could not stop herself. It was like an ulcer in her mind that her thoughts kept touching to see if it still stung. *Cyril was her father.* It hurt – there, what did you expect? Stop thinking about it! Her brother Cyril was not her brother, but her father. Her sister Edie was not her sister, but her mother. It was agony. Edie had been right to run away. If only *she* could run away – but she'd take the stain with her, wherever she went. How Ma had hated her – and with justice. She understood it now. And Cyril – he had been good to her, the only person in her life to show her kindness. It was he who had insisted she go to school. He had wanted her to make something of herself, to be better than her lowly origins. He knew, as she had not, how lowly they were. They had kept it from her, and she had gone out into the world and looked it defiantly in the face. She never could again. She was damned.

Lilian came in with a supper tray, breaking the agonised cycle of thought, and told her with round-eyed breathlessness that Bobby had been killed in action. Ethel felt shock and sadness – she had liked Bobby. Everybody had liked Bobby. They'd be devastated, the family. There was nothing she could do to comfort anybody. The one bit of good about his death was that it gave her something else to think of, to keep her away from the ulcer.

★　★　★

Everything seemed strange and unreal. A heaviness hung over the house, and there was nothing to do. Edward insisted that the boys go to school, and he had to go to work – the war did not stop for them – so Sadie sent a note to Mrs Cuthbert and stayed at home with her mother. Beattie did not want to talk or be comforted, so Sadie's job was to deal with the visitors and keep them from her. In between, there was nothing to do or to think about but that Bobby was dead. He wasn't coming back. It was impossible to believe in Bobby being anything but alive. He had always been so vital, so indestructible. Over in France the war went on, and there were reports in the paper of successful actions, territory gained, German guns captured and prisoners taken, but it meant nothing to her. It was like a work of fiction, and not a very interesting one, because how could it be real when it claimed, impossibly, that Bobby was dead? And so her thoughts went round, like a mouse in a wheel, and the aching boredom of death filled her with emptiness, like hunger.

On Thursday there was a letter in the post, from one of Bobby's colleagues.

Dear Mr and Mrs Hunter,
I hope it may be of some comfort to you in your loss to know something of how your son died. Hunter and I were friends, having been together since cadet school in Shoreham, and we served together from the first day in France. On 1st July we had been busy all day on reconnaissance flights. We went out again at 4.15 to see if German reinforcements were on the road and disrupt them if possible. We were shelled heavily going over the line, then north of Ovillers we met 5 Hostile Aircraft. We engaged them and after about 15 minutes they'd had enough and went down, and landed at their aerodrome. We went on towards Bapaume, where we

dropped our bombs and managed to inflict some damage on the railway lines. On the way back, the Huns must have been expecting us because as we neared the line two HA came up behind us, firing. We managed to drive them off, damaging one quite severely, but Hunter's machine was shot through the radiator and he had difficulty in getting it back to the aerodrome. We did not know until afterwards that one of the shots had gone through his lung. It is a tribute to his great skill and courage that he managed to land his machine before collapsing. He died shortly afterwards. He was a superlative pilot and a good friend and will be deeply missed by all in our mess, but especially by,

Yours sincerely and with deepest condolences,

L. J. Farringdon, 2nd Lt.

Beattie did not think it *was* any comfort to know how he had died. Death is never less than death when it's as close to you as that. It might be noble when someone else's son dies with courage; your own just dies.

But at least it was something to show Mrs Oliver when she called, something to occupy her so that Beattie would not need to talk.

'Oh, my dear,' she said, when she came in. She took Beattie's hands and looked at her gravely, but did not say any more. Beattie remembered she had lost Hank, who had been like a son to her (*ah, but not a son – there's a difference!*) So Beattie gave her the letter, and she read it slowly twice. When she gave it back, she didn't mention it, for which Beattie was grateful.

'I didn't come before because I thought you'd be inundated with visitors,' said Mrs Oliver. 'Is there anything I can do? I know there never is, but one asks in hope.'

'Thank you, but Sadie's here. She's looking after everything.'

'What a blessing of a girl she is,' said Mrs Oliver. She

cast about for a subject. 'Have you heard anything from your sister-in-law in France?'

Beattie brought her own mind back. 'Oh, you mean Laura? Yes, she wrote to tell us she'd arrived safely, and that she expects to be very busy – there's such a shortage of ambulances. We haven't heard any more since.'

'Did she tell you *where* she was? Not too near the action, I hope?'

'She's based in Amiens, and she says it's a lovely town, with some beautiful buildings and good restaurants. She seems comfortable there.'

'But Amiens – that's right on the edge of the battle area,' Mrs Oliver said.

'The ambulance wouldn't be very useful if it wasn't near the line,' Beattie said. She had nothing inside to spare for Laura. Bobby was dead, and until she heard from David – which she supposed wouldn't happen until he came out of the line – she could care about no-one else.

'What a singular woman Miss Laura Hunter must be,' Mrs Oliver said. 'Courage and determination one usually only finds in a man.'

'She is unusual,' Beattie said. She felt suddenly exhausted.

Mrs Oliver must have seen it because, with blessed tact, she stood up and said, 'I won't stay – I know how tired you must be. Don't ring – I'll see myself out. By the way,' she said, and hesitated, then went on, 'I do applaud you for taking in that poor wretched girl, your former maid. I just want you to know I've had words with Mrs Fitzgerald, and I don't think she'll be troubling you about it again. In the meantime, if it becomes too difficult for you, you can send her over to me, and I'll take care of her. We have a big house and she won't be in the way.'

Beattie was touched. 'Thank you. You're a good friend,' she said. 'But she's all right where she is. I'll take care of her. It's my duty.'

'I wish more people thought like you,' Mrs Oliver said, and left.

It was half an hour later, when Beattie and Sadie were having a sad cup of coffee together in the morning-room, that the telegraph boy appeared out in the street on his bicycle. Beattie's cup went down into the saucer with a chattering noise. Sadie held her breath, willing him to ride on past the gate. It was Jackie Hicks, youngest son of their postman, and fellow Boy Scout in William's troop. Sadie urged him in her mind, *Go past, Jackie, go past.* But he stopped, propped his bicycle, opened the gate, walked up the path. Beattie hadn't moved. Sadie realised her mother couldn't, and got up to intercept him.

She brought the envelope to her mother, and watched Jackie through the window as he fidgeted about in the front garden, scratched his ankle, peered into a rose, waiting to see if there was a reply. Out there, beyond the glass, life was still normal.

Beattie made no sound, but a moment later she gave the form to Sadie, got up, and walked quite steadily out of the room.

Sadie spread the paper flat, her heart leaden, and read:

'Regret inform you Captain D. E. Hunter, North Midland Rifles, wounded in action 2nd July.'

By the time Edward came home, there had been a second telegram, saying that David was in hospital in Rouen and seriously ill.

'Wounded on Sunday,' he said. 'Why has it taken so long to inform us?'

Beattie didn't answer. It was like punishment, like persecution. How could she bear it? David, David wounded – seriously ill! Was everything to be taken from her? She heard Edward talking as though from a long distance away, speculating – uselessly – on the workings of the telegraph service,

281

the medical facilities in France. She wished he would stop. At any moment she thought he might wonder how David had been wounded. A lost limb? A lost eye? Something worse? *No, no, don't think about it! Don't let those ideas into your head!* But she saw him now in her mind's eye, in a hospital bed, half his head bandaged, or bandaged stumps where his lovely limbs had been. *No, stop it, stop it!* She thought she might go mad.

Sunday was a heavy day. Edward was at home and everyone was at leisure for the first time, with nothing to do but think about the heavy blows that had hit the family. Beattie had had no respite since the first telegram arrived. When the time came for church, she could not face it, and Edward excused them all for once. Sadie was relieved not to have to endure the condolences of their neighbours. She took Nailer out for a long walk in the woods, and made Peter go with her – William would not come. He stayed in his room, working on a balsa-wood model aeroplane in a sort of numb desperation, saying he *had* to get it finished. She understood the compulsion. Focused activity helped somehow. She tried to keep Peter occupied by talking of fishing and the life-cycle of the frog. He was bewildered by the change to the family, and hadn't the mental resources to distract himself.

They had just finished luncheon when there was a knock at the front door.

Oh, please, God, not more misery, Beattie thought. William and Sadie went out to see who it was. Beattie heard a deep man's voice – not a telegraph boy's. But she had no hope of relief. She was being punished, and she knew why. But hurt me, not my boy! *Let him live*, she thought suddenly and clearly, as though a din had been shut off in her mind: a calm voice she recognised as her own from long ago, when things were normal, said, Let him live, and I'll accept anything else you want to do to me. Just let him live.

A large, bulky figure filled the doorway, following Sadie in, sombre in official blue-black, helmet politely in hand. PC George Whittle, looking older these days, pouchy-eyed, having to do so much more since PC Andy Denton had been called up and all he'd got to replace him was a Special. In the same cool clarity of thought she remembered that Andy Denton used to open for the Northcote XI – a powerful batsman and a good fielder at slip. That would not protect him out in France.

'I beg your pardon for intruding, ma'am, sir,' Whittle said.

'It's a message about David,' Sadie jumped in, her expression torn between hope and fear. 'They say you can visit him.'

Beattie stared, unable to make sense of this.

'What are you saying?' Edward asked. He looked bewildered too.

'That's right, sir,' Whittle said, in his most comfortable tones, out of sheer habit. 'He's in the 8th General Hospital at Rouen, and the specialists there would like you to go and visit him because they think he's at a turning point.'

'Turning point?' Edward asked sharply – too sharply.

Whittle looked miserable, like a dog unjustly punished. 'Not improving, sir. They're afraid gangrene might be setting in.'

'Oh, God!' Beattie's cry was like a wounded animal's.

'But – *how* can we visit him?' Edward asked.

Whittle seemed glad to be back on more practical ground. 'You have to go and see the War Office, sir, and they arrange everything. They'll give you all the information, travel warrants and such. I understand you're met at every stage of the journey so you won't get lost.'

'We must go,' Beattie said.

'Of course,' Edward said.

'Oh, Dad, please can I?' Sadie cried

Whittle began to rumble. 'No, Miss Sadie, I don't think—'

But Edward pulled himself together. 'No, of course not. Your mother and I will go. You'll be needed here, anyway, to take care of things.' He looked at Whittle. 'Thank you for coming to tell us. We'll go up to London tomorrow.'

'Yes, sir. And – I wish you all the best of luck. I hope the young gentleman pulls through.' He pulled out his handkerchief and wiped his face. 'This war's a rotten thing. It doesn't seem right when bad things happen to good people.'

'Thank you, Constable,' Edward said, and gave Sadie a desperate look, which she interpreted correctly.

'I'll see you out,' she said to Whittle.

It was a long day, made longer by the silence in which they travelled. In cases of desperate hurt, silence can be the only thing that holds a situation together. By tube they travelled to the War Office, then had a long delay in an institutional waiting-room of mild green and cream paint and the smell of floor wax. Then by tube again to Waterloo, by train to Southampton, and by ship to Le Havre. The sea was calm, and it was an easy crossing. At Le Havre they were met by an army transport, which took them to Rouen. Whittle had told no more than the truth – they were met at each stage and guided kindly to the next. The kindness sickened Beattie. It was like kindness to the bereaved. They were taking her to see her son die.

A WVR woman met them at Rouen station in the red light of evening, and took them out to a car. 'I've reserved you a room at the Red Cross Hostel for relatives,' she said. 'But . . .' She gave their prosperous appearance a doubtful look '. . . perhaps you might prefer to go to an hotel. The Mercure is quite nice, so I've heard. Of course, you'd have to pay for that yourselves. Your warrant wouldn't cover it.'

Edward answered for them. 'We'll take the hostel room for tonight at least.'

'It's quite comfortable,' she said, 'only not grand, you understand. Would you like to go there now, or to the hospital first? The hospital, I expect.'

'Thank you, yes.'

The hospital was in a large house on the north side of Rouen, approached by tall, handsome gates and a wide drive. Extra accommodation had been made in huts erected in the grounds, but they were taken to the main entrance where they were met by a firm-faced woman in her early forties, wearing Queen Alexandra uniform, smart with its scarlet cape and flowing headdress. She greeted them with a handshake and said, 'I'm Matron Roscoe. Mr and Mrs Hunter – yes, I know all about you. You were expected. I'll take you straight to your son. He's doing a little better today.'

Edward swallowed with an audible click. 'Something was said – about gangrene.'

Matron Roscoe frowned. 'We can't rule it out. It *is* often a complication in these cases, particularly when they were out in the field for a long time before being brought in, but it hasn't set in yet, so we must hope for the best. Come along – this way.'

Inside, what had been a fine old house now looked rather shabby, with signs all around of its new occupation, and the smell – disinfectant, iodine and underneath, barely concealed, the odour of sickness and death. Beattie walked after the matron's rapidly moving figure, aware of the silence of Edward beside her, and her mind empty save for the thought, born of panic and unbearable uncertainty, that they ought to have brought flowers.

CHAPTER EIGHTEEN

Stepping between the car and the hostel, Edward heard a distant rumble, which he took to be thunder for an instant before he realised it was guns. It was a grim postscript on the day.

The hostel room was Spartan but clean. Edward found it rather comforting – it was like being back at school. They were both tired to death and hungry by the time they reached the hostel, for they hadn't eaten since the middle of the day on the ship. The kitchen was closed, but the warden took pity on them and provided them with cheese and biscuits and coffee. It was French cheese, soft and rather pungent, but Beattie noticed it no more than the room.

The images were imprinted on her brain. David, lying in a hospital bed, pale with blood loss and pain. The first sight had laid at least some terrors: his face was whole, and both of his arms. But though his eyes were open, he did not speak or acknowledge them. And the shape of the blanket on the bed said there was a cradle under it.

The doctor, who looked worn to a thread, told them the story. David had been hit by shrapnel from a shell blast, which had seriously wounded his left thigh. He had been in a forward position, an enemy trench his company had occupied, and because of continued shelling it had been impossible to get him back for more than thirty hours. The image for Beattie was of her son lying helpless and in pain

286

with a shattered leg for hour after hour as the battle raged around him.

'What is the prognosis?' Edward had asked.

'I can't tell you at the moment,' the doctor said. 'He's very weak from blood loss and long exposure in the field. Infection could set in, or gangrene. And with wounds like this, pain and debility take their toll. Death from shock, stroke or heart failure is common. That was why it was felt you should have the chance to come and see him.'

'He's strong,' Beattie heard herself say. 'He'll fight.'

The doctor looked at her sadly. 'If he survives, recovery will be a long and complex process. The fracture is comminuted, and there is soft-tissue damage as well, with loss of muscle. He may never walk again. And, at any point, infection could set in.' He looked away from her, and met Edward's eyes, as if that was easier. Edward read the message that he could not say aloud, that death might be the kinder outcome.

They had sat with David for an hour. Sometimes he seemed conscious and sometimes unconscious, but he never spoke or looked at them. Then a nurse came and gave him an injection and gently ushered them away. 'You can come back tomorrow,' she said. 'You look all in. Go and rest, now.'

Rest – as if that were possible! In the bare little hostel room Beattie began mechanically to undress, reaching back for her buttons. She smelt the ghost of Edward's bay rum as he came up behind her, and she stiffened. What she longed for above all just then was to be alone. He undid the buttons for her. Then he slipped his arms around her. 'Don't!' she said.

'Beattie,' he said. 'Don't push me away.'

She removed herself from his grasp and went to the window. The curtains didn't meet properly, and she fiddled with them, trying to close them. Outside there was a narrow cobbled street, and buildings opposite with closed shutters

287

that made them look abandoned. She felt marooned on an unknown planet.

Edward stood watching her for a moment, and then said, 'Married people ought to help each other.'

'You can't help me,' she said.

'Don't *say* that. This is happening to both of us. Your pain is my pain.'

She turned then and looked at him, hardly seeing him. He was tall, narrow, dark – as though modestly not taking up too much of the world, of the light. He was not broad-shouldered and fair-skinned and big with life. 'You don't know my pain,' she said. 'You can't understand. This is my *son*!'

'I've lost my son, too,' he said quietly.

'He's not—' she began, and stopped, a second too late. He was talking about Bobby. Oh, God, in her anguish over David, she'd forgotten about Bobby. *She'd forgotten Bobby!*

She tried desperately to think of a way to retrieve the sentence, but it was no use. She saw it in his face. He knew what she had been thinking. She saw him sigh slightly, as a person who lives with intractable pain will sigh as they adjust themselves to it for yet another day. Then he turned away. 'I'm going to the bathroom.'

'I'm sorry!' she cried, low and desperately. He checked for the fraction of a second, as though acknowledging her. But still he went out.

There were two single iron bedsteads in the room – thank God! The bathroom was down the hall. She would do without it for now. She changed into her nightgown, and was in bed by the time Edward came back. He turned out the light and got into the other bed, and at last Beattie was alone in the dark and free to think – or, rather, to be assailed by her thoughts.

There seemed no change in David the next day. He seemed to sleep a lot of the time, but when he was awake, he neither spoke nor looked at them. Edward sat patiently beside him, talking. 'To let him know we're here,' he said to Beattie. At the other side she sat in silence, holding her son's unresponsive hand. They wheeled him away to change his dressings. They gave him morphine. What frightened Beattie was the thought that he was in pain, and this grim silence was his way of dealing with it. It suggested courage of an order she couldn't face. And if he went too far away, he might not be able to get back.

In the middle of the day the nurses sent them out, while ward duties were carried out. 'Give yourselves a bit of a break,' said an Irish nurse. 'Get a breath of fresh air.'

They obeyed because it was easier, and went out into the grounds to walk up and down a path. At last Edward said, 'I will have to leave tomorrow morning.'

'I'll stay,' she said.

'Are you sure? We can't do anything for him.'

'You think he's going to die,' she accused.

He stopped and looked down at her. 'We have to face the likelihood. And I don't want to leave you here alone.'

'The warrants are for a week,' she said. 'I'll stay for a week, anyway.'

'Would you sooner go to an hotel?' he offered.

'The hostel is good enough,' she said.

They walked on. 'I don't like leaving you,' he said. 'What will you do?' She just looked at him, as if it were a question not worth answering.

That evening he insisted they leave the hospital early enough to get a proper dinner. David was asleep, or unconscious, after a morphine injection. In the town, shops were still open. They dined at a restaurant in a big square with a church in it. Edward thought it was the cathedral. The food was good and he ordered wine, but she didn't eat or drink much. She felt restless away from David. She was afraid not being there might tip the balance in some way. Superstition and prayer were all you had at times like this.

Back in their room, she suddenly found herself dead tired. Once she was in bed with the light off, she began drifting away, and sleep beckoned like the longed-for arms of a lover. Behind her closed eyes, David woke up and smiled and spoke to her. Or was it Louis? It seemed to be both, in a composite person, calling her into a dream of happiness. She was drifting. From the other bed she heard Edward say, 'Are you awake?' but she was too far down to answer, too far down to want to come back . . .

Ethel was sitting by the window, which had a nice view over the treetops and a glimpse of the garden below. Beside her was a basket of socks for darning, but she was sewing a baby-shirt, which gave her a strange feeling, because it made her wonder about the baby, which she had not done so far. The bulge in front of her was merely an inconvenience and a punishment, not a person. But Mrs Hunter had given her some nice sheer cotton and a pattern, and told her the baby would need some things. The Hunter children had been babies too long ago and their clothes and toys had been given away, but there was a cot up here, and the sheets for it were still in the linen closet. The baby would not be laid in a drawer or an orange box, as Ethel had seen it done back in Gosford.

A baby. A little boy, maybe. She thought of herself with a little boy. She skipped over babyhood and jumped to a toddler, trotting along beside her, holding her hand. Was there something enticing about the image? Would he look like Andy Wood? Well, Andy Wood was a decent-looking bloke, but she didn't think she wanted to be haunted by him for the rest of her life. Better she had a little girl, maybe. A little girl who looked like her, with golden curls and—

She pricked her finger because she wasn't paying attention,

and cursed softly. Ethel Lusby and a child? What did she know about babies? And how would she keep it? She couldn't expect Mrs Hunter to keep her on *and* accommodate the child. Terror of destitution was bred deep in her bones, by generations of peasant forebears. It was what had driven her all these years to try to better herself, secure a husband who would provide for her. Much good it had done her! Stuck with this—

There was a knock on the door, startling her out of her savage thoughts. A knock? Nobody in the house would knock. The children weren't allowed up here – she had gathered that from Lilian – and anyone else would come right in.

'Yes – come in?' she called.

The door opened, and the big figure of Frank Hussey ducked under the lintel, making her heart jump with a mixture of dismay and excitement. 'Hello, Ethel,' he said.

'What are you doing here?' she exclaimed, jumping up. Her hands went automatically to her bump as if to conceal it – fat chance now, with the good food she was getting! 'No-one's supposed to know.'

'Mr Munt told me. He wasn't very complimentary.'

'I bet,' said Ethel, bitterly. 'He always hated me.'

'You always hated him,' Frank pointed out, with his easy smile. 'So then I went in and made Mrs Dunkley spill the beans.' Frank was the only person who ever called Cook by her name. It gave Ethel a queer shiver, because she knew he did it to be kind, and she didn't know how to cope with kind people.

'So now you know it all,' she said sourly, because, of course, he didn't. No-one but her knew the really bad thing.

'Not quite,' he said. 'There are a couple of things I'd like to know. Can I ask you a question? Two questions?'

'Why should I tell you anything?' she said defiantly.

'Because I've got your best interests at heart.'

'Heart!' she said scornfully. But she sat down, finding her

legs suddenly weak. 'What d'you want to know, then? Curiosity killed the cat.'

He looked round, picked up a wooden nursery chair, placed it in front of her and sat down carefully. It creaked a bit under him. There wasn't an ounce of fat on him, but he was a big man, with gardener's muscles. 'Who's the father?' he began abruptly.

The answer was snapped out of her automatically. 'None of your business.'

'Why won't he marry you?'

'Is that your second question?'

'No, it's still part of the first. Does he know?'

'No.'

'Why haven't you told him?'

'Because he's married already.'

'Ah,' said Frank. 'I thought it might be something like that.'

She said nervously, 'It's no-one you know.'

'Is that a fact?' He looked at her steadily, but she stared defiantly back. 'Here's my second question, then. Why didn't you come to me?'

It wasn't what she'd expected. 'Come to you?' she said, startled.

'I told you, didn't I, that if you were ever in trouble to come to me, and I'd always help you? Told you more than once.'

Ethel felt herself reddening, and looked down at the baby-shirt rather than at him, and began unconsciously pulling it about.

He removed it from her hand. 'You'll spoil it,' he said. 'Ethel, why didn't you come to me?'

'Didn't think,' she said. Then she looked up at him, despair in her eyes. 'Nothing you could've done, anyway.'

'I couldn't make you not be in the family way, that's true. But there's still a lot I could have done. I could have married you.'

'Married me?' she exclaimed derisively.

He was undaunted. 'Yes, married you. Plain English, isn't it? You need a husband and a father for your baby. Well, here I am. This is me asking you now, in case you hadn't twigged.'

'You want to marry me?' she said slowly, torn between the agony of hope and the misery of missed opportunities.

'Bit slow, aren't you? I'll say it again. Will you, Ethel Lusby, marry me, Frank Hussey? It's an official proposal.'

'But – *why*?'

'Why? Funny question. Because I like you, and because you need me. So, what do you say?'

'I *can't*!'

He didn't blink. 'Why, because of this – married man of yours?'

'No,' she said scornfully. 'I wouldn't have him if he asked.'

'Which he won't. So, go on, then. I've got a steady job and a little cottage. It's not grand, but I'll be head gardener one of these days because Mr Orwell will be retiring, and then I get a better house.'

'You'll get called up one of these days, and then what?'

'No, I won't. I've told you before, they won't take *me*.'

'Because you're a gardener?' she said derisively.

'No, because I've got a medical condition,' he said calmly. 'It's not one that need concern you, but it means the army doesn't want me. I was called up in February, as it happens, and failed the medical, so I've got the exemption papers at home.'

She felt winded. 'You never told me.'

'Never told anyone – and don't you go telling anyone either.'

'Me? I'm no talker.'

'No, you're not. It's one of the things I like about you. So, is it a go?'

She looked at him despairingly. 'I *can't*.'

'You said that already, but you didn't say why.'

'Because you don't know what I am. You don't know – who my parents were.'

With a creak of the chair he leaned forward and took both her hands. 'I don't care who they were. It's you I want to marry, not them. I'll take care of you, Ethel, and your kid, and when we have some of our own, I swear I'll never make any difference between them. Come on, what do you say? Let me get you out of this hole. I can't bear to see you stuck down there and struggling.'

'You'd rescue a wasp out of a water butt, wouldn't you?' she said wonderingly.

He laughed – a big, lovely laugh full of life and hope. 'Probably I would. I'd kill it after, but I can't bear to see helpless struggles. Makes me sick to my stomach, that.'

'So it's kindness, then? You want to marry me just out of kindness.'

He gave her the old smile that had always intrigued and annoyed her – the one that saw through her wiles and found them amusing, like the gambollings of a kitten. 'Gor, you're a hard woman to woo!' he said. 'It's not *just* kindness – I told you, I like you – but it seems to me you're in need of a bit of kindness anyway. What's up? Don't you fancy me, then?'

Oh, yes, she did! That was part of the trouble. She fancied him like anything, and liked him a lot more than was good for her. How could she let him buy the pig in the poke that was Ethel Lusby? On the other hand, here was a lifebelt being thrown, and did she really want to drown? A father for the baby – respectability – a home.

'Have you asked the missus?' she said.

'I will do. But do you really think she won't be delighted?'

'Oh, is that why you're doing it? Sucking up to the nobs?'

He ignored that. 'Come on, Ethel. Say yes. One short little word – it isn't so hard. Shall I spell it for you? Y-e-s. Will – you – marry – me?'

And she heard herself say, 'Yes,' though she hadn't been

sure the instant beforehand that she would. But immediately she felt a huge relief, as though she had been holding up something back-breakingly too heavy, and someone had told her she could put it down.

Frank stood up. 'Good girl,' he said. 'And now give us a kiss. You're allowed to, as an engaged person.'

She stood, but instead of kissing her, he enfolded her in his strong arms and held her close against him. 'Don't be scared,' he murmured. 'I'll look after you.' He cupped her head, and she rested against his shirt and felt the warmth of his skin through it. A tear tried to squeeze out but she refused it passage.

Then his big hand tilted her face up and he kissed her – and it was as well he was holding her up, because it was so lovely her knees threatened to give out.

He set her back on her feet, smiled, and said, 'When Mrs Hunter comes back, I'll ask her. Meanwhile, let's keep this to ourselves, all right?'

'Master's back,' she reminded him.

'This is for her, not him. Don't worry, I won't run out on you. But there are things I need to discuss with her, so keep the secret for now. It'll only be a few days.' He was at the door, but turned back. 'Oh, in case you start thinking this was all just a dream . . .'

He felt in his pocket and placed in her palm a piece of metal in the shape of a funny little imp-creature, capering and grinning. It had a loop at the top as if for hanging on a chain. 'It's a lucky pixie,' he said. 'It's the seal off my watch-chain. My dad give it me. He got it from his boss after twenty years' service. It's real gold. It'll give you something to hold on to till I buy you a ring.'

Then he was gone, and Ethel sat down, feeling bewildered. Yes, she thought, it was just as well he had given her something, or she *would* have thought she'd dreamed it.

★　★　★

Bobby's kit came home. Sadie was glad it arrived while Mother was away, for it fell to her to unpack it. Why, she wondered, would they send a bloodstained uniform to break people's hearts all over again? The undershirt, shirt and jacket were all brown and stiff with it, and there were smears on the trousers as well. His personal possessions were few – his housewife, his brushes, his writing-case, a few books. Meticulously, the army sent back everything that had been his, even a half-used tin of tooth powder and an almost-empty bottle of cologne. It was agony to look at them. Ghosts of his body, which had been shattered and died, and was buried somewhere in the clay of France. The Church said his spirit lived on, and went home to God, but there was no evidence of that here, only of the absence of the body they had loved. It took more faith than she had to be comforted in the face of half a tin of tooth powder.

And his watch, which Dad had given him when he got his wings. Absently, automatically, she wound it, and it came to life, ticking as a cat purrs, the hands beginning minutely to move. If only you could revive the body the same way. *Bobby! Bobby!*

She gave the watch to her father when he came home from work. How tired he looked, these days, how full of cares.

Edward gave it to William, who received it with awe, then had to run away and hide. It was hard for a boy to cry when he was sixteen. But Bobby had been his hero. In the darkness of the airing cupboard, he clutched the watch so tightly his palm hurt, and sobbed as though his heart would break.

Beattie came home. She looked thin, and worn out, and Edward guessed she had not been eating. Everyone gathered in the hall to greet her, and Cook spoke up for the servants, asking how Mr David was.

'About the same,' she said. 'Except they don't think there's danger of gangrene now.'

'Well, that's a blessing, madam,' said Cook, in the strained voice of one trying to find something positive to say.

'Oh, yes, a blessing,' said Beattie, as though it was irony. She stood where she had stopped, like a stalled motor-car, staring at Cook, as though she might get her going again.

Cook said, 'Supper in ten minutes, madam.' And she hustled the servants away.

Edward guided her gently into the drawing-room, and the children followed and sat around, looking at her in a lost way. 'He didn't speak,' she said. 'Not all the time I was there. I don't know if he knew I was there. He must be in pain, but he doesn't show it. Only once, he cried. No sound, but tears coming from his eyes.'

'Will he—' Sadie had to swallow and start again. 'Will he come home?'

Beattie looked at her blankly, as if she didn't know who she was. 'If he lives.'

Sadie got up, took Peter's hand and pushed William gently. 'Let's go in the morning-room and get on with that jigsaw puzzle,' she said.

Alone with Edward, Beattie said, 'I'm sorry.'

It could have been an apology for anything, or nothing. He said, 'No, I'm sorry. This is hard for all of us.'

She nodded. 'Sadie's a good child.'

'I don't know how we'd have managed without her.'

'Edward—'

She seemed on the brink of some perilous revelation, and he shook his head. 'It's all right,' he said. 'No need to say anything.'

'I'm sorry,' she said again, hopelessly. 'I'm no good for anything. I'm so tired.'

'You've a right to be,' he said.

They went up to bed early, and at the door Beattie gave

him a look of such exhaustion and defeat that he said, 'I'll sleep in the dressing-room, so as not to disturb you.' He hoped she might say no, stay here with me, but she didn't.

He lay wakeful in the unfamiliar, narrow bed, lonely, grieving for his sons, and wondering if something had broken that could not be mended.

The next day Diana came to visit. 'Aunt Sonia said you were back.' Edward had telephoned her from work first thing. 'How is he?'

Beattie gave her what news there was, thinking how lovely her daughter looked. At least things had worked out for her. Her clothes were smart, her hair beautifully arranged, her poise queenly. She was wearing a necklace of garnets with matching earrings, an unusual setting, pretty.

Diana saw her looking at them and said, 'Rupert bought them for me. He loves buying me jewels. But it seems wrong to talk about things like that when Bobby's dead, and David—'

'No, it's all right,' Beattie said. 'There are people all over the country who have lost men they loved, and they carry on as if nothing had happened. Put on a brave face, darling – that's the patriotic thing to do. Life goes on.'

'Yes,' said Diana. 'It does. That's the thing, you see. I'm having a baby.' She searched her mother's face. 'I wasn't sure if I ought to tell you yet, if it would be – tactless.'

Beattie looked at her for a long time. 'It's not tactless,' she said at last. 'But are you sure? It's very soon.'

'I'm pretty sure. I've always been . . . regular.' She blushed at the mention of such things. 'Rupert's sure. He says he had a sixth sense about it. It's rather sweet, Mummy – he's so thrilled. Even more than me, really. I had to swear him to secrecy because he wanted to rush out and tell everyone and, well, if it should turn out to be a false alarm . . .'

'I won't tell until you say I can.'

'I know it doesn't make up for Bobby. Nothing can. But it's – new life.' She looked appealingly at her mother. 'David's going to be all right, isn't he? I mean, he won't – die?'

'I don't know,' said Beattie. 'We can only pray.' She roused herself. 'How's the new house coming along?'

'Oh, very well. It will be ready next month, but we won't move in until September, of course. Everyone's going out of London now. Lord and Lady Wroughton are going to Norfolk and then to Scotland for the whole of August, and Rupert and I have invitations to country-house parties all summer. It'll be nice to have a proper home to come back to. I hope the baby will be born there. You will be there when it comes, won't you? I think I'm going to feel very nervous.'

'There's nothing to it,' Beattie said.

'I knew you'd say that.' Her smile was radiant. 'As soon as I'm sure, I'll let you know, and then you can tell everyone.'

Sadie came in just then, and said, 'Tell everyone what?' Her eyes widened. 'Are you having a baby?'

Diana turned to her. 'I think I am. How did you guess?'

'I don't know, it just came to me.'

'It's supposed to be a secret until I'm really sure. You won't tell anyone, Sadie, because if it turned out to be a false alarm—'

'I won't tell anyone, if you say not. Only – you'll tell Father? He's so sad, and tired, working too hard and everything, and it would make him happy, at least for a little bit.'

'You can tell Father, but nobody else just yet,' said Diana.

Beattie was surprised when Ada came to say Frank Hussey would like to speak to her privately. He came, clean-scrubbed, respectful, his cap in his hands, his cheeks red from a really good shave, and said that he would like to marry Ethel.

He was a nice-looking man with a patently honest face, the sort of chap any young girl would be glad to have as a suitor. He was too good, really, for Ethel, she thought, then checked herself, because who was she to cast stones?

'Can you support a wife and family?' she asked.

'It won't be a high living, ma'am, but I have a job and a little cottage.'

'But what if you get called up?'

'I'm exempt, ma'am. I've a heart condition, not bad enough to kill me in the normal way, but there aren't any jobs in the army that wouldn't be too much of a strain. So since I'm engaged in growing food, which the nation needs, they give me my certificate.'

'I'm sorry. I didn't realise,' Beattie said.

'It don't bother me, ma'am. I've got a good healthy outdoor life, the best thing for me.'

'Well, it seems to me an excellent solution for Ethel, and I'm very happy for you both,' Beattie said. 'You have my blessing, if that means anything to you.'

'Thank you, ma'am.' He smiled. 'You been very kind to her, but I guess you'll be glad to have her off your hands.'

'When are you going to marry?' she asked.

'I got a few things to sort out, ma'am, make the cottage suitable for a wife and child, a few arrangements with my master and so on. So, if it's all right with you, I thought next month. August. Baby's not due till October. But that's if you're willing to keep her on a bit longer, because she's nowhere else to go.'

'I took her in, Hussey. I won't turn her out now.'

'Thank you, ma'am. I take that right kindly.'

'And where will you do it – the wedding?'

'Well, ma'am, not the church, in the circs. We'll go for a register-office do.'

'I hope you'll accept a wedding present from Mr Hunter and me for the occasion.'

'Oh, no, ma'am, there's no need – you been so kind already.'

300

'There'll be a lot of things to buy. I expect cash will be the most welcome, won't it?'

He seemed overwhelmed by the idea, but accepted gratefully.

And, thought Beattie, it would be worth it to her to have the Ethel problem resolved so painlessly. And if there was one man in the world who could curb her destructive proclivities, that man must be Frank Hussey.

CHAPTER NINETEEN

Nula had sorted out a pattern and some material – there were lots of spare dress-lengths in the linen room – so that Ethel could make herself a decent outfit for her wedding. She went to Beattie, ostensibly to ask her permission. 'I'll have to give her a hand,' she added, 'because the pattern'll take a bit of altering to allow for her shape, but she can do the work herself. Better she keeps occupied.'

Beattie nodded. 'I've no objection. What did you really want to see me for?'

'This came,' Nula said, taking an envelope out of her pocket. 'It was inside an envelope addressed to me.'

She handed it to Beattie, who stared at it like one mesmerised. *He had written at last!* Such a time had passed with no word from him that she'd thought he'd decided not to. A darker part of her mind feared he had been killed. Of course, no-one would tell her. He would be dead and buried, and she would never know.

'What's going on?' Nula asked bluntly.

Beattie rallied. 'Don't be impertinent. It's none of your business.'

'It was lucky Wilkes had gone to work when it came or I'd have had to explain it to him. If I'm to cover up for you, it *is* my business.'

'Just bring me any letters, that's all you have to do.'

'Who is it?' Nula demanded, setting her jaw. 'I don't like

302

it. It's not like you. And the master's always been so good to you.'

'For God's sake, stop talking!' Beattie said wearily.

'*And* to me. If you're deceiving him—'

'I met him again,' Beattie said. 'In London. By accident. He's in uniform. He's back at the Front now but—'

Somehow Nula caught her meaning. Her eyes widened. 'Oh, my God. You don't mean – *him*? After all these years?'

Beattie raised her head. 'I've been seeing him, at his house, in London.'

'Oh, what have you done?' Nula said in horror. 'Beattie Cazalet, what are you thinking? Are you mad? He ruined you once, and now you want to let him ruin you again?'

'I couldn't help it. I had to see him. How could I walk away? *You* know—'

'Yes, *I* know all right! You've a grand marriage, a wonderful husband—' Something occurred to her. 'Mr Edward's been sleeping in the dressing-room, hasn't he?'

'That's not – that's because of Bobby. And David. He doesn't know. He mustn't know.'

'You're damn right he mustn't,' Nula said hotly. 'He's a good, decent man and he doesn't deserve this.'

Beattie felt a surge of anger, mingled with shame and fear. 'You can't speak to me like that. I know I owe you a lot—'

'Where would you have been if I hadn't helped you? Who do you think got Mr Edward up to the starting line? He was too shy to think himself good enough for you. He's a damned sight too good, if you want my opinion!'

'You're right,' Beattie said, defiance evaporating. She stared at Nula in misery. Bobby was dead – her gay, debonair Bobby. David was wounded, perhaps dying. And Edward was suffering, but she couldn't comfort him. 'I can't help it,' she cried. 'I love him. I've always loved him. Nula, help me. I can't bear it. Everything hurts so much.'

Nula stepped close. 'Baby, my baby,' she said caressingly, 'my little miss.' Carefully she took her mistress into her arms. Beattie tried to hold back, her body stiff. 'I know how much you hurt, my baby. Wasn't I there all the time, from the beginning? But I took care of you. I'll always take care of you.'

Nula held her, stroked her back. She wished there had been tears, but Beattie didn't cry. Tears had never come easily for her. And after those first bitter storms, when Louis had gone away, something seemed to have broken in her, and she rarely cried. It would be better if she could.

Most beautiful, most beloved [Louis had written], did you think this letter would never come? Things are hectic here. We work until late at night, sleep a couple of hours and rise before dawn to begin again. There is barely time to eat, and we survive on picnic meals snatched between crises. So I must be brief. I just wanted you to know I am still here, and still love you more than life itself. Please write to me – address your envelope to my friend Capt F. Fortescue here at HQ and he will pass it on to me. He is a safe hand – don't worry. No more now, but I hope to have leisure in a few more days to write properly. Ever yours, L.

The battle in Picardy ground on, and casualties were brought daily back to Britain. The nation was used to it now, and the sight of those loaded hospital trains moved but did not shock and frighten people as it had last year. The various support and comforts organisations, which had been idling in the first half of the year, roared into high gear. New hospitals opened; soldiers in convalescent blue were a common sight in every town. And in army camps all over the country, the newly conscripted learned their trade, ready to take the place of the fallen at the Front. Meanwhile, the munitions factories worked day and night, providing the millions of tons of shells needed. The war had become an efficient machine.

The August bank holiday was cancelled, as the Whitsun one had been, to increase production; there was a rumour that Guy Fawkes Night was to be banned, in case the bonfires and fireworks attracted Zeppelins. And since the 21st of May, the clocks had all been put forward an hour under a scheme to use the daylight hours more effectively. 'Government Time', the people called it – to distinguish it from God's Time, the real hour of the day it would be if it hadn't been 'messed with'. It was useless for thinkers like Frank Hussey to point out that the clocks had always been set by man: traditionalists like Cook, who hated change, stubbornly averred that no good would come of tinkering with the ways of the Almighty.

Now that Frank was to make Ethel an honest woman she was officially allowed to exist, and though her presence in the kitchen was not encouraged, she did pass through it daily on her way to get a breath of air in the garden. Lilian and Emily gazed at her with big eyes, and Emily had to be restrained from rushing to talk to her. Ada was embarrassed by her pregnant shape, went red and could not look at her directly.

The sight of Ethel made Cook grumpy. She had been forced to accept the creature under threat of dismissal, and no-one likes being coerced. And she felt obscurely cheated by this happy ending. The wicked were supposed to be punished, weren't they? Munt merely opined that Frank was a fool, and that he wouldn't have thought him mug enough to be taken in. Mrs Chaplin, the charwoman, on her days, was eager for details no-one could give her, and was forced to make them up for herself when she was pressed for gossip by her own friends away from the house. Only Nula, when she was at the house, declined to express any opinion. 'I've got worries of my own,' she would say. 'More important ones.'

'She's worried about Mr David,' Cook said wisely. 'Poor young man.'

'But he's out of danger now, isn't he?' Ada said anxiously. 'Didn't the missus say?'

'There's out of danger, and then there's all right,' Cook said gnomically. 'And what about that poor young woman he's engaged to? It must be breaking her heart – such a sweet, pretty, nice girl as she seemed.'

'She'll stand by him,' Ada said, thinking of Len. If that had happened to him . . . Thank God he was in England, training troops, not out in France. 'Mr David *will* get better. I feel it in my water. We'll see him walk down the aisle with Miss Oliphant yet.'

'At least he's got a chance,' said Cook. 'Not like Mr Bobby.' His death had hurt her deeply. And without a funeral, grief felt unfinished. You had to mourn them for ever if you couldn't lay them away properly. The master had ordered his bloodstained clothes burned, but before Ginger had carried them out to the bonfire, Cook had cut off the buttons. 'Waste not, want not,' she had said. But they had not gone into the button-box. She kept them in a little box in her bedroom drawer to remember him by. They were like a talisman to her. In a confused way, she felt they would keep her safe. Bobby would watch over her if she kept his buttons, and the Zeppelins would not get her.

Ethel had been feeling rather unwell all day. It started with breakfast – Lilian brought her up her tray, and the smell of the kipper made her stomach heave. 'Take that away!' she complained.

'But you've got to eat,' Lilian said. 'My ma says you have to eat for two when you're in the family way. Look, it's a lovely kipper, and nice bread and butter. It's what they're

306

having in the dining-room. We had porrage and bacon. I'll just leave it for you – you'll feel like it in a minute.'

Ethel poured herself a cup of tea, then nibbled at a piece of bread, felt a bit stronger, and thought she'd tackle the kipper. She had two or three mouthfuls before she thought better of it. But now she believed it must have been off, because she had a pain in her stomach.

'Rotten kipper,' she muttered. There was some Milk of Magnesia in the nursery bathroom cupboard, so she had a big slurp of that, then sat on the edge of the bath for a bit to see if she would be sick. She rather wanted to be – she felt it would sort things out. But she wasn't. She just had the tight, rising feeling inside her, and that knot of nagging pain.

By lunchtime, the pain had moved round to her back, and she hobbled down to the kitchen clutching it like an old woman.

'What's the matter with you?' Cook demanded, without sympathy. Playing the old soldier, she sniffed to herself. Looking for sympathy. Well she's come to the wrong shop!

'Got this pain,' Ethel said shortly. She was finding it hard to catch her breath.

'Kidneys,' said Cook.

'I couldn't eat a thing,' Ethel gasped.

'No, where you've got your hand – kidneys. My brother-in-law in Folkestone had 'em. Fetched him off in the end.'

'It was that kipper this morning. Must've been bad,' Ethel said.

'It was not!'

'Me uncle had a bad kipper once,' Emily said, coming in with a pile of plates. 'It went right through him, but a bit of it got stuck in a corner inside him, and three days later he swelled up and died. It's true!'

'Never mind your uncle,' Cook said. 'Anyway, this one was as sweet a kipper as I've ever fried. D'you think I'd

307

have bad fish in my kitchen? You et it too quick, that's all.'

'Kippers give me wind,' said Emily. 'But I like that – you get to taste 'em all over again. Here, you look awful white,' she added to Ethel. 'Have a sit-down.'

Ethel reached behind her for a chair. There was a horrid swelling feeling in her ears, and she felt nausea rising. 'Think I'm going to be sick,' she said.

'Not in my kitchen, you're not!' Cook said indignantly.

But Ethel didn't vomit, she fainted.

When the doctor left, Beattie came to her bedside. 'You've lost a lot of blood,' she said, 'but you'll be all right.'

Ethel looked at her from what felt like five fathoms down. Her tongue was leaden and words seemed immensely difficult to form, as though she were trying to speak under water. 'The baby,' she said, with huge effort. 'I never heard it cry.'

'I'm sorry,' Beattie said. 'Two months early, it didn't have a chance. It never breathed. Born dead, poor little thing.'

'Can I see it?' Ethel managed.

'No, dear. The midwife took it away. Would you like a drink of water?' She lifted Ethel's head and held the cup to her lips.

Back on the pillow, Ethel felt an enormous weight of sleep rolling over her, like a great tide. She was drowning. But how could she drown when she was already under water? She forced her eyelids up. Mrs Hunter was turning to leave. 'What was it?' she asked.

Beattie turned back. 'What's that?'

'Boy or girl?'

'It doesn't do to think about it,' said Beattie, firmly. 'Sleep now, and you'll feel better when you wake up.'

Ethel stared at her with all the urgency she could muster from far, far down below the waves. '*Please?*'

Beattie hesitated. 'It was a boy,' she said. 'But too tiny

to live. Don't think about it. You're young – there's plenty of time to have more. Go to sleep now.'

Ethel let go, and felt the tide carry her away.

'She'll have to stay here until she's recovered, at least,' Beattie said. 'The doctor says six weeks.'

Cook looked resentful. All that trouble for a girl like that! 'Couldn't Frank Hussey take her, madam? He was the one wanted to marry her.'

'Of course he can't. He's out at work all day,' Beattie pointed out. 'He wouldn't be able to look after her. I'm afraid he'll have to put off the wedding until she's on her feet again.'

'Lucky if he doesn't call it off,' Cook sniffed, 'now he's no need. Then we shall have her on our hands until Kingdom come.'

'He won't call it off,' Beattie said, with conviction. 'And if he did, she was a maid here before and she can be a maid here again.'

'Yes, madam,' Cook said gloomily. 'I don't know why you're so soft on that girl,' she felt compelled to add. 'She don't deserve it.'

'Which of us gets what we deserve, if it comes down to it?' Beattie said. 'We all need God's mercy.'

'Yes, madam,' Cook assented, because she had to. But she was firmly of the opinion that the world was divided into sinners, and decent people like her, and God ought to show Himself on the side of the latter.

Edward was in his office when Laura arrived, whirled in past doddering old Murchison like a bomb blast. 'Just a fleeting visit!' she said. 'Someone had to come back for some specialised supplies, so we drew straws and I won. One night in a proper bed in a decent house, and then it's back to work, but it was worth it. How one pines for clean sheets – absurd, in the circumstances, but true! I'm staying at Sonia's.'

'Then let me give you lunch,' Edward said, trying to work out what was different about her, apart from a certain brownness of skin, which was not unattractive, though unusual in a woman.

'Dear Teddy, I'd love that, but it will have to be *very* quick, because I've so much to do. I have a shopping list as long as my arm for the Army & Navy – stockings and underwear and so on for the girls, not to mention morphine pills and Horlicks tablets and tweezers and I don't know what – and then I've got to get across to east London for some engine parts. Bessie's got a sore tum, and it's quicker for me to go and get them than to wait for them to reach us across "war-torn France", as the newspapers call it.'

'Speaking of which,' Edward invited.

'How am I getting on? Oh, famously! It's the most tremendous adventure, I promise you, and the best thing is knowing we're making a real difference.'

'But isn't it dangerous?'

'Oh, yes,' she said easily, 'but, you know, one simply hasn't time to be afraid. We roar up to the aid station, load up, and roar back to the hospital. Shells falling all around us, but as long as they don't fall *on* us, what's to worry about? And the men – my dear, they are *so* stoical in the face of such frightful wounds that one hasn't the gall to be upset by near misses. Now, what about that luncheon? Can we go to the Ritz? It's nearby, and I have such a hankering for a spot of luxury before I return to reality. They won't mind my garb, will they?'

'I think not,' said Edward. Everywhere had to be more accommodating nowadays. 'I expect one of these days a female will go in there in trousers, and then we shall see.'

'We'll see the temple come tumbling down! What, are there women in trousers in London?'

'Well, not in the smart places, not yet, but some of the working-class women wear them because of their jobs.'

On the way out, he stepped back for her to walk before him, and coming close behind her, he saw what was different. He had assumed her hair was pinned up under her hat, but now he saw there was no soft bulge there. *She had cut her hair!* He felt cold with shock for a moment. This was his sister, after all. Of course she would not have done it had she not been at the Front, but where would it end? He thought of his daughters with short hair, and knew, if that ever happened, a very important temple would have come tumbling down.

Over luncheon, she told him about her life. They had a base in Amiens – a sort of lodging-house, with very basic facilities – but they were hardly ever there. There was so much to do, so many wounded to move, that they worked fourteen hours a day, sometimes more, and often just snatched a few hours' sleep in the ambulance. 'After we've swilled it out, of course, at the end of the day,' she added, offhand, shocking him again. They had had to adapt Bessie, putting in an extra rack on either side so they could take six stretchers, though it was hard to hoist the top ones into place – 'but better than leaving the men perhaps for hours more'. And sometimes there would be another body in a stretcher on the floor, and half a dozen walking wounded hanging on however they could and trying not to tread on his face.

'Oh, and, my dear, the roads! The ruts and holes and mud! It's quite terrible to think what all the jolting is doing to the men. But they never make a squeak. It's their pride, you see. Now and then we get some poor soul who's raving, and they try to hush him up. "Not in front of the ladies," they say, in shocked tones. It makes me want to cry.'

'What do you hear about the progress of the battle?' he asked.

'Nothing. That's far above our level. The Tommies never see anything but the little space in front of them. All they know is that they have to shoot when they see a grey uniform. Now and then we have a word or share a cigarette with an officer – yes, I've taken up smoking, don't look like that. It's the only way to get through the day. The wounded smell so terrible, and a good gasper is all that stops one making a fool of oneself. What was I saying? Oh, yes. The officers don't know much more than the men, but they say they're making progress, though every yard is hard fought. And the casualties – well, I don't think anyone at home has any idea of the scale of the casualties. But they say the Jerries are worse hit.' She glanced at the clock. 'Is that the time? I must fly. I haven't had time to ask about all of you. I'm so sorry about Bobby. It's hard to believe he's gone. But he died a hero's death – without the RFC, our men would be attacked from the air as well as on the ground. And David – how is he going on?'

'They've sent him home – to England, I mean.'

'Well, that's encouraging! When?'

'He arrived yesterday. He's at the WHC hospital in Endell Street.'

'Oh, but that's our hospital!' Laura exclaimed. 'You know our doctor comes from there? I'm sure I told you. Have you seen him?'

'We haven't been allowed to visit yet. I believe the journey set him back quite badly. We just have to be patient and wait for better news.'

Laura laid a hand on his arm. 'He couldn't be in better hands, you know. Women doctors have to be twice as good as the men to qualify at all. All the officers say if they catch a Blighty, that's where they'd like to go. How's Beattie holding up?'

'Not well,' Edward said. 'She doesn't complain, but I know she's suffering.'

'Yes, he always was her favourite, wasn't he?' Laura said.

'The prognosis isn't good,' Edward confessed, 'but if only she could see him, she might be able to bear it better.'

'Hospitals hate visitors, so you shouldn't read too much into it. My dear, I must go! Give them all my love. And I'd adore a good long letter with all the news. Tell Sadie to write – she's the one who notices everything.' He stood as she did. 'Thanks for the lunch. You're looking tired, my dear. Don't take too much out of yourself.'

'You're looking well – invigorated,' he said.

'I feel it! I believe I'm ten years younger than when I went away.' She kissed his cheek in farewell.

He had time for one last word. 'Laura – your hair!'

She turned back, grinning. 'Like Jo in *Little Women*, I find it so cool and comfortable I don't think I'll ever grow it again. *Now* I've shocked you!' And she was gone.

Ethel looked up as Frank Hussey came in. She pulled the sheet up defensively to her chest. 'What are you doing here?' she asked sharply.

'That's a fine question. Who's got a better right?' He crossed the room with a chair and sat down beside the bed. 'I'd'a been here before, but they said you weren't able for visitors. It's been a long two weeks.'

'Is it two weeks?' she said listlessly.

'It is,' he said. 'They say downstairs the doctor says you're going on all right.' She shrugged. 'Ethel, I'm so sorry,' he said gently, taking her hand. 'I can't imagine how you feel – I don't suppose any man can – but I know you must be upset.'

'I don't feel anything at all,' she said, 'just weak and worn out.'

'You lost a lot of blood. You'll need building up. Lots of rest and good food. Lucky Mrs Dunkley's a good cook – she'll get your appetite back for you.'

She didn't answer. Her hand lay limply in his, and her pale face was turned away from him. It hurt him to see her brought so low, when she had always been so full of fire and spite. He longed for a snippy answer from her. It would not tug so badly at his heart.

'Mrs Hunter's ever so kind,' he tried. 'She's said you can stay here as long as you need to. And the doctor says you'll be able to start getting out of bed in another week, just for a little while each day, and that in six weeks you'll be back to normal. Of course, I had to cancel the wedding, but I booked it again for Saturday the 16th of September. You'll be all right by then, won't you? What do you think about that?'

Ethel removed her hand from his and looked him in the face. 'I think you'd better *un*book it. I'm not going to marry you.'

He studied her expression. 'Why?' he asked, just as bluntly.

'Because there's no need now. I've lost the baby, so everything's all right again. You don't need to marry me.'

'I wasn't marrying you because of need,' he said. 'I want to.'

'Well, I don't want to marry you,' she said, 'so it's off. All right?'

'No, it's not all right. This is just your weakness talking. You wanted to marry me, and it wasn't just because of the baby. You'll feel different when you're a bit stronger. I'm not taking no for an answer, not when you're still all upset.'

'I'm not upset. I never wanted that baby and I'm glad it's gone. Now I can get back to my own life.' She turned her head away again so that she wouldn't have to look at him as she said the next bit. 'And that doesn't include you. I don't need you any more. I'm not going to tie myself down to a rotten *under-gardener*. I can do better than that. I've got plans. I want to make something of myself.'

He didn't say anything for a long moment. Then she

314

heard the chair creak as he stood up. 'All right, Ethel, we'll leave it at that for now. I'll come and see you again when you're more yourself.'

'Don't bother!'

He walked towards the door. She reached under her pillow and held out her hand. 'Here, you'd better take this back.'

He turned. On her palm was the watch-seal pixie. He considered her expression for another moment. 'No, you keep it,' he said. 'I reckon you need the luck more'n me.'

'I don't want it,' she said, and threw it at him. She missed, of course, and he went out and shut the door quietly.

She managed to hold off the tears until she was sure he wasn't coming back, then buried her face in the pillow. She was the child of shame. She couldn't do that to Frank, let him marry her now there was no need. She could have duped and tricked and cozened any other man, but not him.

When Lilian brought up her tea, she saw the pixie at once, and said, 'How did that get there?'

'It's mine. Give it to me,' Ethel said. Lilian put the tray down and brought it to her, and she restored it to its place under the pillow.

'Is that gold?' Lilian asked, with interest. 'Where'd you get it?'

'Never you mind,' Ethel said, but it was without her customary fire.

War or no war, the servants had to have their annual holiday. Cook departed on the 17th, taking Emily with her, to stay with her sister in Folkestone. Usually Emily dreaded these visits, but this time she was intrigued to find out if you really could hear the guns in France.

Ada and Lilian held the fort – Ada was not a bad cook, as long as you didn't mind simple food – and would go when Cook and Emily got back. To take the strain off the household, Edward was to stay at his club. The Palfreys had gone to Brighton for the whole month, and the boys had gone with them – William, in particular, was looking peaky, and needed a holiday. He took his Scouting duties very seriously, and Bobby's death had affected him deeply. He didn't really want to go, until Sadie pointed out that there were bound to be Scouting duties in Brighton, like anywhere else, and he could get Ada to pack his uniform.

That left Sadie and Beattie at home. Sadie didn't want a holiday – her work with the horses was not work to her. Beattie said she had too much to do to go away, and that it wouldn't be fair to leave the servants with Ethel to take care of, in case she had a relapse. She was worried about the girl. Frank Hussey had come to her to tell her that Ethel had refused him, but he was confident that she would change her mind when she felt stronger, and asked Beattie not to mention it to her. Beattie was impressed by his determination, but was afraid that Ethel, who had a stubborn streak, really would refuse to marry him, and then what would become of her? Beattie would be stuck with her for ever.

'It won't be much of a holiday for you,' Edward said.

'I can come up to London on the odd day,' she said. 'And I want to be on hand when they say we can visit David.'

Edward departed sadly, knowing he was not wanted. He would be more comfortable sleeping at the club than in the dressing-room, and the food there would be better than Ada's, but he was lonely, worried about his son, grieving for Bobby, and wondering how he and Beattie would repair the breach between them – or if she even wanted to. If David recovered – *when* he recovered – she might be in better heart; but would she want to take him back into her life? And would he be able to forget she had rejected him? Two separate blows, Bobby and David, had wounded them, and he was afraid they would never be quite whole again.

★   ★   ★

The Endell Street hospital building had been an old work-house, and consisted of two five-storey blocks linked by a glass-covered passage. When the Women's Hospital Corps had taken it over it had been cleaned and painted, the old fixtures ripped out, new plumbing and electricity laid in throughout, and lifts capable of carrying stretchers installed. Each ward had its own kitchen and bathroom; operating theatres, X-ray rooms, laboratories, dispensaries, storerooms and a mortuary were created. It had 520 beds, and though it accepted only male patients – all officers – it was run entirely by women, with around fifteen lady doctors and eighty nursing staff, headed by Dr Louisa Garrett Anderson, who was chief surgeon.

In the early part of the war, every hospital had taken in every kind of wounded soldier, but by 1916 some had begun to concentrate expertise in certain fields, and Endell Street now specialised in head injuries and femoral fractures. That, Beattie gathered, as she climbed out of the taxi in front of the building, was why David had been sent there. It gave her a little comfort to think that there was some kind of reason in all the madness. He had undergone two more operations since his arrival, to remove bone fragments from the wound, and to fix the ends of the bone together with a metal plate. Now, if infection did not set in – and that was always a risk – he might begin to mend.

A very young nurse met her at the door and escorted her upstairs. She seemed nervous of Beattie's grim expression, and chattered as they walked, as if to reassure her. 'It's lovely here,' she said. 'Everyone says it isn't like a military hospital – it's so home-like. Each ward has different-coloured bed covers and screens, and some ladies bring in flowers every day. And there's a dining-room and an entertainments hall where the convalescent patients can go. They have concerts and plays and things, and quite famous actors and singers and suchlike come and perform.'

'How nice,' Beattie said repressingly, and the nurse dropped gratefully into silence.

But the ward *was* pleasant, very light, with windows down both sides, and pale green walls that made an attractive background for the counterpanes and screens, which were in a pattern of pink and blue flowers on a buff background. There were thirty beds. At the near end the men were sitting up, or out of bed in armchairs, and Beattie felt their eyes following her with the minute interest generated by being confined with too little to do. At the far end the men were lying down, and some had screens round them.

And here was David at last. He was propped up on several pillows, and there was still a cage under the bedclothes. His hands were resting on the top sheet. Though he was awake, he wasn't reading or looking about him, but staring vacantly at nothing. He was thinner – so thin, his head was almost skull-like. The short-cut hair seemed to have lost much of its colour, not dark reddish-brown any more but almost sandy. He looked old. If she hadn't known him, she'd have thought him close to forty. Pain had etched itself into his white face in deep lines.

'A visitor for you, Captain Hunter,' said the nurse, brightly.

'David,' said Beattie.

His eyes moved to focus on her, but there was no welcome in them, no light. He nodded slightly, acknowledging her. There was a chair beside the bed, and she sat down, turning it to face him. He watched the movement, looked at her, but did not smile.

'My darling boy,' she said. 'I'm so glad to see you at last. How are you?'

He seemed to have to think for an answer. 'All right, I suppose. What date is it?'

'The twenty-second,' she said. He seemed to want more. 'Of August.'

'Ah,' he said. He looked away, and sighed. 'I lose track.'

He lifted a hand to scratch his nose, and it seemed a feeble, fumbling movement, like an old man's. He looked round vaguely. 'Are my cigarettes there?'

There was a packet and a lighter on the bedside cabinet. 'Shall I light one for you?' she offered. It gave her something to do. Smoking it gave *him* something to do, something to put into the vast chasm between them. He did not seem like her son at all.

At last he said, 'How's everyone?'

She searched for something that might interest him. 'Diana thinks she's going to have a baby.'

'Oh,' he said. He seemed to make an effort. 'That's good.'

There was a silence. She said, 'Have they told you anything – about when you might come home?'

He looked at her with an expression of surprise mixed with something like distaste. 'Home? God, not for a long time. Weeks. Months. I don't know.' He squeezed his eyes closed. 'It was kind of you to come,' he said politely. 'I'm afraid I'm not very good company.'

Beattie pressed her nails into her palms. 'You don't need to be good company,' she said. 'You're my son.'

'It was rotten luck about Bobby,' he said. She thought he had said it simply to deflect her. It came to her that he didn't want to talk to her, didn't want her there at all.

'Is there anything I can bring for you?' she asked in desperation.

'Nothing, thank you,' he said, still heartbreakingly polite. He opened his eyes. 'I'm rather tired – would you mind?' She stood up automatically. 'You don't need to come again,' he said. 'They look after me here all right.'

'Of course I'll come again,' she said; and then, grasping for something that might reach him, 'I'll bring Sophy to see you.'

His mouth turned down. 'I don't want her to see me like this.'

'She won't care about that,' Beattie said. 'She loves you.'

His grim face only grew grimmer, and he stared ahead of him, saying nothing, the cigarette burning down in his fingers.

'I'll go, then,' Beattie said. He didn't respond, and she made herself walk away. The sun was coming in from one side, throwing oblongs of light cut into squares by the shadows of the glazing bars, and she concentrated on them, stepping from light to shade to light down the ward to the door. He was in pain, she told herself, and frightened. But the thought of her son imprisoned in that grim, impenetrable misery made her think it might have been better if he had died after all. And then she thought that perhaps *her son* had. The man in that bed bore no resemblance to the gay and gallant David who had gone off to war.

CHAPTER TWENTY

'Ah, Hunter!' said Lord Forbesson. 'What news of your son?'

'He's out of immediate danger,' said Edward. 'But it will be a long process.'

'Yes, bound to be, bound to be,' said Forbesson. It sounded perfunctory, but with so many people in the same boat, it did not do these days to make too much fuss about any one of them. Stoicism was a national trait, and the war was exaggerating it. He thought Hunter was looking a trifle haggard but, then, who wasn't? They were all working and worrying long hours. 'Spot of luncheon?'

'Thanks. I'd be happy to join you.'

They strolled together into the club's dining-room. 'There's a table, over there,' said Forbesson. He grunted. 'Can't get used to the sight of these females waiting at table. Quite decorative and all that,' he waved a hand, 'but it's the wrong place for 'em.'

'I saw a conductorette on a bus this morning as I was walking along Piccadilly,' Edward offered.

'I don't mind that so much,' said Forbesson. 'As long as they don't start driving the damn things.'

When they had ordered – Edward was amused to note that Forbesson spoke slowly and loudly to the waitress as though she were a foreigner – they discussed finance and business. It was not until the main course had arrived that Edward asked how the war was going.

'Oh, we're making progress, y'know,' said Forbesson, inspecting the cutlets he had chosen to follow the club's excellent consommé. 'We've advanced the line some two miles, over a front of sixteen. It's a hard grind, but the general view is that the situation is satisfactory.'

'Our casualties, I believe they're quite heavy?'

'They're within acceptable limits. The Germans are suffering more than us – and *their* casualties are trained, experienced soldiers, the cream of their professional army, who simply can't be replaced. We're fatally weakening them, just as Haig planned, ready for the kill. It's attrition warfare, y'see – wearing them down more than they wear us down. Damned beastly business, but we didn't start it. That's what the Huns are doing to the French at Verdun – trying to bleed them dry. We didn't start it, but I'm damned sure we'll finish it.'

'I'll drink to that,' said Edward.

'And we've got a new weapon we're working on,' said Forbesson. 'When we unleash it on the Huns, it'll wipe their eye for them. A mobile cannon, mounted on a sort of armoured tractor. The really innovative part is that it lays its own track as it rolls along – can't tell you the technical details, but it means it can get across the worst terrain, mud, ditches, shell holes, the lot! As you probably realise, getting the artillery over shattered ground is hard, sometimes impossible, and horses and limbers get hopelessly bogged down in mud. This new machine will take our fire power right up to the enemy.'

'Extraordinary,' Edward said. 'This really is an industrial war, isn't it? New machines all the time. Zeppelins, submarines, aeroplanes, now these armoured tractors of yours.'

'Started out by calling 'em landships,' said Forbesson, spearing peas, 'but now they're calling 'em tanks. Haig's very keen. Be good if the machines would fight each other without involving us human beings,' he sighed. 'No blood, just oil and petrol.'

Lilian came back from her holiday at home with the news that they were building a magazine at West Hendorp. Because the Hendorp filling factory was expanding now that Darvell's was making the shell casings, they needed somewhere to store the finished shells until they were taken to the Front. The magazine was to have twenty huts, with a guardroom and mess, general stores and a forge. Tracks connected it to the main railway near Hendorp Junction.

'There's lots of extra work on the buildings and the lines,' she said excitedly, 'and they're digging a big sort of pond thing to hold water, in case of fire. My dad says it'll keep our lads out of the army for months. Only everyone's cross because they've got a band of Irish navvies actually laying the railway lines. My mum says they're a rough lot, the navvies. They get drunk and cause trouble.'

'I know!' Ginger said excitedly. 'I seen some of 'em. They live in this camp, sort of, down the end of the woods. They get into fights with the sojers from the army camp. I heard one of the sojers got beat up bad last week down Chalkpit Wood.'

'My Len says the Paget's Piece soldiers are going at the end of the week,' said Ada. 'Salisbury Plain for two weeks' brigade training, and then off to France.'

'We'll have to make sure and give 'em a send-off, brave lads,' said Mrs Chaplin, whose day it was.

'Off to France,' said Cook, mournfully. 'And who knows how many'll come back?'

'Don't talk like that,' Ada said.

'When you think how many of our local boys have give their all . . .'

'I heard Cliff Lanson, the groom from Breakspeare's, he copped it last week,' said Mrs Chaplin. 'And those two

323

officers that lodged at Mrs Wilkins's last year? Both of 'em gorn.'

'Oh, my Lord!' said Cook. 'I hadn't heard. She must be upset – she said they were like sons to her.'

'It's a tough old war,' said Mrs Chaplin.

'You don't need to tell anyone that in this house,' Cook retorted.

Sadie heard about the incident in Chalkpit Woods from Stanhill. They were in the paddock, backing a horse, a bay he had named Rhubarb. She had accustomed the horse to the saddle and bridle and to carrying a burden, in the form of a sack of bran slung over his back, but it was always a nervous moment when mounting for the first time. Horses were unpredictable. Some people advocated backing in the stable where there were fewer distractions and the horse couldn't get away; but Sadie liked room to fall clear if necessary, and she worried that if the animal reared it could hit its head and contract poll evil, which was often fatal.

It was good to have someone both strong and calm at the other end of the reins. Podrick would have been her man of choice before, but she and Stanhill had worked together a lot now, and she trusted him completely. She began by standing beside Rhubarb and leaning over the saddle, gradually putting more of her weight on him. The horse flicked his ears enquiringly and shifted his feet, but did not seem alarmed. 'All right,' said Sadie, quietly. 'Put me up.'

Still holding the horse's head, Stanhill took Sadie's lower leg and smoothly hoisted her until she could slide the other across the saddle. This was the potentially explosive moment. Rhubarb snorted and took a step forward, as if trying to get out from under the burden, then he swung his head round, ears back, teeth ready, to see what had caught him. Sadie leaned forward to offer him her hand to sniff, so he should know it was her. Stanhill spoke quietly to the horse, stroking his neck, and gradually the steel-spring tension went out of the legs and spine.

'I think he's going to be all right,' Sadie said. 'Try leading him forward. Take it slowly. And if you could keep talking, that'd help.'

Stanhill obliged, but instead of talking sweet nonsense to the horse, which was what she had meant, he told her about the Chalkpit Wood incident. He, however, had more detail than Ginger.

'It was a sergeant, name of Woods,' he said. 'He's well known, not just at the camp, something of a womaniser, apparently. And he's generally reckoned to be pretty handy with his fists, able to take care of himself.'

'How do you know all this?' Sadie asked.

'There's a sergeant from the camp I'm friendly with,' said Stanhill. 'We meet now and then for a beer. I knew him before the war – he's from Bradford too. I think he's settling in nicely,' he added, referring to the horse. Rhubarb was walking, rather in fits and starts as he tried to adjust to the movable object on his back, but quietly enough, his ears going back and forth like semaphore flags.

'Yes, he seems all right,' Sadie said. 'Go on about this soldier.'

'Well, everyone was surprised that he got himself knocked about, but he said four of them had set on him at once, so it wasn't a fair fight.'

'How horrible,' Sadie said. 'Did they find who did it?'

'That was the odd thing,' said Stanhill. 'The redcaps wanted him to go down to the navvy camp and pick them out so they could be handed over to the police, but he refused.'

'Why?'

'He wouldn't say. Just refused to co-operate. So then they put *him* on a charge for brawling.'

'That seems rather hard on him, if it wasn't his fault.'

'If,' said Stanhill enigmatically.

'You think there's more to it than there seems?' Sadie queried. 'But Mr Stanhill—'

He turned his head back to look at her with a wry smile. 'You oughtn't to call me "Mr", you know. I'm not an officer. I'm just "Stanhill".'

Sadie coloured a little. 'I couldn't possibly call you that.'

'You manage all right with Podrick and Bent and Oxer. And the ineffable Higgins.'

'That's different,' Sadie said, wondering why it was. 'You just seem to me to be naturally "Mr Stanhill".'

'Ah, it's the schoolmaster thing, isn't it? It's like a stain that ingrains itself and won't scrub off. I've been called "Mr Stanhill" by so many hundreds of little boys, I shall never be free of it.'

'Do you want to be?' Sadie asked, intrigued. 'I'd have thought being a schoolmaster was a thing to be proud of.'

'Bless your innocent heart, Miss Hunter – there are all sorts of schoolmasters, as many different sorts as there are of people, saints and rogues and wits and numbskulls and everything in between. But in general people think of a schoolmaster as a chap in a tweed jacket sucking on a pipe – a good sort, reliable, but ever so dull. Not likely to set the world on fire.'

Sadie was amused now. 'I think there are enough people setting the world on fire at the moment. You should be glad to be called Mr Stanhill.'

'I'd prefer *you* to call me Hugh,' he said very quietly.

Sadie felt her heart trip uncomfortably. He had suddenly come much too close to her. 'I can't do that,' she said, equally quietly, and then, to cover the embarrassing moment,

326

went on, 'I think Rhubarb's getting used to this. Let's try him with dismounting and mounting again. Make sure it wasn't a fluke.'

And no more was said on the subject.

When Edward told Élise de Rouveroy he was living at his club, she was fascinated by the idea. It was somehow very English for men to have a second home like that – and one that women were absolutely banned from entering. 'But your schools, I think, are very odd, too. That's what makes you so shy around women.'

He smiled indulgently. 'I'm not shy around women. How can you say so?'

She nodded. 'Oh, but you are. It is a very pretty thing, however. I like it very much. French men are so businesslike, one feels one is nothing very special. But, Édouard, where shall you eat while your house is closed to you? Not in the club every night?'

'Why not? The food is very good there.'

'There are excellent restaurants all over London,' she said, 'but it is not the same as eating at home. *Tiens*, you must come here. Solange has been reading many books of *cuisine* so that I should not become bored with the same dishes over and over. It would be a kindness to let her practise on you.'

'I couldn't possibly impose on you like that,' he said.

'It is not imposing. *Please*, Édouard! It would be so nice to have a man at my table again. I am born to be a hostess, me, and it is very hard to be *twarted* like this.' She beamed. 'I have discovered this new word. It is a good one, *hein*?'

'Very good, but it's pronounced *thwarted*.'

'*Twarted*. Pff! I cannot say it.'

'Stick your tongue out, like this.'

'Th-twarted.' She practised and he demonstrated until they were both laughing. And he found he seemed to have agreed to dine with her every night without realising it.

The idea was beguiling – but he felt a little guilty all the same. This was beyond the bounds of business. But he was lonely, sad, anxious, worried and tired. The tribunal work was ever-increasing, and he often found the cases upsetting. There were his normal duties at the bank, and there were Treasury meetings of increasing frequency. His son had been killed, he had another son seriously wounded, and there was no comfort for him at home. Wasn't he entitled to a little kindness, even if it was from an unconventional source?

All the same, he knew how easily he could feel more than he should for Élise. Beattie didn't want him any more; Élise did. Whom would it hurt? But he was not that sort of man.

Yet he had lived in the world enough to know that anyone could fall from grace. Even as he was laughing with her, he told himself he must be on his guard.

Letters from Louis were all that kept Beattie going. Visiting David was allowed once a week, but her second visit had gone no better than her first. He seemed sunk in a desperate gloom, and she could not reach him; and when she got up to go, he had said again, almost irritably, that she did not need to keep visiting. It hurt her, even though she told herself that he was not in a normal state of mind. She was his mother, and she ought to be able to ease his suffering.

He had refused absolutely to allow Sophy to visit, though she had written to Beattie several times asking if she could. But when the next visiting day arrived, Beattie swallowed her pride and asked Sadie to go in her place. 'He won't talk to me, but perhaps he will to you. You were always a favourite with him. And you're nearer his age.'

So Sadie took the day off from Highclere, and caught the train to London. She hadn't been up since Diana's wedding, but though that was only two and a half months ago, she saw changes. Many of the buses had conductorettes now. She saw a woman posting bills on the side of a building, and three women walking along carrying ladders and buckets – evidently a window-cleaning team. Jobs that men used to do, women were having to take over. And though she didn't see any women in trousers (Peter had urged her particularly to keep a look-out) she noted that everyone's skirts were well above the ankle now – five or six inches in many cases.

There were more wounded about, too, convalescents, mostly, in hospital blue, but also men who must have been discharged, making their way slowly on crutches, or with an empty sleeve, or in one terrible case a silk mask over his face. The eyes that looked out were like those of a trapped animal.

A man with no legs was selling matches outside the station. She bought a box from him, though she didn't need them. She noted that he was sitting on a sort of platform on wheels, and that he was wearing fingerless leather gloves. The knuckles of the gloves were much scuffed, and she realised in a flash of understanding that that was how he got about, scooting himself along. As she walked away, she had to fight back angry tears that a strong man should come to that.

She was impressed with the hospital. They had tried to make Mount Olive nice, but it was not a patch on this. But every other thought went out of her head when she saw David. He looked gaunt and almost old, and the front of his hair had gone quite grey. The nurse had told her on the way up that he was doing quite well but, she had said, he was still in pain – fractures of the femur were particularly painful, and especially comminuted fractures, and they had to limit the morphine because of its debilitating effect on the patient.

'But will he walk again?' Sadie asked urgently.

'Let's hope so,' the nurse said. 'The leg will never be

what it was, but if we can get it to take his weight, at least he'll be able to get around.'

Sadie was shocked to silence. She had expected the answer 'Yes, of course.'

David expressed no curiosity about her presence. She said, 'I brought you cigarettes and chocolate. Oh, and matches.' She put them on the bedside cabinet. Without asking him, she lit a cigarette and gave it to him, put the ashtray on his chest, and then sat quietly, not looking at him, while he smoked. She knew from her visiting at Mount Olive that they hated to be plagued with questions, and when they were very sick, they hadn't the energy to be interested in what was happening outside. Telling them the news from home comforted only the visitor, not the visited. To be there, a sympathetic silence, was all you could do for them.

Out of the corner of her eye she saw when he had finished, took the ashtray away and put it on the cabinet. After another silence, he said, 'You're restful. I'm glad you came.'

Her heart sang, but she didn't make a fuss. After another silence, she said, 'Do you want to tell me about it?'

He squeezed his eyes shut, but no tear came from them. Morphine had dried him out. 'Give me some water?' he said.

She filled the glass and handed it to him, took it back empty. Then he said, 'We were in the second wave. We were advancing over the bodies of the first wave. Cast about, like old clothes. The dead don't look like dead people, just something not wanted any more. My own men were falling all around me. Only a handful of us reached the trenches.'

She lit him another cigarette, and he took it with a trembling hand.

'German trenches. Full of dead Germans. Then the shelling started, and we were pinned down. Those shells . . .' He paused, and smoked. 'You can't imagine how loud they are.

After a while, your brain can't take any more, and the noise becomes a silence. And you stop – feeling. My men, being blown to bits all round me, and I couldn't feel it at all.'

'I know,' said Sadie.

'How can you?'

'The officers tell me. The wounded I visit.'

'The wounded,' he repeated. 'We've become a single entity: "The Wounded". Like "The Dead". Not individuals. Not people. So many. There were so *many*!'

'Yes,' Sadie said, to keep him going.

He was staring ahead of him, at nothing – no, at his memories – his eyes wide and appalled. 'It wasn't meant to be like that,' he said. 'I wanted to do something noble.' He stopped with a choking sound. A single tear rolled out of one eye, and he dashed it away impatiently with his free hand. 'There was nothing glorious about it. The glorious dead, they call them. But they haven't seen them. They're foul. Rags and blood and bit of flesh, trodden into the mud. I can never— I can never— I can never—' He seemed to have stalled.

Forget, she imagined was the next word. The cigarette was burning down too quickly. She took it from his fingers and stubbed it out for him. He gave a great sigh.

'You did what you had to. That's all anyone can,' she said.

A look of great bitterness came over his face. 'I did *nothing*,' he said. 'None of us. We never reached the Germans. Never even saw them – only their dead. I wish *I* was dead, then I'd have some peace. I ought to have died. Why did *I* live?'

She had no answer for him. She gave him water, and sat quietly in the prison of his silence. After a while she saw his hands relax and, risking a look at him, found he had fallen asleep. It was not a quiet sleep, but perhaps it was better than being awake.

★   ★   ★

Stepping out into the street, she was surprised to find it was still light, and rather surprised to discover it was summer. Darkness and snow would have been more appropriate to her lacerated feelings. But he had talked to her, and that was something. That was a great deal. She stopped at the kerb and wondered what to do. She didn't want to go straight home. They would ask her questions and she didn't want to have to talk to anyone yet. She wandered down to the Strand, thinking she might look at the river, but she spotted a Lyons, and realised she was hungry. So she went in, feeling very bold and somehow liberated. She had never been to a restaurant alone.

She ordered a poached egg on toast and a pot of tea and, while she waited, looked with vague interest at the people all around – mouths moving, talking, chewing – and wondered who they were, and why they were here, and what secrets they were concealing. People didn't wear black armbands much any more, so you couldn't tell the bereaved from the lucky, but the odds were that some of them – perhaps many of them – had lost someone. There was an airman across the other side of the room with a girl, and she thought about Bobby. She was glad the girl he was with was pretty, and hoped it wasn't just his sister.

A shadow fell on her and she looked up, expecting the waitress, but it was an officer in uniform – young, with the sort of pink, undefended face that told you he had a loving mother and probably sisters too. He said, 'I say, I'm frightfully sorry to disturb you, but would you mind awfully if I sat here? There doesn't seem to be anywhere else.'

'Of course I don't mind,' she said. 'Please do.' Nothing was too good for our boys in khaki – that was the automatic response – but as he sat down, he looked at her, grew a little pinker and looked away, and she realised with surprised enlightenment that he had asked to sit here because she was a *girl*. The sort of girl a man might like to get to know.

It had never happened to her before, and she was as much intrigued as pleased because she didn't think of herself in that way. She was just Sadie, and she was the supervisor at Highclere and good with horses, but she had never been a girl. That was Diana's province.

She smiled, and said, 'On the way out, or on the way back?'

He looked at her, eagerly taking the opening, and said, 'On the way out. I've just been home on leave, but I pretended my train was earlier than it was. I wanted to have a bit of time on my own in London. I mean, I love my family, but they can be a bit smothering. I don't suppose you know what I mean?'

'You have sisters,' she said.

'Four,' he said. 'How did you know?'

'And they treat you like a pet.'

He laughed. 'Always have. They're older than me, you see. I'm the baby.'

'I'm the middle one,' Sadie said. 'It has its advantages. You don't get noticed.'

'That sounds lonely.'

'No, it's good. People tell you things because they don't really see you.'

'I'm sure that's not why they tell you,' he said. 'I think you're the sort of person people just naturally tell things to. Look at me – I'm usually stupidly shy around girls – I mean women – oh, gosh, *ladies*.' Sadie laughed, and he looked relieved. 'You see? I'm a clumsy ass. But I spoke to you and, believe me, normally I'd never do a thing like that.'

'It's the war,' she said. 'It changes us. Are you going to France?'

'Yes. We've been in a cushy sector, but I've a feeling we'll be moving once I get back.'

'To Picardy?'

'They won't tell us until we get there.'

'I have two brothers there,' she said thoughtlessly.

'Gosh, do you? Are they all right? I mean, one hears—'

Nothing was too good for our boys in khaki. He looked so young. She smiled brightly and said, 'Yes, they're all right.'

The waitress came with Sadie's meal, and took the young man's order. When she had gone, he said, 'Have you seen any shows lately?'

She hadn't, but he had, so she got him to talk about them while she ate. It was an odd little encounter, she thought, and one that could never have happened before the war – for so many reasons.

In September Diana and Rupert moved into the house in Park Place, and the news was formally announced that she was with child. The earl and countess were told first, so that the announcement could come from them. This, Rupert told Diana, was what was called Tact, something she seemed singularly lacking in.

That was how he talked to her – not like a lover or how she had ever heard a husband talking to his wife, but like a brother talking to a sister. She found it rather refreshing, especially since she could talk back to him in the same way – though she could never annoy him, only make him laugh.

The countess was pleased with the news, and was more gracious towards Diana than she had ever seen her. 'Of course it will be a boy,' she decreed. 'Boys run in the family. You will have two boys – then, if you wish, you may have a daughter, though it isn't necessary. I would rather have liked a daughter but, after all, when one's sons marry one has a daughter-in-law, and that does instead. You will come here for the birth, and you will be attended by our own physician, Sir Maurice Enderby. He has delivered several royal babies. Now, as to names – I will give you a list of suitable ones. You may wish to name him Algernon, after

Rupert's father, or Thomas after my father. And Charles, of course, is a traditional family name.'

Rupert had warned Diana beforehand not to argue with his mother. 'It only makes her stubborn. Don't worry, she won't get her way. I'll arrange everything the way *we* want it.'

Afterwards, he reassured her. 'You shall have the baby at home, and old Enderby won't be invited. He's about two hundred years old – besides, I think he delivered *me*, and that would make me feel very odd.'

'About the names,' Diana said.

'We shall *not* be calling the poor little thing Algernon,' Rupert assured her. 'Don't worry, we've plenty of time to find the right name.'

Diana hoped he wouldn't settle on Charles. That would make *her* feel odd.

Now the secret was out, she had dozens of visits of congratulation. Those, plus settling into the new house, and their usual engagements, kept her busy. She had not always enjoyed the country-house visiting. Going from one gathering to another seemed to her too much of a good thing, as they all seemed to follow the same pattern. She was quite glad to get back to London and the new house, though Rupert immediately absented himself, saying he was going away for a few days. He wouldn't tell her where or why, but when he came back he told her, in an unusually expansive mood brought on by a particularly good claret, that he had gone away with Erskine.

Her heart sank a little. She just couldn't like Erskine, and she'd hoped that when he was called up, it would take him out of their lives. 'How did you manage that,' she asked, 'when he's in the army?'

'He finished his basic training and transferred to officer cadet school, and he got his four days' leave, so I borrowed a motor-car, picked him up in Cambridge, and we went to

Dersington, seeing that the Aged Ps are in Scotland, so the coast was clear.'

Dersington Manor was the Wroughtons' place in Norfolk, handy for Sandringham.

'You've never taken me there,' Diana said. 'I'd have liked to see it.'

'Oh, you'd have hated it,' Rupert said dismissively. 'You wouldn't have been comfortable. It's only habitable when my parents are there with their army of servants – and then, of course, *my parents* are there so it's not habitable at all.'

'So how come you and Erskine were comfortable?' she asked.

'We both went to public school,' he said, and laughed as if it were a great joke.

Apart from that incident, she had nothing to complain about. Rupert was very *odd*, different not just from Charles but from any other man she had met, but it was an easy oddness to live with. Apart from his hours at the War Office, he often went off alone and didn't tell her where he was going, but she had lots of friends now and plenty to do, so she didn't mind. And when he was at home, he was very attentive. He brought her presents, and was always interested in how she felt and whether she was comfortable. He took a great interest in her appearance, and chose her clothes for her, and liked to escort her in public and have people admire her. He took her to all the plays and exhibitions and parties she wanted. He introduced her with pride, almost gloating, to his friends and acquaintances.

And he was so excited by the baby, that she sometimes struggled to match him in emotion. He was already planning the conversion of the top floor into nurseries.

'You *like* this house, don't you?' he asked her. 'You'll be happy to stay here for a long time? Years and years? Good, then it's worth making the alterations. This will be our home

336

until Papa shuffles off and I have to take on the mantle and the strawberry leaves.'

'Strawberry leaves?' She often didn't understand his references.

'Strawberry leaves and pearls. The earl's coronet.'

When they were first married, Rupert had slept with her every night, and while she did not find *that thing* they did particularly wonderful, she did sometimes begin to feel some slight tremor inside, some faint revival of the yearning sensation she had had towards Charles when he kissed her. She began to feel that she might come to like it, given time. But as soon as she told Rupert she thought she was pregnant, he had stopped doing *it*. He did still come to her bedroom once or twice a week, though. He seemed to like the cuddling, as she did. He would slot their bodies together – 'like two spoons in a drawer', as he put it – and wrap his arms round her, and they would go to sleep like that. But he was always gone when she woke in the morning.

A frequent visitor to Park Place, and more welcome than most, was Obby.

'You've done this so prettily,' she said, when she saw Diana's private sitting-room for the first time.

'All Rupert's doing,' Diana said. 'I haven't an artistic bone in my body.'

'I don't know anyone with better taste than Rupert,' Obby said. 'And that's a compliment to *you*.'

She was glad of Obby's friendship. Her friends from home, from Northcote, hadn't translated, and otherwise her circle consisted of upper-class girls, who were nice but different from herself, and Rupert's 'Bohemian' friends – who were different from everyone. With Obby she felt comfortable, and they often had tea together. She always made Obby put her feet up on a footstool, and ordered a lavish tea. She knew now what nurses wanted.

'I hope you'll be around when the baby actually comes,'

337

she said one day. 'It would be nice to have a nurse near by.'

'I'm sure you'll have the best midwife money can buy,' Obby said.

'I'd sooner have a friend,' said Diana. 'Obby, do you think you could tell me exactly what happens? I'm terribly ignorant. It isn't something anyone ever tells us, is it? But if I could talk about it with you . . .'

'I don't know much myself,' Obby said. 'I haven't done any midwifery. No call for it in an army hospital. But I tell you what – I could get a book. There's sure to be something in the hospital library. And we could look at it together – if you wouldn't be too embarrassed?'

'I'm sure I will be, but I'll get over it.'

'Well, I applaud your spirit,' said Obby. 'So that's what we'll do. It'll come in handy for me, too, one day.'

'You're not thinking of becoming a midwife after the war?'

'No, I'm thinking of getting married after the war,' Obby said, laughing. 'If the war ever ends. Sometimes it seems as if it's been going on for ever, doesn't it?'

The house was dark and silent; even the servants weren't astir yet. It was chilly, too, and comfortless with no fires lit. Beattie had been awake for a long time, thinking about the Somme. Another phase in the battle had started. Another two miles had been taken, and the army was regrouping for a further assault. That's what the papers said. Louis had written to say that he was moving from General Headquarters to the 4th Army headquarters, to be more closely involved in the strategy. She knew what that meant. He would be in more danger. She longed for him so much that it was like a dull ache inside her. Half the time she wished they had never met again. She had grown used, over the years, to the old pain of losing him. She had learned to live with it. This new pain was debilitating. But, no, she wouldn't lose the memory of those weeks they had spent together in the dusty little house, not for anything. If at the gates of Heaven they said, 'Give them up or you can't come in,' she would wander in exile for ever.

She was cold in the bed without Edward. Her body didn't generate enough heat to warm the sheets. She thought about going to the kitchen and making herself a cup of tea, but couldn't quite get up the momentum. She felt in the grip of a grey lassitude. She rose, put on her dressing-gown, and stepped quietly out into the passage, listening. Edward was asleep in the dressing-room nearby. He had seemed different since he came back from his stay at the club. She couldn't quite put her finger on it, but he was different. Yet he seemed just now so little to do with her that she did not care enough to find out what it was. It did not occur to her for a moment to go in to him. There was no comfort for her there.

She went instead along the passage to the room David and Bobby had shared when they had all first moved here from Kensington, and which later had become David's own. It was tidy and lifeless now, the relentless tides of household cleaning having smoothed away all traces left by him. It smelt anonymously of furniture polish. Once, it had smelt of him. But there were things still, books on the shelves, outgrown treasures put away in cupboards, clothes he'd had no need of in drawers and wardrobe.

The curtains were open, but there was no light coming in from outside. It was dark of the moon, and the streetlamps, dimmed in any case against Zeppelin raids, were turned off between eleven and six to save electricity. There had been more raids at the beginning of September. Bombs had been dropped on Wood Green and Waltham Abbey, but one of the airships had been shot down by a BE2c from Suttons Farm, which had cheered everybody. She remembered what type of aircraft it was because she remembered Bobby talking about them.

They said the pilot was going to get the VC for it. The VC for one woman's son, the cold clay for another.

She found David's bed by feel, with its eiderdown of blue sateen. She lay down on it, liking to imagine there was a lingering sense of him here, where he had put his head and pursued his boyhood's involved dreams. She remembered the first time she had held him, cradling that same head in her palm – so tiny, so surprisingly thatched with thick dark hair. His fragility had both frightened and enraptured her. She had looked down at the tenuous scrap of life in her arms, and fallen instantly and irrevocably in love. Even then she had sensed his otherness. He was made of her flesh, had grown inside her body, but he did not belong to her. He was only on loan, and she had known one day she would lose him.

They had been wonderful, terrifying years, watching him grow up, receiving his grave and passionate love. Remembering them, thinking about him as he was when he was whole and unbroken, she fell asleep where she was, on top of the bed, deeply asleep, at last without dreams, waking only when Lilian, passing and wondering why the door was open, looked in, saw her, and let out a little muted shriek, thinking she was dead.

CHAPTER TWENTY-ONE

In mid-September, Jack came home on four days' leave. He and Beth and the Hunters all met at the Palfreys' house, as there was too little time for separate visits. Beattie thought he was looking better than when she had seen him last – more rested and not so thin. It seemed he had got away from Ypres at last, and had been for some weeks in the Champagne, a 'cushy' sector where the front lines were so far apart you never saw the enemy. It was like a rest cure, Jack said. On his return to France he expected to be going to Picardy, where the battle was still going on around the Somme.

'Everyone has to have a turn,' he said lightly. 'It's the genius of the British Army that they don't leave anyone too long in one place. A few days in the line, then back to rest. A few days in the heat of battle, then out to a quiet sector.'

'But here you are now,' Sonia said comfortably. 'It's good to be all together again.'

All together, Beattie thought. Bobby would never be coming back, and David was in hospital. Donald was absent, in officer cadet school. Sonia was a tactless fool.

And she and Edward were not together. Even here in the Palfreys' drawing-room, they were sitting on opposite sides of the room, and he never looked at her, never met her eye.

Jack asked how David was doing.

It was Edward who answered. 'He's being released from hospital in two weeks' time. And discharged from the army.'

'Will he be coming home?'

'Yes,' said Edward. 'We spoke to the doctor at the hospital yesterday. A rather distinguished-looking woman.'

'How do you like having a woman doctor?' Jack asked.

'She seems to know what she's talking about,' he said. 'She had plenty of sensible advice for us. She said we ought to consider hiring a trained nurse for the first few weeks. And he ought to have manipulation and massage of the affected limb, too, so she's going to find someone trained in it, from the Almeric Paget Massage Corps.'

'We're going to turn Bobby's room into a sitting-room for him,' said Beattie, 'because he won't be able to get downstairs while he's on crutches.'

'Oh, what a good idea,' said Beth. 'Being confined to one room can be depressing. How long will he be on crutches?'

'We don't know,' said Beattie, flatly. The doctor had said it would be a matter of time and gradual progression, from two crutches to one, then two sticks, then one stick. He was young, she had said, and the healing abilities of the young were remarkable. Probably he would always limp, but he might be able to walk without a stick at all, in time. Much would depend on his own determination. But the thought of repeating all that defeated her.

During the evening Diana called in for a brief visit, with Rupert, on their way to an engagement.

'I wish we could stay,' Rupert declared, 'you all look so cosy and comfortable. But we were invited by Lady Tockwith weeks ago, and the mater will be there, so we daren't chuck.'

Beattie thought that was merely tact, but it went down well with Sonia.

'How well you're looking!' Beth said to Diana. 'Positively blooming!'

They discussed the progress of her pregnancy, while

Rupert seized Jack for five minutes of eager quizzing about the war, and then they were off again, like a whirlwind, leaving behind a sense of vacuum, until Jack asked Audrey how she was liking her job, and the family talk revived. Aeneas was proud of how well his daughter was doing, and said laughingly that, when the war was over, Donald might have to find himself another job.

The news that David would be coming home coincided with the end of Ethel's period of convalescence, the moment at which some decision would have to be made about her. Though passed as fit for work, she was not her old self, seeming listless, lacking the fire that had made her a less than ideal servant. Beattie supposed it was the loss of the baby, hoped that she would shake herself out of it and marry Frank Hussey – if he would still take her. But she felt tender about casting the girl out when she had nowhere to go, so David's coming home provided a good excuse to keep her on.

'Mr David will need waiting on,' she told Ethel, in a private interview in the morning-room, 'and I don't want to burden the other servants. Also there will be a trained nurse living here for a few weeks. So I'm offering you a position as housemaid, with the special duty of looking after Mr David's rooms, and the nurse's room, waiting on him, and helping the nurse as and when she needs it. You won't do any other housemaid duties, though I may still give you mending to do. Well? Do you accept?'

'Yes, madam. Thank you, madam,' Ethel said, in a colourless voice that concealed her relief.

'There will be a lot to do to get the rooms ready. You can help, and I'll resume paying you from tomorrow. You'd better go down to Rice's this afternoon and get a day uniform. I suggest blue, to distinguish you from the others. Plain cap and apron, of course.'

Sadie threw herself into the preparations. David's room had to be rearranged, moving the bed so that there was access from both sides, and taking away unnecessary clutter. Then the guest-room next door was prepared for the nurse, and Bobby's room, across the hall, was turned into a sitting-room. That involved removing all Bobby's things, which no-one had had the heart to touch yet. Sadie packed them away tenderly, shedding many tears. It seemed to her that Bobby often got overlooked in the agitation surrounding David. It was understandable: the living must always come first. But as she laid things in the trunk – clothes that had known the shape of his body, possessions she had seen him handling, things he had thrust carelessly into his pockets when he was full of life and warm blood and cheerfulness – it seemed almost like doing away with him for good. *Go free, poor ghost*, she said in her mind. *You don't need to linger here. I shall never forget you.*

A little sound behind her made the hair stand up on her head, and she turned stiffly, slowly, afraid that she would see him there, longing to, but knowing it would be too frightening to bear. In the doorway, watching her, was Nailer; he made the little sound again, a muffled whine in his throat. She held out her hand and he came to her, wagging his tail eagerly. The thought occurred to her that he was lonely. Ridiculous! But she stroked his head, remembering how Bobby had tried to teach him to walk on his hind legs, by dint of holding up the front ones so he had no choice. That had been on the day David had told them he'd volunteered. She remembered it clearly; and for an instant, Bobby was there beside her, the scent of him, the sense of him, his eyes screwed up in laughter, his long brown forearms where his sleeves were rolled up, the sound of his voice. Just for an instant he was *there* – and she wanted to cry out, because she knew she would never have this feeling again. You remembered only the *fact* of people: everything else faded away.

344

He smiled at her, his old Bobby smile, and then there was nothing but the stale air of his unused room.

With tears on her face she went back to her task. Nailer stayed by her until she had finished.

David was home, installed in the newly arranged and cleaned bedroom. The journey had fatigued him, and Sister Heaton, a sensible Yorkshire woman in her forties, advised them to let her get him to bed and not bother him until the next day.

Sadie was disappointed. She had wanted to show him his sitting-room, which they had taken great pains over. They had imported the most comfortable furniture and the best rugs; Sadie had chosen books for the small bookcase brought down from the old nursery, and had arranged vases of flowers to make it bright and cheerful.

Above all, she wanted him to see the splendid present Uncle Aeneas had sent, which stood proudly on a small round table in the window: a gramophone, in a handsome walnut case, together with a selection of disc records – popular songs, ragtime, piano music and operatic arias. It was like Uncle to think of the exact thing most likely to beguile someone through the listlessness of suffering.

The next day, Sister banned visitors in the morning. Only Ethel went in and out, looking almost nurse-like in the plain blue dress with white cap and apron. It annoyed Cook, who had hoped they would be rid of her once she was better, and who resented her new status as sick-room maid. She resented it even more when Ethel 'gave herself airs' and refused to tell them anything about Mr David. Ethel was a newcomer, where Cook had known him since he was a baby.

But in the afternoon, the nurse insisted he get up, and walk a little on his crutches. 'You must practise every day,' she told him, 'or you'll never see any improvement.'

'What's the point?' he said dully. 'I'll never be well.'

345

'You won't with that attitude. Come along, up we get. You can walk over to your new sitting-room and hold court.'

And so they saw him, Beattie and Sadie and the boys – Edward was at work. Each in their own way was shocked at the sight of David lurching slowly and painfully, crutches under his armpits, his deformed leg held clear of the floor. It took him minutes to cross the passage from one room to the other, and then he had to be lowered into a chair, exhausted. He did not have the energy to look at the room, and admire the arrangements. Peter was disappointed, William embarrassed at the sight of his elder brother brought so low, and ashamed of his embarrassment. Sadie was afraid, having expected him to be more mobile.

But as the days passed, the household settled down to the new routine and the presence upstairs of the wounded god, and the rawness went out of the situation. Peter went from tiptoeing to having to be told not to make such a noise on the stairs. William tried politely to interest David in what was going on outside, but when he had been rebuffed a few times, he gave up and managed, for at least the busy part of the day, to forget. Sadie went back to her horses, visiting him every evening, though there was no sign he welcomed it.

It was Beattie who suffered every day the pain of knowing there was nothing she could do for him. When he wanted something, he would forestall her, saying, 'No, let Nurse do it. She knows what to do.' Beattie liked the nurse, who was quiet and pleasant and efficient, but she hated her for the way David turned more and more towards her. He didn't talk much, even to the nurse, but sometimes Beattie would come into the room, and have the sense that a conversation had broken off at her appearance.

The chilly morning mists and golden days of September gave way to the soft fogs and quiet greyness of October. In Picardy the battle went on, the army slowly creeping forward, trying to gain the high ground above Thiepval and Beaumont-Hamel, trying to reach the Péronne–Bapaume road. David moved daily from his bedroom to his sitting-room and back. They would hear from downstairs the irregular thump of the crutches on the floorboards. Sometimes he would dab the foot of his injured leg down for an instant, but it hurt him too much to take the weight on it.

One day when Sadie was with him, he reached for his cigarettes from the table beside him and knocked his pocket book to the floor. 'I'll get it,' she said, stooping quickly. A white fold of card fell out and, retrieving it, she recognised what it was. 'Oh, it's the white heather I gave you,' she said. It seemed impossibly childish now, to have stuck a piece of her white heather onto a card for him to take with him when he went for a soldier. But they'd had no idea then what the war would be like. It had seemed like something from which the luck of white heather could save you.

David looked at it blankly, as though he hadn't known it had been there. 'Throw it away,' he said. 'I don't want it.' Sadie shoved it into her pocket, to dispose of downstairs. His eye followed the movement, and perhaps he realised he had hurt her, because he said, 'It didn't save me, you see.'

'No,' she said. 'I think this war's a bit bigger than lucky charms.'

When David had been home a fortnight, Sophy was allowed to visit him. The prohibition had been both on medical grounds and from her parents, who did not want her upset. David had been longing to see her, but when the time came, Sister Heaton had to persuade him not to put her off. He was suddenly in a cold sweat of fear at having her see him like this.

'I never would have taken you for a coward,' Heaton told him shortly. She tried from time to time to needle David into annoyance: she felt it was healthier.

'You don't understand,' he said.

'On the contrary, self-pity is very easy to understand.'

So he was up and dressed and established in an armchair in his sitting-room when Sophy arrived, escorted by her mother. Heaton went downstairs to fetch her, and could see at once why any man would fall in love with her. Her dress of soft cobalt-blue wool enhanced her exotic colouring, the white skin, thick dark hair and sparkling dark eyes. Women these days were becoming more robust, brisk-moving and – frequently – weather-tanned, and to see someone so delicate, and utterly feminine in the old-fashioned way, was almost a shock. Sophy was like a porcelain figurine: you'd be afraid of breaking her.

Heaton could see she was nervous. She also saw that the mother would be a hindrance to the young people: large, ponderous and all Edwardian, from her crimped hair to her carpet-brushing hemline, with four strings of pearls and a variety of chains decorating her bolster of a bosom. Beside her, Sophy seemed tiny and quick-moving, a wren to a wood-pigeon. So, as Mrs Oliphant began to rise, Heaton said, 'Just the young lady for the present, if you don't mind. We don't want to overtire him.'

Sophy was nervous. She had been asking to see him, and the longer she was forbidden, the more anxious she became. A leg wound, they had said. That didn't seem too bad. She had felt one could get used to a leg wound. But after three months of his being 'too ill to be visited' her imagination had begun to run wild. How long could it really take a leg to heal? Was there something they weren't telling her?

She wished she could think of something sensible to ask the nurse as they walked upstairs, but her mind was an inconvenient blank of panic. As they approached the door, the nurse glanced at her, and said, 'He's still in a lot of pain, so don't worry if you don't find him chatty.'

Chatty? Sophy thought wildly. He had never been chatty:

he had talked, magnificently, eloquently, his Viking head held high, his blazing eyes set on far horizons. He was always so different from her other suitors. Humphrey Hobart had been *chatty*, not David. 'Um—' she said, but it was too late to ask anything. They were there.

She was so churned up with nervousness that for a moment she could not see him. There was someone sitting in the armchair, but it was just a male shape. Then something like David's voice, only without the vibrancy, said, 'I'd like to stand up for you, but it's rather a performance and I can't manage it without help yet. Sorry.'

'It's quite all right,' she said, in a faint voice. She was trying not to stare, but at the same time, trying to find David in the person before her. She had carried his image in her mind all this time. Where was he? This was an older man, gaunt, grey over the temples, lined in the face. She could see by the hang of his clothes how thin he was. And there was nothing in that haggard face of the spirit and life of David, nothing proud and strong.

David's heart had lifted at the first sight of her, so beautiful, so unchanged. But she was too young to hide her feelings. He saw her shock at his appearance, and her struggle to assimilate the change in him, and his heart failed. The smile that had been coming to his lips faded; his mouth turned down again. The familiar feeling of defeat crept back over him.

'I'm sorry,' he said. 'I know I don't look the way you remember me.'

'Oh, no, really,' she managed to protest. 'You're – I'm sure—'

Heaton intervened. 'Why don't you sit down,' she said, gently urging her to a chair, 'and have a nice talk? I shall sit over there with my book, so I shan't hear you.'

Sophy sat down. Her legs felt weak. She couldn't think of a thing to say. *How are you?* seemed pitifully inadequate.

Talk of love, of having missed him and so on, seemed inappropriate against his suffering. And she wished she could stop herself *staring*! The old David would have carried the conversation himself, allowing her to ride along on the swift wings of his intellect. Rather than let the silence extend itself further, she said at last, 'It's quite a nice day outside. Not sunny, but quite warm.'

'Is it?' David said.

'Do you get out much?' she tried.

'No, I haven't been outside. I haven't tackled the stairs yet,' he said. 'Getting about up here is as much as I can manage.'

'Oh.' She was disconcerted. *He couldn't walk! He couldn't go out!* All the things she usually talked about when making polite conversation were ruled out – tennis, dancing, shows, parties. The latest dance tunes. Summer picnics and outings. Even the war, and the charitable activities she undertook with her mother. The whole of life had become an unapproachable subject. She realised at last what a disaster she was facing. 'Oh, David,' she said, and her voice trembled.

'Please don't cry, Sophy,' he begged. 'I know it's a shock to see me like this.'

'Do – do you want to tell me about it?' she asked bravely.

He looked at her with sad, defeated eyes. 'No,' he said, 'I don't think I do. Tell me what you've been doing.'

Tears filled her eyes. 'I *can't!*' she whimpered. 'Talk about my silly doings when you're – you're— Oh, *David!*'

He pulled out his handkerchief and pushed it into her hands, and waited in pain as she covered her face, and her slender shoulders shook. It seemed to him one of the bravest things he had witnessed when she emerged, in control again, a little pink at nose and eyes, pressing her lips firmly together so they shouldn't tremble. She was so *young*, he thought. Young and beautiful and still perfect. How could he tie her to the saddened wreck he had become?

350

'Better?' he asked. She nodded, rather than try to speak. 'Sophy,' he said, 'I want to talk to you seriously. About us – about our engagement.'

A faint look of alarm came over her face. 'There's no need—' she began.

'Yes, there is,' he said. 'I love you, and I know you loved me when we became engaged. But things have changed. I'm not the same person you promised yourself to, and it would be very wrong of me to try to hold you to that promise.'

Her eyes became dangerously bright again. 'What do you mean? Don't you want to marry me? Don't you love me?'

'Dearest Sophy, I love you more than ever. But I can't tell you when I would be in any position to marry you. You deserve the best of everything, and how can I provide that? So I want you to understand that I am releasing you from any promise you made, and I'll completely understand if you want to break off our engagement. In fact, it's the only sensible thing to do.'

'Sensible!' she cried. 'How can you talk about sensible when you're—' She waved a hand to encompass all his suffering. She touched his handkerchief again to her eyes, sat up straighter, and said, in a determined small voice, 'I wouldn't dream of breaking it off. How could you think it? I'm not the sort of girl who—'

'Abandons a chap who's in trouble?' David finished for her. 'But that's what worries me. I know you're a splendid girl, and I don't want you to tie yourself to me because you think it's the right thing to do.'

'But I *love* you,' she protested, and just then it was true. Just then, she was talking to the David who had kissed her in the old nursery a lifetime ago. 'And I'm not breaking off our engagement, so that's that.'

She smiled at him, and inwardly he saluted her valour.

351

'Thank you,' he said, and his voice sounded weak even to him. He was suddenly exhausted. 'I'm sorry,' he said.

She stood up. 'Perhaps I'd better leave you to rest. I can see you're tired.'

'I'm afraid I'm not very good company today. I'm sorry I can't see you out.'

'That's quite all right,' she said politely.

'It was nice of you to come and visit me.'

'I'll come again soon,' she said, and smiled uncertainly, and left him.

Heaton followed her out. David sat staring at nothing, too exhausted to feel anything much. Sophy had stood by him, and that was good – that was wonderful – but it changed nothing, really. He was a helpless cripple, and she was a beautiful young woman, a creature from a different world. What ending could that story have?

On the stairs, on the way down, Sophy asked the nurse, 'How long will it be before he's better?'

'Better?' Heaton glanced at her, 'We're a long way off that. A long way. But I think we should see an improvement in six weeks or so.'

Six weeks? Sophy thought. *Improvement?* 'But – he will get well? I mean, completely well?'

Heaton gave her a pitying look. 'He'll probably always need a stick. He'll always limp. But in time, he ought to be able to get about pretty well.'

'Oh,' said Sophy. She asked nothing more, and Heaton delivered her to her mother looking thoughtful and unhappy.

She went back upstairs to David, looked at him, then said briskly, 'You haven't tried your gramophone yet. It looks like a good one. Shall I put a recording on for you?'

He neither assented or refused. She picked one at random and started it playing: John McCormack's voice issued like magic from the horn, singing 'Somewhere A Voice Is Calling'.

She didn't think he was listening, but when it finished, he said, 'Again.'

So she wound the gramophone and played it again.

Working at her dressing-table, Beattie finished the letter to Louis, sealed it in the envelope and addressed it. Then she just sat, thinking.

Battle was raging in France at Ancre Heights, hampered by bad weather and counter-attacks from the enemy. But the Germans were exhausted by the months of battle: they were fatally weakened, and the British Army was setting itself up in a strong position for the campaign of the following year.

Louis had explained all this in his last letter. She had written to him of her misery over David and her frustration at his slow progress. Sister Heaton had been with them almost a month, and she had been hinting that she should be thinking of leaving. Beattie didn't know how they would cope without her. It was only through her bullying that David attempted to walk; otherwise he would sit all day in his room, playing his gramophone records over and over. He didn't read or write letters, or express any interest in anything that was going on. The boys had abandoned attempts to engage with him, and seemed to have closed a door in their minds so that they could get on with their own lives without him. Sadie doggedly attempted to talk to him, would tell him of her day's activities up at Highclere or Mount Olive, but he did not respond or offer any thoughts of his own.

There had been air raids at the end of September and the beginning of October – the latter alarmingly close: one Zeppelin circled over Harlow, Stevenage and Hatfield and was finally brought down by a BE2c at Potter's Bar, killing all the crew. It had reawoken Cook's and Ada's fears – Hertfordshire was the next county, and Potter's Bar was no distance as the Zeppelin flew.

There were shortages, in paper and matches, in sugar and dried fruit – the latter worrying to Cook with Christmas approaching. The price of coal, butter, milk and bread had doubled; and coffee was increasingly hard to find.

And Mrs Fitzgerald had been plaguing her again, wanting her to join a campaign to ban women from frequenting the local pubs. It was aimed, of course, at the munitionettes who, as far as Beattie could see, caused no more trouble than taking up a lot of room on buses and trains as they travelled to and from work. But a group of them had gone into the Station Hotel one evening and, finding soldiers in the bar, had patriotically stood them all a drink. 'Treating' had been banned quite early in the war, but it was unofficially ignored when the 'treatee' was a soldier in uniform. Don Weaver, the landlord, had mentioned the incident to Mrs Fitzgerald after church one day with a wry shake of the head – only in a my-goodness-times-have-changed sort of way, but since then she had been out for blood.

All these worries, serious and petty, wearied her. Louis was her escape. In the back of her mind there was a country of permanent summer, where he dwelled, and she visited him there. What the future held she could not guess: she supposed only more pain, trouble and, for her and him, separation. But in that green and pleasant land, for a little while at least, they could be together.

In mid-November the fighting on the Somme was ended because of increasingly bad weather. The Allies had advanced over six miles across a front of sixteen, and had taken many important positions, from Beaumont-Hamel almost to Péronne, though they had not managed to take Bapaume, the original objective. It was a hard-fought victory against a numerically superior and experienced foe, and it had placed a strain on the old, professional German Army from which it could hardly hope to recover.

Edward had a visit from Warren, on leave, who called on him at the office, looked about him wistfully, and accepted his invitation to drink tea. They talked first about the Budget, McKenna's 40 per cent tax rises and the tax on war profits, then about the situation in general.

'I remember when the war started, sir. I and a lot of us chaps were worried it would be over before we had a chance to get in it,' said Warren.

'I remember,' said Edward.

'No fears of that sort now. It's going to be at least another year, perhaps more.'

'Kitchener was right all along. He said from the beginning it would be four or five years. And costing us five million pounds a day. When will you finish training?'

'As I understand it, we'll be going to our battalions in January. Time to get used to things out there before the campaigning season starts again.'

'You'll make a good officer,' said Edward.

'I hope so, sir.'

'You'd better – I don't want to have given you up for nothing.'

'Are things – not to your liking?'

'They never have been since you left,' Edward said. 'I suppose I was spoiled before. You understood my ways.'

'I wish I could find someone for you, sir, that you liked and were comfortable with.'

Edward smiled at Warren's creased brow. 'It isn't your problem any more, my dear fellow. And we all have to make sacrifices. Mine are small compared with others'.'

'How is your son doing?' Warren asked diffidently.

'How did you hear about that?'

'Oh, word goes around. When one's interested, the name stands out.'

'He's making slow progress. Sometimes it seems so slow as to be invisible.'

'A great shock like that takes time to get over,' Warren said sensibly. 'Even after the body has healed, the mind needs time too. A friend of mine from school volunteered right at the beginning. He was wounded in 1915, and it was a year before he was really himself again.'

Edward felt comforted. 'A year. Yes, I suppose it's only been four months, four and a half, for David. Of course, you're right – one must be patient. Thank you. You've cheered me up a little.'

'Glad to be of service, sir,' said Warren, with a smile.

CHAPTER TWENTY-TWO

David folded his arms under his head and stared at the ceiling while Sister Heaton's cool fingers moved enquiringly over his upper leg. He hated to look at it. He had not been a vain person before, but there is in all young creatures a wordless sense of satisfaction in being whole and unscarred and nimble. Now the leg was a horrible thing, not like his own but something he had to drag around with him, as a horse is harnessed to a cart. It was misshapen, where flesh and muscle had been torn away, and puckered and seamed with livid scars. Only Sister Heaton could be allowed to touch it. No-one else must ever see it.

She finished her examination. 'Well,' she said, 'there's no inflammation. No sign of any infection. The scars are healing nicely. You're lucky, my lad.'

'Lucky!'

She looked stern. 'You've still got it, and a lot haven't. And you're alive – that's the luckiest of all.'

'It doesn't feel it sometimes,' he said.

'If you dare to say you wish you were dead, I shall smack you!'

That raised the faintest smile. 'Are you allowed to strike your patients?'

She glanced at the watch on her bosom. 'In another twelve hours you won't be my patient any more. I'll risk it.'

'I wish you wouldn't go. Why do you have to go?'

357

'You don't need me any more. There's others that do.'

'I *do* need you.'

'No, you need *yourself*. You've got to buck up and take responsibility. You don't want to be dependent your whole life, do you?'

'I shall never—'

She raised a threatening hand. 'I'm warning you! No self-pity today. I've got you to one crutch, and today we're going to get you onto one stick.'

'I thought the next thing was two sticks.'

'You're going to skip a stage – that's how much faith I've got in you. And if you practise, like a good boy, you'll be able to go downstairs in a week or so.'

'Not without you,' he said, alarmed. 'I couldn't manage the stairs without you.'

'The maid can help you – she's a sensible girl. I had my doubts about her at first – thought she was too pretty to be any use. There!' She smiled. 'I've exposed myself. The prejudices of a plain woman.'

'You're not plain,' David said seriously. He examined her face. 'In fact, I think you're beautiful.'

She seemed amused rather than flattered. 'Which is why so many nurses marry their patients. It's called rose-tinted glasses.'

'Do they really marry their patients?'

'They do – but I'm too old for you. You're going to get yourself mobile again, and then you're going to marry that nice young woman who's madly in love with you.'

'Like this?' he said, gesturing at his leg.

'Oh, a limp is very romantic,' she said airily. 'And no woman worth her salt will care about a scar or two.'

He met her eyes. 'What right have I, a deformed cripple, to tie the most beautiful girl in the world to me?'

'That's for you to decide,' she said. 'My job is to get you on your feet. I want you to set your sights on getting downstairs in time for Christmas. And you won't do it if you soak in self-pity. There, now I've upset you, and *you* want to smack *me*.'

'You don't understand,' he said.

'Of course not,' she said comfortably. 'I'm just a nurse. What do I know about life? Now, then, are you ready to throw that ugly old crutch away? Let's get you up, and get you walking with a stick. Don't look like that – where's your pluck?'

'Down the drain,' he said hollowly. But she only laughed. There was no defeating *her* spirit.

'Come on, my handsome lad. You'll find it's much easier than you think. Up and at 'em! Steady the Buffs! No surrender!'

'Will you stop saying things like that?' he said irritably, as she helped him to his feet. 'I'm not in the army any more. And, anyway, I was light infantry. The Rifles.'

'And what was your motto?' she asked, her shoulder under his armpit as she got him upright and reached for the stick.

'"Swift and Bold",' he said. 'Ironic, isn't it?'

When the nurse left, Ethel wondered what would happen to her job. Would she be turned off? But Mr David told her he would depend on her more than ever, and the mistress said nothing. As David got better, Mrs Hunter seemed, by contrast, to get more distracted and vague. She had resumed her canteen duties, so she was out a lot more, and the servants all thought it was a good idea. It wasn't good for her to mope about the house, when there wasn't really anything to do for her son.

It was Ethel who answered whenever he rang, who took his meals up to him, ran his bath, laid out his shaving tackle. And at other times she would sit in what had been the sister's room and do the mending, so that she would be on hand if he wanted anything. She liked her new responsibility, and the distinction it gave her from the rest of the servants. It improved her spirits, as the stillbirth dropped further behind her and her health recovered. But she still didn't know what she was going to do with her life. Her old plan had lost its appeal. To marry a man she didn't care for, just so he would keep her? To bed with him and bear him children without feeling anything for him? She wondered now how she could have thought of it. Damn that Frank Hussey! He had spoiled everything.

She remembered the short time she had been engaged to him, his visits and his kindness and how he could make her smile, and what it had felt like to be kissed by him. She missed all that. She took pains to stay away from the kitchen on Sundays, the day he had most often visited, and since she didn't speak about him to the others, she didn't know if he still did come. He didn't come up and see *her*, she knew that.

She would sit in the nurse's room and listen to Mr David playing his gramophone records over and over. She liked it when he played the sad songs, like 'Somewhere A Voice Is Calling'. It suited her mood. He played them when the pain was bad. He had a photograph of Miss Oliphant, in a frame, which he kept on the table beside the gramophone where he could look at it while he played the sad songs. He was thinking, Ethel guessed, that he would never be well enough to marry her. It was very affecting.

Sister had taken Ethel on one side before she left and warned her she must make the young master use his leg, and not sit around all day feeling sorry for himself. 'Otherwise he'll never improve,' she'd said. 'I trust you to keep after him.'

'Me?' Ethel had protested. '*I* can't tell him what to do.'

'Your head's screwed on tight,' Sister Heaton had said. 'You'll find a way.'

Ethel's method was just to assume he would do it, and

to present herself at certain regular times to help him, as if it were taken for granted this was what they did at that hour. On the whole it worked. On good days he walked without help with the use of the cane, though it was slow, and she knew it still hurt him – too much for him yet to tackle the stairs. On his bad days he went back to the crutch. Now and then, when it was fine, he would sit by the window looking over the garden and smoke a cigarette and watch the clouds. But nothing – not even when a robin flew down onto the windowsill and sat looking at him – really brought him to life. He was sad and depressed and he thought everything was hopeless. She knew, because she felt like that herself, and recognised it.

David was listening to 'Roses Of Picardy' for the eighth time that morning, when he heard muted voices muttering on the landing. Outside there was an icy November fog, with nothing to see but the black branches of the nearest tree, dripping. Here in his sitting-room, he had the lamps on, and Ethel had recently made up his fire. Sadie had arranged some holly and pine in a vase in lieu of flowers, and the warmth was bringing out the pine smell, reminding him of a wood they had been stationed in back in 1915. He had company: Nailer had followed Sadie upstairs one day, discovered the fire in his sitting-room, and now often crept in to curl up on the hearthrug.

David had every comfort, but he felt no relief. The weeping day outside and the sorrowful words of the song fitted his feelings. 'And the roses will die with the summertime, and our roads may be far apart . . .'

The record came to an end, and behind the quiet, rhythmic creak of the needle at the centre, he heard the voices on the landing and called out, 'Ethel! Who's making that row?'

Ethel appeared at the door. 'There's a visitor for you downstairs.'

'I don't want any damned visitors.'

'That's what I said, but they seem to think you'll want to see him.'

'Who is it?'

'It's Mr Freddie Oliphant.'

His heart jumped. Jumbo, his closest friend ever since school. And, best of all, Jumbo had been there, on the Somme – he would understand, as no-one else did. He yearned for the comfort of old friendship.

'Bring him up.'

He got up and turned the gramophone off. And by the time he had arranged himself, standing, opposite the door, he had heard the tramp of feet on the stairs and the familiar figure in khaki, puttees and Sam Browne had appeared in the doorway, a breath of army, too big and real for a domestic setting.

They looked at each other for a long moment. David saw, with the new eyes of distance, that Jumbo had changed, had broadened and hardened and grown up, had a man's face now, with the firmness of responsibility in it. He was brown from the weather, and there was nothing of Sophy in him. Jumbo had brown eyes, not the sparkling dark eyes of a wood nymph, but the sad round eyes of an elephant who had seen too much and knew that life hurt.

Jumbo stared, too, and his lips worked a little, rehearsing openings; and then he just said, 'Oh, David, I'm so sorry!'

And that seemed to cover everything. David held out his hand, Jumbo crossed the room to him, they shook heartily, and it was all right.

Ethel brought tea. They were seated in armchairs on either side of the hearth now; Nailer had left them, affronted by all the chatter when a fellow was trying to nap.

'It's gone quiet now,' Jumbo was saying. 'Shocking weather – snow, sleet, driving winds. We're dug in for the winter. So they're giving us all leave, while they can. The Boche are licking their wounds and the brass are totting up the accounts. I've heard rumours that the casualties were pretty high. Maybe three hundred thousand. But the Germans lost twice as many. And we'll get 'em next year.' He paused awkwardly, realising that his friend would not be there.

'You will,' said David. 'I have every confidence in you.'

Jumbo picked at a hangnail, looking troubled. 'I – I don't know if I ought to say anything. I don't want to worry you. But – have you heard from Sophy recently?'

'Not for a week or two,' David said. 'But I haven't written to her, either. It's my turn, but it's hard to think of anything to say. My days are all pretty much the same. Why?'

'It's just that . . . well, she's been out enjoying herself quite a bit lately. Going to parties. Dancing and so on.'

'No reason why she shouldn't,' he said. ''Tis the season to be jolly, isn't it? I can't expect her to stay in every night just because I can't be there to squire her.'

'I know, but . . .' Jumbo said, dissatisfied. 'Humphrey Hobart's home on leave,' he added, after a moment. 'I'm sorry to say my mother's been encouraging him. Inviting him to supper and so on.'

'Can't blame her for that,' David managed. 'He's a better prospect than me.'

'You're worth ten of him – a hundred!'

'With a leg like this?' David gestured.

'The hell with the leg! You're the better man, I tell you.'

David looked away, at the fire. 'You're a good friend, but I'm not any kind of a man. I did try to release her from the engagement, you know, but she wouldn't have it. Perhaps I should have tried harder.' He was silent a moment. 'Do you think she's interested in this Hobart fellow?'

'I shouldn't think so for a minute,' Jumbo said. 'It's all Mother's doing. He's dull as ditchwater. If she even thought about it, I'd never speak to her again. What kind of a girl would ditch a fellow just because he had a gammy leg?'

'I'll write to her,' David said painfully. 'Let her know that I wouldn't hold her to the engagement, if she's had second thoughts.' Jumbo only looked angrily at his hands, not knowing what to say. David went on, 'Do you remember how we sat under the trees that summer – 1914 – and dreamed of doing something grand and noble and important? We were sick of reading books about life, we wanted the real thing.'

'I remember.'

'It seems I shall be confined to reading books for the rest of mine.'

'Oh, rot! You're walking about, ain't you? Maybe you won't play cricket any more, but what's cricket? I won't either, for that matter.'

David leaned forward suddenly. 'You'll take care, won't you? You won't take any unnecessary risks?'

Jumbo looked puzzled for an answer. War was what it was. You did what had to be done. It was just luck – the shell hit you or someone else. You shot the Hun or he shot you. You didn't pause before you did something to work out if it was risky or not.

David recognised the thoughts running through Jumbo's mind because they had run through his own before he had been wounded. He had had a soldier's way of thinking then. He waved a hand, cancelling the question. 'Silly thing to say. Forget it. That's civilian talk.'

Jumbo nodded. But he understood. 'When you were missing, I thought you were dead,' he admitted, in a low voice.

'How long?' Beattie asked, her head on Louis's chest. 'How long have we got?'

'The campaigning is finished for the year,' he said. 'Haig

364

declared the battle over on the 18th. I'm back in London at least until the New Year – probably longer. Perhaps until the new campaign starts in spring.'

They were silent a while. 'Spring,' she said. 'It used to be something you looked forward to. New life. Blossom. Lambs. Green grass.' She thought suddenly of Bobby, playing cricket for his school, his whites dazzling against the green, squinting into the sun from under his cap's visor. *Bobby*. 'Now it just means more war.'

'Don't think about that,' he said. He stroked her head. 'We've six weeks at least, six weeks, two months, maybe more, to be together. I wish we could be together all the time. I wish you didn't have to go back.'

She knew he said 'go back' rather than 'go home'. 'You know I have to,' she said. He didn't argue. She said, 'My daughter will be having her baby in March. At least that will be new life.'

'And if it's a boy,' he said, 'one day you'll be grandmother to an earl.'

'Don't mock me.'

'Ah, no, I wasn't. Don't you know I'm aristocratic myself? The blood of the Plunketts runs in me.'

She rolled over on top of him and kissed him savagely. 'Make sure it only runs in you, not out of you,' she said. They kissed for a long time, his hand wound in her hair.

Later, he said, 'It's good to think about new life. Over there, there isn't much grass any more, and the trees are all smashed to matchwood. I don't know where spring will spring when the time comes. I suppose we'll find it some-where. In our hearts, perhaps.'

'In our hearts,' she repeated.

'It hurts me to think of you with him. I hate that you're married to someone else.'

'He's a good man,' she said.

'Yes,' said Louis. 'A better man than me.'

'No—'

'He's cared for you all these years. Oh, Beattie, what are we doing to that poor man?'

'You know what we're doing.'

'Yes,' he said. 'And I can't help it. I love you.'

'I love you.'

'But it doesn't make it right.'

'No,' she said. It took courage to say, 'Do you want to end it?'

'*No!*' he cried. 'I can't live without you, now I've found you again. You don't want to, do you?'

'No,' she said. She was betraying Edward, her good husband, and that was agony. And soon enough it would end: she knew that. But not yet. Please, don't let it end yet. The clock in the corner ticked on, slicing off thin seconds, taking away time from her. Everything was taken away from you, piece by piece. All you had that belonged to you was time, but you couldn't hold it, any more than you could hold water in your cupped hands. She would have to go soon, back to her other life, to try to keep up the pretence of normality. But there was a little while longer to lie in his arms and be at peace.

When she got home, Ada came to take her coat in the hall, and said, 'There was a message from the master, madam. He's had to work late, so he's staying at his club for the night.'

'Very well.'

'Did you have anything to eat, madam? Shall I get you some supper?'

'No, I'm not hungry. I'll look in on Mr David, and go to bed.'

He was already in bed, and she went very quietly into his room just to look for a moment at him sleeping. In sleep, some of the lines softened, and he looked a little more like

366

his old self. She remembered him as a baby, as a little boy, as a youth growing into strength and purpose, and her heart cried out. It couldn't end here, it couldn't all be for nothing. *Be well, David. Recover your spirits. Live a full, long life.* It couldn't be for this that she had suffered, borne him and suffered, loved him and suffered. It couldn't end like this.

He stirred in his sleep, and frowned, and she crept quietly away, so as not to disturb him, and went to her own bed, and wished she could weep.

A fine day came at the end of November, one of those days when suddenly warmth comes back into the air, and with it the smell of grass and fallen apples and woodsmoke; when the morning fog lifts to a gauzy sky, and the sun shines with a sad, gentle radiance as though saying goodbye.

David saw it from his window, and suddenly wanted to go out. It seemed like a last chance. He wanted to feel the sun on his face one last time before winter set in: spring seemed too far away to contemplate as a possibility.

He called for Ethel. With her help, he managed the stairs as far as the turn, but then had to sit down, catching his breath in pain.

'It's too much,' Ethel said. 'You'd better go back.'

'No,' he said. 'I'll do the rest sitting down. I must get *out*.'

He bumped on his behind from step to step, feeling almost dizzy with the new perspectives as 'downstairs' came slowly into view. He'd forgotten so many things. There were chrysanthemums in a vase on the hall table. The clock had an uneven tick. Was that a new rug? From the kitchen passage came the smell of beef roasting in the slow oven. It was Sunday, so there would be roast beef and Yorkshire pudding and apple pie, but for the moment everyone was at church, so there was no fear that anyone would catch him and want to talk. He hated being asked how he was. His mouth these days was set in a permanent down-curve, which ought to have warned people off. Ethel knew better than to try to talk to him, and he was glad of it.

At the foot of the flight he got upright again, and she helped him through the side door and into the garden. His leg was hurting fiercely now. 'The bench,' he said, through gritted teeth. It was against the wall of the house, sheltered and giving back warmth from the brick. She got him to it, helped him sit, watched him light a cigarette with a shaking hand. He didn't want her hovering over him; but she mustn't be too far away in case he needed her.

'Have a walk around the garden,' he said. 'Get some fresh air – it will do you good.'

She said, 'All right. Just five minutes,' and walked away down the garden, the fuzzy sunshine making a halo of her fair hair. He sucked on his cigarette, and lifted his pale, lined face to the sun's rays. His leg jangled like a rotten tooth, misery lay deep in him like stagnant water. He didn't exactly revel in the sunshine, but the touch of it on his face was benign. It made him want to cry.

Ethel walked along the paths. Halfway down, by the hedge to the vegetable garden, there was a rose bush, with a single dark-pink bud that had somehow survived, and was struggling to open in the unexpected warmth. She stopped to look at it. 'What do you think you're doing?' she said to it. 'Coming out this time of year? What a mug!'

Nailer appeared from under the hedge and looked up at her from under his eyebrows. 'I wasn't talking to you,' she said. 'Get off, you mangy article.' But she didn't kick out at him. She'd had to get used to leaving him alone now he was allowed in Mr David's room – a big mistake in her opinion. Give some people an inch . . .

'You'd take a yard all right,' she said. Nailer wagged his tail, just in case.

And Frank Hussey came through the gap in the hedge.

'I'd take a what?' he said.

'Nothing,' Ethel said, her mouth dry. All the trouble she'd taken to avoid him, and now this! 'They're all at church,' she said.

'I'm a bit early,' he said. 'Couldn't waste such a nice day. I wondered if I'd see you.'

'Well, now you've seen me,' she said.

He was not repulsed by her hostility. 'Come and have a little walk with me.'

'I got no time for walking,' she said.

'I know – you've got new responsibilities. I'm pleased for you. It's an important job.' She shrugged. 'You've been avoiding me.'

'Avoiding *you*? I never think about you from one day to the next.' Which was a terrible lie. Mentally she crossed her fingers.

He smiled, as if he saw them. 'Still got the lucky pixie?'

'D'you want it back, then? You can have it.'

'No, you keep it. I can wait.'

'Wait for what?'

'For you to change your mind.'

'You not still going on about marrying, are you?' she said, trying to sound scornful, though her heart was tripping.

'Why not? Everyone's got to marry someone. Unless you want to end up like Mrs Dunkley.' Cooks were always called 'Mrs', even when, like Cook, they were middle-aged virgins.

'You think you're my only choice, do you?' she said.

'I don't think that at all. I know how much choice you've got, which is why I'm sticking close. Got to keep off rivals.'

He said it lightly, with a smile, but something occurred to her. A story she'd heard a while back and paid no attention to.

'There was one of the soldiers from down the camp,' she said, 'got beat up. He said it was the navvies from the railway. But he wouldn't go and identify 'em.'

Frank looked at her, a bright, cat-like look that gave nothing away. 'Man's got some pride, I suppose,' he said.

'Pride? He said it was four men. Couldn't be expected to beat four of 'em.'

'It wasn't any four men. Just one. Said it was four to cover for himself.'

'How do you know?'

'I hear things.'

'I heard it was a sergeant,' Ethel said. Frank looked away down the garden, whistling softly. 'Frank Hussey, look at me and tell me the truth. Did you beat up Andy Wood?'

He didn't say yes and he didn't say no. 'He had it coming,' was all he said.

'You could've got arrested, thrown in jail!'

'He wasn't never telling. He'd never hold his head up again if the truth was known.'

Ethel felt something unwelcome tug at her heart. 'Why did you do it?'

'Like I said, he had it coming.'

'You did it for *me*?'

He looked at her. '*You* couldn't hit him. So somebody had to.'

She stared at him a long time. 'You daft devil,' she said. 'I don't know what to think about you.'

'Yes, you do,' he said, smiling. That smile made her knees go weak.

'Don't start that. I'm not marrying you.'

'Okey-doke. We'll start small. Walk out together on your day off. See how it goes.' With infinite gentleness he reached up and picked off a small leaf that had blown into her hair.

'I got to go,' she said. 'Mr David's out in the garden.'

'Next Sunday,' Frank said. He was a great, calm, strong interruption to the sunshine, so much more *there* than anything else in the garden that he should have had a big black shadow, not that feeble grey thing at his feet. 'Your afternoon off. We'll catch the bus and go to the Copper Kettle in Coneys and have tea.'

'Maybe I will, and maybe I won't,' Ethel said, turning away so as not to see him smile any more.

'I'll come for you at two o'clock, all right? I'll wait by the front gate.'

'You'll have a long wait, then,' she said, and stalked off. But she knew already she'd be there. Maybe she'd be late – one had to keep some power – but she'd be there.

One grim day a week before Christmas, David was dozing by his fire. He hadn't been downstairs again. He'd told Ethel not to mention that outing, and the weather had been foul, anyway. He preferred to keep to his room. He liked his things around him, his gramophone particularly, and he didn't want to talk to anyone. Conversation was an unbearable effort, like trying to lift a great weight far beyond his strength – a motor-car, say, or a gun limber.

Sophy had written, one of her well-crafted letters saying very little. She apologised for not writing sooner but said she had been busy helping Mother, with Christmas coming up. She mentioned Jumbo's leave, but not Humphrey Hobart's. She spoke of coming to visit him when the weather was better, and sent her fondest love. He tried to get up the courage to write to her and offer again to release her, but he couldn't quite manage it. Without her, his life would be completely grey. He wasn't sure he could face it.

Downstairs the boys were home from school and playing a game of some sort with Sadie, whom bad weather had kept away from Highclere. In between records he could hear the rhythm of their voices. In a little while, he thought, Mother would come upstairs and try to persuade him to dine downstairs with them tonight. He felt tired, tired to death. Winter was like a continuation of the war, a grimness he could do nothing about. His thigh ached with a beastly pain, and he was holding off from taking a morphine tablet. He was afraid to take too many, terrified that they would lose their effect through overuse and leave him defenceless.

He got up and put on 'Un Bel Di' from *Madama Butterfly* again. The anguish in that final note helped him, one pain distracting from another. As it finished, Ethel appeared in the door. 'Visitor,' she said.

'No visitors,' he replied.

'Come a long way,' Ethel said, 'and it's cold out. Go on, just five minutes.'

'I don't want to see anyone,' he said. But the visitor had not waited below to be fetched. She had come up after Ethel, and now appeared behind her, looking apologetic but determined.

'Just long enough to say sorry,' she said, 'and then I promise I'll go.'

His heart lifted a fraction of an inch out of the stagnant water with the first pleasure he'd felt in five months. 'Antonia!'

She crossed the room to him. Ethel disappeared. He took both her hands (they were like ice and faintly damp – inadequate gloves, he surmised). She was smiling at him, a very troubled smile. 'I know,' he said. 'I look ghastly.'

'What? Oh – no! I wasn't thinking that. Oh, David, I'm so sorry. About not writing. I didn't know, you see – I had no idea.'

'Come and sit down,' he said. 'You're shivering.' She took the chair opposite him by the fire. She hadn't so much as glanced at his leg, not once. 'You don't need to apologise,' he said.

'I honestly didn't know,' she said. 'When I didn't get any reply to my letters, I thought you'd tired of the correspondence. I didn't want to sound as though I was nagging you, so I just stopped writing. But I never stopped thinking about you, wondering how you were getting on. Daddy and I often speculated. He misses your footnotes very much.'

'I should have written and let you know,' David said. 'I'm sorry.'

'No, no, you had other things on your mind,' she said. 'If I'd known, I wouldn't have expected you to write.'

'How *did* you find out?'

'Captain Oliphant wrote to me. He told me about your being wounded and said that you wouldn't mind my visiting. Well, I thought about it a good bit, and then I had to come up to London with Daddy, so I asked him if he thought I should come, and he said an act of genuine friendship can never be resented. So here I am.'

'I can just hear your father saying that. How is he?'

'Oh, very well. The reason he's come to London is to see his publisher. He's finished his book – his commentary on Tacitus – and they're publishing it in the New Year.'

'But that's splendid!'

'Yes, he's very pleased. We're proud of him.' She smiled shyly. 'I've been writing, too. Nothing as grand as Daddy's *oeuvre*, but it's rather fun.'

'Tell me.'

'It's a children's book. The adventures of Ben, the Circus Pony.'

He actually smiled. 'You carried on with it?'

'No, I started again. You and I were just playing about, but this is a serious attempt at a proper book. Daddy's publisher says there's quite a demand for children's literature, though with the paper shortage he doesn't think it could be published until after the war. But I haven't finished it yet anyway. It keeps me occupied, when the tea room isn't open. Keeps my mind from things.' She looked at him. 'A lot of our boys haven't come back. I hear from their friends sometimes, or their parents. Oh, David, so many have fallen. Thank God you weren't killed.'

He had never heard anyone say 'Thank God' more as if they meant exactly that.

'I'm out of the army now,' he said. 'Discharged unfit. I'll probably never walk without a stick.'

'That's hard for you,' she said. 'But you got out alive, and there's nothing wrong with your brain. That's the most important thing.'

'You think so?'

'Of course! The brain is the seat of all that makes us human, makes us ourselves. The body is nothing.'

'Well, I was rather fond of it,' he said. And she laughed. No-one ever laughed around him now, he realised.

Ethel peeped in ten minutes later and saw them talking busily, and concluded the young lady was staying. When she came back a quarter of an hour later with tea, they were still at it, and there was a bit of colour in Mr David's face, such as she'd not seen before. She couldn't make out what they were talking about – booky stuff, it sounded like, half of it in a foreign language, she reckoned – but it seemed to be what he'd needed because he barely noticed her presence as she laid the tea within reach. She checked the coal scuttle was full, and went away.

The fire shone red, and after a bit Nailer stuck his head round the door, smelling muffins on the air, and sidled cautiously to a place on the hearth-rug where he could get the benefit of the warmth and still keep an eye on their plates. He didn't know the strange female taking up the spare seat, but his sense of her was comfortable.

Outside, the December greyness gave way before the early winter dark, the dim streetlamps came on, and it began to snow again. The fresh snow like feathers gradually built up in a line along the glazing-bars, and in a soft heap on the window sill; and if they hadn't been talking so much, they would have heard the high, laughing voices of Peter and William down in the street, with half a dozen other local boys, having a snowball fight.